VENGEANCE SQUARED

Ginna Leatherbury

ISBN: 0615996809
ISBN 13: 9780615996806
Library of Congress Control Number: 2014905964
Ginna Leatherbury, Manassas Park, VA

DEDICATION

I dedicate this book to my believing mirrors, a group of women so special that when I fly it is by the support of their wings.

Special thanks to Diane K. Bergeron – her editing and commentary were invaluable.

And of course my deepest gratitude to my husband, who has put up with me over the past several years while I give this art of writing a go.

"**T**he goddamn champagne is warm."

Rebecca Grande's perfectly painted lips spat out the words, her accusing eyes aimed directly at her maid of honor.

Nancy shrugged, the small gesture causing the entire bodice of her dress to ride up her torso, chafing her skin. She struggled with the yellow chiffon, pulling the material back into place and vowing that she'd never do a stint like this again. What a pain in the ass, throwing the bridal shower and being Becca's slave for the entire engagement period.

Nancy's stomach growled, reminding her of the diet she'd subjected herself to in order to squeeze into the gown. "No wonder, it's hot as hell up here. Do you want me to pop open a new one?"

She didn't wait for an answer, knew what Becca would say, as she walked across the small room to the cooler. She took her time pulling out another bottle, smiling as the cold water soothed the heated pulse of her wrist.

"I wish you'd stop complaining," Becca said as she emptied her glass into the peace lily sitting in the corner. "I told you, small private wedding chapels are the *in* thing. Chic; that's the word Cosmo used."

"Hopefully we'll get a nice ocean breeze and everything will be perfect."

Drops fell from the chilled bottle of Moet as Nancy wrapped it with the oversized tee-shirt she'd worn to the church this morning, the Harvard logo still visible on the faded fabric.

"You're the one not happy with the champagne," Nancy said defensively. "I'm not a freaking sommelier; you try keeping it chilled in this old cooler."

There was a soft knock at the door, then someone calling out, "You girls aren't arguing again, are you?"

"It's my knight in shining armor; he said he had a surprise for me," Becca said as she pulled the bottle away from Nancy and filled her glass.

"You can't see Henry now. It's bad luck." Nancy crossed the room and opened the door slightly, her wide berth blocking Becca from view. Before she had the chance to chastise him for ignoring tradition, he said, "Don't you look pretty."

Nancy looked out at a dashing Henry Fullington, nicely outfitted in a tailor made tuxedo that fit his lanky form to perfection. It even looked like he'd used a bit of hair gel to keep the cowlick that always stuck out on the left side of his part under control.

"Henry, you're the worst liar I know. What I look like is an over-ripe banana ready to burst," Nancy said, her hand absently pulling at the bra strap that was cutting off her circulation. "You, on the other hand, look quite dapper."

Henry bowed slightly, smiling. "May I have a moment with my intended?"

Nancy never could say no to Henry. "Fine," she sighed. "If you need me I'll be in the bathroom. I think one of my eyelashes is coming loose."

She grumbled to herself as she went, but loud enough for Becca to hear. "I don't know why I have to wear these fake things anyway. It's not my wedding."

Once in the tiny bathroom, Nancy slammed the door behind her, leaving the love birds alone.

• • •

Becca walked into Henry's arms, eyes sparkling up at her dream man. He was kind, generous, and great in bed. Oh, and one other thing; he was rich.

"Where's my surprise?" she said, clapping her hands in anticipation.

Henry extended his right arm, fist closed. "It's in here."

Becca pulled back three of his manicured fingers before recognizing the small glass vial in his hand.

"I thought you couldn't find any of this stuff for our honeymoon," she said as he offered up a little golden spoon. She put a finger against her left nostril and snorted the cocaine as daintily as possible, felt the delicious rush course through her body. "Yum, this is the best snow I've tasted in ages. Give me another hit."

While Henry scooped up more of the cocaine and brought it to her nose, he said, "I found a new source. I'll tell you all about it when we get out to Montauk. Baby, I'm going to do all kinds of naughty things to that beautiful body of yours."

"Do you want a drink before you leave?" Becca called over her shoulder, her body swaying as she went to refill her champagne glass.

"No, I'm good," he said, remaining at the door.

She turned, looking at her beloved. Henry. The man who saw more in her than just the personal shopper he'd met two years ago while she was working at Saks. The man who saw past her lack of pedigree. The man who, by marrying her, would bring her into the world of high society. Champagne wishes and caviar dreams? Hers were about to come true.

"Are you sure?" Then she laughed. "You don't believe that silly wives tale about seeing the bride, do you?"

"We've hit enough bumps in the road getting here, and I don't want to tempt fate at this point," Henry answered as he turned to go. "I'll see you downstairs soon. Oh, and did I mention that you look exquisite?"

She was wearing a Vera Wang gown, her long dark hair piled on top of her head with tendrils gently falling around her face. An incredible crown made of pearls contrasted with her almost jet black hair, the effect stunning.

She tilted her head to the side and smiled. "I know."

Henry winked, blew her a kiss.

And then he was gone.

Old man Damson stood at the back of the small church, looking out at the sea of guests furiously fanning themselves with the wedding programs he'd so carefully left on each seat. The Gulf Cove chapel was quaint; no fancy altar, no stained glass windows, and regrettably, no air conditioning.

He wiped the sweat from his brow, relieved that everything seemed to be in order, and shuffled over to the screen door. Outside sat two lucky young boys chosen to ring the bell that morning – something that was considered a big honor amongst the children at Gulf Cove.

"Cal, Tony; it's time to get things rolling."

Cal shot up off the ground first, absently wiping his dirty hands over his white dress shirt as Tony ambled forward nervously. Mr. Damson whispered to the boys as he ushered them to the alcove on the right. "Now remember, all you need to do is pull down on the ropes a couple of times. That'll tell the bride it's time to walk down the aisle."

Cal took hold of the thick twine in front of him while Tony clamped onto the other rope, both boys looking at Mr. Damson for the signal.

"OK," the old man said. "Time to go."

Cal rolled his shoulders and reached up for his first pull. His hands wrapped around the rope and, holding tight, pulled down the same way he had done hundreds of times before.

But this time nothing happened. Cal stood back for a moment, looking up toward the bell before approaching the rope again and giving it several strong jerks. There was no give; the rope just hung lifelessly in front of him. He rubbed his hands together and jumped, grabbing hold of the thick cord high enough so that his full body weight was now added to his effort, but the rope still would not budge.

"Don't just stand there, help me," he said to his friend, his smile replaced with frustration.

Tony leaped forward, gripping the rope just below Cal's hands and pulled, moaning from the effort. But still there was no motion and no chimes.

"Hey, Mr. Damson, the bell is stuck or something. It won't move."

"What do you mean it won't move? Are you playing with me, boys?" the old man answered as he held out a hand to delay the bride's entrance into the church and shuffled over to the ropes.

"No, Mister Damson, s-s-sir, we wouldn't do that," said Tony, the stutter that only made an appearance when he was really nervous surfacing. "It's r-r-really stuck."

Cal and Tony moved their hands closer together so there was room for Mr. Damson to add his weight to theirs. The three of them were straining against the immovable thick twine when Mr. Damson felt something land on top of his hairless head.

He pulled his left hand free, wiped it over his scalp and then looked down at the dark crimson liquid. "What in the world?" he mumbled, raising his hand closer to his eyes so he could get a better look.

"I think something's leaking up there," Cal said just as something dripped onto his sleeve.

Mr. Damson, confused, gazed up into the bell tower. The dark chute was nothing but shadows.

"Gross, what is this stuff?" Tony whined as he threaded his fingers through the slimy substance tangled in his hair, finally using his fingernails to scoop it away.

Mr. Damson glanced over at the child, a rush of concern as small droplets continued to shower down around them.

"Boys, shush," he said, placing a quivering finger over his mouth. "Do you hear that creaking sound? What in the world?"

Cal looked up, eyes wide as something landed on the side of his face with a splat. His entire body stiffened as he raised his arm to brush it away. "Gross," he screamed, his voice catching as the goop slid down his cheek, leaving a runny film behind before dropping onto the floor.

Mr. Damson reached over and gave the young boy's shoulder a gentle squeeze. "No need to be scared," he said. "There's probably a nest up there and we've gone and upset things. No need to be scared," he said a second time as he drew in closer to the children.

"I've never seen bird poop like that," Tony managed to say, tears threatening as he pointed to what had just hit ground.

It looked like a small pile of worms, clinging and writhing and held together by some kind of gelatin.

Whatever the hell it was, it was now raining down on the three of them, splat splat splat, wads of grossness landing on their clothes and their faces, splashing onto the floor all around them. They stood frozen, their bodies paralyzed except for their eyes looking at each other with horror.

The sudden snap was loud and distinctive, jarring them out of their shock. Something up in the bell tower had broken free and was barreling down the chute.

Tony turned and dove away, landing hard on his chest, while Cal staggered backwards, tripping and falling on his butt. But the old man's reflexes weren't as fast as theirs and he didn't move away in time to avoid the large mass that spilled from the tower, a flailing limb knocking him onto the ground.

The body of Henry Fullington finally came to rest at the bottom of the belfry, torn apart like a rag doll, his skull split open, brain matter splattering all over Mr. Damson and the two lucky boys.

3

"Noooo." The strangled scream wrenched through the air. Becca was standing at the back of the church next to her mother, who was about to be escorted up front by one of the groomsmen, when the chaos erupted. From the corner of her eye she saw two little boys scrambling away from something falling from high above. She tried to focus her eyes, tried to make sense of what she was seeing.

It was a person, wearing dark slacks and a white shirt. She saw a quick flash of satin running down the pants, a cummerbund. The one she had given Henry as a wedding gift, pale yellow to match the bridesmaid's gown.

Again, the word exploded from deep in her chest. She dropped her bouquet of white roses and lilies and covered her mouth, her denial futile; her entire body started trembling as comprehension flooded through her.

One of the boys lying on the floor, inches from her beloved, pushed himself up and sprinted toward the exit. Becca watched as his little body seemed to move in slow motion, his mouth open in a silent scream, coming straight in her direction. She was paralyzed, unable to move and prevent the bloodied child from running right into her, his short frame folding into her wide skirt and tripping. Her mother grabbed her arm, steadied her, as the boy leaped up and continued his flight, running out the door just seconds later.

She reached down, touching the organza and tulle of her Vera Wang original, blood and viscera now clinging to the thin netted fabric.

And then people were pulling her away, commanding her to keep her eyes closed. Her legs gave way as she crumbled toward the ground, arms catching her just in time and propelling her forward. She felt vacant, strangely detached, as her mother's voice floated in space around her.

"No, not back upstairs. Put her in the limousine," ordered Glenda Grande.

It dawned on her that her mom sounded oddly authoritative. Unusual. But the people carrying her complied as she felt herself lifted into the back of the limo. Her wedding dress suddenly felt like a vise as she fell into the leather expanse.

"I can't breathe." She grabbed the left shoulder strap of the gown with both hands, yanking and pulling until she heard the fabric start to give way. "Get it off of me," she screamed, her hands clutching at the cinched waist and coming away with nothing more than the small pearls and sequins carefully sewn into the tulle.

"Go get something for Becca to put on," Glenda called out to Nancy before she crawled into the back seat of the limousine next to her daughter. "Turn around, honey, let me unzip you."

Instead of a zipper there was a long row of tiny pearl buttons. Glenda's fingers fumbled, her long red acrylic nails struggling with the fastening.

"I need it off, now." Becca was screaming, her arms and legs thrashing around so wildly that Glenda backed away, just missing an elbow to the jaw.

"Here, let me try."

Glenda turned, relieved to see that Nancy had returned, a tee shirt in hand. They traded spots, Glenda now on the sidewalk and Nancy in the car. She looked at her best friend, mascara streaming down her face, nose running; she was a complete mess. Then their eyes met; trust.

Becca turned her back to Nancy, who grabbed the fabric and yanked hard. The buttons gave way, flying into the air, until the dress was opened from neck to waist. Becca felt her arms being guided out of the gown and into something else, much softer against her skin and loose.

"Raise up a little so I can pull it all the way off," Nancy said. Becca did what she was told, an automaton as she leaned her back against the seat, planted her feet on the floor, and arched upward while Nancy slid the dress past her hips and down her legs.

When Becca felt the weighty material down by her ankles she dropped back onto the seat and picked up her feet.

"That's good, Becca. It's gone now, OK?" Nancy dragged the dress out the open door, out of sight, while Becca scooted to the far side of the car and curled into the corner, sobbing.

A small form approached Glenda, white haired and limping with the aid of a cane, winding her way through the group of onlookers at the limo's side. "Is there anything I can do to help?"

"Oh God am I glad to see you." Glenda hugged Monica Adams, her neighbor and closest confidant. "I'm going to take Becca home. Will you come with me?"

"Of course, dear," Monica said, taking Glenda's hands in hers. "My guest has the car keys; she'll find her own way home."

4

A New York State park police cruiser skidded to a stop in front of the church, kicking up a cloud of dirt and debris from the gravel surface. The passenger door jerked open and Officer DiMitri jumped out, immediately putting his hand on his holster and looking through the crowd loitering in the parking lot.

His partner, Officer Calhoon, finished the urgent phone call sure that he had the important details and rushed after DiMitri. They made their way to a small group that remained rooted in the vestibule, some on cell phones, others just standing blankly by.

"They look like they're in shock," commented DiMitri.

Calhoon ignored his partner's chatter. "Can anyone here tell me briefly what happened?"

A man who looked like he was most in charge answered. "I heard a scream and then a loud thud, like something had fallen. A couple of people got up to see what happened, and when they started screaming I knew it must be something really bad. Henry, the groom," he choked out. "Someone killed him and threw his body down the bell tower."

"OK people, you need to go outside right now," Calhoon said, putting his hand on the man's back and pushing him toward the screen door, the rest of the group following. "Officer DiMitri here will start taking your statements in just a minute."

Calhoon visually panned the rest of the church, seeing a little boy hovering over to the left in a small pantry area. He was covered in blood and God knew what else, doing his best to stifle the flow of tears. An old man was also there, bent over a small sink and ringing a cloth before turning to the child and washing off his face.

To the right was the body of a male Caucasian, bloodied and battered and spread out over the floor, arms and legs splayed at unnatural angles. There didn't appear to be anyone else inside the chapel.

"Why don't you start by getting those two out of here," Calhoon told DiMitri, pointing toward the kitchenette. "Once you get them settled outside, see if you can get a statement from them. If they're too upset to talk, move on to other witnesses. And don't forget to ask how and where they can be contacted if we need them later on.

"I'll take the inside and make sure everything is sealed off until reinforcements get here."

"I'm on it," said DiMitri without hesitation as he walked over to the pair and ushered them outside.

Calhoon moved closer to the fallen body, his mind flashing back to his time serving in Iraq where IED's caused similar pulverization. Damn government made him clean up the mess, like he was some glorified janitor or something. He knew one thing for sure: whoever's job it was to remove this carcass was going to need a rake.

He moved around the corpse carefully, trying not to step in the splatter. A portion of the torso lay intact on its side, ribs protruding through the skin. The limbs had landed askew and it was hard to tell if they were broken away from the rest of the body or severed. The victim's tailored shirt and slacks did nothing to hide the catastrophic wounds; they too were shredded. He would not have been able to make out the head were it not for a section of short dark hair that seemed to cradle what used to be a portion of his cranium.

It was the cries of a woman somewhere from above that pulled his mind back to the task at hand. Refocused, he climbed the spiral staircase leading to the belfry.

"Park police," he called out as he reached the top landing.

A woman was trying to pull an older gentleman away from the bloody vicinity around the bell, tugging at his shoulders. "He's gone, Arthur, there's nothing more you can do. Please come downstairs with me," she implored.

Calhoon approached, knowing he had to move these people as soon as possible. "Sir, this is a crime scene. I'm sorry; you're going to have to leave."

"But my son," the man sobbed. "Look what they've done to my son."

Calhoon was indeed looking. His insides rumbled as he scoured the small area with his eyes, searching.

Parts of the victim's corpse were still tied around the bell, somehow not coming loose when it was swung. Small clumps of this body debris periodically peeled away, splashing to the ground below.

There was a large pool of blood in the corner along with a coil of rope, what looked like tape, and a knife that he couldn't really make out from where he was standing. He noticed the dark fabric of a discarded tuxedo jacket that lay on the floor nearby, somehow clean of any blood or even grime from the dusty room.

With more force, he said again, "I'm sorry for your loss. But you need to leave the premises." He leaned over the grieving mass that was Arthur Fullington and, despite the fact that he was a good eight inches shorter than the man, pulled him up by his arm pits and practically dragged him down the stairs, the woman trailing behind.

Calhoon got them through the alcove and to the exit before shouting again, "Everybody out."

The sound of sirens was quickly approaching, no doubt backup from the Nassau County Police Department. Gulf Cove was technically their jurisdiction. However, since the chapel was located on land immediately adjacent to what was defined as a state park, park police had received the call as well.

With one quick glare to make sure his instructions were being followed and that the church was empty, he ran back to the stairwell and to site of the crime.

5

"**T**his is the biggest clusterfuck I've ever seen. Are you telling me that the entire crime scene is contaminated?" Chief Hartman's jowls flapped as he threw his head back and forth, demanding an answer.

Captain Langly stuck a fresh stick of Nicorette into his mouth as he stood in the church parking lot and tried, for the tenth time that day, to explain to his boss how the clusterfuck occurred.

"Frank, half the people in that church ran straight out the back door once they realized what was going on. Guess what the other half did?" Not waiting for an answer, Langly continued. "They went to see if they could help the victim. Or ran up the tower stairs to see what was going on there. There are so many foot and hand prints in that church that it'd be a miracle to isolate which ones belong to the perp."

"Don't call me Frank, goddamnit. I might not get any competency from you but I will at least get some respect," he said, furiously swatting at the fly that buzzing around his face.

"Sorry, Chief," he responded, chomping on his gum. "I keep forgetting."

Chief Hartman pounded his way around the rear of his Crown Vic, mumbling, "Just because we were in the same class at the damn police academy doesn't make us buddies."

"No, but playing poker every week does," Langly laughed as Hartman opened his car door and reached in for a bottle of water. He opened the top, poured some into his cupped hand, and splashed it on his face.

"Listen, I get it," Langly added. "I know appearances are important."

Hartman sighed. "Not as important as tying up this investigation. And fast. Now tell me what you've got."

"We've got a tight timeline, that's what we've got. The old man who watches over the church got here at 7:30 a.m. to open the upstairs bridal chamber. The bride and her friend arrived at the church at approximately 7:45 a.m. At about 8:00 a.m., two little boys showed up to be first in line to ring the bell, and the caterers arrived soon after that. Damson said that's when he sat down to rest, just wanted to close his eyes for a minute. Forty five minutes later he woke up; preparations were already in full swing and guests were starting to arrive.

Langly adjusted his NCPD cap, double protection for his nose that already sported zinc oxide, and continued. "The last time anyone saw the victim was at approximately 9:20 a.m., when he went up to have a private word with his fiancé."

"What about the best man, Aiden Ellsworth? I've got the governor crawling up my ass wanting to find that guy."

"He's still missing. So far as we know, the last time anyone physically saw him was over there in the parking lot, sitting in the car with the groom having a drink."

The color in the chief's face turned an even deeper red as he pounded his fist on the car's roof, looking like he was about to explode. But before he had the chance to fire off more expletives the sound of an approaching car got his attention.

"Thank God, he's here," Hartman said, his frustration deflating just a little as he watched Xavier King arrive.

6

X drove his SL 550 Roadster into the parking lot with seemingly no rush in the world. He was obeying the 10 mph speed limit signs that were posted, mentally preparing himself for the task ahead of him. He liked going into a crime scene focused and alert, with no outside distractions.

He sat for a few seconds after turning off the ignition, watching two of his favorite people in the world standing by a Crown Vic talking. Frank Hartman, chief of police. Hard ass but soft heart. Even in this heat he was wearing a suit, seersucker, always looking the part of a senior official. And he did look senior, more senior than his sixty four years of life.

Then there was Langly. Dockers pants, short sleeved shirt, his self-designated standard issue uniform. He was standing in the small area of shade provided by the parked car, the pale skin of his arms pink despite the constant application of sun screen he fastidiously used. X knew his first name was Matt but had never used it. The guy was the best; humor when needed, hard core investigator all the time.

X took a deep breath and climbed out of the car, waving to a couple of cops as he approached the Crown Vic.

"Hey, Langly, glad to see you're working this case. How's it going?"

"Peachy," he responded, swatting X's arm as he passed by toward the chief. "I see you haven't lost your touch."

"Huh?" X said.

"Every woman in this parking lot just stopped what they were doing and watched you sashay over here."

"Yeah, right," X laughed as he reached out and shook the chief's hand. "Well, we've certainly gotten the press' attention. I haven't seen so many news vans since I don't know when."

"Are those cocksuckers still lined up outside the front gate?" Hartman pulled a crumpled McDonald's napkin out of his pocket and wiped away the sweat falling down his forehead.

"I guess it's the nature of the beast."

Chief Hartman acknowledged the statement with a grunt. "Thanks for coming in on this. I know you and Ann were supposed to leave on vacation today." His eyes roamed over X's appearance before adding, "Really sorry. Looks like you were ready to hoist the sails."

X's chino shorts, tee-shirt and white sneakers were definitely not standard issue for him, but when he got the chief's call he jumped off his boat and into the car without even thinking about changing. He tended to dress conservatively, though not nearly as starchy as the chief.

"Don't worry about it, Chief; you know I'm available whenever you need me."

And X was stating the absolute truth. Not only had Hartman been a good friend of X's father, he'd also worked like a dog in helping to put away the man who murdered him 20 years ago. Since that day, X vowed to repay him whenever and however possible.

"So what are the talking heads in the media saying so far?" Hartman asked.

"Not much. Everything they're reporting is pretty vague. Henry Fullington, son of wealthy philanthropist, found gruesomely murdered seconds before he was supposed to get married."

"Did you get anything out of the bride?" the chief questioned.

"Unfortunately, not much. I went over to her house as soon as I got your call, but by the time I got there a doctor had given her a sedative and she was pretty loopy."

"That's just great," Hartman said, waving away the fly that was buzzing around his head. "First she leaves the scene before police arrive and then is too incapacitated to give a statement."

"How'd that happen anyway?" X asked. "The bride's mother told the limo driver to bring them back to her place in Massapequa and he just agreed?"

"Apparently so," Langly confirmed. "The park police cruiser saw it pulling out of the gate just as they were arriving."

"Dumb sons' of bitches. Any cop with half a brain would've stopped the damn thing," Hartman said, squeezing the half empty water bottle he was holding in the middle until it collapsed. "So what did Becca Grande have to say?"

"She was able to confirm that she saw Henry about forty minutes before the wedding was scheduled to start and that he didn't look nervous or agitated. He was looking forward to the honeymoon, didn't have any enemies, and everyone loved him."

"That's it? We already knew all that," the chief said, his voice increasing in decibel with each word.

"Sorry," X said, wishing he had more to tell the chief. "The woman was one blink away from oblivion. I was lucky to get that much."

"How many uniforms are there?"

"Four. Plus an old lady from across the street," X added. "She's a feisty one; she held her cane across the stairwell and told me that I was not allowed upstairs to see the bride unless the doctor said it was OK."

"That's just great. Thwarted by the aged and disabled," Hartman said as he took the cap off the water bottle and tried to take a sip from the scrunched up container. The log jam prevented any flow at all; frustrated, he threw it into the nearby sea grass.

X watched the bottle hurl through the air and land, a halo of dry sand indicating its final resting place. Langly, at age 36, stood next to him contributing sound effects, a long whistle that slowly petered out once the bottle landed. Sometimes he acted more like a six year old.

X turned to his friend, the distraction over. "What about on this end? Do we have any witnesses?"

"Nope," Langly answered, his eyes squinting at the sun's glare. "Nobody remembers seeing anything suspicious."

The chief cut in. "Xavier, how much do you know about the Fullington family?"

X considered for a moment. "I don't have any personal knowledge of them, though I am fairly certain that Dad interviewed Arthur Fullington at one point."

Hartman grinned for the first time that day. "I bet your old man skewered him. I still miss him, you know."

X nodded, remembering his dad. A single father, he'd worked hard to provide a loving home for his son, even before he became famous. Then Timothy King was discovered by a small cable network and became known for his zealous and probing interview style; his TV program was an instant hit.

Timothy King's celebrity was cut short when he was tragically murdered by a stalker during X's senior year at Fordham University.

X dragged his mind away from the memories and back to the business at hand. "Blue blood. Old money. Real estate. Philanthropy." X listed off things he associated with the name Fullington.

"You forgot politics," added Hartman. "The name Fullington carries a lot of weight in the state. And Henry being murdered in Nassau County means we have a lot of eyes on us. It's imperative that we move on this case quickly and effectively."

Chief Hartman crooked his finger and motioned for the two officers to come closer.

"This isn't something you'd necessarily find in the ordinary course of your investigation. It came to me through the governor, who's a personal friend of Henry's father.

"It has to do with Aiden Ellsworth, the missing best man. Apparently Arthur Fullington is convinced that Aiden has been embezzling money from his son's company for at least the past 6 months."

X asked, "Does he have any proof?"

"No, that's the problem. Just last month Arthur talked Henry into letting the family CPA review the company's books and there was nothing that looked irregular."

"So what makes him think Aiden's been stealing?"

"It seems our missing best man likes to play the ponies. Arthur happens to own several racehorses, keeps an ear to the ground on what's going on at the track, and heard that Aiden's been on a losing streak. Apparently Aiden's paid off some big losses lately and Arthur is convinced he doesn't have that kind of money. Rumor has it he's still in the hole sixty big ones."

"So you're suggesting that somehow Henry found out that Aiden was skimming money from him, that they fought, and Henry ended up dead?" X asked.

"It's a possibility. And one that I want you to explore. The governor assured Mr. Fullington that we'd follow up on the lead," Hartman said, pressing his finger into X's chest.

"An APB went out on Aiden Ellsworth as soon as I got here," added Langly, "and we've got two teams with dogs scouring the entire Gulf Cove vicinity looking for him."

"Good," said the chief as he opened the car door and dropped into the seat. "We don't want to disappoint the governor. Is that understood?"

Not waiting for a reply, Hartman slammed himself inside, put the car in gear and left the two cops staring at his tail lights.

7

"I know our guys have already scoured this place," X said as he walked into the church, "and I trust their work completely."

"I know, I know. 'You just want to get a feel of the place,'" added Langly.

X smiled, dimples appearing on cue, his blue eyes set off by dark hair and brows. "I'm that predictable?"

"You say it 99 times out of a hundred," Langly answered as he unconsciously rubbed some of the menthol he always kept with him under his nose. "So, there are two main points of entry. The doorway we just came through and the one to the right of the altar."

He tossed the small container over to X, who caught it in one hand and immediately brought it up to his nose. "Thanks. It smells like hell in here."

"Yeah, apparently some of the brave souls who wanted to see where the groom landed weren't so brave after all and lost their lunch. Between that and the dead body, it reeks pretty bad."

X's eyes travelled down the center aisle toward the altar. "It must have been a real free for all in here; half the chairs are on the ground." X pushed a section of the trampled and dirty white satin runner aside with his toe and leaned over to pick up one of the chairs, a bundle of now wilting flowers tied to its back.

"That's what we're hearing. Most people headed straight for the exit door. Except for the brave ones," Langly added, winking.

"Why anyone would want to see a corpse is beyond me."

Langly nodded and pointed to the right as he walked, a cloth partition to the small alcove pulled aside. "So here's where all the action happened. The two little boys were standing there, along with the old man who oversees things at the church. When the bell rang the groom and best man were supposed to enter the church using the door up by the altar. Then the bride would enter the vestibule, the organ would start playing, and she'd walk down the aisle."

X stood, shaking his head. "I can't believe I had my cell phone turned off and missed the original call." He looked at the blood stains, splatter, and the inordinate amount of yellow police tape spread around the floor and said, "I would have preferred to see the remains before they were taken away."

Langly shrugged. "I figured you would. But the coroner insisted that the body be moved a.s.a.p. Something about accelerated decomposition due to the nature of the injuries and the heat."

"Yup," X said as he moved around the yellow markings, trying to visualize how the body had looked lying there. "Not the typical outline of a murder victim."

"No, this one was definitely spread around."

X eventually looked directly up to where the bell hung some 30 feet higher. It was hard to make anything out other than the two twined ropes hanging lifelessly from above.

"The body must have been pretty beat up; the fall alone would have made a mess," X commented before heading for the spiral stairwell tucked into the far corner of the room.

X took the stairs two at a time and ducked his head as he entered the dimly lit attic, the only light coming in from the louvered air vents on each wall. The space was about eighteen by twelve feet, with a large circle cut out of the center of the wooden floor where the bell hung. "These are pretty tight quarters; there wasn't a whole lot of working space for the killer," he remarked, turning around and looking for Langly.

"I know," Langly answered, huffing as he finally reached the top of the stairs. He leaned over, hands on his knees, and took a second to catch his breath.

"Geez, Lang, you need to get into better shape. You're too young to be so old."

"Are you kidding me," he answered, stretching out his arm and flexing his muscle. "I'm lean and mean."

X shook his head, laughing. "You look more like Popeye in big need of some spinach." Then, "So do we know how tall Henry Fullington was?"

"Five feet 10 inches. Not huge, but getting him laid out and tied to that thing," Langly answered, pointing to the bell "couldn't have been easy."

"Looks like the confrontation happened over there." X walked to the far corner and squatted down, touching the blood stained floorboards that were Henry's deathbed. "It's still wet." He rubbed his moist fingers together, the blood now coloring his own skin. He was caught up for several moments, staring intently at his stained fingers before he turned his head and noticed the tuxedo jacket discarded and rumpled on the floor.

He stood up, stooping his head to avoid hitting the vaulted ceiling, and approached the heap of dusty clothing. "This should have been the happiest day of his life," he said softly to himself.

He finally looked over to Langly, who was leaning against the wall and waiting, a big yawn in process. "Sorry. Where were we?" X asked.

"That tape on the floor is where the knife was found. CSI said it looked like a surgical scalpel. And there was a body suit that was discarded to your right, drenched in blood. The tech said, folded up, it would probably be the size of a napkin. Anyone could've walked in with it undetected. They're working on prints, and our guys are looking into where you can buy one of those outfits."

X paced, marking the distance between the bell and the red-soaked floor. "It doesn't make sense. Henry would have tried to fight back, or at least screamed like hell. And not even one person heard or saw anything?"

"At least not that anyone remembers so far, but we'll be re-interviewing. Maybe if we're lucky we can shake something loose in someone's memory."

X took a last look around, shadows falling in slats across the bell, the blood, the jacket. "Thanks, Langly. You'll keep me posted?"

"You know it," he answered as the two descended the stairs and headed back out into the hazy, hot and humid sunshine smoldering away the afternoon.

• • •

X was walking toward his car, running through scenarios of how Henry was killed, logistically, when he heard someone calling out his name.

"Are you Detective King, sir?"

X raised his hand across his forehead to cut the glare of the sun but didn't recognize the approaching officer. "That's right. And you are?"

"Sergeant Calhoon, with park police." The man stood in front of X, his posture ramrod straight. Shoulders back, chest out, stomach in. Legs straight, heels together and toes pointed out at an angle. Arms at his side.

Given his stance, shaved head and the way he emphasized the word sir, it was an easy guess. "You're ex-military?" X asked.

"Once in the military, always in the military." Calhoon didn't move; he stared into X's eyes, his five foot six frame conditioned to standing at attention.

A second park officer jogged over from their squad car and joined the struggling conversation.

"What's going on? Did I miss anything?" X watched as the young man bounced from one foot to the other, seething with energy, a big smile on his face.

Calhoon's face tightened into a grimace. "This is my partner, Officer DiMitri. He's still a little wet behind the ears, doesn't remember how to respect those in higher command."

Whether the chastisement went over DiMitri's curly haired head or he simply didn't care, X wasn't sure. Instead he blurted out, "I've read everything written about you, Detective King. That last article in *Newsday* describing how you nailed the guys who robbed the Empire National Bank was awesome. You're like a living legend."

X smiled, but brushed the compliment aside. "It's always team work; I couldn't do it alone."

That got a nod from Calhoon, which X was happy to see. They had at least that philosophy in common.

X's cell phone sang the distinctive 3-tone ring that told him Chief Hartman was calling. "Excuse me for a second, I've got to take this call."

He took a few steps backwards and turned, grabbing his phone from his pocket. "What's up, Chief?"

"I just spoke with the coroner."

"That was fast."

"The governor's riding his ass, too," Hartman said. "Anyway, he did a quick once-over on the body looking for something other than the obvious and found cocaine residue in Fullington's nasal cavity. Which is a miracle, considering the condition of the head."

"Cocaine?" X looked over his shoulder at the parkies who were standing idly by, Calhoon's head tilted in X's direction.

"Yup. The lab's rushing toxicology tests on it as we speak. Did the bride say anything about drug use?"

"Not to me, directly. But one of the uniforms who was already at the house when I got there told me he'd asked whether she or Henry used recreational drugs, and Becca told him no."

X pulled the cell away from his ear as he listened to the chief's screaming voice reverberating from the small phone. "Well go back over there and wake her up, find out the truth. We can't be wasting time while she's getting her beauty sleep."

When he heard the noise quiet down X placed the phone back to his ear. "It won't do any good. I spoke to her physician and he said that she was in deep shock and bordering on hysteria. He wanted to admit her to the hospital for observation but she refused. That tranquilizer he gave her is going to knock her out for a good 12 to 18 hours."

"That's just fucking fabulous," Hartman answered, his frustration dripping off the words. "OK, then, change of plans. I want you to go see Arthur Fullington, try to calm him down, assure him that we have everything under control."

"Why, is he causing trouble?"

"Yes and no. It appears he's exerted his influence on the press, who are taking the high road and not detailing the gory aspects of the murder. And he's offered a $100,000 reward for any information on the missing Aiden Ellsworth.

"But on the negative side, he's called every high ranking official in the state asking for help in finding his son's killer. And every single goddamn one of them is calling me for information and updates. It's only been four hours since the murder; we need some breathing room."

"Alright, I'm on my way there next."

"And for God's sake, don't show up wearing shorts."

The next sound X heard was the click as the chief hung up on his end, his way of saying good-bye.

X looked down at himself; he was already so consumed with the case that he'd forgotten that he was dressed for sailing, not detective work. The chief was right, he didn't look very professional. He turned back around to the park officers. "Listen, I've got to run. I'm sure I'll be seeing you."

"Detective King, one last thing?" DiMitri chewed on his bottom lip as he inched his way forward. "If there's anything I can ever do to help you out, just call. It doesn't matter if I'm on duty or not; it'd be an honor to work with you."

"You can start by calling me X," he said, laughing.

X watched a grin explode across DiMitri's face as his surly partner pulled him by the arm, dragging him toward their car.

• • •

"Could you have acted more juvenile?" Calhoon kicked the back tire of the patrol car with the toe of his boot, looked at DiMitri's face, and then kicked it again.

"What did I do wrong?" DiMitri asked, his face blank.

"You were kissing up to him. How is he ever going to respect us if that's the way you act?"

Calhoon balled up his fists and stomped around in a small circle before continuing his tirade. "Do you remember when you were sworn in? Part of the pledge was that you would wear your uniform with pride and dignity, because each officer is a representative of the entire force."

Kicking the tire one more time, he went on. "I could tell as soon as the county cops showed up at the church this morning that they were looking down at us. They already have a superiority complex; having you look like an idiot in front of the lead detective isn't going to help our reputation at all."

Calhoon yanked open the driver's door so hard that it swung against its hinges, snapping back and slamming closed again. He turned to DiMitri. "Aren't you going to say anything?"

DiMitri stood there, his mouth wide open. "I … I'm sorry. I didn't think …"

"That's your problem. You don't think." Calhoon grabbed his door again and pulled it open, getting behind the wheel. He looked up at DiMitri and yelled, "Aren't you going to get in?"

"Where are we going?" DiMitri asked as he ran around to the passenger side of the car.

"To Aiden Ellsworth's place. Maybe we can find something that the county cops missed."

He turned his head and looked in DiMitri's eyes and for the first time since his rant smiled. "Wouldn't that show them?"

● ● ●

Calhoon stopped the car directly across the street from Aiden Ellsworth's house and put it in park.

"Four squad cars and I don't see anyone outside. I bet you any amount of money that they haven't done a thorough search of the property." Calhoon got out of the car and pounded the top of the roof. "Are you coming?"

DiMitri pulled his seat belt off and followed his partner to the front lawn. "They've been here for at least a couple of hours; I'm sure they must've checked out here."

"Yeah, maybe. But you know what I learned when I was overseas?" Not giving DiMitri a chance to respond, Calhoon continued, "I learned that you never take anything for granted. Especially when it comes to the competency of your comrades."

Calhoon marched off in another one of his huffs, stopping at a line of overgrown shrubs. He kicked at a large bag of mulch that was leaning against a nearby poplar and was emptying it by the time DiMitri got to his side.

"Why don't you check through that first," Calhoon said, running the toe of his boot around the edge of the smelly pile. "Then move on to the bushes. They're pretty thick; it'd be a good place to hide something.

"I'm going to see what's in the back yard."

Calhoon marched toward the side of the house, leaving DiMitri to the task at hand. He used his foot to spread the mound around more evenly before stepping into the middle and squatting down.

DiMitri unfastened his watch and put it in his pocket before digging in, both hands at once; he wanted to get through this exercise as soon as possible. He'd barely started sifting through the fertilizer when the tip of his finger brushed against something.

DiMitri shifted his hand so he could move his fingers around the object, tugging at the corner of what felt like some kind of packaging. Whatever it was, it had a different consistency than the mulch.

"Calhoon," he called out. "I think I've got something here."

"If I can just grab hold ... I got it." DiMitri pulled his arm out, fertilizer now caked all over his shirt, holding a large plastic zip-locked bag.

Calhoon jogged the few feet he'd moved back to DiMitri and squatted down next to his partner. He took one edge of the dirtied baggie, brought it closer to his eyes, and then did something highly unusual for him. He gave his partner the thumbs up sign.

"Score one for the park police."

"Is that what I think it is?" asked DiMitri.

"You bet," Calhoon grinned. It's cocaine. And a lot of it."

8

X made the drive into New York City in 45 minutes, summer traffic on the expressway light. Arthur Fullington's penthouse was on the corner of 88th and Fifth, a prime location with spectacular views of Central Park. X was waiting in the formal parlor wearing the just in case outfit he always kept in the trunk of his car. The one he forgot to throw on before leaving his sailboat that morning, the extra one ready to wear in the event he got dirtied up at a crime scene.

He felt the vibration of his cell phone in his pocket and pulled it out, reading the text from Langly. "Approximately five kilograms of cocaine just found at Ellsworth's. FYI."

X was punching in a reply when a butler entered the room. He was wearing a starched white shirt and black slacks and had a square jaw and sallow complexion. A definite Lurch lookalike from *The Adams Family*.

"Mr. Fullington will see you now. Follow me, I'll show you to the library."

They walked down a hallway that boasted signed photographs of famous politicians and actors before entering a large study. The man who stood up from behind a long rectangular desk was almost as tall as X and appeared to be in good shape. He had a full head of silver hair and a nice tan, but his red eyes gave away the pain he was suffering.

"I'm sorry to have kept you waiting. I was in the middle of an important call. Condolences already," he said, leaning against the desk for a second, a tear running down his face. "Can you believe it?"

X watched as Arthur Fullington shook away the tear, straightening up and trying to reclaim his composure as he took a deep breath.

"We're all very sorry for your loss," X said as the two shook hands, surprised at the older man's fragile grip.

"I appreciate your coming by to give me a briefing," Arthur said as he guided X to a small seating area in the corner of the room, sitting in one of the chintz armchairs.

X took the other seat, thankful for the text he'd just read; that was the only real news he had to share.

"Mr. Fullington, I understand you believe that Aiden Ellsworth might have something to do with your son's death. Do you have anything tangible you can share that might substantiate your claim?"

"Unfortunately, no," he answered, his thick white eyebrows forming one strong line across his forehead. "But every instinct in my body leads me to him. Have you found the coward yet?"

"I'm sorry to say, no. We did, however, retrieve a sizable amount of cocaine at Ellworth's residence."

"Well there you go," Mr. Fullington said, hitting the table in front of him. "He's dirty. I knew it."

The grieving man's eyes searched X's face, apparently waiting for more information. Since that was basically all X had, he moved forward with the generic line he used so often.

"I want to assure you that we are working every angle, and I'm confident that we'll pin Aiden Ellsworth down soon."

Arthur scooted forward in his chair, pointing a shaking finger at X's chest. "Soon is not good enough. I want that bastard behind bars, and I want it now."

He reached over to a small silver bell that sat on the table and rang it, the tinny sound bringing the butler to his side immediately.

"A little of the Bowmore White, please. The '64."

Arthur didn't offer X a drink, just waited, his hands clasped together and his eyes fixed on the ceiling, as Lurch made the four step walk to the bar. He opened the Sub Zero freezer and shifted around several bags of ice before using silver tongs to place cubes into a crystal glass. He then added a generous amount of the whiskey, placed a linen towel over his forearm and returned.

Arthur Fullington had excellent taste. Not only was the single malt whiskey expensive, it was quite rare. X sat silently, gazing around the room, trying to allow Henry's father some semblance of privacy as the butler handed him the drink and disappeared back down the hallway.

Arthur brought the glass to his nose, inhaling the rich scent, and then took one long sip before settling into his chair.

"I've taken the liberty of putting together some paperwork I've compiled on Henry's company. There's the most recent audit I insisted on being done, and some other paperwork that my people came across and copied, information they thought I might be interested in seeing."

Mr. Fullington didn't seem at all embarrassed that he'd had his lackeys not only snooping, but copying his son's private files.

"I want to make sure you relay to Chief Hartman the urgency of this situation. Every hour that goes by allows that murderer 60 more minutes of life than my son had. I don't care what it takes; I will personally cover any additional resources the department might need to close this case. Money is no object."

Lurch materialized once again, bowing in front of his employer. "Sorry to interrupt, sir. The boxes you requested have been delivered to the lobby."

"Those are the documents I told you about," Arthur said as he stood up, steadier now that he'd had some liquid courage. "I expect your best forensic accountants to get to work on them right away."

X rose as well, was about to gently suggest that Mr. Fullington perhaps back off a little and let the police do their jobs without outside interference, when Fullington added, "By the way, I've contacted Judge Martin and he's already issued a search warrant for anything that might pertain to Aiden Ellsworth's finances. If you have any problem accessing his accounts because it's a weekend, let me know immediately. I can open any door you might need."

Arthur Fullington wasn't bragging; from what X could tell he was simply stating a fact as calmly as he might have just said that the Yankees were playing tonight.

But his countenance changed as he spoke his parting words, his eyes steely hard and focused, his voice authoritative. "My son's murderer will be behind bars before he is laid to rest."

It was not a prediction or a request.

It was an order.

9

X balanced the Starbucks cup on a fresh stack of files as he opened his office door. He ran his right elbow along the wall until he felt the familiar bump, hit the light switch and was halfway to his desk before realizing there was someone sitting on the couch.

"Langly, what are you doing sitting here in the dark?" X carefully lowered the folders onto the only remaining open desk space before retrieving his coffee and plopping down next to his friend.

"The chief sent me over to help you weed through Henry Fullington's business records. I must have just nodded off."

"Maybe some caffeine will help," X said, offering Langly the cup. "It's espresso, guaranteed to ruin your sleep if we're lucky enough to get to bed tonight."

"Talking about beds, how'd your pillow mate take your cancelling the vacation?"

"You know Ann, she's a pro. In fact, the first thing she did when she heard about those two little boys at the church was to offer their families counseling. They're already on her schedule."

"Don't think I could handle dating a shrink." Langly yawned, reaching over for the coffee and taking a long sip of the hot liquid. Passing the cup back, he continued. "So have you found out anything interesting about Henry's company?"

"Not really." X got up and retrieved a yellow legal pad that was on top of one of the piles. "Universal Technology. It's an internet tech firm that Henry Fullington founded a little over 3 years ago. There are 23 employees, and Aiden Ellsworth is listed as Vice President and Chief Operating Officer."

"Nothing incriminating on Ellsworth?"

"Not so far. He only has one senior staff member working directly under him, a Kelly Winston. When I called her, guess how she answered the phone?"

"Tell me it was something exciting, like 'What are you wearing?'"

X slapped his shoulder, grinning. "No. She said, "Aiden, is that you?""

Langly sat up straight, said, "Well isn't that intriguing; she was expecting Ellsworth to call."

"He was supposedly going to stop by to pick up a project they'd been working on, but my sense is that there's something more personal going on.

"All I could get from her is that Aiden is a technical engineering genius and that he's undervalued at Universal Technology."

"That sounds like a girlfriend talking," agreed Langly.

"We've got our numbers people looking at tax returns and accounting spreadsheets, profit and loss statements, that kind of thing. I'm actually more interested in hearing from Ryan. He's supervising the search at Aiden's home, and I'm hoping we might get lucky and find a smoking gun in his personal papers."

Three loud knocks at the door interrupted the discussion as Calhoon stepped into the room, holding his park police Stetson against his chest like a badge of honor. "Did you hear? We found a stash of cocaine in Aiden Ellsworth's front yard. Looks like we located Henry's supplier."

DiMitri rushed in behind his partner, moving around him so he was standing in front of X. "I'm the one who found it," he said, the perennial smile on his face dialed up a notch. "It's my first bust."

X dropped the legal pad onto his desk and extended his arm. "Yeah, we heard the news. Good work," he said as he shook both men's hands.

"Kudos," Langly added from his perch on the couch.

"We're here to fill out all of the paperwork," Calhoon said, putting the hat on his head and giving a nod. "Just thought we'd stop by, let you know so you don't waste your resources on looking for some local coke dealer.

"Come on, DiMitri, let's go."

DiMitri gave one last smile before trailing out of the office behind his partner like an eager puppy following his master.

X looked at Langly, saw the familiar cocky tilt of the head, the wide eyes and raised brows that meant he was skeptical.

"Are you thinking what I'm thinking?" asked X.

Langly sat forward on the couch, clasping his hands together. "If Ellsworth had that much coke, he was worth what, maybe a hundred and fifty thousand dollars?" Shaking his head, he relaxed back, crossing his leg over his knee. "So I don't see him having a problem paying off a bookie, do you?"

"Nope," X agreed. "Or it could be that Fullington senior is wrong about Aiden being in trouble. I was actually surprised he didn't hire someone to tail the guy. Fullington certainly isn't shy about how he goes about gathering information."

X looked around, finally spotting the coffee cup on the floor between Langly's feet, and grabbed it. "But since cash flow doesn't seem to be a relevant issue for Ellsworth at this point, I say let's get out of here. I'm tired of looking at files."

"What'd you have in mind?" Langly asked as he held out his arm, waited a few seconds, then shook it at X. "Aren't you going to help me up?"

X reached over to the couch and pulled until Langly was standing. "You're like an old man; you need to start working out." He hit the light switch and added, "Think you can handle a drive?"

10

They drove past the nearly empty parking fields of Jones Beach, the sun worshippers' gone for the day, and arrived at Gulf Cove just as dusk faded into nighttime.

The front gate was now being manned by the police, the television crews that had been stationed just outside the entrance blessedly gone for the evening.

X downshifted as he approached, his window down and his arm resting on the doorframe. "Hey, it's Rhoda, right? Anything going on?"

The female officer lowered her eyes, blushing. "All's quiet. You guys going back to the church?"

Langly cleared his throat and leaned across X's chest from the passenger seat. "Actually, per my suggestion, we're going to talk to Mr. Damson first, see if he can fill in some of the blanks from this morning."

X put his hand on Langly's forehead and pushed him back into his seat, nodded at Rhoda, and drove on.

"What on earth was that?" wondered X.

"That's me flirting." Langly pulled down his visor and opened the mirror. "How do I look?"

"Desperate," X answered absently as they turned into Mr. Damson's driveway, his focus now on the house in front of them. "Well he must be home, all the lights are on. Wonder why he didn't answer his phone?"

"Maybe he's taking a snooze and didn't hear it," Langly answered as he snapped the mirror back in place and got out of the car, approaching the front door. "I don't see a doorbell, do you?" He leaned closer to the screen and peered through the mesh. "Hello is anybody home?"

X shouldered his way to the door and looked closely. "Shit," he said as he grabbed the doorknob and tried to open it. "I think that's him on the floor."

The old lock rattled when X tried to force it, but it wouldn't give. He pulled his army knife out of his back pocket and sliced through the screen; Langly's hand shot through the tear and slid the locking mechanism open from the inside.

X rushed through the galley kitchen into the next room, kneeling by the old man's side, while Langly called for an ambulance.

"Mr. Damson, are you OK?" X leaned down, on auto pilot as he placed his index and middle finger against the soft hollow area of the man's neck looking for a pulse. He repositioned his fingers once, then again, and then a third time, searching for any glimmer of hope that the carotid artery was still doing its job, even if weakly. But it was as lifeless as Mr. Damson.

X could hear Langly on the phone telling them to hurry. He bowed his head, rubbing the bridge of his nose, the first feeling of fatigue creeping through his body.

"It's too late, Lang," X called out. "He's gone."

X took a big breath, let it out slowly, and refocused on the body in front of him. He lifted first one, and then the other of Mr. Damson's skinny arms, running his hand from shoulder to fingertips, the saggy skin and age spots free from any obvious wounds or trauma. Next he patted down his legs and torso, but everything appeared normal. Then finally he brought his attention to the man's face, gently closing the lids of his bulging eyes, a trail of dried saliva leaving a stain that went from the corner of his mouth down past his chin.

"His face looks symmetrical; probably not a stroke," commented Langly as he walked carefully around the room. "As I remember, he was 84. Could've been a heart attack," he added as he stopped at the side of a worn La-Z Boy Recliner, Damson's body just inches away.

X sat back on his heels, his eyes scanning the room. "There's no sign of a struggle. Maybe the poor guy just nodded off for a nap and died in his sleep."

"Who are you trying to convince, me or you?" Langly poked at the TV remote control and a highball glass that were on the small side table. "I know you believe in coincidences about as much as I do."

Langly sighed, and squatted down next to X. "This guy was one of only a very few people that can describe everything that happened at the church this morning. He was the first one there and, other than the cops, the last to leave. And now, by day's end, he's dead too?"

He stood back up, shrugging. "I don't like it."

• • •

X didn't like it either.

He was standing in the kitchen, looking at an unopened frozen dinner that was sitting on a butcher block table, moisture beading down its sides and now room temperature. Mr. Damson's last meal, but not.

His mind journeyed to a night years earlier, sitting at The Capital Grille on East 42nd in NYC and waiting for his father to arrive for their scheduled dinner. They both loved that restaurant; it had great steak, aged to perfection.

But his father never showed up, never enjoyed that meal. It was the night his father was killed.

X pulled himself out of the silent reverie as one of the CSI cops walked through carrying an evidence bag filled with prescription bottles. "Don't forget to get the contents of all of the trash containers," X told him. "We don't want to miss anything."

He stepped outside onto the deck and joined Langly, then leaned closer to his friend. X took a few obvious sniffs and smacked Langly. "You've been smoking."

"A lot of good those breath mints did," Langly mumbled under his breath.

"I heard that," X said. You've got to be serious about quitting or it's not going to happen."

"I am serious. I just had a momentary lapse of judgment, that's all. No need to get all excited about it.

"Saved by the bell," Langly said, turning away when X's cell phone sang the 3-tone tune.

"Hey Chief, we're just wrapping things up ..."

The familiar voice on the other end blared through the phone, "Forget about Damson. Aiden Ellsworth's body just washed up on the beach about two miles west of Gulf Cove. I want you there.

"Now."

angly held onto the dashboard of the Mercedes Coupe, white-knuckled, as X sped down the highway.

"There, that's where the chief said to go," Langly said, pointing at the Tobay Beach parking lot. X made the turn wide, crushing the beautiful array of wildflowers that curtained the entrance.

The car screeched to a stop, tail spinning. X was out of the automobile first, holding up his badge to the night watchman.

"Don't let anyone in or out of the area, got it?" he yelled as he ran towards the beach. He could see two police cruisers leave the highway and drive right over the sand dunes directly onto the ocean front.

"Your fancy car can't do that, can it?" wheezed Langly sarcastically as he tried to keep up with X.

The smell of grease and stale beer pervaded the air as they sprinted through the concession area. Seconds later they were on the beach and running through the sand, Officer Ryan's jeep parked just to their left, lights flashing. There was a young man sitting in the back seat, his wrist handcuffed to a grab bar and another eight teenagers sitting around a bonfire, huddled together and heads bent.

Officer Ryan was directing the four cops that had just arrived, pointing three of them in the direction of the group and the other to the person in the jeep.

"Ryan, what've you got?" The red and white beams flashing from the three patrol cars sent a kaleidoscope of colors across the sand, Ryan's dark police uniform at times blending into the darkness as he led them to a large form that was covered by an old beach towel.

"It's Ellsworth. He must have floated west from Gulf Cove, or been carried by the tide."

"How'd the blanket get there?"

"One of those kids," Ryan said, nodding his head in the direction of the fire. "I got here five minutes after the 911 call was made, and nobody's touched a thing since."

Seagulls dove wildly at the object, their squawking an eerie backdrop to the sound of the waves breaking on the beach.

X knelt down, threw an arm out to wave away the birds. "How can you be sure it's him?"

"Well I can't be positive, but whoever it is looks a whole lot like the picture posted on the BOLO, and the guy is wearing formal wear."

"Sounds like our man," X agreed. "Hey, would you mind turning off your brights? There's a little too much glare."

Ryan jogged back to the jeep and dimmed the headlights as X slowly pulled the towel to the side. Sure enough, he was looking into the face of Aiden Ellsworth, his body swollen and blue. His left eye was missing, a small minnow trying to swim out of the vacant eye socket.

"Looks like a classic dump." Langly squatted down on the other side of the corpse as X lifted the formal white shirt Aiden Ellsworth was wearing.

"See, there's a mark around his abdomen," X continued, pointing to the deep chafing around Aiden's waist. "I'd guess it's from a rope, and that whatever was tied to the other end was meant to keep him from surfacing."

Langly stood up, looking out to the ocean. "The knot must have come loose. No way will we find out what was on the other end now." He shrugged his shoulders. "I guess it doesn't really matter."

X ran his hands through his hair, shaking his head. "Are you kidding me? Of course it matters."

He resumed his inspection, leaning down closer to the decaying skull so he could get a better view. He carefully put his index finger against Aiden's temple and gave a firm push. The head lolled over to the side before flopping down to the chest, stopping at an unnatural angle.

X said, "His neck's broken."

He looked up at Langly and asked, "And the last time anyone saw Aiden Ellsworth alive was sometime around 9:20 a.m., sitting in a car with Henry having a drink?" X stood up and brushed the sand off of his hands.

"Affirmative. It's only a 3 minute walk from the church to the ocean; maybe he just strolled over to check out the view and was taken by surprise once he got there."

"But no-one remembers seeing him on the beach?"

"Nope. We went door to door, to every house in Gulf Cove. Other than a couple of dog walkers, there weren't many people out on the beach that early. And they didn't see any strangers."

X looked down at the mound, water lapping around the edges closest to the tide. "He's not wearing his tuxedo jacket. That could be important."

"Actually, we found it hanging in the back seat of his car."

"I wasn't aware of that," X said, irritated. "I went over every report generated on this case and don't remember seeing that piece of information."

"They probably just haven't had enough time to enter the data yet," answered Langly. "Regardless, it looks like we have a dead end as far as Ellsworth goes. Literally." Langly smirked, then said, "What? Not even a smile?"

X frowned back, his dimples disappearing into the now rigid jaw line.

Langly took the hint. "OK, really. What's the likelihood that Ellsworth killed Henry first and then was himself murdered by a totally unrelated person? I'd say it's an unlikely scenario."

"You're right," agreed X, "it makes more sense that they were both victims of the same perp."

X took one last look at the mound that was Aiden Ellsworth and turned, walking back up from the shore to Ryan's side.

"I want you to take the lead on the scene. You were here first, plus you look a heck of a lot fresher than either of us," X said, acknowledging Langly with a nod.

"I don't know about that," his colleague responded, "but I'll do you proud."

The beach around them was totally deserted except for the small group still sitting around the dying embers and a growing number of police. The distinct scent of marijuana was wafting from the fire, as well as melted plastic.

"So I guess those kids were partying when they found the body?" X guessed.

He was looking at Officer Ryan, thinking that he looked like a kid himself. Maybe it was the long sideburns, or the way his dark bangs were fluttering across his forehead because of the wind. But X knew otherwise; Ryan had a wife and two toddlers at home, had been on the force for almost a decade.

At Ryan's affirmative nod, X continued. "What are you going to do with them?"

"The guy in the jeep only had a joint on him. They must have thrown the rest of the stash into the fire, as you can obviously tell.

"They're all scared shitless as it is. If it's OK with you, I'm thinking I'll just give them a warning. They've had a traumatic enough evening as it is."

X looked back at the draped body of Aiden Ellsworth, seagulls dive bombing it from above. Yes; there'd definitely been enough trauma for one evening.

● ● ●

X threw his keys on the kitchen counter as he entered his house through the garage. He went directly to the refrigerator, opened the door and grabbed a Heineken. After one long pull, he leaned his head inside, looking for something to eat. There wasn't a whole lot in there; he was supposed to be away for the next week on his vacation with Ann.

He gave up, turned the lights off behind him and trudged up the free-standing mahogany staircase to his bedroom. His father had loved mahogany, said it was one of the reasons he bought the sprawling estate in Sands Point to begin with.

X sat on the side of his bed, thinking about the three victims the day had brought into his life. He would find the person responsible, make them pay.

No one deserved having the life of a loved one stolen away by murder.

No one.

12

It was already 85 humid degrees when X arrived at the Grande's home at 8:00 a.m. on Sunday morning. He rang the doorbell, looking around as he waited for someone to answer. He'd called in advance and knew they were expecting him.

It was a nice neighborhood in the town of Massapequa, homes spaced decently apart so each had some privacy. If he had to guess, he'd say that this one was a good 40 years old; its pink shingles, though weathered, still stood out among the other more traditional houses surrounding it.

He heard the chain lock slide before the door opened widely. Glenda Grande stood in front of him wearing an orange sweat shirt and matching pants and sporting a totally different hairstyle and color than when he met her yesterday. X tried not to stare at the wig, a Dolly Parton knock-off which was a little off center.

"Well good morning Detective," she gushed. "Oh my, you're even more handsome than I remember."

X cleared his throat, hoping to cover his embarrassment, and said, "Is your daughter available to talk?"

"She's just getting dressed. Come on in," Glenda said, taking hold of his arm and pulling him inside.

The scent of fresh chocolate chip cookies wafted from the kitchen at the far side of the house, the familiar older woman from yesterday making her way across the living room to the foyer. It looked like she might suffer from scoliosis, her upper back curved unnaturally, but she walked with good energy and a crooked smile on her face as she came to a stop directly in front of X.

"I hope you aren't here to arrest me," Monica Adams said smiling sheepishly.

"No, Ma'am," X laughed, "you look too tough for just one man to bring down."

Monica reached for the crucifix that hung from a fine chain around her neck. "Being nice to an old lady; that'll get you good marks from above.

"Now don't forget to tell Becca that my houseguest made those cookies from scratch," Monica told Glenda as she made her way to the door. "Camille was already so grateful to be able to accompany me to the wedding, especially since you don't even know her. But with the way things turned out ... well, she just wanted to do something nice to show her support."

X lingered in the small foyer while the women said their goodbyes, looking intently at a framed picture hanging on the wall. It was of a younger Glenda, with long dark braided pig-tails and a bandana tied across her forehead. Her tie-dyed shirt had a huge peace sign across the front and in her arms was a small baby, dressed in pink.

Distracted, X peered into the adjoining family room, guessing the style was minimalist. There were only three pieces of furniture; a couch with a nearby coffee table and an old blue trunk that sat against a wall adorned with stickers of some of the hottest Rock and Roll bands of the '70's. Other than a dozen or so large multi-colored seat cushions spread around the room and a few house plants, that was it.

X heard the front door close and glanced up just as Becca was coming down the stairs.

"Oh good, you're here," Glenda said to her daughter. "Do you remember Detective King from yesterday?"

Becca looked a hundred percent better than yesterday, when she could barely keep her tear-drenched eyes open or speak. She was dressed in a white tank top and short lime green skirt, wearing the highest heeled sandals X had ever seen. Her jet black hair was pulled back in a simple ponytail which showed off long dangling earrings made of what looked like real emeralds. The heavy necklace she wore hung right to the top of her cleavage, making it difficult for his eyes not to momentarily travel to exactly that spot. When he quickly jerked his head up, he noticed a brief smirk on her face before resettling into a composed grief.

Becca stopped two steps from the bottom of the staircase so that she was looking down at X. "I'm having a really bad day," she said, crossing her arms over her chest. "Why do I need to talk to the police again? I've already told you everything I know." A tear appeared at the corner of her eye as if on cue, hanging onto the edge of a long eyelash until it fell and slid slowly down her cheek.

They'd gotten precious little out of Becca yesterday; with the enormous pressure to make an arrest there was no way X was going to fall for crocodile tears.

"Ms. Grande, there are still a lot of unanswered questions regarding yesterday's events, many of which we are hoping you can answer."

Becca descended the last two stairs and stood directly in front of X. Even in her heels, she was a good five inches shorter than he. She took her time looking at him, starting at his head and moving slowly down to his shoes. "Gucci," she commented, her voice somewhere between surprised and impressed.

X looked down at his feet, shifting his weight from one to the other. "Yeah, well. About yesterday."

Becca laughed, a short snort of derision. "You mean that debacle that was supposed to be my wedding?"

"Yes, ma'am. There's been a development and I'm afraid I have some more bad news. We recovered the body of Aiden Ellsworth late last evening."

Becca stiffened, frozen for several seconds before she lashed out. "What do you mean you recovered?" She took several steps backwards, raised a trembling hand to cover her mouth, before advancing on X again. "But he's OK, right? He better be OK, because I'm going to kill him when I get my hands on him. How could he have just run off like that, especially after what happened to Henry?"

Becca's loud, hysterical voice ended in barely a whimper as she uttered her fiancé's name.

"I'm sorry, ma'am," X said. "I'm afraid he is deceased."

"Oh my God, how can this be happening to me?" Becca turned to her mother, as though she might be able to provide an answer, before stomping her way over the white shag carpet to a pile of the pillows. She reached down and grabbed the one on top by its sky blue tassels and threw it at the potted dracaena in the corner, sending it crashing onto the floor. "I just can't believe this," she said softly, looking overwhelmed.

Her mother rushed over and grabbed her hand. "You should sit down, honey." She led the now silent Becca to the couch, gently pushing her back until she was sitting.

Glenda turned back to X, ringing her hands. "What happened to Aiden?"

X lowered his head, trying to show at least a little respect for the dead. "It appears that he was killed sometime yesterday morning and his body disposed of in the ocean." It was as brief and concise an answer he could think of. He didn't see any reason to give the gory details.

"That bastard," Becca said, a spark of fire flashing through her eyes. "He was never a good friend to us. I don't know how Henry could have chosen him to be his best man. I'm glad he's gone." She pushed herself off the couch and started pacing.

"Becca, honey, you don't mean that," Glenda said before turning to X. "She's obviously still in shock; she doesn't know what she's saying."

"Yes I do, Mom." Becca's voice was firm, her dark eyes looking defiantly at her mother. "Ever since the trial, Aiden's been a total jerk. It's not as though I was the only witness who testified. I wasn't going to perjure myself just to help his cousin out."

She stopped talking abruptly and took a deep breath. "I'm sorry Detective, you said you had questions for me? And please call me Becca," she added, suddenly in a more conciliatory mood.

The obvious change of topics didn't go unnoticed; X knew they would get to the story about Aiden's cousin soon enough. He actually already knew all of the details, had read the police report just this morning. But Becca didn't need to know that.

Instead, he smiled. "OK, it's Becca then. I understand that you told investigators that you and Henry didn't use drugs. That's problematic, because we've gotten the preliminary autopsy reports on Henry and there is confirmed cocaine residue inside the nasal passage."

Becca looked blankly at X, offering nothing.

"So there are a few possibilities here," he continued. "Either Henry was doing cocaine and you didn't know about it, or you did know about it and possibly even participated."

Becca's eyes took a leisurely stroll around the room, looking anywhere and everywhere except in X's direction.

"Your honesty about this could be crucial in finding Henry's murderer. It's possible that the cocaine was tainted with something that would have knocked Henry out. That's the most likely scenario."

X didn't elaborate that it would have been next to impossible for the murderer to tie Henry's body around the bell without him already being unconscious.

"But if you did some of the same cocaine and didn't have any adverse reaction," X continued, "then that theory is less plausible. We want to make sure we don't waste our resources on false leads."

Glenda Grande glared at her daughter, looking as eager for a response as X.

He pressed a little harder. "Remember, you're not on trial here. I'm not with the DEA and I promise you that my only interest is to find out if it's possible that the cocaine Henry snorted was doctored."

"Can't you test the coke you found?"

"We've already done that and it appears to be pure. The problem is that some substances can't be detected by our general tox screening. It's going to take 48 hours to get back a complete report to positively rule out foul play."

Becca fidgeted with the large diamond ring on her finger before she finally responded. "OK, yeah, I did some coke with Henry before the wedding. But it was a total surprise to me; the guy Henry usually scored from got busted and is in jail up in Westchester."

"You promised me you were done with that stuff," Glenda said, grabbing onto Becca's arm when she tried to turn away. "I didn't go through the hell of raising a daughter on my own, working two jobs so you could have the best in life, just so you could waste it all doing drugs."

"Why do you have to make such a big deal over everything," Becca said, finally pulling her arm free from her mother's grasp. "Everyone experiments."

Becca watched her mother stomp into the kitchen and shrugged. "Mothers," she said, as though the word were some universal code for pain in the ass.

X wouldn't know; his had died when he was an infant. But he doubted there were many out there who would condone drug use by their children.

X smiled because he didn't know how else to respond and quickly moved on to more questions.

"Why Westchester County?"

"How am I supposed to know; I'm not a lawyer. All I know is that it was a freaking pain in the ass driving up there every day for the trial."

Becca walked over to the coffee table and yanked open a drawer, pulling out a pack of cigarettes and lighting one.

"Are we talking about Aiden Ellsworth's cousin here?" X asked.

Becca tilted her head, considering. "What the hell," she said, "you might as well hear the whole story.

"Aiden's cousin, Sean, was our dealer. Not that Henry and I did big time drugs or anything," she added, looking into the kitchen where her mother stood with her back to them, making a pot of coffee. Lowering her voice, she added, "We just used them recreationally. Sean lives up there in Westchester County."

She blew tiny smoke rings into the air and went on. "Anyway, when we wanted to party Henry and Sean would hook up, usually in the city, and make the deal. I assume you know Henry worked downtown on Wall Street?"

"Yes, we have that information," confirmed X.

Becca took another long pull of nicotine before going on. "So everything would have been great, but Sean blew it. He ended up selling 4 grams of cocaine to an undercover cop, and the rest, as they say, is history."

GINNA LEATHERBURY

"So how come you were subpoenaed?" questioned X.

Becca looked around for a non-existent ashtray and finally settled on grounding the smoldering tip of her cigarette on a nearby decorative plate of a unicorn.

"I had the unfortunate luck of witnessing the entire event. That coke was supposed to be ours. Henry's and mine. I almost never did a pick-up, but Henry had a last minute meeting so I showed up at a Starbuck's where they were supposed to meet.

"I guess Sean was looking for Henry and didn't recognize me when I walked into the store. Thank God for small favors," Becca added, "otherwise I might be in jail too."

It was always fascinating to X, the difference between reading a police report in black and white versus having a witness tell the same story in full color. He listened to Becca's account without interrupting.

"Before Sean and I could connect, an undercover cop showed up. I can still see her like it was yesterday," Becca laughed, shaking her head. "She was dressed like a hooker; trampy clothes, fishnet stockings and cowboy boots. And she headed straight for Sean, like she knew he was carrying.

"I could see his pecker get hard from where I was standing and figured there goes our stash, he's going to leave with that slut. So I hurried up over there, trying to get his attention.

"Fat chance of that," Becca said sarcastically. "I could have lit my hair on fire and he wouldn't have even noticed. He was definitely otherwise occupied. Personally, I didn't care if they hooked up or not. I just wanted to get the ... well, you know, the coke."

Becca went back to the sofa and plopped down, spreading her arms. "And that's the story."

X was silent for a second. "So they called you as a witness because you saw Sean give drugs to the cop?"

"I heard the whole thing too. Sean quoting prices and amounts, and then suggesting that they do a trade, sex for drugs. That's when she pulled out her badge and arrested him for possession, dealing, and soliciting.

"And do you want to know the biggest shocker? Amazingly," she said, drawing the word out, "I was the only one there who witnessed anything. I tried to get the hell out of there, like everyone else, but I was practically on top of them when it went down. The cop looked me straight in the eye and ordered me to stay put, said I was a material eyewitness to a crime."

X gave her the most sympathetic look he could muster before asking, "Was Aiden a user too?"

"Aiden got off on anything he could," Becca answered matter-of-factly. "Liquor and drugs were his preference, but he'd drink mouthwash and sniff glue if that's all there was available."

X remembered Kelly Winston swearing up and down that Aiden was clean. Of course it wouldn't be the first time a guy kept a bad habit from his girlfriend, if indeed that was what Kelly was to him.

"I appreciate your candor, Becca. It's very important that we be aware of anything that might be relevant to Henry's and Aiden's death. Is there anything else you can think of that might be important? I know you said that Henry didn't have any enemies, but sometimes things occur to you after you've had some time to think about it."

She shook her head no as she got back up and started pacing again. "You know, I wish I could think of something. None of this makes sense."

An hour later, after pushing and prodding her memory, X let Becca lead him to the door.

"You have my card; please contact me if anything comes to mind, even if you think it's not that important."

"I do have one question," she shouted out as X walked to his car. "When do I get my belongings back? I left my make-up bag in that closet they call a bride's changing room. And the cooler. I hope you kept those bottles of champagne chilled. And the caviar, oh my God, I forgot about the beluga! I have the name of the cop I told to put everything in a refrigerator. His name was DiMitri."

13

X followed the warden down a long hallway of the Westchester Penitentiary, the sound of his footsteps reverberating off the walls. His curiosity was piqued; he had two conflicting reports about Aiden Ellsworth's drug use despite the fact that a sizeable stash of cocaine was found hidden outside his house. And add to that a cousin in jail for dealing. X wanted to conduct this interview himself, see if the cousins shared more than just a blood relationship.

When they arrived at the door X looked through the small window, taking a good look at Sean Baker. He was sitting at a bare table in an otherwise empty room and appeared to be studying his cuticles. His thinning blond hair was combed straight back on his head and looked greasy under the fluorescent lights, the standard prison uniform a little baggy over his chest.

At the sound of the door opening, Baker looked up expectantly before a frown took over his face. He narrowed his eyes, leaned his head forward and studied X. "I don't know you, do I?"

"No, you don't. I'm with the NCPD."

X was pulling his badge out to show Baker when the prisoner cut him off with a wave of the hand. "I don't need to see it. You say you're a cop, you're a cop."

He refocused his attention to his hands. "But what I'm wondering is what a nassau county cop wants with me?"

"I'm sorry to say I'm here with bad news." X took a chair on the opposite side of the table.

"Hey, I'm used to bad news," Baker said, spreading his hands, pointing them at the four walls surrounding them. "I'm here for the next three years, two if I'm lucky and get parole. And I can't count on that. You see, I ain't no choir boy, you know what I mean? I seem to attract trouble. It's like I'm just sitting around, minding my own business, and boom, trouble comes along and bites me in the ass." He laughed hard, tapping his hands on the table like he was beating a drum.

"This news is about your cousin Aiden. He's been murdered."

Sean's fingers abruptly stopped their movement, his hands curling into fists. He bent forward at the waist, his head hanging limply as he drew in several deep breaths, before sitting back up.

"Murdered?" his voice squeaked. "Who the hell would murder Aiden? He's the nicest guy I've ever met. I can't even believe we're related, you know what I mean? It's like he's so good, and I'm – well, me, not so much. No one who knew Aiden would hurt him. Murdered?" he repeated. "Holy crap."

Sean leaned over again but this time smacked his forehead against the table, bam bam bam, fast and steady, much like he'd done with his fingers just moments before. X let silence fill the room as he watched the man opposite him. If this were a performance, if Sean already knew that Ellsworth was dead via some drug cartel pipeline, he deserved an Academy Award.

Sean finally looked back up, rubbing his eyes. "Aiden's mom must be freaking out, she loved him like crazy." He rested his back against the chair, explaining. "He was her only kid. I used to go over to their house for sleepovers and she always took real good care of him, made real dinners and always had ice cream for dessert, every time. It was like heaven for me."

X continued his silence, waiting to see where Sean would lead the conversation. Finally the question came.

Sean leaned forward, asked in a conspiratorial whisper, "So what exactly happened?"

"His body was found last night, but we believe he was killed earlier in the morning." X paused before adding, "He wasn't the only victim. His good friend, Henry Fullington, was also murdered."

"Son of a bitch," Sean said, smacking his hand against the table. Henry Fullington is the reason I'm locked up in here. I can see why someone would want to take out Henry, but not Aiden. Aiden's a good guy."

"Why do you think someone might want to kill Henry?" pressed X.

"Because he's an asshole," Baker declared simply. He looked down as his dirty nails before polishing them against his shirt.

"That's it?" X asked. "Nothing more specific?"

"Nope." He put his elbows on the table and smiled back at X.

X pursed his lips, his frustration mounting. "You seem to like short sentences. Here's one for you. Was your cousin a user?"

Sean shook his head. "No way, he never touched the stuff. He had asthma when he was a kid and it totally freaked him out. He'd never do anything that might screw up his breathing. But don't get me wrong, Aiden could definitely party. He drank like a fish."

X noted that this made the tally two to one in favor of Ellsworth not being a drug user and moved on.

"So you were Henry's supplier?"

Sean shrugged. "I guess there's no point in denying it. That's why I'm inhabiting this hell hole."

"What I don't understand," X said, ignoring the urge to correct his grammar, "is why use you when Aiden was dealing too."

"Aiden deal? There's no way my cousin would touch the stuff, even for a profit."

"Are you sure about that? When's the last time you even spoke to him? Were you close?"

"We were like brothers when we was kids, just like this," Sean answered, holding out his hand, his pointer and middle fingers crammed together. "And we stayed close," he said defensively.

"He stood behind me at the trial, even though I let him down. Like what a brother would do." Sean looked down, shaking his head. "But I could see the disappointment in his eyes, that I was selling drugs. He told me it was a bad thing to do, that I was responsible for kids getting hooked and people losing their jobs and families.

"That's how I know he could never deal. Not Aiden. No way."

Baker looked genuinely ashamed as he spoke, and X sensed that he was speaking the truth.

"Do you know where Henry might have gone to get drugs after your arrest? Is it possible he went directly to your supplier?"

"You're kidding, right?" Sean shifted in his seat, crossing his arms over his chest. "My lawyer warned me about this kind of thing, people fishing for information that I wouldn't give at the trial.

"See, here's the thing. I ain't no snitch. I've been, ah, doing what I do for almost 30 years now. Started when I was in middle school. Some guy came up to me and asked if I wanted to make easy money, and I say, 'Sure, what do I have to do?' Guy says it's like being a waiter. I take an order from someone, bring it to the chef, he makes it all up, and I deliver it back. But I ain't really a waiter, see what I mean? That's what you call a ufism."

"You mean euphemism," X corrected.

Sean looked at him with a blank expression. "Huh?"

"Never mind," X said, sorry he'd interrupted him. "Just go on with what you were saying."

Baker looked up to the ceiling, closed his eyes, and said, "Where was I? Oh, right. See, if I don't ask no questions, I don't get no flap. Cash and carry. That's what my job is. And I make good money, too. Didn't need no fancy college degree to get ahead. Check it out if you want to. I own a big house in Dobbs Ferry right on a golf course. I can buy any woman I want. Well, they have to be for sale, I sure as hell learned my lesson on that one," he laughed, gave X a wink like they were fraternity brothers sharing war stories. "Wouldn't want no fancy educated cunt anyway. I like my women to be professional, if you get my drift.

"So I been doing business with the same couple of guys since I started. But I don't know nothin' about any of them, who's who's boss or anything like that. You see, I don't care! Don't give a rat's ass! Because me, I'm just happy being their delivery man."

He gave X a wide smile. "And they like that about me. They don't have to worry I might accidentally spill the beans on them."

Sean Baker leaned back in the chair, relaxed, looking like he believed his life really was that simple.

"OK," X sighed. "So let's pretend I believe you, that you don't know anything about your own outfit. What about rivals?"

Sean shrugged. "I'd be just as dead if I snitched on them."

X stood up, pulled the car keys from his pocket, and pushed his chair in. "You said Aiden was like a brother to you. Yet you're telling me that you don't have anything to say, even if it's possible someone in your organization killed him?"

Sean stood up too, shaking his head vehemently. "I'm telling you man, it couldn't have happened that way. I'd stake my life on it, Aiden was clean."

"That's an interesting choice of words," X commented, giving Sean a once over. "Because if you're wrong, they'll know I was here.

"And your life won't be worth shit."

14

X looked at his watch as he ran up the stairs two at a time, finally reaching the third floor and heading into the chief's office almost ten minutes late for the 6:00 p.m. interagency meeting. There were five chairs planted across from the chief's desk occupied by the two parkies and Officers Langly and Ryan. The last seat was intended for X.

When X walked into the room, Hartman was standing in front of DiMitri, his finger pointed into his face. "Listen, son, I know you don't have a lot of years under your belt. But you never refer to a dead body as being hog tied to anything, much less a bell. Especially to the press."

The veins on the side of the chief's neck were bulging and the sweat stains under his arm pits were almost halfway down his shirt. "Do we need to check and make sure that your fucking brains weren't mixed in with Henry Fullington's at the bottom of that belfry?"

DiMitri shrunk into the chair and hung his head, looking like he wanted the floor to swallow him. The room was otherwise silent.

Hartman turned, saw X had arrived, and said, "You're late," as he stomped around him, his tie swishing back and forth across his big belly, and sat behind his desk.

X looked around the room, waiting for someone to offer up an explanation as to what he'd walked in on, before approaching DiMitri. He touched his shoulder, gave it a reassuring squeeze. "What's going on?"

It was as if X had somehow transferred courage to the park police officer. DiMitri corrected his posture, calmed his quivering lips, and spoke. "It's my fault, Detective X. A couple of buddies of ours," he said, glancing at Calhoon, "took me out for a drink to celebrate my first big bust. You know, finding the cocaine at Ellsworth's." His lips curved into a momentary smile, a fleeting sign of pride, before he continued. "Anyhow, we got to talking about the case and everyone kept buying me shots and … well, there's no excuse. I don't remember saying anything like what Chief Hartman just said, but I guess I must have."

"And there was a reporter there?" X asked, confused.

"No, but somehow parts of our conversation ended up being posted on a blog."

X turned to face the chief. "Frank, what's the big deal? We have bloggers saying crap about us all the time. Everyone knows that half the stuff they say is garbage. And the other half is just their opinion."

"Right now my name isn't Frank," the chief sputtered. "This is business. And why are you in such a good mood anyway? Have you solved the case? Or I should say cases," he added, with heavy emphasis.

He didn't give X a chance to respond, he just charged on, shouting, "I'll take your silence as a no."

Hartman stood up and grabbed his jacket from the back of his chair before kicking it backwards, sending it crashing into the wall and adding another ding in the already beat up surface. He put his hands on the desk and leaned towards X. "You think you can do better with this group, have at it. The next time the governor calls wanting to know the status of this investigation, I'll let you give him the news that we're no closer to solving this thing than we were yesterday morning when we got the original call."

He grabbed his briefcase and stomped out of his office, the sound of the slamming door reverberating behind him.

"Well, that was fun," X said as he pulled the vacant chair so that it was facing the others and sat, extending his long legs. "It's always good to see the chief in a good mood."

No one looked particularly amused by the comment until Langly laughed. "Yeah, right." Then he turned to DiMitri and said, "Try not to let Hartman get to you; he's hard on everyone. If I had a dollar for every time he chewed me out I'd be a rich man."

X saw a smirk cross Ryan's face, noticed that DiMitri let go of the death grip he had on the arms of his chair. Calhoon, as usual, was unreadable. But all in all, X would say mission accomplished; Langly had lightened the mood in the room.

"So," X said, "as the chief so kindly reminded us, we have a few cases to solve and the pressure is on. There've been a couple of major developments since Fullington's murder. Calhoon, why don't you start with a summary of what you've been working on."

Calhoon stood up, his body perfectly perpendicular in his starched uniform and cleared his throat. "After leaving the Gulf Cove crime scene I took it upon myself to go over to Aiden Ellsworth's place of residence and search for any evidence of criminal behavior. My partner and I were there, inspecting the yard, when he found the drugs." He nodded for DiMitri to pick up the conversation, the first time he'd even looked in his direction since X had entered the room.

DiMitri did a double take; his mouth opened in surprise and whispered, "Me?"

Calhoon clenched his jaw and said, "Yes, you," the words *you idiot* left unsaid but loud and clear.

DiMitri shrugged, leaned forward and said, "I was searching through the contents of a bag of fertilizer and felt a plastic bag. When I pulled it out I saw that it was filled with white powder. Calhoon verified that it was cocaine," he added before scooting back into his chair, his statement finished.

X looked over to Ryan. Compared to Calhoon, the county cop looked like he'd just come through the spin cycle. His shirt was wrinkled, his hair was disheveled, and his sideburns were uneven, the right side looking neatly trimmed and the left totally forgotten. "And our guys didn't find it during their search?" X asked him.

"At the time we were focused inside the house. I'm sure we would have uncovered it in due course," Ryan added, raising his chin just a bit, his voice a little defensive.

It was more of a snort than a laugh, but it was loud enough to get everyone's attention.

X pulled his legs in and shifted in his chair, looking up at the offending party, Calhoon. "Is there a problem?"

Calhoon was still standing, giving another snide laugh. "So much for the working as a team speech you fed me and my partner yesterday, Detective King. What, just because your guys didn't find the drugs at Ellsworth's home the evidence is now suspect?"

X blinked, looking at a snarling Calhoon and not sure he could believe his ears. "That's not what I meant at all," he said, standing up so they'd be on more equal footing. "I was just thinking out loud, try-ing to make sense of things. I happened to just come from interviewing Ellsworth's cousin, who's incarcerated up at Westchester Penitentiary for dealing. He swears Aiden would never have anything to do with drugs, and I found him to be very convincing."

"So a convicted felon who also happens to be related to our stron-gest lead in the case tells you some story and you automatically accept it as true?

"I know I don't have the decorated title or experience that you have, sir," Calhoon said, a fine mist of spit coming out with his words, "but I was taught to follow the laws of logic in an investigation. And I don't see how it could be more obvious. Henry was a drug user. And we have the evidence that proves that Aiden Ellsworth was a drug dealer. Now both of them are dead, along with a third victim, and there are no other suspects, not even a single person we've found that might have a grudge against either of them.

"Our focus should be on Aiden Ellsworth and the fact that his house is a hub for drug dealing. In my humble opinion." He bowed and then added, "Sir."

If that was supposed to be a sign of respect, Calhoon had failed miserably. X felt like he'd just been given the finger. X pursed his lips, wanting to consider what was just said without judging that view point based on the way it was presented.

In a very calm voice, he finally responded. "You raise some very good points, Officer Calhoon. I didn't mean to insinuate that a drug angle be ruled out completely."

Calhoon nodded, the only indication that he'd been heard, and sat down.

X rubbed his jaw, noting he needed a shave, as he paced around the group. "I've got two sources who say Aiden stayed away from drugs. His girlfriend and his cousin."

"And I'm sure they wouldn't lie," Calhoon piped in.

DiMitri was looking like he wanted that hole in the floor to reappear. "What's the matter with you?" he whispered to his partner.

X ignored them both and kept talking. "Ellsworth was also rumored to be in some trouble with a bookie he could have easily paid off with that much coke."

Calhoon shrugged his shoulders. "You're assuming the guy was capable of making rational decisions. There's no telling why druggies do anything; their minds are warped."

"I don't know," pressed X. "Something just feels off."

"Feelings aren't facts, Detective," Calhoon said, remaining stonily silent for the remainder of the meeting.

● ● ●

When X finally called it a night, Calhoon was the first out the door, walking rapidly down the hallway and into the stairwell just as Langly caught up to him.

"Hey, you."

Calhoon didn't stop at the harsh words, just continued on down the stairs.

Langly grabbed the handrail and followed, catching up to him on the landing. When he opened his mouth to speak he started wheezing and had to lean over to catch his breath.

"You OK?"

Langly straightened up and nodded, shocked that the parkie had bothered to stick around.

"So are you going to ream me now for being disrespectful to the detective?" Calhoon asked.

"Naw," Langly said, swatting at him with a laugh. "X is a big boy; he can take care of himself."

"I'm here to ream you for treating your partner like an asshole. The kid is obviously intimidated by you, and from what I've seen you aren't doing anything to help the situation."

Calhoon leaned against the wall, raised his eyebrows. "You're serious?"

Langly walked over and stood so that they were side by side, the paleness of his skinny arm in sharp contrast to the parkie's stiff gray uniform.

"When Hartman was up there chewing DiMitri up and spitting him out, you didn't say one word to defend him. Man," he said, knocking his elbow against Calhoon's, "it doesn't matter what the situation is, you got to always have your partner's back, no matter what."

Langly pushed himself off the wall and started walking back up the stairs slowly, adding over his shoulder, "No matter what."

15

"**D**id you hear him?" screamed Calhoon for the thousandth time as they walked through the parking lot of park police headquarters. "He couldn't have been more condescending. 'You raise some very good points'" he said, mimicking X's voice. "Who does he think he is?

"It's just like when I was in the service. The higher the rank, the more bullshit they deal out. Add a few bars to their uniform and all of a sudden they think they're God. You've got to watch out for people like that, DiMitri. They'll steal your ideas and take credit for your actions, you can count it. It happens every time."

DiMitri was dragging along beside Calhoon pretending to pay attention. He was used to Calhoon being difficult, but the way he'd spoken to X was appalling. They finally made their way through the side door and into the locker room. It was 11:00 p.m. and a good dozen or so park officers were in the process of either coming on or going off duty. A chorus of 'Hey, how ya doing," echoed through the room as DiMitri went straight to his locker, ignoring the group.

O'Rourke, a middle-aged Irishman and one of DiMitri's drinking buddies from the night before, was at his side in an instant.

"So how'd it go today, me friend," he asked, the brogue a little thicker than usual.

DiMitri shrugged the man's hand off his shoulder, avoiding looking at him. "Fine. The usual."

"He's a little touchy." Calhoon walked over and joined the two, putting a foot up on a bench that ran down the center of two rows of lockers. "The brass over at county just ripped him a new one."

DiMitri leaned his head against the locker, wondering why his partner couldn't just keep his mouth closed. "It's no big deal," he said, hoping to end the conversation.

But O'Rourke didn't let it die. "Why? I can't imagine anyone getting mad at you. Especially after your big score yesterday."

"He had a big something yesterday," Calhoon said, laughing. "Unfortunately, it was his mouth." He gave DiMitri a slap on the shoulder and moved to his locker, two rows away, chatting with some of the other guys in the room.

DiMitri turned to face O'Rourke. "Some of the stuff I said at the bar last night ended up on a blog. The chief wasn't very happy."

O'Rourke took a step back. "No way. We were in a booth way in the back; no one could have overheard us talking." Then, a split second later, "Wait a minute. You don't think one of us had anything to do …"

DiMitri held his arm out, shaking his head. "No. Absolutely not," he said with a lot less conviction than he'd intended.

O'Rourke folded his beefy arms across his chest, see-sawing on his toes. "I know you haven't been here long, but trust me. What's said in confidence around here stays that way. I know every man who was at that table last night personally and would stake my life on any one of them."

"I know, I know," DiMitri said. "It's just been a long day."

He sat on the bench and leaned over to pull his boots off. O'Rourke parked his body at his side, leaned over and whispered. "I can see this is bothering you, so I'll tell you what I'm going to do. I'm going to have a one on one with every person there last night, ask them point blank if they might have inadvertently spread some of the info we were talking about. But I wouldn't count on it.

"If there's a leak, it didn't come from any of us."

16

X arrived at the coroner's office at first light on Monday morning, a large double espresso in his hand. When he finally got home last night, he was disappointed not to find Ann's small body curled up in the middle of the bed. She probably decided to stay at her place assuming he'd be working late. He smiled, thinking of how she always ended up dead center of his california king, leaving all 6'2" of him to somehow navigate around her.

He pulled his wandering mind back to the present and to Dr. Dormer, who was standing at a long countertop bent over a microscope, deep lines on his forehead as he concentrated on what he was looking at. X tapped on the door as he entered.

"I've been expecting you." Dormer glanced up at the wall clock before pulling off his glasses and absently let the chain around his neck catch them.

X knew the man had a penchant for organization; his files were organized, his staff was organized, and his thoughts were organized. And apparently so were his scheduled appointments.

"Sorry I'm a little late," X apologized, double checking his watch and noting that it was running a few minutes slow. "But I'm anxious to hear what you've found."

"You're not the only one. I've never gotten so many calls from the chief; he is really pushing to get these autopsies done. Apparently he's getting a lot of heat from the governor."

Dormer walked over to his desk, totally cleared except for three legal size files that lay side by side. "Shall we begin?" he asked as he sat down and rolled his chair in, reaching for the file on his far right.

Down to business right away; X appreciated that. Everyone was equally under the gun on these cases; there really was no need for pleasantries. "Shoot," he said, sitting in one of the folding metal chairs opposite the coroner. If they were going for comfort, whoever chose this particular piece of furniture had failed miserably.

"Henry Fullington," Dormer recited as he opened the folder. "Parts of the victim's head were found intact and I was able to confirm extensive and prolonged cocaine use based on the partial nasal passage examined."

X nodded. "The chief relayed that Henry was a user, but it's good to know to what extent."

"Well here's something you haven't heard before." He put his glasses back on and flipped through a few pages before stopping.

"It appears that Henry Fullington was poisoned, and the source was not the cocaine. We haven't been able to identify the toxin yet, but the amount was lethal. He was already showing signs of multiple organ failure at the time of his death."

"Poisoned? Are you sure?" X looked questioningly across the desk, knowing it was a stupid question to have asked. Dormer was one of the most highly recognized medical examiners in the country; yet it was hard for X to wrap his brain around this new curveball.

Dr. Dormer slid his glasses down to the tip of his nose and looked at X. "I'm positive. The tox screens don't lie. In combination with the coke he snorted and the amount of alcohol in his system, it's my opinion that there was a simultaneous overload to his central nervous system. My guess is that he suffered a sudden and acute loss of body function in the minutes right before his death."

He slid his glasses back on and referred back to his notes. "Which would explain how the murderer was able to arrange him around the bell."

"I've been wondering about that," X said. "Logistically, it couldn't have been easy."

"It would have been impossible without the slashing," Dormer said as he opened a drawer and pulled out a silver letter opener, using it as a prop. "There were several long deep cuts around each of the limbs," he said, demonstrating on his own body where they'd been made, at each arm pit and then up and around the shoulder and then at the groin area, "with a serrated knife. It looks as though they were made purposefully to avoid immediately severing the limbs, but deep enough for them to dismantle given the moderate movement of the bell."

Dr. Dormer glanced over at X. "Are you OK? You're looking a little green."

"I'm fine," X answered, swallowing down the bile that just rose unexpectedly. He usually had a stomach made of steel, had never once gotten sick at a crime scene, or even during an autopsy.

Except for that one time. When they found his father, dismembered, body parts stacked on top of each other in a neat little pile in the back of a closet. It had taken years of therapy to get that image out of his head, yet it still maintained the power to reappear at any moment, to force its way to the forefront of his mind and claim his heart and soul, fill him with sorrow. He squeezed his eyes shut, refocused back to the present. "I just can't believe the lengths this guy went to."

"It was carefully planned out, I'll give you that," Dr. Dormer said as he laid the pseudo knife on the desk. "Whoever it was even thought to cover the wounds with a solution designed to reduce bleeding, and then wrapped them with gauze. The result was to avoid copious bleeding until the moment that the limb detached from the body."

X's stomach did one more flip flop. "Were you able to determine cause of death?" he asked, a hand unconsciously covering his mouth.

"That's the million dollar question. In this instance, time of death pretty much establishes the cause. I can't say with certainty whether he was dead before being draped around the bell or if the massive head trauma from crashing against it is what killed him. The two events happened so closely together that I had to send tissue samples to pathology for a more detailed analysis. It'll be a few days before I can pinpoint what actually killed him."

X ran a hand through his hair, knowing the delay could hold up their entire investigation. "This is not the kind of news I wanted to give to the chief."

"I don't envy you that job, X." Dormer closed the file and replaced it neatly on the desk before picking up the one in the middle. "Now, are you ready for corpse number two?"

"Do I have a choice?" X mumbled as he shifted his weight on the chair, trying to get comfortable.

Dr. Dormer cleared his throat and continued. "The Aiden Ellsworth case is quite interesting. Again we have high levels of alcohol in his system, though evidence of recreational drugs, namely cocaine, is not evident.

So the girlfriend and cousin were telling the truth, thought X as Dormer continued speaking.

"That said, however, does not make him any less a candidate than Henry Fullington for having a catastrophic reaction to the toxin that he ingested."

"Ellsworth was poisoned too?" X didn't remember standing up; he was on automatic pilot as he walked around Dormer's desk to see the report for himself. "But I was there right after he got pulled out of the ocean. It looked to me like his neck was broken."

"Indeed it was," confirmed Dormer. He scooted his chair to the side, X standing next to him and leaning over to see the paperwork. "But that wouldn't necessarily be atypical if in fact he drowned due to the poison."

"I'm listening," said X, waiting for further explanation.

"If the cause of death was drowning, Ellsworth's body would have sunk to the bottom of the ocean. Between the waves, the current and the topography of the ocean floor, it could well end up quite battered and have sustained broken body parts.

"So Ellsworth's neck was broken post-mortem?"

Dr. Dormer smiled. "That's not what I said; I was merely making a point."

X shook his head, confused. "I'm not following."

"There was no water in Ellsworth's lungs, which allows me to say with almost certainty that he was dead when he hit the water."

"But," X said, waiting for the punch line.

"There's something called a dry drowning. It's a bit technical, but I'm happy to explain if you'd like."

"No, that's OK," X said, patting Dormer's shoulder before returning to his chair. He stood behind it, his fingers tapping on the cold metal. "You know, when I saw Ellsworth it looked like his head was almost ripped off his trunk. A clean break, straight through the cervical bones. It's an assassin's dream kill; the only weapon you need to carry are your own hands."

"I tend to agree with you," Dormer answered matter-of-factly. "But the chief doesn't want me to make any assumptions."

Dormer opened his desk drawer and pulled out a piece of paper, handing it across the desk to X.

"Here's the most recent e-mail I got from Hartman. He wants every i dotted and t crossed in these autopsies, and that's what I'm doing."

X read the note and blew out a long breath. "It says the Fullington funeral is scheduled for tomorrow. Have you even released the body yet?"

"A hearse showed up at 10:00 p.m. last night and descended on us like the cavalry. And there was no negotiation, either. They came for Henry Fullington and by golly they left with him." Dr. Dormer looked a little perturbed that his turf had been violated, but his practical side resurfaced with a sigh. "I guess it doesn't really matter anyway; I had all the samples I needed."

X slid the e-mail back across the desk, said, "And Ellsworth. From a practical standpoint, what do you think happened?"

"I'd say, off the record, that cause of death was the broken neck. I was able to get a good look at his organs, thanks to getting him out of the water when we did. Decomposition was minimal, and though there was more poison in his system than in the Fullington case, it's not what killed him."

Dormer leaned back into his chair. "Do we know how Mr. Ellsworth's body made its way to the waterfront?"

"Based on the lack of evidence to the contrary, I am assuming that he went willingly."

"Really," said Dormer. "That's surprising."

X explained. "Other than being bodily dragged there in full day-light, the only way to have gotten him there would be by vehicle. And no-one reported seeing any on the beach that entire day."

"Hmm." Dormer closed the file, moved it to the side of his desk before opening the third. "Onto Mr. Damson, the elderly gentleman that oversaw the church."

"Tell me he just died of old age," X sighed.

"Sorry, can't do that Detective. And this one wins the prize for the most poison ingested, which precipitated a massive heart attack."

"This is crazy. The connection between Fullington and Ellsworth is obvious, but how does Damson fit in?"

"I'm assuming that's a rhetorical question since that's your forte. All I can tell you is that, in all three cases, there was enough poison in each of their system to eventually kill them."

"Yet two of the three victims were murdered before the poison did its job," X commented as Dormer closed the file in front of him and pushed away from his desk.

X saw the cue that the meeting was over and stood up. "How long before you can nail down that toxin?"

"It's on the fast track. I can't close any of these cases without that information, and I want to clear my desk of all three."

X believed him. No-one was more organized and efficient than Dr. Dormer.

• • •

"All three were poisoned," X told Langly, speaking into his cell phone as he made his way back to headquarters for the meeting he'd just scheduled with Becca Grande. "Call the parkies, have them check out the restaurant where the rehearsal dinner was held. And I want Ryan over to the caterers, and tell him to turn everything upside down. We need to find out the source of that toxin; for all we know, it's still out there.

"The last thing we need is more dead bodies."

17

Glenda was watering the small petunia plant on the windowsill when Becca came into the kitchen.

"Where did you hide my suitcases mom?" she asked as she poured herself a cup of coffee.

"I didn't hide them; I just put them back in the garage. "Why?"

"Because I need them for the honeymoon."

Glenda turned around, sure she must have misunderstood. "What did you just say?"

Becca was wearing a yellow halter dress, a big floppy sun hat in her hand. "Mom, I have to get away from here. With everything that's happened, it's just too much for me to handle; I think Henry would want me to go on out to Montauk Manor without him. I can relax, have some spa treatments, and start the grieving process."

Becca looked down at her recently painted nails, still wet, and blew on them. "Anyhow, it's already paid for and I can't get the money back."

"What do you mean you can't get the money back?" Glenda squeaked. "Did you tell them what happened?"

"Of course I did. I said that my fiancé was murdered just minutes before our marriage and that we obviously would no longer be coming for the honeymoon."

"And they refused to refund you the money?" Glenda asked, shocked.

Becca averted her eyes. "Well, not exactly. The lady told me that since Henry made the reservation and confirmed it with his credit card, his card would be credited.

"It's a one bedroom super deluxe suite," Becca moaned. "That's a lot of cash. I told her I wanted a check refund made out to me instead, and she got all self-righteous on me, said that it would be impossible.

"It's just not fair," Becca moaned, stamping her foot just like she used to when she was a child. "I would be Mrs. Henry Fullington right this minute if it weren't for some crazy person out there. I'd be set for life. Now I have nothing."

Becca looked down at the four carrot engagement ring she was wearing. It looked lonely without the diamond band Henry was planning on giving her on their wedding day, swearing his love to her.

One damn band that made all the difference.

• • •

Becca walked back and forth across the badly lit reception area at the NCPD waiting to speak to Detective X. One of the fluorescent bulbs was blinking on and off overhead, emitting a faint buzz.

She couldn't believe she'd rushed over here and now was being kept waiting. At least it gave her a chance to see how the brand new Lexus Coupe that Henry had given to her as a wedding gift handled. Thank the gods he'd thought to put the title in her name. She didn't know what she was going to do now that Henry was gone, but at least she didn't need to worry about transportation. She hoped the car would be safe where she parked it; this place really needed a valet service.

She looked up as the minute hand on the wall clock moved to the next tiny black mark, indicating that it was now 9:15 a.m. She fished a tissue out of her shoulder bag and wiped it over a plastic chair that looked like someone had pulled it from a garbage dump, finally sitting on it with distaste. She had been waiting for almost half an hour and was getting angrier by the minute.

When X finally came into the room, she rose quickly.

"How dare you keep me waiting after summoning me here," she said in her most frosty tone. "It was my understanding that you would see me immediately."

"I'm sorry about the delay," X apologized, "my meeting with the coroner ran a little late. The reason I wanted to see you is because the autopsies of your fiancé and Aiden Ellsworth have been completed." X raised the file he was holding against his chest, said, "There are some disturbing results that I need to discuss with you."

Becca looked at the folder, crinkling her nose at it like it smelled. "I don't know what could be more disturbing than having the man I was about to marry end up swinging from the church's bell tower." She blinked up at him, daring him to come up with something that might be worse than what she'd already experienced.

"I can appreciate that," X said. "But aren't you interested in how that happened? And aren't you curious about Aiden's death?"

A resigned sigh escaped her lips. "OK, then. What did the coroner tell you?"

X pulled out a chair and sat, waiting for Becca to do the same. She tapped her foot, as though considering her options, and finally said, "Fine. I'll sit." She repeated the ritual of cleaning the chair before smoothing the back of her yellow dress and taking a seat.

She regarded the man sitting opposite her, wondering how she'd not noticed what a good looking guy he was. His dark hair was cut in layers, the summer look of the season, his blue eyes a nice contrast to the dark coloring. She recognized the gray slacks and silk blend shirt as Burberry, calculating in her head that the outfit retailed at about $800. It was one of the by-products of being a personal shopper; she couldn't help herself.

Add to that the Gucci belt and loafers and you ended up not only with a good looking guy, but one with money. She didn't think detectives made that much. Interesting.

Becca heard X talking and realized that she should be paying attention.

"It looks like the cocaine Henry used was not tainted."

"I could have told you that. I already said I tried the same coke and I'm OK."

X verified with a nod then cleared his throat. "The coroner did find something else, though." He scooted his chair closer to hers, paused for a second and then jumped in. "There's no easy way to tell you this, but there was a poisonous substance found in Henry's bloodstream. At this point we're not sure exactly how long the toxin was in his system, but it was there long enough to have damaged his organs."

Becca tried to absorb the nonsensical words, shaking her head. "I'm not sure I understand."

X leaned toward Becca and said gently, "Henry was poisoned. Even if he had gotten to a hospital as soon as he started feeling sick, the damage would have been irreversible. It's unlikely that he could have been saved.

"It appears that a similar, if not identical, poison was used on both Aiden and the elderly caretaker of the church."

Becca closed her eyes tightly for several seconds, wishing that X and everything he was telling her would just go away. She was tired, frustrated, and confused. When she finally found her voice, she lashed out, "OK, Mr. X," with heavy emphasis on the Mr., "what does this new information mean?"

"It means that I need to know what Henry and Aiden did over the past 72 hours."

"Well, they've been dead for most of it," she said.

X looked up at the ceiling for a second, took a breath and tried again. "How about the 72 hours before the wedding?"

Becca puckered her lips, tapping her long fingernails on the plastic seat. "Let's see. I didn't see Henry at all on Wednesday. On Thursday morning I had my final fitting and was busy with the details for the rehearsal dinner the entire afternoon. Henry was at work. When he called late that night, he said it was a really long day, trying to get any loose ends tied up so he wouldn't have to deal with business over the honeymoon."

"I thought the two of you lived together in Henry's apartment in the city."

"Not that it's any of your business," Becca said, brushing invisible lint off of her arm, "but we decided to live apart for the month before the wedding. You know, so our wedding night would be special."

"I see. Do you know if Henry saw Aiden at work that day?"

"As far as Aiden goes, I have no idea what he was up to."

She thought a few seconds longer and said, "Wait a minute, now I remember. I was upset because Aiden was going out of town on Thursday and wasn't due back until mid-day Friday. I was worried that he'd screw up, as usual, and forget to pick his tuxedo up in time."

"So Aiden screwed things up a lot?" X asked.

"Oh let me count the ways," Becca said, not bothering to hide her contempt. "Henry insisted he was a computer genius, but as far as common sense goes, forget it. Aiden could get lost in a paper bag; he had absolutely no sense of direction. And he was never on time, and I mean ever. He could be either an hour late or an hour early; you never knew when he'd show up."

Becca shifted in her seat, crossed one long tan leg over the other. "It's a good thing he got along with computers so well because his people skills were in the toilet. Henry explained it away, saying he was just analytical and linear, whatever that's supposed to mean. But if you ask me, he came across as being pushy. And condescending," she added, remembering all of the times Aiden had talked down to her, treating her like she was stupid.

"Interesting," X commented, jotting down notes as she spoke. "So Henry didn't see Aiden at all on Friday?"

Becca tapped a manicured nail against her chin, lost in thought as her brain went on rewind. "Not until we saw him at the rehearsal dinner that night. We had it at this great restaurant and Henry and I were sitting at the bar when Aiden walked in. He came straight over to us to say hi.

"Scratch that," she said, directing her gaze at X. "What he really came over for was to get a drink. He said his business meetings went OK, but the flight back was delayed and because of severe turbulence they didn't offer the beverage cart."

Becca opened her purse, pulled a pack of tic tacs out and popped one into her mouth. "I knew immediately what he meant. He was pissed because he didn't get his oh so needed cocktail. But he made up for it. He ordered a double shot of Stoli on the rocks, downed it in one swallow, and was on his second before I had a chance to sit back down."

"I'm assuming that the bartender used whatever liquors were available there at the bar?"

"What are you insinuating?" Becca said, insulted. "That I'd choose a place that wasn't classy enough to have the good stuff? That my guests would have to brown bag it?"

X reached a hand out and put it on her arm. "No, of course not. What I am wondering is whether it's possible for someone to have poisoned that particular bottle of vodka knowing Aiden drank Stoli. Did Henry drink vodka that night too?"

"No, he was drinking scotch. And Aiden was an equal opportunity drinker. Gin, scotch, vodka, rum, it really didn't matter to Aiden so long as it was top of the line. I don't see how anyone could have guessed what he'd be in the mood for that night."

Becca looked down at her watch and then the clock on the wall. "Are we almost done here?"

X quickly went through the remainder of his questions. The rehearsal dinner started at 6:00 p.m. and ended at 10:00 p.m. Yes, everyone ate and drank the same foods and wines. No, she didn't spend the night with Henry. Yes, the boys were going to go out for a night-cap afterward but NO, it was not a bachelor's party. Henry was not that crass. No, she didn't know where they went. And finally, could she tell him the names of some of the guys who might have gone along.

"Try one of the ushers from the wedding, they should know," she said as she stood up, taking the car key out of her purse.

"Can I go now? I really need to get on the road if I'm going to make my spa appointment out in Montauk."

She didn't appreciate the look on X's face, crossed her arms defensively. "What, do you have a problem with that?"

"No, I'm just surprised you're going all the way out to Montauk, what with the funeral scheduled for tomorrow."

Two red circles flamed across Becca's face, anger and embarrassment dueling for top honors. "What? Where did you hear that from?"

"Through the department. Didn't Arthur Fullington get in touch with you about the arrangements?"

"No, he hasn't been in touch." She stomped her way to the door, turning around before leaving. "I don't know why that man hates me so much. He's treated me like dirt ever since Henry and I started dating; he never thought I was good enough for his son."

Becca wanted to punch something and reached for the doorknob with too much force. "Just great," she said, tears welling. "Now on top of everything else, I broke a nail too."

18

Camille Lopez sat in the front row at Monday morning Mass and allowed her mind to drift for just a moment.

She had befriended Monica Adams a little over two weeks ago, right there at St. Rose of Lima's Church after just a few days of attending daily Mass. Her selection of the elderly woman as a friend was made easy, especially after scrutinizing the parish directory which listed the names and addresses of all parishioners. Monica had virtues other than her address; she was a good Catholic and very generous. When she found out that the friend Camille had supposedly come all the way from Italy to surprise was away on vacation, she took her under her wing. Monica insisted that Camille move from the local hotel she was staying at and be a guest at her home instead.

"You would be doing me a favor," she said to Camille. "I'd love to hear all about your adventures of living in Rome."

And so Camille ended up staying in the small guest bedroom, where she settled in like a tick.

Camille realized that the Mass was about to end and looked up just as the priest and two altar servers walked by her row. Recognition hit her like a shot, and with it realization; it was time to get out of Dodge.

• • •

"Come along, Monica, why are you moving so slowly?" Camille hurried the small gray haired woman across the church parking lot, pulling her by the arm. "Here, give me the keys. I'll drive," she said, grabbing them out of Monica's hand.

Camille opened the passenger side door and pushed Monica in before hurrying into the driver's seat. She had the car in drive and was out on the main road before Monica had time to reach for her seat belt.

Over the car's warning beeps, Camille announced, "It's time for me to return to Rome. As soon as possible, hopefully today."

"Well my goodness, this is so sudden. Is everything alright?" Monica asked as she reached for Camille's arm and gave it a gentle squeeze.

"Everything is fine," Camille snapped, roughly moving her arm away and shifting the old car into third gear. God she hated Monica's sickly sweet voice sometimes. She glanced to her side, where Monica sat looking like she'd just been slapped, her mouth covered with the white lacy handkerchief she always kept tucked under the cuff of her sweater. The blue veins in her hands seemed to stand out more than usual, reminding Camille that she was just an old lady after all. She took a breath, turned on her own sugary voice and said, "It's just that I've been praying that God tell me His will about the length of my visit, and today during Mass He answered. He says I'm needed back in Italy." She sped through a stop sign, continuing. "I have no idea why, of course. But you know what they say, 'We walk by faith and not by sight.'"

They arrived home in record time. Camille was half out of the car before she remembered her arthritic friend. "You'll be OK getting yourself unbuckled and all? It'll be good exercise for your hands." Not waiting for a response, she added, "I'll see you inside."

• • •

By the time Monica made her way to the kitchen, Camille was on the phone, walking around the small kitchen like a caged animal. Her blue A-Line skirt that ended just below the knee swung back and forth, actually billowing when she made the quick turnarounds. She watched as Monica sat at the table, a front row seat to the dialogue she was having with a particularly stupid airline agent.

"My name is Camille Lopez and I would like to book my return flight from Kennedy Airport to Rome." She then dutifully gave all of her flight details, including her reservation number, airline record locator number and her ticket number.

Camille's side of the conversation went on. "Today if possible, tomorrow at the latest."

Seconds later, she said, "What do you mean the first available ticket in that class is Saturday? That is unacceptable. What if I leave from one of the other New York Metropolitan airports? You can't be serious. Why would I have to pay a surcharge?"

Camille slammed the phone down and then re-dialed the airline. "Hello, this is an emergency. My mother died and I need to return to Rome immediately."

Camille saw surprise cross over Monica's face as the elderly woman grasped onto the end of the table and attempted to rise. Monica got as far as a partial squat before having to sit back down and try again. At each attempt she made she'd gain a few centimeters, but Monica never did make it to a standing position. She eventually gave up, exhausted from the effort, looking at Camille like she had two heads.

In the interim, Camille recited all of her ticket information yet again into the phone.

"The end of the week? My mother will be buried by then. OK, let's forget about whatever class my ticket is in. How much would it cost to leave today or tomorrow? Five hundred dollars! Don't you have bereavement fares?"

Again she crashed the receiver down. "What is wrong with those people?"

Camille planted her fingers against her scalp and pushed against the throbbing pain that was quickly escalating while Monica finally won the war against gravity and stood up, ambling over to Camille. "Come sit down for a minute. I'll make you some herbal tea to calm your nerves."

"My nerves are fine," snapped Camille. "Can you believe the airlines want to gouge $500 from me? That's the best they can do, even as my poor mother's corpse is waiting for burial."

Monica leaned over and put her hand on Camille's arm, rubbing gently. "Honey, you told me that your mother died years ago. I think you might be getting a little too caught up in the story you just told. Just try to relax a little."

"I do not need to relax." Camille enunciated each word with mounting anger, condemning Monica for even suggesting such an absurdity. She snatched her arm away from Monica, leaving the old woman swaying unsteadily on her feet.

"What I need is to get out of this godforsaken place." Camille stomped up the stairs, not bothering to stop when one of the old picture frames that lined her ascent fell off the wall.

Five minutes later, like a change in wind direction, Camille came back downstairs and into the kitchen, where Monica was standing at the stove. "Please forgive me, Monica. I'm sorry I was so sharp with you. I'm just so anxious to return to Rome as soon as possible. Maybe together we can think of a way."

Camille took the tea kettle and filled Monica's favorite mug, the one that had 'JOY!' written in big red letters, and put it on the table where Monica always sat. When she turned back around, Monica was standing with her arms opened, apparently wanting a hug.

Camille complied reluctantly, dragging her feet as she leaned down to the stooping 5 foot tall woman who insisted that she'd lost three inches over the years. But as soon as Camille felt their bodies connect, she backed away. She knew better than to get too close to people; if you were careful to always protect yourself, you could never get burned.

"Of course, dear, you know I'll help you in any way I can," Monica said as she slowly made her way back to the table.

Camille paused, weighing her words carefully for full effect. "I need you to lend me five hundred dollars. I promise to pay you back every cent, with interest."

The smile on Monica's face disappeared, the sagging skin around her mouth and eyes falling into a sympathetic frown. "I'm so sorry Camille, but I don't have that kind of money."

"Sorry," Camille lashed out. "Well you should be sorry. If you didn't hoard every penny you have you might be able to help a friend in need."

Monica slid back into the chair, mouth wide open, grasping the crucifix around her neck as Camille snatched up the phone and again dialed the airlines. Camille's one way dialogue continued.

"I'd like to speak with a supervisor immediately."

Monica watched mutely as the minute hand on the clock slowly moved 10 minutes during which time Camille extended her pacing area from just the kitchen to the entire first floor of the house. Camille felt her temper slipping away, couldn't control the little tantrum she was having that included ranting and cursing. But as soon as she heard the supervisor's voice she pulled herself together.

"My name is Sister Camille Lopez. I am a nun and am visiting the States from my convent in Rome. The Pope has asked that I return immediately to aid him in a crisis situation. This is a matter of life or death."

As soon as the words were out of Camille's mouth, she heard something break in the kitchen. Camille moved to the doorway and watched as Monica wiped away the hot liquid spilling over the place-mat in front of her, a large piece of the cracked porcelain mug now reading 'OY!' on the floor at her feet. Camille disconnected the phone and approached the kitchen table slowly.

"What are you looking at?" Camille hissed. "And take your hand away from your mouth, for goodness sake. Everyone tells little white lies, it's not such a big deal."

The sound of the doorbell chimes interrupted the awkward moment.

"I've got it," Monica said, this time getting up from the table on her first try and limping past Camille to the front door.

"Oh look," she said. "It's my neighbor."

• • •

Like a dog picking up a scent, Camille forgot everything else that was going on and instead focused her attention on this new development. From where she was standing, she could make out Glenda Grande coming through the front door and giving Monica a hug.

Camille's antennae were on high as she leaned back slightly so that she was out of view and eavesdropped on the women's conversation.

"How is Becca holding up?" Monica asked.

Camille heard a dreadful hoooooonk, apparently Glenda blowing her nose, and then, "Not so good. She's acting delusional; she wanted to go on the honeymoon without Henry. Can you imagine anything so sad?"

This was too good to miss; Camille wanted a visual along with hearing what was going on.

She patted down her hair, making sure her bun was intact and any loose strands were behind her ears, and breezed what she hoped looked innocuously toward the ladies.

"I recognize you," she said as she got closer to the two, "even though we've never met. I'm Camille Lopez, and you are Glenda Grande. You were so kind to allow Monica to bring me to your daughter's wedding as her last minute guest." She put her arm around Monica and gave it a slight squeeze before adding, "It's just terrible the way things ended."

Tears immediately appeared in Glenda's eyes.

"I didn't mean to upset you," apologized Camille. "Come sit down in the kitchen, let me put on some fresh tea. Silly Monica here just spilled hers all over the table."

Within minutes, Camille had a coffee cake warming in the oven and a pot of water on the stove. She joined the ladies' conversation midstream.

"Did I hear you say that the funeral is tomorrow?" Camille sat down at the table, her antennae still hard at work, scooting her chair next to Glenda's.

"Yes, that's right. At Saint Patrick's Cathedral, in New York City. My daughter is so pleased. Becca desperately wanted to be married there, but there was some sort of problem, I'm not exactly sure what. You see, Becca doesn't always confide in me," Glenda said, dabbing her eyes with a tissue.

"Well that's just terrible," cooed Camille with exaggerated sympathy. "It must be very painful to have your own daughter distance herself from you."

Glenda turned her tear-stricken eyes to Camille, a long line of mascara dripping down her face. "Thank you for being so understanding. Becca says I'm overbearing. After all, she's not a child anymore; she's 30 years old."

"That's no excuse," Camille said, passing a fresh napkin to Glenda who dabbed at her eyes, succeeding in smudging the mascara stain even more.

The kettle whistled, the shrill noise screaming through the kitchen. Camille looked over at little gray haired Monica, sitting there with weathered hands covered with age spots and said, "Are you deaf? The tea's ready."

Then she returned her attention to Glenda. "So are the police telling you anything?"

"Becca actually just called from the police station. It ends up Henry was poisoned." Glenda took a moment to blow her nose into the napkin with a loud productive snort and continued. "Can you imagine that? And apparently his best friend, Aiden, and some old man who lives at Gulf Cove were too."

Camille's mind leapt into overdrive as she tried to assimilate this news. "But what about whoever stabbed Henry? Aren't the police looking for that person? I mean, I'd think that would be their priority."

"I honestly don't know," Glenda answered. "I'm so tired, trying to be strong for Becca. I'm praying someone will call into the hotline that Henry's father set up; there's a $100,000 reward for anyone who can lead them to the killer."

"That's a lot of incentive for someone to talk," commented Camille, tossing this new element into her musings.

And it could be an answer to a lot of prayers

19

arry LaFitte was a walking advertisement for his business, Can-Do Caterers. He was wearing a tee shirt, apron and a baseball cap all with the logo Can-Do embroidered on them. And he was complying with everything that Officer Ryan asked of him.

"Becca Grande hired me in early June to cater her wedding at Gulf Cove. It was supposed to be a simple affair, something for people to nibble on while the bride and groom were busy with the receiving line and taking a few photos. Then they would cut the cake, have a champagne toast, and that would be it.

"The serious reception was scheduled for after Labor Day, in New York City." Larry looked up at the ceiling of the old warehouse, lamenting "If only I could get a gig like that, I'd prove I could make it in the major leagues."

Officer Ryan coughed, interrupting Larry's dream fest. "My understanding is that there was a limited bar also."

"That's true; if someone specifically asked for a drink I was supposed to take care of them. We kept a couple of bottles under one of the tables, out of view. You'd be surprised at how many people knew to ask, even though it was before ten in the morning."

"Did you supply the beverages?"

"Yes and no. I had bought the labels Ms. Grande requested, but at the last minute I got a call from her saying that there were a few extra cases of champagne from the rehearsal dinner and they were sending them over. Apparently it was superior to what she'd ordered from me, so we were going to start off with that."

"When did that happen?"

"I got the delivery at about 11:00 p.m. on Friday night. Put it right into the walk-in frig to keep it cool, and the ice went into the freezer."

"And what about the food? Did you see either Henry Fullington or his best man eating anything you'd provided?"

"Nope. It was so freaking hot that morning that most of the appetizers were still in the truck. I was waiting for the ceremony to start, then we'd quickly bring everything out so it would be nice and fresh for the toast."

"So what happened after the incident?" Ryan asked, jotting down notes as he spoke.

"It was pandemonium, man. Everyone was running out of the church, screaming and yelling. But believe it or not there were still a couple of diehards who slowed down long enough to grab a drink. One for the road, as Frank would say."

"Frank?"

"Sinatra." Larry said the name like he was completing a sentence with the only conceivable word that would fit and give it true meaning.

"Anyhow," Larry continued, "the first two cops there didn't tell me not to serve people, so I kept pouring. Eventually a policeman, Officer Langly was his name, he told me I needed to clear the area so they could investigate."

Larry continued his walk around the warehouse, pointing out certain areas. "This is where we store the dishware, utensils and glassware. When we get back from an event everything gets washed first and then replaced in these cabinets."

Ryan's eyes roamed the area, resting on a map-sized calendar that hung on the wall. "You keep a pretty busy schedule."

Larry smiled. "That's the idea. Right now we're a small outfit, but business is steady."

"How many employees do you have?"

"Eight. Kenny there," he said, pointing to an average sized man outside unloading a truck, "is my only full time employee. He's worked for me since the beginning, almost eight years now. The rest are part-timers; they seem to come and go.

"Except for Chris Hill and Billy McGhee; they're in high school and have been with me for a couple of years now, summers and weekends. They're good kids. They worked the wedding on Saturday so you'll probably want to talk to them again too." Looking at his watch, he added, "They should be here any minute. They're altar boys at the Catholic church and Mass should just about be finishing up."

A Fed Ex truck pulled into the lot and Larry excused himself for a second to sign for a package. It gave Ryan a chance to watch Kenny Mensti, his dark head of hair bobbing in and out of view as he transferred boxes to one of the storage areas close by.

Larry passed by Mensti on his way back, tapping him on the shoulder and then pointing over to Officer Ryan. Mensti nodded and followed his boss, his eyes focused on the floor.

"Officer Ryan, this is Kenny Mensti, my full time man," Larry introduced, putting an arm around Kenny's back.

Kenny didn't look nearly as good as his boss did in the company tee-shirt, the Can-Do logo hanging loosely over his skinny frame. His baggy pants were cinched by a back brace that circled his midsection, the overall image not of someone who earns their living moving heavy loads.

"I told the officer we'd help in any way we could, so don't hold back, you hear?" Larry added before heading off to his office, leaving the two alone.

Ryan spotted some chairs nearby and said, "Why don't we sit?"

There was no conversation as they got situated, Kenny opting to keep his mouth shut.

"There's no need to be nervous," Ryan said, watching Mensti tug on his beard, perhaps a nervous habit. "I know you already spoke with the police on Saturday, I just want to go over a few things again. Would that be alright?"

Usually asking a witness' permission to talk worked to make them feel less anxious, gave them some semblance of control. But Mensti's body language didn't change at all. He scooted in his seat, giving his beard a break and pulling at the strap of his brace instead. He finally looked up, nodded. "What do you want to know?"

"Did you see anything unusual on Saturday morning? Did you leave the truck unattended at any time? Did anyone approach you wanting to enter the truck? Did you see anyone at the buffet tables looking suspicious?" The questions came one after the other and Kenny gave the same answer to each question, a resounding "No."

"My job is to load up the truck on this end and then unload it on the other. I'm not paid to talk to people, I just deliver the food and drinks, wait until the party's over, and then bring it all back to the warehouse."

"Do you think either Larry or the two high school kids acted in any way different on that particular day?"

Kenny licked his lips and, leaning toward Officer Ryan, lowered his voice. "I don't want to get anyone in trouble," he said. "But Chris and Billy, they sometimes skim leftovers. And I'm not talking about the food. I think I saw Billy stashing some booze under his shirt when we finally clocked out that day."

Ryan stopped jotting down notes and looked up. "You think?"

Kenny squirmed on the chair before finally saying, "OK, I definitely saw him take a bottle. But hell, they're just kids. No harm no foul, right?"

Just then Larry came walking through the warehouse, Chris and Billy trailing behind.

"Don't mean to interrupt, but these are the other two that worked the Fullington wedding with us."

"We're done here anyway," Ryan said as he stood up, observing the boys in front of him. They looked like they were in their mid to late teens, one with dark hair and a blotchy complexion and the other blonde, his deep tan striking against perfectly aligned teeth that looked like they'd just been whitened. They were wearing the same green company shirt that their boss had supplied them and jeans. The fairer skinned one had acne scars on his cheeks, and was wearing sunglasses.

Kenny shot out of the chair and was a good ten feet away when Ryan called out to him. "Mr. Mensti, one last thing."

Kenny turned around and retraced his steps, his eyes again rooted to the floor. Ryan needed to work on his bed-side manner; the guy looked like he was walking down death row.

"Here's my card," Ryan said. "If you can think of anything else, I want you to call me."

"No problem." Mensti grasped the small piece of paper and shoved it into his back pocket without even looking at it before walking away.

• • •

"Sorry if we kept you waiting, Officer."

Chris initiated the conversation. He appeared to be the alpha dog, talking for the two of them. And although they wore the exact same outfit, Chris' didn't look like he had slept in it the night before.

"No problem, you're here now." Ryan scratched his head. "What's with the glasses?"

Billy reluctantly pulled the dark lenses to the top of his head, squinting as his red eyes adjusted to the light. "Allergies," he said, shifting his weight from one leg to the other.

"Ah ha," Officer Ryan said, the stale scent of gin wafting around the adolescent a persuasive clue that in fact the kid was probably hung over. Ryan scribbled a quick note before moving on, asking virtually the same questions he had posed to Kenny Mensti.

"I'm not sure you could say the truck was unattended," answered Chris. "I mean, once we parked we all started unloading and getting set up in the foyer of the church. There might have been a minute or two when all four of us were away from it, but I don't think more than that."

"Was anyone hanging around the truck or asking to get inside?" continued Ryan.

"Naw. Sometimes I think Larry painted it that ugly green just to keep people away from it!"

"Wait a minute," said Billy. "There was that woman who wanted a bag of ice. I told her no. It was hot as hell already, and we can't just be handing out bags of ice. But she said that it was for the bride and if the bride didn't get what she wanted, all hell was going to break loose."

"So did you give it to her?" asked Ryan.

"Yeah. I figure it's the bride's gig anyway, she can have whatever she wants."

"What did this woman look like?"

"She was kind of fat. Brown eyes. And she was wearing a Harvard tee shirt. I saw her going up the stairs to where the bride was getting ready."

"That was the maid of honor," Ryan said mostly to himself. He knew someone was going to talk with her again today; he'd make sure to confirm the account. Pressing on, he asked, "And you're sure you didn't see anything or anyone who looked suspicious? Go back in your mind and try to remember every detail of that morning. Something that might not seem that significant to you could be the exact information we need."

Chris shrugged and looked and his buddy for confirmation. "Nope. Sorry."

Officer Ryan held out two of his cards. "I want you each to keep one of these, in case anything comes to mind."

Chris reached into his back pocket and pulled out his cell phone. "I lose everything," he explained as he took one of the cards and added Ryan's information into his phone.

But as Billy reached out his hand to take the other, Officer Ryan slowly pulled it away.

"Oh, and a bit of advice," he said, taping the card against Billy's chest. "I'd re-think the whole pocketing of open bottles if I were you; taking property that's not yours is a crime. And so is underage drinking."

Billy slid the sun glasses back on and stammered a 'Yes, sir," almost tripping over his own feet when he turned quickly around to leave.

• • •

Billy was sitting on a box, elbows on his knees and head lowered. "How do you think that cop knew we were taking bottles?"

"Gee, I wonder?" Chris said, exasperated, as they did inventory in the storage room. "I can smell the alcohol on your breath from here. I swear, this morning at Mass I was afraid you might go up in flames if you got too close to any of the candles."

Billy raised his head and asked morosely, "Oh oh. Did I screw up on the altar?"

Chris used his teeth to pull off a piece of masking tape from the roll and used it to reclose the lid of a box of tapered candlesticks before answering.

"No, but what was the deal? Who were you staring at?"

"It was that woman in the front row sitting next to old Mrs. Adams. I know I've seen her someplace else before but I can't remember where. Did she look familiar to you?"

"You mean the mousey looking one?"

"That's the one. Did you see that bun? If she had her hair pulled back any tighter her scalp would have peeled off."

"I never laid eyes on her before," Chris said as he ripped open another box. "She's way too old for you anyway."

"As if," Billy laughed. "Pray that I never get that desperate."

20

The park police cruiser rolled to a stop in one of the handi-capped parking spaces of Corbinian's, the restaurant where the Fullington/Grande rehearsal dinner was held on Friday night. DiMitri's eyes were glued to the blue sign in front of the vehicle bla-tantly featuring a wheelchair as his partner opened the driver's door and got out.

"Are you coming?" Calhoon banged on the roof of the car just like he always did when he was impatient. He saw DiMitri looking at the sign and added, "We're the police. We are entitled to park wherever we want."

DiMitri opened his mouth to say something and then promptly closed it, deciding it wasn't worth the effort. They entered the restau-rant and were greeted by refreshingly cool air and a lot of noise as they walked through the door.

"Look at all these civilians, just wasting away the day," Calhoon said, disgusted. The hostess who was stationed at the front door looked up from the seating chart she was studying. "Table for two?"

Calhoon pushed his chest out, as though the woman might not have noticed that he was wearing a uniform. "We're here on police business. Can you please let the manager know that we have a few questions for him?"

She motioned a harried waiter, who led them to a back office. "I'll tell the boss you're here," he said as he rushed back in the direction of the dining room.

The room was immaculately clean, the desk top free of clutter except for a few leather trays neatly labeled "pending," "in," and "out."

A large ceramic mug with some kind of bird on it held pencils and pens, and a telephone sat at the far corner.

Calhoon paced around the room, looking at his watch every fifteen seconds, while DiMitri took one of the two leather arm chairs that faced the workspace. Eventually he pulled a pad out of his back pocket and started flipping through.

"What's that?"

DiMitri jumped, startled. "It's just a notebook. I write down stuff that seems weird about a case. There's no place for things like that when we make out an official report."

The door opened abruptly and a man entered. "Sorry to keep you waiting. What is it that I can do for you?"

"And you are?" The question sounded like a challenge coming from Calhoon's lips.

"Mark Bramm. I own this place," he said, matching the tone. His physique was tall and burly, somehow corresponding perfectly with the deep timbre of his voice.

Calhoon planted his legs apart before having to tilt his head up to look into Bramm's face. "We have some questions about the private party that was held here on Friday night."

"The rehearsal dinner?" Bramm said, wiping his hands on the apron hanging around his waist. "Sure, what do you want to know about it?"

"Did anything happen out of the ordinary that evening?" Calhoon asked. I'm assuming you were here."

"I'm here every evening. And every morning; it seems like I'm here 24/7." Bramm walked over and adjusted the thermostat so that more cool air came through the vents before sitting down at his desk chair. "I have deliveries coming in as early as 6:00 a.m., prep work for the lunch crowd, cleanup before the cocktail circuit comes through, then the diners who show up for the early bird special. We have people eating dinner as late as 10:00 p.m., which is when the kitchen closes. There are usually a good half a dozen people still sitting at the bar while we're trying to close up for the night."

"I understand you closed down the entire restaurant for this party. Does that happen often?"

"That was actually the first time. I run a pretty good business, and I hate to turn my customers away. But I'd heard about this wedding months ago, knew that the groom was some big hot shot from New York City.

"I actually solicited his business. I met with Henry, sold him on having the rehearsal dinner here, and walked away with a nice chunk of change for the effort."

Bramm leaned forward and confided, "If I'd have known what a pain in the ass his fiancé was, no amount of money would have been worth dealing with her. Becca Grande rode me about every single detail, called me constantly. She was a real piece of work."

"I understand that cocktails were served before dinner?"

"That's right, though it was open bar the entire evening. I special ordered the wines and champagne they wanted served during dinner and the ice, if you can believe that."

Calhoon changed direction with his next question. "Have you had any recent complaints from your customers about feeling unwell after dining here? Or have any of them died suddenly?"

Bramm laughed out loud. "That was subtle, officer. Are you thinking that something those two dead guys ate or drank here on Friday night caused their deaths? There's no way. First of all, I had the Health Department show up that morning for a random inspection and my bar and kitchen passed with flying colors. And before I purchase any food, I taste it myself first to make sure it's fresh. And I'm still alive and kicking."

DiMitri dared a glance at Calhoon. He didn't take put-downs very well and Mark Bramm had just laughed in his face.

Calhoon's eyes turned into daggers, aiming straight at the restaurateur. "What about the bar? Specifically the Stoli and Dewar's."

"Let's find out." Bramm smacked both hands on top of his desk and got up, moving around the parkies and opening the door. "Are you coming?" The question hung in the air, spoken as if to an errant child, as he left the room and walked down the hallway to the bar, not waiting for the cops or even looking back to see if they were following.

DiMitri had never seen Calhoon so mad. He was seething, could barely make out the words, "That guy's an asshole. He's got no respect."

Then he marched after him, DiMitri following a few steps behind and hoping Calhoon wouldn't make a scene.

When they got to the mirrored bar area, Bramm was already behind the counter. He pulled out four shot glasses, pushed two in front of Calhoon.

Calhoon pushed them right back across the bar. "I can't drink; I'm on duty."

Bramm smirked, grabbing them up with one hand and taking them off the counter. "We wouldn't want you to do anything against the rules."

Of the two glasses still on the bar, Bramm filled one with a shot of the vodka, the other with the scotch.

"Here's to your health, gentlemen," he said, raising first the one and then the other to his lips, swallowing each while managing to sneer at Calhoon. "Now that'll put hair on your chest," he said, wiping the back of his hand across his mouth.

Calhoon was not enjoying the performance.

"Are you mocking me?" Calhoon said, leaning as far across the bar as was physically possible.

"Do you know what your problem is?" Bramm wiped his hands on his apron, untied it from his waist and threw it on the bar. "You take yourself too seriously; get a life."

DiMitri grabbed Calhoon's arm, knowing that his partner was about to blow, and hoping to deflect the tension asked, "Would you mind if we took some samples with us back to the lab?"

Bramm looked at DiMitri like he'd just noticed him for the first time. "Sure, no problem." Turning to the bartender, he said, "Cheryl, help these gentlemen out with whatever they need. I've got to get back to the kitchen."

By the time they'd collected their samples and left the restaurant, Calhoon's seething rage had simmered into a vindictive vow. Once they got into the patrol car, he turned to DiMitri, jabbing a finger in his chest.

"Mark my words, I'm going to teach that guy a lesson he'll never forget. He's going to find out that he's not dealing with a gentleman.

"He's dealing with me."

21

"**N**ancy Lubinowitz; she's expecting us," Calhoon told the woman who was sitting behind a beautiful cherry wood desk in the reception area of one of the most prestigious law firms on Long Island.

Nancy stood in her doorway, watching every head turn as the two policemen were led down the long corridor toward her office. She'd considered taking the day off but thankfully decided otherwise. She was an instant celebrity when she walked into the office that morning. Everyone knew she was in the now infamous bridal party that ended up so tragically. Nancy had become a star, the center of attention, and she loved it. She doled out tidbits of information to her colleagues like breadcrumbs to a gaggle of geese. She intended to ride this wave of popularity for as long as possible.

"I'm Officer Calhoon and this is Officer DiMitri. We spoke with you on Saturday at the murder scene."

"Yes, I remember you both. How can I help you?" Nancy spoke loudly enough for her colleagues to hear, sweeping the policemen into her office with a conspiratorial wink to everyone in general and no-one in particular. She made sure to leave her door wide open before sitting behind her desk.

Calhoon started the interview, DiMitri opting to sit in one of the barrel chairs at his side. "We have the time-line that you provided, Ms. Lubinowitz, which has been very helpful. I just want to verify a few things. You and Ms. Grande arrived at the chapel at approximately 7:45 a.m., at which time you saw no familiar cars in the parking area."

"That is correct."

"You then took three immediate trips from the car to the bridal chamber, via the outside stairwell, carrying garment and travel bags, as well as a cooler."

"Yes, and that damn thing weighed a ton."

DiMitri appeared to make a note of her comment as his partner went on. "I'm curious, why did you go back down and get a bag of ice when the caterer's truck arrived?"

Nancy answered, "Thank you very much, that's what I said," seeming vindicated by the question. "But Henry has this thing about ice cubes; they have to be a certain size and from pure water. He special orders them from some company; his father apparently got him into it."

"So what was in the cooler that you carried upstairs?" DiMitri asked, scratching the side of his head with the tip of his pen.

"Oh, that was just ice to cool the champagne. It came from the freezer at the Grande's house."

"Was there liquor in the chamber in case Henry wanted a mixed drink?"

"Ha, that's a good one." Nancy pulled at the lapels of her blazer in an effort to fasten the button at her waist before giving up, irritated. "It wasn't necessary. His father had a $5,000.00 bottle of Scotch delivered to Henry's hotel room sometime Friday night. Can you imagine that? What a freaking waste. It was sitting there on the counter with a bow tied around it when Henry got in from the bachelor party. He even remembered to provide the ice, left a cooler in the bathroom.

"Geez, I wish I had an old man like that," Nancy added. "My dad can't even remember my birthday."

Sucking in her breath, she tried one more time to close her jacket. She had temporary success before the button came loose, flying through the air and landing on her desk as soon as she exhaled.

Three sets of eyes watched it eventually roll to a stop before Calhoon coughed and asked, "Did Henry bring the bottle with him when he came to the room?"

"You know, I'm not sure." Nancy nonchalantly put a hand on top of the button and slowly retrieved it, adding, "He did tell Becca he didn't want a drink, which is rare."

"How did you find out about this high dollar scotch in the first place?"

"Aiden told me. I called his room at about 7:00 a.m. Saturday morning to make sure he was up. He and Henry were already toasting the day."

The remainder of the interview went exceedingly quickly, from Nancy's point of view. She didn't think the cops had been there for more than fifteen minutes before they were giving her their cards, asking that she call if she remembered anything that might seem relevant.

Nancy ushered the two cops to her door. "Can I ask you for one little favor? What you said about me being careful? Would you mind repeating that while I'm walking you through the office? And make it loud."

Because, for Nancy, any attention was good attention.

22

There were too many people to fit into X's small office at head-quarters so the mid-day Monday meeting was held in the conference room. X looked at the clock on the wall; it was going on 1:00 p.m. and they still had a lot of ground to cover.

The coroner was giving an overview of his findings. "Mr. Damson's time of death was approximately 7:30 p.m. My best guess is that he ingested the poison relatively close to that time. Because of his age and a weak heart, he reacted to the toxin virtually immediately."

Dr. Dormer continued his very succinct explanation of the three deaths and answered questions in a way a layman could understand.

"How do we know the poison was ingested and not delivered in another manner, say by needle injection or inhalation or even topically?" asked X.

"That's a good question, Detective. Especially given the traumatic injuries sustained by Mr. Fullington and the degree of decomposition of the Ellsworth corpse.

Basically speaking, evidence of the poison was found in the digestive tract of each victim, as well as trace proof in their esophagus. Interestingly, Mr. Damson had quite a bit of residue on his gums and teeth, as well as the upper palate of his mouth."

DiMitri's head jerked up as he reached for his back pocket, pulling out the small pad and rapidly turning pages.

"Does that mean something to you?" X asked.

DiMitri cleared his throat, said, "Well, I spoke to the victim's nephew who lives out in California. He told me that his uncle sat down every night at the same time with his one drink of the evening, just in time to watch Wheel of Fortune. Gin and tonic. And that when the drink was gone, he'd chew on the ice cubes, get as much kick as he could."

"You might be on to something there," said Dr. Dormer. "That could explain the excessive poison residue in his mouth."

"Are you suggesting that the ice cubes themselves were poisoned? Couldn't it just as easily be whatever liquid was in the glass?" asked X.

"It's possible," Dormer said, "but less likely."

"OK, I want everyone in this room to think back," X said. "Whether or not it might be relevant, I want to hear anything you heard or saw regarding ice."

Calhoon stood up, his chest thrust forward as though he were about to receive a medal of honor. "I have two sources who indicated that Henry Fullington had some kind of ice fetish."

X pulled at his ear, not sure if he heard correctly. "A what?"

"You know," DiMitri added, "he had a thing that his ice cubes be made from purified water and be a certain size and shape."

Langly's laughter cut through the room, and even Calhoon cracked a quick smile before X wagged a finger for everyone to calm down.

"Can you please explain in greater detail what you're talking about?"

"The maid of honor said she went down to the caterer's truck to get a bag of this special ice, that Henry could tell the difference between regular and …"

Calhoon stalled for a second before DiMitri chirped, "Luxury ice. Some company out in California makes it, from …"

"I know, I already heard. It's from pure water etcetera," X said.

Officer Ryan spoke up. "I interviewed the two high school kids who work for the caterer and they can confirm that Lubinowitz did indeed take a bag of ice from the van."

X let this thought settle throughout the room for a few seconds before continuing.

"I want to go back to the first crime scene. All three victims were there at the Gulf Cove church. It makes sense that it's the location where they were either exposed to or had access to the poison. But if the ice was somehow contaminated, why don't we have more victims? The ice was available to everybody."

"I'm not so sure about that," Ryan said. "The owner of the catering company told me that the plan was to serve champagne after the ceremony. He had a couple of cases chilling on blocks of ice in large tubs.

"But he also had a small bar that they kept under wraps for people who specifically asked for something stronger. Whatever ice he used for those drinks wouldn't have been circulated to everyone."

Ryan shifted in his chair, stretched out his legs. "Whether or not he used this luxury ice, I can't say. But I do know that there was a huge icemaker in the warehouse, and a walk-in freezer next to it."

X walked over and nudged Ryan's foot. "I want you back over to Can-Do now, and I want samples from both ice units. And close them down until we get results back from the lab."

"You got it."

"Whoever's patrolling Gulf Cove today, I want them over to the Damson crime scene to check the freezer. I want to hear from them pronto."

"OK," Langly said as he stepped out into the hallway to make the call.

"We still have that cooler from the bride's changing room, don't we?" he asked no one in particular.

"I'm guessing it's still in evidence," answered Ryan.

"Can you track it down? It needs to get over to the lab like yesterday. Tell them it's a priority."

"I'll take care of it," he said, heading for the door and bumping into Langly as he re-entered the room.

"There's an ice bag in Mr. Damson's freezer; they're bringing it over to the lab now."

"Call them back, tell them to rush it. And find that ice company and see if they've had any problems recently. Shake them down, find out about disgruntled employees, the whole nine yards."

"You got it, boss," Langly said.

"OK, let's move on this. Unless Dr. Dormer has anything to add," X asked, looking to the coroner.

"No. I'll notify the lab and be waiting for the samples."

The room emptied rapidly, leaving X and Langly to walk toward the elevator together.

"So where are you off to?" Langly asked.

"To see a pretty lady," X said, his dimples a precursor to the wide smile that appeared milliseconds later.

"What, don't look at me like that," he laughed, throwing an arm up to block Langly's slap, "it's strictly business. Ann met with the two little boys from the church this morning; I'm going to get an update."

• • •

"Strictly business, my ass," Ann giggled as she rolled away from X, pulling the sheets up to her freckled chin.

X turned on his side and pulled her closer, their bodies molding together like they were made for each other. He rested his chin on the top of her head, leaned down and inhaled the musky scent that followed her everywhere. He remembered her laughing at him when he'd asked what kind of perfume she wore. She said she didn't really go for that kind of thing; she was more the au natural type.

"You know I hate to ruin the moment," he started, but she was up and off the side of the bed before he even finished the sentence.

"I know, you have a big case to solve," she said as she shrugged into his discarded shirt, her 5'1" frame almost disappearing inside of the blue short sleeved tee.

X sat up against the headboard while Ann took a file from her briefcase and hopped back on the bed facing him, getting cozy seated in a yoga position that looked excruciatingly painful to X.

"So you said you might have gotten some useful information?" X asked as he craned his neck, trying to read the pages she had in front of her. It was no use; they were upside down from his angle.

"First," she said, shaking two sheets in front of him, "are the signed parental consent forms waiving doctor-patient confidentiality."

"Oh yeah, I guess I forgot about that," X said sheepishly.

X recognized the satisfied look in her eyes, and grinned. He knew how much she loved being the one to throw around the law for a change.

"Did the boys happen to mention anything about bags of ice?"

Ann stopped rearranging the papers in the folder, brushed aside a wayward curl that had fallen in her line of vision. "Not bags, just the big blocks that were chiseled down for the tubs. Why?"

"There's a possibility that some of the ice at the wedding was poisoned."

She scrunched up her face, skeptical. "Geez, someone really had it in for Henry Fullington. Poisoned and cut up into pieces. Classic overkill."

"Ain't that the truth," X said as he walked his fingers over the bed-spread toward the folder, finally getting close enough to grab hold at its corner and tug.

"All you had to do is ask, silly," she said, swatting at his hand before letting go of the manila file.

X reached over to the bedside table and grabbed his reading glasses, quickly paging through what looked like a transcript of the entire session.

"You recorded them?"

"It's pretty much standard practice these days," she answered, moving out of her lotus position and crawling so she was sitting next to X. "But look at my notes on the session, there they are," she said, pointing to several pages held together with a pink paperclip. "I think there's some information that might be important."

X was already scanning the typed pages, devouring them with his eyes. He stopped abruptly and looked at Ann.

"They saw Henry Fullington talking to Kenny Mensti?"

"They didn't say so by name, but if he fits their description, then yes they saw that and more."

X continued reading. "This is good information, Ann. Now we have Mensti following the victim into the church."

"And both kids were pretty sure they didn't see Henry come back outside," she added.

X took her chin in his hands, brushed the tip of her cute little upturned nose. "Ann, this is great. I owe you, baby."

A soft gentle whisper of a laugh escaped her lips, the one he loved so much, the one he knew came more from lust than from anywhere else. "And I intend to collect," she said, moving aside as he got off the bed and headed for the shower. "At some time, and in some place where you least suspect it, I shall collect."

• • •

"Mensti? Now that's interesting." Langly was sitting on a barstool at Starbuck's, his turkey and Swiss sandwich halfway to his mouth as he spoke.

X nodded as he wiped his mouth, taking a breather from his Panini. "It's certainly not enough for a search warrant. And the guy's record is clean."

"So what are you thinking?" Langly wondered as he leaned down for another bite. Then, with his mouth full, "Isn't that your phone?"

X's cell phone was vibrating across the tabletop; he grabbed it and read the text. "The lab has something back from ice taken from Mr. Damson's freezer. I gotta go."

He stood up, pulling his car keys out of his pocket and jiggling them while he thought. "Why don't you see if you can find Mensti. But don't approach him yet; just keep an eye on him so we know where he is."

"Got it," Langly said, then added, "Hey, if you're not going to take that with you can I have it?" Langly was already pulling the remainder of X's Panini across the counter top.

"You know how hungry I get when I'm on a stakeout."

23

"We've got less than a day to find out who killed Henry Fullington before his funeral. What the hell is so complicated that you can't figure this out?"

X was just outside the lab, anxious to get the results on the ice found in Mr. Damson's freezer. He closed his eyes, not wanting to get into it with the chief yet again. "Listen, the guy was a coke addict, plus he was poisoned, then carved up and stuck around a belfry. We have to look at each of those facts individually, then collectively, then potentially linked in tandem with each other, in every possible combination. Plus there are two other victims."

X heard the frustration in his own voice and hated it. He knew he was more than just capable. His knack of putting things together, seeing them in a way that others missed, is what drove him up the ranks within the department so quickly. But was he was the stuff of legends? Despite some positive commentary from the press on several cases he'd solved, the answer was no way. His Achilles heel had always been working on a deadline.

He ran a hand through his hair, croaked into the phone, "You've got to know I'm doing everything I can."

"Do more." Then silence. Hartman had hung up on him.

X hated calls that ended like that. He considered calling the chief back when he heard Kato's voice calling him.

"Tell me you have good news," said X as he entered the lab.

Kato Rueger, the lead forensic pathologist who ran the lab, nodded in the affirmative, smiling like a Cheshire cat. "This is so rare I have only heard of it killing a human once."

He moved to a microscope and peered down at a slide. "The top layers of ice from the bag retrieved from the Damson murder scene contained an inordinate amount of selenium."

"I thought that stuff was good for you," X said. "In fact, I think it's in the glucosamine I take."

"Getting to that age too, are you?" laughed Kato. He was a native of Alaska, a proud finisher of the Iditarod some twenty years earlier and a recent recipient of a brand new hip. "I take it too, and you're right, in the proper amounts selenium is a good thing. It's an antioxidant. But in high levels, it can be dangerous."

"How so?" X wondered.

"A person who consumes toxic levels of selenium would typically develop selenosis, which is rarely fatal.

"The more benign symptoms are a garlic odor to the breath and hair loss, possibly even neurological disorders. In more extreme cases, and over a prolonged period of high quantity ingestion, cirrhosis and pulmonary edema can occur."

"I don't see how this ties in to our cases. Dr. Dormer said that our victims suffered from an acute assault to their organs and central nervous system."

"And that's where things get interesting," said Kato.

Turning to his computer he leaned down and clicked a few buttons, finally retrieving what he was looking for.

"I found this article published by the Mayo Clinic that was most illuminating. It was about a woman who died suddenly several years ago; despite several autopsies, no cause of death was determined. The husband continued to strongly suspect foul play and eventually months later the body was exhumed and sent to the Mayo Clinic.

"They performed additional scientific tests which were reviewed by an expert on exotic toxins. It was determined that death was caused by a fatal dose of selenium."

Kato straightened his body, turning back to face X. "They never were able to determine the source of the selenium, though her case is still considered an open homicide."

X asked the obvious. "How much selenium was in the ice?"

"One hundred and sixty four thousand micrograms. To put that amount in context, exceeding the tolerable upper intake level of 400 micrograms per day can lead to selenosis."

"It doesn't sound like your average Joe would know about something like this," X said.

Kato responded by shrugging his shoulders, agreeing. "I don't know who would have this kind of knowledge. If I didn't have the opportunity to test an individual ice cube affected, it's doubtful I would have been able to figure it out."

"Were all of the ice cubes poisoned?"

"No, just ten of the cubes at the top of the bag, which I estimate was about three-quarters full."

X paced around the lab, thinking out loud. "I don't see any motive for murdering Mr. Damson unless he saw something he wasn't supposed to. It's either that, or the poor guy just saw an extra bag of ice at the church and decided to bring it home."

He paused at the microscope and took a quick peek through the viewer; all he could see was a canvas of tiny pink and yellow dots on a dull gray background. It meant nothing to him, yet death for the old man.

"How about the cooler that was taken from the bridal chamber? Did you find any of this selenium in there?"

"There was an empty ice bag inside with no poison residue. And the tox screens on the three inches of water that remained in the cooler came back negative. But," Kato said, holding out his hand, "those results aren't necessarily conclusive."

"What do you mean?"

"It's possible that the selenium was so diluted by all of the melting ice that my equipment wasn't sensitive enough to detect it. I sent the entire contents of the cooler to Albany; they've got a new machine that should be able isolate and identify even the most miniscule amounts of a substance."

X raked his hand through his hair. "How long before you get the results?"

"The governor has one of his lackeys flying it upstate as we speak. The testing itself shouldn't take more than a few hours."

X glanced at his watch. It was now going on 5:00 p.m. Looking at Kato, he said, "I just hope we hear something before another person dies."

24

Monday's late day sun shone through Monica's kitchen window as she worked on a crossword puzzle. At the sound of footsteps coming down the stairs, she took off her magnified reading glasses, rubbing her fatigued eyes.

The Camille who entered the kitchen barely resembled the woman who had been living with her for the past several weeks. Gone were the modest clothing and natural appearance. Instead she was wearing a tight-fitting skirt that was at least 2 inches above the knee, something that would be prohibited in most of the churches in Rome. Plus she had on a sleeveless shirt with a plunging neckline. And what had she done with her hair? She usually wore it very simply, pulled back into a bun. Monica was surprised to see the blond tresses falling loosely down to Camille's shoulders in a stylish cut and blown dry expertly. The finishing touch was way too much make-up and bright red lipstick.

"Well my goodness, Camille, you look so …" Monica stammered before finally coming up with a word. "Different."

"Thank you," Camille said as she plopped her big handbag right on top of the puzzle, causing its small pieces to scatter apart. "I'm going over to meet Becca and offer her my condolences. I don't know how long I'll be, so don't wait on me for dinner."

There was no suggestion to take Monica with her, no offer to help her with supper when she got home, and no warmth in her voice.

• • •

"Mom, stop fussing over me," Becca said, pushing her mother away as she pulled a dress over her head. "I'm trying to get ready for tomorrow and I can't do that with you constantly interrupting me."

Becca stood in her bra and panties amidst a sea of outfits that were piling up around the room. She picked up a dress that was lying on the bed, held it up in front of her and looked in the mirror.

"Black is just not my color," she said, throwing the offensive clothing on the floor. "It washes out my complexion. Plus I colored my hair to highlight the ivory of my wedding dress. It's altogether wrong for black."

She rolled her shoulders and stretched her neck before leaning closer to the mirror to inspect her face. "Look at those bags under my eyes. Damn Henry's father for scheduling the funeral so quickly. I really could have used some TLC out at Montauk before dealing with all of this."

"Well at least they're letting you move the dates without a penalty. You know, I've never been out to that part of the island. Maybe you'd like some company when you go?" her mother said, moving in close so they were reflected side by side in the mirror, Glenda's face full of hope and Becca's with no way written all over it.

The doorbell interrupted the moment. "It's probably the florist with more sympathy flowers. I wish people would just send cash; that's what I really need."

"I'll take care of it; you just go on with what you're doing," Glenda said as she headed down the stairs.

After a quick peek through the peephole, she opened the front door wide. "Camille, what a lovely surprise. Won't you come in?"

• • •

Camille was through the door and inside the house before the invitation was out of Glenda's lips.

"I hope I'm not disturbing you, but I was hoping to offer my sympathies to your daughter." Camille took a look around, the main living area an open floor plan that was filled with plants and flowers, small cards attached expressing sorrow of Henry's passing and offering condolences. She felt disgust rising in her, the sea of monuments nothing more than a lame attempt by the ungodly to assuage their discomfort of the naturalness of death.

"What a waste of money," she spat.

"I was just saying the same thing," said Becca as she descended the stairs. "Do I know you?"

Camille's head snapped around as she watched the woman who had caused her so much pain approach. "We haven't met, but I feel like I know you," answered Camille. "You have no idea how much you've been on my mind lately."

Camille's eyes came to rest on the woman who was the bane of her existence: Rebecca Grande. There was a sudden rush of blood behind her eyes, the pulsing making her light headed, and her vision blurred. She long knew that Becca was a curse upon the human race; after all, it was she who single handedly caused the demise of the only man Camille had ever loved. Henry. Only evil incarnate would be able to affect her this way, cause her to literally lose her breath in its presence. And that evil was Becca.

And my God, just look at her physical appearance. Clearly Henry's taste in women had deteriorated since he left Rome five years earlier. What she saw was a painted harlot, about 5 foot 5 inches tall, with cleavage that didn't resemble God's original creation and which was spilling out of a black bra she was wearing under a sheer white bathrobe. The belt was tied around a teensy weensy waist that screamed anorexia. And those squatty legs reminded her of the heavy coliseum pillars back in Italy.

Glenda interrupted the awkward silence. "Honey, this is Monica's houseguest, Camille."

"You must be my guardian angel," Becca said, clapping her hands together like a child. "I can see that you have great fashion sense. Would you mind helping me choose what to wear to the funeral tomorrow?"

Camille tried not to laugh at the irony of the request. She looked down at the clothes she had so carefully chosen to wear to this meeting; she'd taken great pains to look her secular best, to outshine the other woman. And she had. She swallowed her sense of satisfaction and simply said, "I'm happy to help."

Camille followed Becca up the stairs, thinking of the countless hours she'd spent preparing for this meeting. She knew she might only have one shot at implementing her plan, so getting it right was imperative. Who would have guessed that it would end up being so simple, penetrating her foe's personal space. As she stood at the threshold of Becca's bedroom, she gave thanks to her mentor for helping her disguise the utter loathing and hatred she had for the woman.

The entire bedroom was done in various shades of pink, from the shag carpet to the walls, the canopy over the bed to the curtains. It looked like Pepto Bismol run amuck. She watched as Becca wandered around the room, picking up discarded wads of Kleenex, a few candy wrappers and a soda can and shoving them into an already full pink wicker trash container.

"Sorry for the mess," she called over her shoulder. "Come on in, there's a chair buried under here somewhere."

Glenda arrived at just that moment, carrying a box of wine and 3 glasses. She smiled at Camille, her thick lipstick smudged on her two front teeth. "In honor of our company, I took out the good stuff. It's Cabernet Sauvignon."

Camille repressed a shudder just looking at the carton of wine and grimaced when she took her first sip. Compared to the wines she was used to enjoying in Italy, this tasted like vinegar. But a few glasses later, she decided the alcohol was definitely her friend. Becca's inhibitions, if she ever had any, were gone. She had modeled every outfit she owned, notwithstanding the color.

"I'm not so sure you should wear red, honey. People might think it's disrespectful," said Glenda of the chiffon cocktail dress her daughter was wearing.

"On the other hand, red symbolizes love," offered Camille. "It might be the perfect way for you to express your feelings for Henry."

Even saying the words repulsed her. What kind of a person would wear anything other than black to the funeral of a loved one? But she was bound and determined to make a fool out of her adversary.

Camille plunged on. "I don't want to hurt your feelings, Becca, but do you know what you need?"

Becca came to a dead stop, mid pirouette, eyes confused. "What?"

"You need to look more refreshed. I have the perfect cream, it's better than any facial I've ever had," she said, pulling a jar out of her bag. "Here, let's get you out of that dress and I'll put some on for you."

Glenda grabbed the chiffon number that Becca tossed her way, putting it back on a hanger, while Camille grabbed a wad of nearby tissues and applied the thick cream to Becca's face.

"It smells good," Becca commented. "Is that lavender?"

"That's right, among other things. Not only will this stuff reduce inflammation, but it'll make any redness or dark circles disappear. The longer it stays on, the better."

Becca turned to the mirror, her dark eyes peeking through the balm. "I don't how to thank you, Camille. You are a godsend."

• • •

Calhoon was not a happy camper. He looked down at the torn skin on his knuckles, grimaced, and banged on the door again. "Why isn't anyone answering the door? It's obvious they're home."

"That's the understatement of the year," answered DiMitri, a wide smile on his face as he stood in the yard peering at an upstairs window. The silhouette of a woman removing her clothes had his rapt attention.

Calhoon strode past his partner toward their car, knocking into him on the way.

"Hey, you did that on purpose. What's up with you?" DiMitri asked.

"I didn't spend three years in the service, where my life was on the line, and then go into law enforcement just to be summoned by my superiors to retrieve ice from the Grande's freezer. Who does X think he is, anyway?

"And why can't you show some professionalism for a change," added Calhoon as he returned from the car with a bullhorn. He clicked the on switch and spoke into the megaphone.

"Ms. Grande, this is the police. It is imperative that we speak with you right away. Please come to the door immediately."

Calhoon pushed the bullhorn into DiMitri's chest and stomped to the front door, looking at his watch while he waited. "Detective King said he wanted the ice from the Grande's freezer a.s.a.p. It's going to make us look bad that it took so long to get it."

The door finally opened. "There's no need to yell my business all over the neighborhood; all you had to do was knock."

Becca stood in front of them, looking like a mime. Cream was spread over her entire face and neck, the only surfaces spared being the areas surrounding each eye and her mouth. "What's so important anyway?" The thin robe she was wearing opened as she shifted, putting her hand on her hip.

DiMitri blushed profusely and nervously stammered out, "We're here to collect ice samples from your freezer."

Camille was halfway down the stairs as the two cops came into the house. Head bent, she proceeded forward, brushing past them and out the door.

"Thanks for the help," Becca called after her, then shrugged. "Wonder what her rush was?"

25

DiMitri and Calhoon finally arrived at the lab with the Grande's 6 Rubbermaid ice trays at the same time Officer Ryan was leaving. He looked up, smiling at the parkies. "Hey, how are things?"

"Great, if you consider wasting your time cleaning people's freezers worthwhile," Calhoon answered, his face a painting of irritation.

DiMitri ignored his partner and changed the subject. "Anything new on your front?"

"Have you heard the news about Kenny Mensti?"

Calhoon's already rigid form straightened even further. "Who's that again?"

"He's the guy who works at the caterers," Ryan answered. "Anyway, apparently those two little kids at the church met with a psychiatrist today and they remembered that Mensti and the groom went into the church together and were headed in the direction of the bell tower."

"You really think anything those brats have to say is true? It's been three days since the murder; no way are their memories better now than they were then, when everything was fresh," Calhoon scoffed, adding, "Leave it to a shrink to help someone manufacture what they remember."

"Geez, tell me how you really feel," said Ryan defensively.

DiMitri jumped in before Calhoon had a chance to get even uglier. "You interviewed Mensti, didn't you? How'd he seem to you?"

"Nothing struck me as unusual when we spoke," Ryan answered, "and his background check was clean. He said his job was to load up the truck at one end and unload it at the other, that he's basically a deliveryman. And when I was over there today he was acting normal.

"But X is taking a serious look at him now."

"Whatever," Calhoon said, cutting Ryan off and dismissing him with a wave of his hand. He turned to DiMitri and added, "I guess X didn't think we were important enough to the team to be let in on this new information.

"You know what? I'm out of here." Calhoon let go of the Styrofoam cooler he was holding and let it fall to the floor.

"Tell X if he needs his shirts starched not to call me. I'm off the clock until Thursday." Disgusted, Calhoon turned and started walking away.

"You're going to leave now?" DiMitri followed him down the hallway, grabbing his arm to stop him.

"You got it, partner. If you want to use your time taking orders from a prick, go for it. I'm getting some shut eye."

Shaking his arm free, Calhoon continued out the door.

26

X was sitting at his desk, typing on his computer with one hand and tearing open a Snickers with the other when Ryan knocked.

"Where's your better half?" X asked sarcastically when he noticed that DiMitri was with Ryan.

DiMitri stammered something unintelligible before Ryan broke in, "Long story. But listen, DiMitri came up with an interesting thought on the drive over."

"You've got my attention," X said as he crumbled the empty candy wrapper and tossed it into the trash.

DiMitri pulled his notebook out of his back pocket, flipping to the earmarked page. "I remember your account of the interview you had with Sean Baker. You mentioned, several times in fact, that he described himself as a delivery man."

"That's right," X confirmed, remembering Baker's crude reasoning.

"Mensti told Ryan the same thing. Which got me to thinking," DiMitri said.

X waited, expecting more, before he caught on. "I have to admit, it never made total sense to me that Aiden was Henry's dealer, despite the evidence found in his front yard."

X moved around his desk, pacing. "So let's assume Mensti was pushing drugs. He goes up the bell tower stairs to sell Henry some cocaine and ends up killing him. And then he stays around to help serve at the party?" He paused, shaking his head. "I don't think so.

"Every single person there was searched, Mensti included. He didn't have any drugs on him. And we went over that catering truck with a fine tooth comb; there was nothing there."

He turned to DiMitri. "You were there first. What did you see in that tower?"

"I never actually did see it. Calhoon took the inside of the church, I focused outside."

X's memory was rolling with images of the scene. The blood on the floor, its sweet sickly scent consuming all of the oxygen in the room. The coiled rope that was used to tie Henry to the belfry.

And Henry's tuxedo jacket, folded neatly in the corner, a solitary footprint on the sleeve.

X strode back to his desk chair, dropping down and hitting his laptop keys at the same time. Turning the computer so everyone could review the itemized inventory list he had just retrieved, he scrolled down the list before jabbing a finger at the monitor. "Look. The tuxedo jacket was one of the last pieces of evidence collected. It was still there when I arrived, which was hours after the fact."

He punched a few more keys. "That's odd. There's no report on the jacket."

X sat back down, running a finger across his lip as he concentrated. "When I spoke with Becca Grande on Sunday morning, she asked me why the coke we found couldn't be tested."

He raised his head. "But we never found any cocaine, just some residue in Henry's nostrils."

X slammed his hands on the desk. "Damn. Henry had to have had more cocaine somewhere; it must have been stashed it in his tuxedo." He stood up abruptly, irritated. "I'm going down to the lab, see what the hell is going on."

DiMitri stumbled out of X's way as he rounded the desk and made his way to the door. He stopped and turned around, gripping the door frame, trying to keep his anger in check. If someone had tampered with the evidence, he'd find out soon enough. In the meantime, he wanted to keep the ball rolling on the investigation.

"Listen, Mensti's at his place and I've got Langly babysitting him. Why don't you go on over there, see if he needs a break?"

He pushed away from the door, said, "I'll be in touch," and marched down the hall. X was not happy and soon, whoever had screwed up by not producing a report on the tuxedo jacket, would not be happy either.

27

Officer Ryan pulled slowly down the road. They could see Langly's standard Crown Vic parked diagonally across from the basement apartment where Kenny Mensti lived. He dimmed his headlights and continued on down the street.

"I don't see Langly in the car, do you?" asked Ryan.

"Nope. It looks empty."

"Why the hell isn't he picking up his phone?"

Ryan made a u-turn at the end of the street and approached the house from the other direction. Looking at it one might assume that it was a Cape Cod. But it lay on a slope, and from an angle view the lower back level was evident. Lights were on and everything appeared to be normal.

Ryan parked so his black and white couldn't be seen from the house. "OK," he said to DiMitri. "We're going to go the rest of the way on foot. Remember to stay in the shadows. And don't make any noise."

The parkie nodded his agreement and followed Ryan's lead. The evening was still, the crickets' chirping a quiet distraction.

Ryan poked DiMitri, and then pointed down to his revolver. DiMitri nodded, and as they crept forward in the darkness, he kept his hand on the gun.

When they finally got to the sedan, Ryan waved for DiMitri to stay low to the ground. Slowly, Ryan rose and looked into the window.

"Oh my God," he screamed, dropping his firearm and yanking open the door.

DiMitri sprung up, looking in the car. Nausea overwhelmed him. Langly's body lay in a heaped mass on the front seat, his eyes wide open with a look of shocked disbelief frozen on his face. The steering wheel was covered in blood, with more splattered on the windshield behind it, a huge circle of red with spray lines that spread across the glass like a spider's web. It had dripped down the vinyl upholstery to the floor mat, pooling in the center, such a massive amount of blood from just one body.

Ryan pulled his radio out and screamed, "Officer down. I repeat, officer down."

DiMitri could hear the hysteria in Ryan's voice and grabbed him. "You've got to keep it together. Mensti might still be inside. We don't want to blow our cover."

"What cover? He obviously knows the cops are watching him. That's why he killed Langly, the poor bastard," answered Ryan, biting back his tears.

"We don't know that for sure." DiMitri looked at the silent house, then back at Ryan. "X would want us to cover all the angles."

Ryan leaned into the car, verifying the obvious: Langly was dead, the gash across his neck deep and thorough, slicing through both the jugular veins and the carotid artery.

He pulled back out, gagging for moment, before asking, "I don't see the murder weapon, do you?"

The crickets continued their song, squeaking in the otherwise quiet neighborhood.

"Oh shit," Ryan said to no-one. "DiMitri's gone."

• • •

DiMtri raced toward the back of the house, his gun drawn. What if Mensti was at that very moment getting away, fleeing to parts unknown where he'd never be found and held accountable for taking Langly's life? He wasn't going to let that happen. He was ready for battle, even though this would be the first time he actually discharged his weapon anyplace other than the shooting range.

He heard sirens in the distance and figured stealth was no longer needed. Unless he was deaf, Mensti would know the police were coming.

There was only one entry visible to the basement apartment. It was a screen door which opened easily when DiMitri's foot connected with the flimsy handle, kicking it open. The sound of Seinfeld was the only noise he could detect, the TV sitting in a corner of the room.

He held his gun out in front of him, moving it from left to right and then back again as he traversed the room with his eyes. No Kenny Mensti in this room. Crouching, he moved down a dimly lit hallway.

Black seemed to loom on black, phantom images in front of him as he progressed, warring with himself between getting through the apartment quickly and being cautious. He didn't see the body at first, his eyes trained directly in front of him and totally neglecting the floor. In fact, he almost tripped over it, catching himself at the very last second by throwing a hand against the wall and steadying himself. He felt cold pinpricks of fear run up his spine as he aimed his gun down, finally able to recognize where the man's head was located.

DiMitri screamed, "Don't move or I'll shoot."

He waited a few seconds; there was definitely no movement from the body. But what should he do now? If he checked for a pulse he'd only have one hand on his weapon, which could make him vulnerable if this was a scam. Kenny could lurch up and grab the gun and then he'd be dead.

On the other hand, it would look pretty idiotic if he was found holding a gun to a corpse's head; he knew backup was coming and they'd be swarming in at any moment.

He backed away from the body, feeling his way along the wall until his fingers connected with a light switch. He flipped it on and looked at the most grotesque scene he'd ever witnessed.

At least since the wedding on Saturday.

Kenny Mensti was lying on the floor, long vertical slits cut at each eyebrow, then moving lower over the lid and down the remainder of his face. His eyeballs had been pierced and were now seeping across the plane of his face, a filmy white liquid oozing from the now vacant hollows.

The other facial wounds were two deep cuts like a "t" across his lips. It looked like a knife had been placed inside his mouth at each corner before slicing through the skin all the way to the ear. The same procedure was used from the middles of the upper and lower lip, the first moving up to the nose and the latter down to his chin. The end result was horrific; the man's entire face had basically been filleted.

His jugular veins had been cut also, just like Langly's. An insurance policy to make sure he was dead? DiMitri didn't know. His hand shook, the gun moving wildly as he rotated, looking for the killer. From the corner of his eye he saw a shadow moving down the hallway before getting lost in darkness, then the sound of a back door swinging shut.

Without thinking, DiMitri was in pursuit. He could feel his feet sliding over the blood soaked linoleum floor as he moved around Mensti's body and thought he would fall for sure this time when the soles of his boots finally gained traction. He charged forward knowing that the possibility that he might have to actually use his weapon had just increased dramatically. His hands were sweating, his grip on the gun slipping.

Once outside he slowly crept forward, willing himself to find the right direction to proceed. The crescent moon shone down on the tall trees, making eerie shadows that took on the appearance of the monsters that used to scare him in his youth. Despite the screeching sirens in the background, he could hear the crunch of dried twigs beneath his feet. He stopped and listened carefully; something was off to his left. Garnishing as much bravado as he could, he clicked the revolver and screamed, "Police. On the ground. Now."

• • •

DiMitri could make out the silhouette of two arms going up in the air as a body started to slowly turn around.

"I said on the ground," DiMitri yelled again, watching as the person finally faced him.

DiMitri lowered his gun arm a few inches, stunned. "Calhoon, is that you? What the hell are you doing out here? I could have shot you."

Calhoon was wearing his civilian clothes, jeans and a dark shirt. He licked his lips, his head moving from side to side scoping the area like a lighthouse beacon. "Same thing as you. I heard the radio call and was close by so hightailed it over." He nodded in the direction of the house and added, "Mensti was already dead when I got here. I thought I heard something out here so I'm checking it out."

Sweat was glistening off of Calhoon's forehead, dripping down his face, yet he remained still.

"You know what, partner, I'm probably going to catch some grief for even being here. I got reprimanded for leaving you at the lab and clocking out mid-shift; they temporarily took my badge. Assholes," he snarled, the familiar raising of his upper lip, the feral focusing of his eyes as good as a road sign. Calhoon was pissed.

He took a few tentative half steps toward DiMitri, leaned his head to the side, and put on the kind of smile a child wears when he's asking for a cookie before dinner. In a surprisingly conciliatory tone, he said, "What do you say you just forget you even saw me? I'll slip away and no one will even know I was here. You'd be doing me a big favor."

Hands still in the air, Calhoon winked as he brought them down slowly, rotating his shoulders as though they'd gotten stiff.

DiMitri was about to speak when Calhoon's right arm thrust upwards, lightening quick, before powering down, the momentum staggering as his elbow connected with the bottom of DiMitri's rib cage.

It happened so fast DiMitri didn't have time to react. Blinding pain seared through his body as he crumbled to the ground. His head hung down like a dog's as he gagged, trying to ward off the vomit that was already forcing its way up his throat. And then he was heaving, the contents of his stomach spewing out, splashing back up onto his face as it hit the ground. He shook his head groggily, trying to rinse his mouth with his own saliva, to spit out the foul taste when he noticed his gun from the corner of his eye. He must have dropped it when he fell to the ground.

He reached out his arm, trying to make a grab for it, but Calhoon kicked it farther away.

"I'm sorry to have to do this," said Calhoon as he pulled a knife out from under his waist band. "I kind of liked you, even though you are the stupidest partner I've ever had."

DiMitri looked up at Calhoon, confused. "You killed Mensti?"

"A gold star for my protégé."

Nothing was making sense to DiMitri. "I don't understand. "Why?"

"You want an explanation?" Calhoon laughed, his grip on the knife loosening as he finally wiped away the sweat dripping down his face. "I've held your hand this far, I might as well go all the way.

"Didn't you find it odd that I took a private call on my cell phone when we were on our way to the Fullington murder scene?"

DiMitri remembered the call, mostly because Calhoon had yelled at him to turn off the siren because he couldn't hear the person he was talking to.

He tried to answer but his tongue stuck to the roof of his mouth, swollen and dry and at the moment useless. He shook his head, hoping the gesture would keep Calhoon talking.

"It's all about power," Calhoon started, his agitation growing as he spoke. "I tried to achieve it by the book, but that never works for a guy like me. Not in a world where favoritism rules, where climbing the ladder of success depends on the people you know and how much money you have. So I decided on another route."

DiMitri kept his eyes glued to the knife that Calhoon was waving around as the rant continued.

"So I decided on another plan, to take an opportunity of a lifetime. All I had to do was erase a business deal, make it go away like it never happened. And I was the only one in a position to make that happen.

"Who had the power then? Me; I did." Calhoon was laughing, looking insane as he thumped his chest in a display of dominance.

DiMitri fought the urge to pass out, knew he had to stay alert if he had any chance of surviving. He peddled his legs against the earth, trying to get a toehold, to push himself farther away from Calhoon, but his body barely moved. He swallowed several times, ran his tongue across his teeth, finally moistening his mouth so at least he was able to talk.

"Look, we're partners. Everything you just told me means nothing; I'll forget I saw you here, forget I heard a word."

Calhoon laughed, said, "You're a terrible liar, partner."

It was no secret that Calhoon had never thought very highly of him. But the way he spit out that last word, with such derision and hatred, took DiMitri by surprise.

"Look at you, acting like a puppy that got thrown out a car window. You're so damn easy to mess with. That blog that got you in so much trouble?" Calhoon bowed as though receiving an award, snickering. "I'm the one who wrote it, not any of those poor dumb groupies you went out drinking with. I knew it would blow up in your face; seeing the chief ream you was cinematic."

The sirens were closing in, the flashing red and white lights sending a prism of light across the dense cluster of trees and bushes.

"Sounds like I need to be on my way," Calhoon said as he inched closer to DiMitri. "You, my friend, will be the second cop I kill tonight."

Comprehension surged through DiMitri at the same speed as the spurt of energy; Calhoon was the one who killed Langly. DiMitri threw his arm out with ferocious force, catching the knife on its downward spiral. The blade easily sliced through his skin, blood pouring from the deep wound. He instinctively cradled the injured limb as Calhoon kicked, his boot finding the exact spot of the incision. An animal sound escaped DiMitri's mouth, a shriek of unbearable pain.

DiMitri watched as the hazy form of his partner leaned over him, dazed and in shock as the knife descended to his neck. He could feel its chill, already wet with his own blood, resting against his jugular. He closed his eyes, waiting for death.

The noise of the gun didn't immediately register as Calhoon's body fell on top of him. DiMitri rolled, holding his wounded arm, trying to get the heavy form off of him.

Then footsteps running in his direction and a flashlight in his eyes.

"Are you OK?" Ryan bent over, out of breath, before yanking the corpse away from DiMitri. "Boy do you have a good set of lungs on you. If I hadn't heard you scream I don't think I would have found you in time."

28

X strode down the hospital corridor, trying to clear his head. The news that Langly had been killed, murdered by a cop, was simply unbearable. And had it not been for Ryan, DiMitri would have been lost as well. As for Mensti's death, well that didn't even register; as far as X was concerned, it was a risk he assumed by being in that line of work. Drug dealing; a blot on humanity.

He stopped and looked into the emergency room cubicle. There was DiMitri, his arm propped up on a high pile of pillows, a nurse adjusting the I.V. feeding into his other arm.

X stuck his head into the room. "I was told out front that Officer DiMitri could have visitors?"

When he saw the protective reaction on the nurse's face he was glad he'd posed it as a question. "I'll be brief, just a few questions."

She yanked the curtains open, her way of saying OK, he figured, and left scribbling notes on a clipboard. DiMitri waved for him to come on in.

X swallowed the lump in his throat, a sudden flood of emotions overwhelming him. His heart was hammering as he looked carefully at the young man lying on the bed, the sunken cheeks and dark circles under his eyes a testament to the ordeal he'd been through.

"DiMitri." X pulled a chair to the side of the bed and sat down, the men's eyes now on a more equal plain. "God, I'm so sorry." He dropped his head, shaking it miserably, not finding the words he wanted to say. "If I had just figured it out a little sooner."

"What are you talking about?" DiMitri said, grimacing as he adjusted himself on the bed.

"Right after you and Ryan left, I went down to the lab. The IT tech was able to verify that the original report on Henry's tuxedo jacket was purposefully deleted. Thank God he was able to retrieve it from a dump file relatively quickly. As it turns out, there was close to a gram of loose cocaine at the bottom of Henry's jacket pocket. The best guess is that it spilled out of whatever it was stored in when it was removed from the tuxedo."

X leaned over, resting his elbows on his knees. "That's when the pieces finally came together. The first person up that belfry was Calhoon; it would have been easy for him to snatch the drugs out of the tuxedo. And he knew, as a cop, that he wouldn't be subject to a body search.

"Then, by chance, you guys arrive at Aiden Ellsworth's place and within minutes discover a stash of cocaine that a dozen other officers somehow missed during their three hour search?"

X pressed his lips together, his anger simmering just below the surface. Or maybe it was regret? He wasn't sure, couldn't identify the feeling, just knew it was eating a hole through his heart. "It was just too coincidental. I figured Calhoon had to be involved, somehow. I decided to just jump in the car and head over to Mensti's, run it by you."

X stood up and walked to the back of the cubicle, where a window overlooked the vast hospital parking lot.

"I was just leaving the station when the report of an officer down came over the wire."

Neither man spoke for several seconds, DiMitri finally breaking the silence.

"What I don't understand it why? Why would Calhoon go to all of that trouble, risk everything, his career, just to move evidence? I could see it if he kept the drugs to sell them later on; that would be some good cash. But how did he profit by planting them at Ellsworth's?"

X rubbed his jaw, thinking. "When you were out there tonight, did Calhoon say anything at all to you about Saturday morning?"

DiMitri shifted his head against the pillow, closing his eyes. "Yeah, he was going on about a phone call he'd gotten. And some business deal that happened earlier at Gulf Cove that needed to be erased."

"He must have been talking about Mensti selling the coke to Henry." X moved back to DiMitri's bedside, thinking it through out loud. "If the cops had found all that cocaine at Gulf Cove, whether it was on Henry or Mensti, or even if it was just dumped in the trash, the next question would be to find out where it came from, who sourced it."

"That makes sense," DiMitri said. "But that same question came up when it was found at Aiden Ellsworth's place. What's the difference?"

X's mind flashed back to his talk with Sean Baker at the Westchester Penitentiary. "It's in a different geographic territory. By moving the stash, Calhoon effectively rerouted the entire investigation away from the specific drug cartel that operates in the Gulf Cove area."

"As soon as Calhoon heard that Mensti was being looked at as a possible suspect, he bolted. He literally drove away from the lab in our squad car without me," DiMitri said.

"He must have been afraid that Mensti knew about his involvement in moving the cocaine and might talk if he was arrested. So Calhoon made good and sure he wouldn't be able to.

"And Langly ..." X bent over, forced a breath into his lungs. It physically hurt just to say the name. "God, I'm the one who sent him over to Mensti's in the first place. Who knows why Calhoon killed him. It didn't look there was any kind of confrontation, no chance for Langly at all; he was ambushed."

"I know I'm green," DiMitri said, "but I'd have never guessed Calhoon capable of anything like this."

X dropped back into the chair, putting his hand on DiMitri's good arm. "There's no way you could have known." X knew the same applied to him; he just wasn't ready to let himself off the hook yet.

The overhead fluorescent light cast a yellowish glow on DiMitri's already pale face, his cracked lips parched. "I've replayed everything in my mind a hundred times, every word Calhoon has ever said to me," DiMitri said. "He was an opportunistic jerk with an authority complex, and it didn't seem to bother him a bit killing either Langly or Mensti. But he didn't have anything to do Henry Fullington's murder. I'm sure of it."

X tended to agree. "So we're back to square one." X sighed as he got up again and walked back to the window, leaning against the sill and resting his head against the pane. "Whatever the reason was for killing Henry and the others, it wasn't related to drugs."

He turned back to DiMitri. "You've proven that you've got a good head for details. Tell me, what were your impressions of the people you and Calhoon interviewed? Did you write anything else down in that little notebook of yours that in hindsight might raise a red flag?"

The sound of the machine monitoring DiMitri's blood pressure beeped a steady melody as he excitedly used his good arm to point to his boots in the corner. "My notebook is in there. Can you get it for me?"

Despite his grief, X couldn't help but grin as he brought the worn book to DiMitri. "I appreciate your enthusiasm, especially under the circumstances."

"I told you it'd be an honor to work with you."

DiMitri scooted against the pillows, settling into a comfortable position. "There was so much commotion going on at Gulf Cove that Saturday morning that not any one person stands out."

His fingers started tapping in time with the medical instrument's beeping. "We had the follow up interview with Nancy Lubinowitz, the maid of honor, and everything seemed kosher there. She said Becca and Henry loved each other and couldn't imagine anyone holding a grudge against either of them.

"Honestly, the only person who had anything out of the ordinary come up was the guy who owns Corbinian's, Mark Bramm."

DiMitri opened his notebook, took some time turning the dog-eared pages one handed before finally saying, "Here we go. I ran the guy's name and it turns out he used to be called Mark Pullister. He legally changed his name 10 years ago. I checked, and both names are clean."

Impressed, X wondered, "That's above and beyond. What in the world made you look into something like that?"

DiMitri stifled a yawn, apologized. "Calhoon. This Bramm guy got in his face, mocked him big time. Calhoon was determined to find something on him, anything in fact, just so he could go back there and make Bramm's life miserable. We dug deep but there wasn't any dirt on the guy, just that he'd changed his name. I wrote a detailed report; it's in the system."

DiMitri's eyelids fluttered shut as he ineffectively tried to suppress another yawn.

"I'm going to let you get some rest," X said as he stood up, not wanting to overtax DiMitri. "What are the doctors saying?"

"I've got a couple of cracked ribs and the arm," DiMitri said, lifting it slightly. "They're keeping me overnight for observation but I'm hoping to out by morning."

"Don't rush it; I want you to take care of yourself."

X looked down at this young cop who had just cheated death, watched as he finally gave in to the exhaustion and the medications dripping through his I.V. and drifted off to sleep.

And when he left the room, he was relieved that the rookie hadn't seen his tears.

• • •

If bad news travels fast, news that an officer is down moves at a meteoric pace. By the time X arrived at headquarters, it was flooded with cops, x-cops, fire and rescue and every other person who was or ever had been a public servant in any capacity of service and protection. It's a tight knit community and when one of their own is slain, there's an unspoken pledge to rally and to hunt down and dismantle the guilty party.

Only in this case, the person responsible was one of their own. And was already dead.

The makeshift memorial to Langly was impressive. The people gathered were holding candles, a shrine of flowers and notes already at the entrance of the building.

Rather than try to squeeze through the throng, X aimed for the rear entryway, the sound of people crying and chanting Langly's name following him.

He put his hand on the door and was pulling it open when he heard the unmistakable voice of Chief Hartman coming from behind him.

"I was on my way out to my car and I saw you."

X turned, his blue eyes rimmed in red as he allowed tears to flow down his cheeks.

They both leaned in, hugging and clapping each other on the back awkwardly.

Hartman backed away first. "I know now's not the best time. But don't let Langly's death be in vain. He wanted to bring in whoever killed Henry. Are you going to let whoever that mother fucker is win?"

X could hear the challenge in his boss' voice. "Not a chance in hell," he responded. "Not a bloody chance in hell."

29

Officer Ryan stood in the Gulf Cove church, alone and in the dark. He wasn't exactly sure why he'd come. He didn't consider himself a religious person, but he felt the need to say a private prayer, to ask God to watch over his deceased friend Matt Langly.

He was bone tired, could barely keep his eyes opened. But allowing himself to rest felt like a betrayal to his dead comrade.

The croaking of frogs was interrupted by a distant noise that came and went intermittently. Ryan focused his attention and, realizing that it was not his imagination, followed it out the front door. He moved slowly, turning right toward a field of sea grass but quickly readjusted his course when the sound weakened.

Ryan berated himself for leaving his flashlight in the car, a stupid move but he didn't want to go back for it now, he knew he was getting close; the pitch was coming from the immediate vicinity. He knelt down, moving his hands through the sand and dirt and grit around him, crawling a few inches in every direction until his fingertips connected with something small and solid. He closed his hand around the object, hurried back to his car and opened the door, the overhead light casting a glow over the cell phone he'd just found. On its screen he could see that the battery level was low; in fact, it was the drone of its warning that he had heard.

He looked up to the stars, offering a thank you, and then threw the car in gear. He needed to get back to the station; maybe this was the clue they were looking for.

• • •

Ryan stood in the hallway peering through the small opening of X's office. There he was, conked out on the couch, a can of Mountain Dew on the nearby table.

Ryan pushed the door open a little wider, the light from the hall slowly filtering into the darkened room. X startled, jumping off the couch and reflexively standing ready to defend himself.

"Oh, it's just you," he said, his body relaxing. He nodded toward the empty soda can. "Obviously it didn't work."

X noted that Ryan had changed out of the uniform he'd been wearing earlier that night, the one that had blood stains all over it. Most of it Langly's blood.

He sat back down, patted the empty space next to him. "How you holding up?"

Ryan sighed as he joined X on the couch. "Don't know. I think I'm still in shock."

The two men sat, looking forward at nothing in particular, lost in thought. Ryan finally asked, "What's all that?"

There were two open boxes under the far window and stacks of paper were spread around them on the floor.

"It's some of the stuff you collected from Aiden Ellsworth's house. I've been going through it, and look what I found."

X reached for some papers that were serving as a placemat for his soda, turned the lamp on, and leaned back against the couch.

"Henry Fullington wrote Ellsworth a personal check for $12,000 back in March. On the memo line it said 'Reimbursement for Trip to Rome.'"

"Had it been cashed?" Ryan wondered.

"Yeah, it looks like it. Ellsworth made a copy of it for some reason, along with another check that was left blank and marked 'void.'"

X held up the piece of paper for Ryan to see, the four big bold letters written across the Xeroxed check. Then in a different pen on the empty space below, Aiden had written, 'Sorry I couldn't help you out on this one. You're right; she's a bitch.'

"It was in with his receipts from that trip. Apparently he was looking for some woman named Camille Lopez. He hired an Italian private eye to help track her down. It turns out she was living and working at a convent that takes on paying guests; apparently that's a big industry in Rome, kind of like a religious B & B."

Ryan took the pages that X held out, glancing through until he came to the last sheet. It looked like an application for employment and listed Camille Lopez as an American citizen with a birth date of October 5th, 1981. Next to the lines marked 'Numero Di Pasaporto' and 'Numero Di Sicurezza Sociale Degli Stati Uniti' were a garble of numbers that were unintelligible; everything else on the form was in very precise block handwriting.

"Interesting. Think she did this on purpose?" Ryan asked, pointing to the lines that were impossible to read.

"It sure looks like it. I've gone through every single state registry and there are no matches for a Camille Lopez born on that date and year."

X rubbed his eyes, trying to suppress a yawn. "I don't know who she is, but I'm damn well going to find out."

X stood up and walked over to his desk, grabbed his phone from the docking station attached to his computer. "Think it's too early to call Arthur Fullington?"

He was dialing the private number as he spoke, not really caring what time it was. Henry's father had been riding them all, calling at all hours of the night and day pushing hard for any information on his son's murder. Turnaround was fair play.

"Yes." That was Arthur Fullington's greeting, a single syllable, loud and firm that implied that whatever was going to be said should be of adequate importance to merit the call.

"It's Detective King; I have you on speakerphone. I've been going through the personal documents we seized from Aiden Ellsworth's home and discovered that Henry paid him $12,000 from his personal account, apparently to go to Rome and track down a woman named Camille Lopez. Do you know anything about that?"

He could hear the exhale on the other side of the phone, a pre-dawn clearing of the throat. "That's his ex-wife. I didn't know he'd sent Aiden over there, though."

"Henry was married before?" X said, stunned. "I didn't see any record of that."

X started pacing across his littered office, five steps to the couch before he had to turn around and head back toward the desk.

How could he not have known that Henry Fullington had been married? He felt the need to keep moving or else risk having his irritation spill out in some less suitable way. He was, after all, talking to a personal friend of the governor.

"Yeah, well believe me, it happened. About five years ago, when Henry was traveling through Europe after his graduate studies." X heard the patter of footsteps and the opening of a door on the other end of the phone as Mr. Fullington continued. "He met her in Rome, and apparently they fell for each other in a big way. But she was a strict Catholic girl and didn't believe in premarital sex. So he married her, if you can believe that. It was a quickie, lasted only three days. Henry said it was a huge mistake, wanted it erased from his memory and never wanted to think about it again. The divorce went smoothly; it appears that they both agreed that it wouldn't have worked out.

"So my wedding/divorce present was to call in some favors and get it cleansed from the records. I didn't see why a failed marriage should dog Henry for the rest of his life."

X waited while he heard Mr. Fullington asking someone for coffee, then asked, "Why did Henry want to track her down? What did he want from her?"

"My guess is an annulment. Becca had her mind set on getting married at St. Patrick's Cathedral, here in the city, and Henry was hell bent on giving her anything she wanted. But even I couldn't make his first marriage totally disappear. In the eyes of the law and the Catholic Church, he was a divorcee."

"I'm assuming the annulment didn't happen."

"If it had, I'm positive Henry would have let me know. All we needed was Camille's signature; the bishop was ready to walk the paperwork through the tribunal himself, as a personal favor. That would have given Henry and Becca the green light to be married in any Catholic church they wanted."

Ryan picked up the job application Camille had filled out and brought it over to X, pointing to the illegible portions.

X nodded, and asked into the phone, "Would you happen to know Ms. Lopez' birth date or social security number?"

"I'm sure I have hard copies of the paperwork somewhere; I'll have my assistant pull the records first thing and get back to you, though I don't know how it's relevant."

More sounds came through the receiver, a spoon clinking against china, a muffled thank you, and the sound of Henry's father taking a deep sip. And then, "I'm sure I don't need to remind you, Detective that I'm going to be burying my son in less than eight hours. That doesn't leave you a lot of time to identify his killer. Don't waste your time on Camille Lopez; she's a non-issue, trust me.

"Eight hours," Mr. Fullington repeated. "I want a name, the name, by then."

X dropped the phone back on the desk, conversation over, cradling his forehead in his hands. Then he reached for his laptop. "Unbelievable. Cleansed? I don't know if I'll ever be able to fully trust public records again."

And as he logged into the department's heavy duty search engine and typed in the name Camille Lopez, the irony of using a source that could be so easily manipulated was duly noted by the acid burning in his stomach.

Ryan peered over the computer, checking out what X was up to. "Guess you don't trust his judgment?"

X's lips curled into a smile, the first since he'd heard about Langly. He knew his buddy would deliver a good line right about now, so in his honor X said, "Don't you read any crime novels? The ex always does it."

X appreciated Ryan's big toothy grin, a little balm on his raw heart.

"Well I have some news," Ryan said. "I drove out to Gulf Cove after ..." Ryan looked down, swallowed hard. "Well, you know. Anyhow, I found a cell phone, thrown in the brush near the church. The lab's looking at it now; want to go see if they found anything interesting?"

"Hell yeah," X said, the first seeds of enthusiasm pumping through his blood. "Why didn't you say something sooner?"

"Well, it might not be anything, just a lost cell phone."

But X could tell that Ryan was excited.

"Only one way to find out," X said. "Let's go."

30

The sun was just rising when X and Ryan pushed through the doors of the lab. The smell of burnt coffee wafted through the air as Bart, the IT guru, dragged an empty pot off of the Mr. Coffee burner.

"Good thing we're not here for your cooking skills," X called out.

"Hey man," Bart said, his heavy Jamaican accent bellowing through the room. "I was just getting ready to text you; I finished my preliminary on the phone Ryan brought in."

"Whatever you have, we want to hear it," X answered as he and Ryan followed Bart to a long counter on the far side of the room.

"Let's start with the bad news," Bart said, rubbing his hands together as he started to speak. "There were two sets of prints on the phone. I ran them through our data base, but we got no hits. And not surprisingly, it's a prepaid model so it's untraceable."

The newly discovered cell phone was now connected to a computer monitor, where its brief call history was scrolling.

Bart swung his long dreadlocks over his shoulder and leaned closer to the screen.

"I know you're interested in Saturday, the day of the Fullington wedding, so that's where I started. This cell sent two text messages that morning, both to the same number. The first one was at 7:36 a.m., which went unanswered. The second was at 9:42 a.m. Within 90 seconds, it received a reply." Bart pulled a piece of paper out of the printer, handing it to X. "They're all in code; here you go, I printed you out a copy."

X took the page and held it out so Ryan could read it as well.

Text sent: 7:36 a.m. SK XLCW TFIA AASUP WFA STKZFS

Text sent: 9:42 a.m. YW UASU SCC TCASA

Text received: 9:44 a.m. CFJA GYFSA NZCC TSCC GG SK 12

"By the way," Bart added. "The other phone involved was a throw-away too. So there's no trail to follow there."

X rotated his head in a circle, heard his neck cracking from the tight muscles. He could really use one of Ann's massages right now. His brain was more muddled than he'd realized, and what he was looking at didn't make any sense to him at all. "Don't we have a decryption program that'll figure this out?"

Bart pointed to one of the other computers along the countertop, the screen a swirling emblem that indicated that it was busy processing something. "It's working on it as we speak."

"What else does the cell show?" Ryan wondered.

Bart scrolled through the phone's brief calling history. "It was activated nine days ago. You'll notice that other than these text messages, all calls either made from or to this little baby were to the same phone number. A pay phone."

A list of approximately two dozen calls were noted on the screen, a long column of the exact same telephone number.

X looked at the sheet of paper, the three coded texts in front of him. "Assuming that each group of letters is a separate word, that last text includes a word with two of the same letters," he said, pointing to the 'GG.' I don't know of any words that meet that criteria."

"Maybe 'G' refers to a number?" Ryan commented. "It could be '11' or '44' or any other number."

"Or," said X, putting the page next to the cell's calling history, "it's an abbreviation. 'GG' for 'pay phone.'"

Bart leaned down, his nose almost on top of the screen. "I wonder if it could be a simple Augustus's code. And if that's the case, why the computer hasn't come up with a resolution yet?"

X was already writing out the alphabet, A through Z sequentially and on a single line, as Bart walked back over to the other computer, which was still churning away. "It's still processing," he called over his shoulder.

Directly under the letter 'G,' X wrote 'P,' then continued in succession with 'Q,' 'R,' and 'S' under the standard alphabet until he'd gone through all 26 letters.

"OK, if I replace each letter of the coded text with the correct alphabetical order, the message would say 'LOSJ PHOBJ WILL CBLL PP BC 12.'"

"Lost phone will call payphone at 12." Ryan called out the words as though he was a contestant on *Wheel of Fortune.* Then, seconds later, "No, it's 'Lose phone.' Someone was telling him to get rid of the evidence."

"Impressive," X said, feeling a rush of heat as he started translating the other two texts. "The middle one says "HF DJBD BLL CLJBJ."

"It's clearly not a standard Augustus; there's some kind of key being used," said Bart. "But we can probably piece it together. It looks like 'B' replaces the letter 'A.'

"And the first two letters must be an abbreviation for Henry Fullington," Ryan added.

X stood back, resting his chin on his fist. "Let's see what the first text looks like."

Pencil in hand, he transcribed the coded language. 'BT GULF CORJ JJBDY FOJ BCTIOB.'

Again, Ryan was quick to come up with a few of the words. "At Gulf Cove, something something action."

"Ready for action," X said, knowing in his gut that they'd just found the smoking gun. This cell phone could lead them to the person responsible for killing Henry. Maybe it was possible to meet Arthur Fullington's deadline after all, give him the name of his son's killer before he was laid to rest.

Ryan pulled the pencil from X's hand, leaned over the piece of paper and wrote out several variations of the middle text. "I bet it says 'HF DEAD ALL CLEAR.'"

"May I see that," Bart asked, taking the page and bringing it closer to his eyes. "Interesting. If that's the correct translation, the letter 'J' is represented by both a vowel and a consonant. I wonder if the key is a word or a number."

X could practically see the wheels turning in the tech's head as he continued to play with the puzzle.

"Keep working on it, Bart; I know you'll get it. In the meantime, were you able to identify which pay phone the cell dialed?"

Bart's hand fisted, crumpling the paper in frustration. "Yeah, it's in downtown Massapequa; hold on, I have it right over here," he answered as he walked over to his desk and looked down at his note-pad. "834 Park Street."

X looked at Ryan and asked, "Want to take a drive?"

31

834 Park Street was in the middle of the block and just outside a deli, which was a beehive of activity with people streaming in and out.

X found a spot nearby and parked his Mercedes. "That place looks like Grand Central Station," he said to Ryan as he got out of the car.

"Lots of traffic," Ryan agreed. "But so far I haven't seen one person use the pay phone; everyone has a cell."

The two stood in front of the public phone, looking for some clue. "I guess we could brush it for prints," Ryan said. "See if they match what's on the cell I found."

X opened the phone book that hung precariously from a metal cord, ripped a page out and then carefully picked up the receiver, his hand shielded from the phone by the torn sheet. Just in case there were fingerprints to retrieve.

"That's disgusting." Ryan was pointing to the mouth piece which was spattered with small crumbs of food and condiments.

"Well I'm not planning on kissing it," X said as he placed his other hand over the number pad, closed his eyes and waited, thinking that some divine intervention right now couldn't hurt.

Ryan stood by, watching basically nothing as X remained in this pseudo telepathic stance.

"I'm going to get some coffee. Want some?" Ryan finally asked as he abandoned his friend and went into the delicatessen.

When he emerged several minutes later, X was still standing at the payphone. But now his eyes were wide open and he was smiling.

"Two sugars, one cream," Ryan said, handing him a large cup. "What are you so happy about? Did you find something?"

X pointed across the street. "Don't you think it's a coincidence that Corbinian's happens to be located on the same block as this pay phone?"

"Yeah, I guess." Ryan absently opened the brown bag he was holding and took out the glazed crawler. "But what motive would anyone at Corbinian's have? I know Fullington's rehearsal dinner was held there, but the cell phone history shows calls coming to and from this pay phone for five days before then."

"Thanks," X said, taking the doughnut and heading back to his car.

"Hey, that was mine. I got you a chocolate." Ryan trotted after X and got into the passenger seat, gingerly holding his coffee so it wouldn't spill.

X had already swallowed the last piece of his breakfast and was loading up his computer.

"DiMitri told me that the owner of Corbinian's changed his last name from Pullister to Bramm. I wonder why?"

"Who knows?" Ryan said as he struggled to peel back the perforated section of his coffee lid. He finally gave up and removed the plastic top altogether. "Maybe he hates his family and it was a show of disowning them."

X clicked away on the keyboard until DiMitri's report was on his screen. It was relatively short, basically a bio detailing Mark Pullister's history. He was 35 years old, born in Upstate New York, and graduated from Stony Brook University on Long Island. He'd never been married, sued, or arrested. Twelve years ago he started his first restaurant, named Pullister's, in Babylon, which was still in business. His father, Mark Sr., co-signed the loan documents.

"Look at this," X said, tilting the screen so Ryan could see. "DiMitri even checked out Bramm's father; he's a restaurateur also, has five places upstate in and around the Rochester area." He scrolled down, the five listings all called Pullister's.

"Then we have Mark Jr. changing his surname to Bramm seven years ago. And two years later, he opened Corbinian's. This time around he was able to finance it on his own."

"There you go," Ryan said, chomping away on the last of his doughnut. "He changed his name because he wanted to distinguish himself from his dad."

"Yeah, I guess. Wonder how he came up with Bramm?"

"Does there have to be a reason?" Ryan asked. "Maybe he just liked the sound of it."

"Or maybe it has some significance to him," X said as he opened Google.

He typed in the name "Bramm," said "Hmm, that's interesting," and then entered "Corbinian."

Ryan sat silently, watching as traffic picked up with morning commuters making their way through town, while X punched more commands into his computer. X suddenly high fived the steering wheel, yelling, "Yes."

Ryan jumped, hot coffee spilling onto his lap. "What the hell?"

"The words Corbinian and Bramm? The origins of both words have the same meaning: raven."

"Raven?" Ryan repeated slowly.

"I don't know how it's relevant, but let's go with this for a while," X said. "What comes to mind when you think raven?"

"Well I certainly don't get the warm fuzzies. I wrote a paper on Edgar Allen Poe's poem in high school. As I remember, the raven represented darkness and doubt."

"It says here that from a historical standpoint the word stands for death and destruction; it's a bird of ill-omen," X recited as he read from the screen. He started talking faster as his excitement increased.

"Look at Henry's murder, how dark and depraved it was. Maybe the person responsible, perhaps even Mark Bramm, wants to be known as the raven."

He saw the skepticism in Ryan's eyes, saw him briefly look away, maybe trying not to offend him, or perhaps just trying to quell the runaway train that was coursing through X's mind.

"I know it sounds farfetched," X conceded, "but think of it. How many serial killers use aliases that have special meaning to them? We had Son of Sam right here on Long Island back in '76 and '77."

"But motive?" Ryan asked the question a second time.

"Some mass murderers don't need a specific motive. They want to kill in a particular way, which is what drives them. The victim is secondary.

"In the case of Henry, the goriness of his death is the key."

"And Ellsworth and Damson?" Ryan challenged.

X let his head drop back against the seat and stared at the roof of the car.

"I'm just playing devil's advocate," Ryan added, "not slamming your theory."

X appreciated the semi vote of confidence. "I don't know, I don't have all the pieces yet. But I want to talk to Mark Bramm. It can't be a coincidence that the cell phone you found at Gulf Cove happened to only have calls made to a payphone on the same block as Corbinian's." He turned to Ryan, his eyes questioning. "Are you up for some double teaming?"

● ● ●

Ryan stood at the front door of Corbinian's, where the closed sign hung, ready to play his part. It would not take a lot of acting experience; all he was supposed to do was give a thumbs-up sign if and when X pointed to him from inside the restaurant. That, and to confirm whatever X might say to Bramm, if things ended up going that far.

In the interim, X walked around the side of the building and into a narrow alley. He could see a pickup truck parked outside a rear entrance with crates of vegetables and fruits in its bed. Just as he was about to move forward, his cell started ringing. He quickly hit the mute button, took a quick peek at the screen. It was Bart calling.

X spoke softly into the phone. "Hi. It's not the best time; it is important?"

Bart's Jamaican accent sang back to him. "I think so. First, I was able to check out the pay phone's log and a call was received at three

146

minutes past noon on the day Fullington was murdered; it came from the same throwaway as the one that texted the cell that Ryan found."

"OK, good to know," X said as he shifted his position, trying to get a better view of what was going on in the alley. "Anything else?"

"The computer just came up with the key to the encryption. It's the letters AENRV.

X was hoping that the code would mean something to him, but he came up blank. He repeated the letters out loud, committing them to memory, thanked Bart and then hung up.

As he continued to approach the truck, he could make out two men who'd been blocked from his view. One of them was almost as big as X but probably a good ten years younger, the other medium height with tanned arms and neck and wearing worn out jeans and a dirty sleeveless tee shirt. X finally got close enough to overhear parts of their conversation.

"I picked the squash this morning Mr. Bramm," the man was saying. "And the beets are the best we've had in years."

He silently thanked the farmer for identifying Bramm. He was standing at the rear of the truck, one foot on the rusty back bumper as he chatted with the farmer. He was dressed in dark pants and a collared tee shirt, and it looked like he was in pretty decent shape. No bulging muscles, but no overhanging gut either. X watched as Bramm handed a check to the farmer, a casual movement made more so when he jerked his head around suddenly, staring down X.

X had no choice other than to act normal and introduce himself. "I'm Detective Xavier King," he said as he approached, pulling his badge out and offering it for inspection.

Mark Bramm wiped his hands on the apron he had around his waist, peered at the identification, and said, "Can you excuse me for a second?" He put two fingers in his mouth and whistled. Seconds later two young Latinos came through the alley door and looked at their boss for instruction.

"Grab those crates and lay everything out on the large butcher block. I want to use the riper stuff for lunch and save the rest for the dinner crowd."

Bramm glanced in X's direction briefly. "I'm a little busy this morning, my chef is out sick with the flu. Do you mind if we talk while I work?" He then grabbed one of the crates and carried it into the kitchen without looking back.

X was willing to go along with the game and picked up a flat of strawberries, following a few feet behind. He came through a door and into a large, impeccably clean and well organized kitchen, handing off the fresh fruit to one of the workers. Bramm was already shouting orders to a woman at a small sink about how to peel the beets, then checking and rearranging prep trays on their way to the walk-in cooler. He seemed to be able to see what needed to be done all in one glance.

Bramm stopped at the stainless steel stove, removed the cover of a huge pot of what smelled like vichyssoise, and dipped a spoon in. "This needs a little more oregano," he told the woman at his side, licking the spoon and handing it over to her before he seemed to remember X was even present.

"So what is it can I do for you Detective?" Bramm called over his shoulder as he continued on his way to a larger work sink in the corner where a young man was holding a fish in both hands, looking confused. "This is my sous-chef, Julio," he semi-introduced. "Julio, are you still having a problem filleting the trout?"

"I'm sorry, I no have good experience with this," the man said, bowing down in apology. He was wearing a red apron covered in fish guts, the vacant and dull look in his eyes just like those of the cutthroat trout he was holding.

X watched as Bramm picked up a knife, flicking his finger on its tip to make sure it was sharp. "All you have to do," he told Julio as he demonstrated, "is lay the fish on its side and gently cut along the belly all the way to the throat.

"Then you insert the knife here," he pointed, "between the gills and the collarbone and cut outward until you can remove the head. Then all that's left to remove are the guts like so," he said, pulling out the entrails and throwing them into a nearby trash container. "Got it?"

Julio nodded yes vigorously while Bramm picked up some liquid soap and cleaned the knife, first the blade and then the handle.

Grabbing a dish towel he carefully dried it before handing it back to Julio.

X watched the scenario carefully, from the way Bramm held the knife in his hand and unconsciously caressed its hilt to how he instinctively removed any trace that he had touched it.

"What are you looking at, Detective King was it?" Bramm drew up close, standing in X's personal space.

X knew it was a power play, an attempt to make him feel uncomfortable, or if truly successful, even vulnerable. There was no way that was going to work. X countered by inching even closer to Bramm, so close that X could see the green specks in Bramm's otherwise brown eyes.

"I was just admiring your technique," X answered as he forced a smile.

The men stood that way for several seconds, two hulks sizing each other up, before Bramm turned his back on X and opened the walk-in refrigerator door. "To what do I owe the pleasure, Detective?"

A cloud of fog leaked from the opening as Bramm pulled out a large container and reclosed the door.

X waited to speak until Bramm finally stopped what he was doing and acknowledged his presence by looking at him. "You owe it to your own stupidity, my friend. You've been pretty slick so far, but your mistakes are catching up with you."

Bramm laughed. "What mistakes?" He gestured toward the stove. "You think the extra oregano was a bad idea?"

X knew that what he was about to imply was a reach, knew he couldn't let that uncertainty show. "No, I'm talking about your communication techniques."

X pulled the discarded cell phone that Ryan had found from his pocket and put it on the counter. "We found the phone that was hidden at Gulf Cove. It was a lucky break, I'll admit. If the battery hadn't been low we might never have found it. Those cheap pay as you go phones sound like a squeaky wheel when they are low on juice."

A flash of surprise crossed over Bramm's face before being quickly replaced by a look of boredom. He flicked the phone back in X's direction. "Looks like you made the trip for nothing; I use a Blackberry."

He took a quick look around the kitchen before walking through the main dining area toward the bar.

"It was clever, using the pay phone across the street to make contact. No way to trace anything directly back to you that way," X said as he slowly followed behind.

Bramm turned abruptly, standing solid and still, a cocky pose and a snarl as a smile. "Just what exactly are you trying to accuse me of?"

X looked out the front door where Ryan was standing, thumb up in the air as planned.

Nodding in that direction, X said, "My partner there just had a nice talk with the deli owner. It looks like you use that pay phone pretty frequently.

"I find that very odd, especially since you could use your own telephone right here, which has got to be less of a hassle than going all the way across the street and standing outside, in the elements, just to talk to someone."

Bramm shrugged. "Big deal, so I use the pay phone. It works great when I'm trying to collect on bounced checks or when running tabs get too high. When I call from the pay phone, people don't recognize the number on their caller I.D. and are much more likely to pick up the phone. Then they have to deal with me, for a change."

X raised his eyebrows. "Impressive. You can lie on your feet, I'll give you that."

"Listen, I really am busy. If you don't have anything more important to talk to me about than my use of a public phone, I'm going to have to ask you to leave."

Bramm raised his chin, folding his arms across his chest. His version of an ultimatum?

At the moment, X was wishing he could think on his own feet. Instead of moving forward with the conversation, his mind was stumbling with the letters that Bart had just given him, the key to the coded message. AENRV.

The letters twirled around his consciousness, tickled a chord in him that screamed they were important. He knew he couldn't just stand there, stuttering around what his brain was trying to put together.

He was just about to speak, just about to ask Bramm why he changed his name from Pullister when the pieces came together. AENRV. RAVEN.

X tried to calm the electricity that shot through his body. He needed to play this right; if the man standing in front of him really was a violent killer, how would he react to the accusation? X knew that how Bramm responded to what he was about to say next would make or break his theory.

So he changed topics midstream, hoping to trip Bramm up. "So you have a thing about ravens?"

Bramm literally flinched, his surprise obvious. He opened his mouth to speak, seemed to reconsider, and then closed it again, his face white as a sheet. He pulled out the neck of his shirt and blew down onto his chest, then went to the air conditioning control and dialed it down. The cool air came on instantly, blowing through the vents.

"I'm done with you making pretend I'm not here," X said, moving closer to Bramm. "I know you changed your name, know the linguistic connection to ravens. And the decryption key for the cell phone texts? Using the word raven was clever.

"What I want to know is why you call yourself the raven? Is that the nickname you planned on using for your killing spree?"

"You think I'm the Raven?" Bramm said, jutting his neck forward with a major smirk on his face, snickering. "Somebody here is adding one plus one and getting eleven. You have no idea what a joke you are, buddy."

Bramm's laughter was overcome by a phlegmy coughing fit that echoed from deep in his chest, the sound seeming to surprise even him. He looked up at the nearest vent. "God it's hot in here," he said as he went to the wall unit and turned it down some more.

He stood there for a second, leaning his head against the wall, before walking behind the bar and pulling out a Budweiser longneck. When he looked up, X had his service revolver raised and aimed straight at him.

"All you have to do is ask for one, you don't have to shoot me."

"I don't appreciate the sarcasm," X said as he put the gun down to his side. "And I want you to keep your hands where I can see them."

X watched as those hands shook, the beer swishing over the lip of the bottle. Bramm raised it to his lips, attempted to take a sip. Instead the liquid flowed down his chin.

"I don't know what you're trying to pull ..." X stopped talking midstream as Bramm clutched his chest and fell onto the floor. Foam started to accumulate around his mouth as he struggled for breath.

"Shit." X holstered his gun as he ran to the front door and opened it to Ryan. "Call 911. Something's wrong with him."

X sprinted back to Bramm, who was crunched over in pain, blood now trickling down the sides of his mouth.

"Bramm, can you hear me?" When there was no response, he tried with his surname. "Mark. Open your eyes."

Slowly Bramm's lids opened. His eyes had dilated and were now bloodshot, the whites of the eyes a sickly jaundiced yellow.

"Did you just take something?" X asked, berating himself that he hadn't thought of the possibility that Bramm might rather take his own life than be collared for murder.

"No way, I'd never do that," Bramm mumbled. Then understanding slowly crept into his face. "Oh my God," he said. "It's that bitch; she fucking double-crossed me."

Tremors took over Bramm's body as he tried to crawl toward X. "In my office, there's a syringe. Top drawer. Hurry."

X raced down a short hallway, assuming the office would be in that direction. There it was, the first doorway to the right. The room was cluttered, stacks of files thrown around and the desktop barely visible there was so much crap on it. The hairs on the back of X's neck rose as he opened the top drawer. It was empty.

It took a second for him to realize that the mess covering the desk's surface was in fact the contents of the drawer. He spread the fingers of both hands and sifted through the array of note pads, envelopes, paper clips, business cards and everything else one would typically find in a desk drawer. Seconds were ticking by yet he did not see or feel anything even closely resembling a syringe. He finally came upon an Epipen, one of those auto-injector shots that people with severe food allergies use.

X wasn't a doctor, but he'd bet the farm that Bramm wasn't suffering from an allergic reaction. Then it dawned on him; it must be the same poison found in the systems of his three murder victims.

He ran back to Bramm and knelt down, jamming the pen into his thigh before moving to his head, holding it up in his hands. The last thing he wanted was for the guy to choke on the fluids coming out of his mouth.

Bramm reached out and grabbed X's shirt, trying to pull him closer, his voice panicked. "The antidote, it's not working."

"I didn't find a syringe in your desk, just an Epipen. That's what I just gave you."

A terrible rattling sound started deep in Bramm's chest and his breathing became labored. With wild eyes, he was finally able to say, "Are you sure? Look again; it's taped to the front right corner."

"I'm sorry. Someone got to the desk before me. Your entire office is trashed."

X watched as comprehension flittered across Bramm's face, shattering the hope that was present just seconds earlier. The widening of his dilated eyes; the opening of his speechless mouth; the tears that appeared and started to flow.

X tried hard to keep his voice calm. "Tell me the name of the antidote. The hospital can start making up more."

"I don't know. The poison was her doing." His body convulsed, sweat now soaking through his shirt.

"Ryan, get me some cool towels," X yelled out before turning his attention back to Bramm. "Are you saying a woman was responsible for the poisonings at Gulf Cove?"

He weakly nodded yes before slumping over on his side. His eyes rolled back into his head, his shallow breaths coming further and further apart.

"Fire and Rescue are here," Ryan said as he put a cool compress on Bramm's head.

X hadn't even heard the sirens; when the two EMTs arrived he moved away to give them more room to work.

"Anyone know this guy's medical history?" the woman tech asked.

Over the drone of the portable EKG machine X answered. "No. I can't be a hundred percent sure, but I believe he's suffering from acute selenium poisoning," he said, watching the EMTs work. "Apparently an antidote exists for it."

The male tech pulled his stethoscope from his ears and stood. He looked down at the patient, who was going in and out of delirium. "Well if he doesn't get it pronto, he isn't going to make it."

"Well then what the hell are you just standing there for?" X's frustration was mounting as he watched his new key witness failing. "Call the hospital, get a doctor's advice. We need this man alive. He's involved in the Fullington murder spree and knows details that can close the case."

X couldn't believe what was happening in front of him, covered his eyes in denial. He felt Ryan pulling at him arm, dragging him back a few feet.

"Yelling at them isn't going to help," Ryan said. "Just hang tough; they know how to do their job."

The EMT pulled out his radio and started talking as X looked on. Bramm's lips and earlobes took on a bluish tint and his breathing was strained.

It was obvious that Bramm was fading fast. His color was now ashen and his body was limp. The paramedics looked at each other, the one with the radio shaking his head no.

Then Bramm rallied, lifting his head and searching around him. He grimaced at the effort of reaching out an arm in X's direction.

X pushed his way through the medical equipment and knelt down next to Bramm, bending so he could hear what he was trying to say.

"None of it needed to happen," Bramm whispered, his voice rattling. "But she blackmailed me, said he had to die. I returned the favor by killing him in spectacular fashion, a show of my superior and escalating power."

"You're talking about Henry Fullington?"

Bramm nodded yes, the blood that was trickling from the side of his mouth now a steady stream. Then his body went rigid and his eyeballs rolled back, leaving a sickly yellow void.

X bowed his head and put his hand slowly down to close the lids of the dead man's eyes.

Bramm's hand shot forward suddenly, grasping onto X's and pleading with his eyes. Then from somewhere deep inside, he commandeered one last surge of energy and spoke his final words.

"Kill the bitch for me."

32

X stood by, numbly watching as the paramedics put a tablecloth over the body of Mark Bramm.

He vaguely heard a cop tell the restaurant employees to wait in the kitchen so that their statements could be taken; after that they would be free to leave.

"Excuse me," the female tech said for the second time, her voice finally penetrating X's consciousness. "These were on the body; I'm going to document that I gave them to you. Is that OK?"

"Right, chain of custody," X said as she placed a sports watch and a ring in his hand.

The noise around the restaurant came into sharper focus. X could hear Julio, the sous- chef, complaining about finding another job. "All that ass kissing for nothing. I do everything for that man."

Ryan was sitting at a large table, taking in the dour scene, while a parade of police and crime scene techs moved about. X joined him, wearied, and put the jewelry on the table.

"Nice ring," Ryan commented. He picked it up, turning it carefully. "Eighteen karat gold. Looks like onyx." Putting it back down, he turned to X. "You're distracted."

"I just hope old man Damson didn't suffer like that." X rested his elbows on the table, his forehead leaning on his hands. "Hopefully Fullington and Ellsworth were already gone before the poison got to them."

"Are you sure Bramm was poisoned with the same stuff?"

"It's the only thing that makes sense." X scooted back his chair, standing up. "He was positive there was an antidote taped to the inside of his desk drawer. Did you see his office?"

"Yeah, someone definitely tore it apart." Ryan followed X to the doorway as they looked into the room. "But why are all of the files open and thrown all over the place? You wouldn't hide a syringe in one of them."

The air conditioning, set on automatic, turned on. Even that slight air flow caused the papers on the desk and floor to flutter, pages whispering against each other.

X took a few steps forward, looking carefully. "Nothing's moving on the left side of the desk." He moved to the air vent and put his hand in front of it. "Something in there is blocking the air flow."

He took the Swiss army knife out of his pocket and jiggled it alongside the vent cover until it popped out.

He reached his hand inside and immediately felt something. "Look what we have here," he said, holding up a Ziploc baggie that contained a small leather notebook. "I wonder if whoever is responsible for the redecorating was looking for this."

Moisture clung to the outside of the bag as X carefully opened it and pulled out a 5 by 7 inch ledger.

"It's cold from the A.C.," X said, the well-worn leather protecting the pages inside.

"What's written in it?" Ryan asked, craning his neck to get a view.

"Let's find out." The two men returned to the table they'd been sitting at earlier, a pot of coffee waiting for them. X put his hands around the carafe, warming them for a second, before he opened the book and started turning pages.

"It looks like Bramm's journal. He has notes on everything from his personal calendar to phone calls he needed to make." X turned another page. "Or made. He jotted down his comments after certain calls, almost like a summary of what was discussed."

X pushed the book over to Ryan, who scanned down the page in front of him. "It looks like a cheat sheet to me."

"What do you mean?" X asked.

"See here," Ryan pointed, "Bramm wrote down that he talked to someone named Mr. Michael Donavan on June 12th and that he has a wife named Mary Lee and 3 kids. It lists their names and ages, what grades they're in, and that they all love soccer and can't get used to American football. Says that Michael is looking forward to going home for the next assemblage."

X still didn't understand what Ryan was trying to get at, motioned for him to continue.

"So the next time Bramm happens to speak with Mr. Donavan, he's got all of this information at his fingertips. Instead of saying something generic, like how's the family, he could say, 'How is little Michelle enjoying kindergarten?'"

Ryan slid the journal back to X. "People in marketing and sales take notes like that all the time and use them to build a rapport with the customer; it makes them more susceptible to whatever you're trying to sell."

"Hmm," X said as he continued to scan pages. "He has a calendar on his desk, so what makes these appointments so special that they needed to be hidden? And who is this Mr. Donavan or any of the other names in here?"

X flipped back to the last entries and stopped, picking the journal up and bringing it closer to his eyes. "You're not going to believe this," he said, and read out loud, "Camille Lopez."

"Are you talking about that crazy lady?" The sous-chef was carrying in a large tray with several more pots of coffee, the fresh aroma wafting through the air and gaining the attention of the many officers now documenting the crime scene.

"You've heard of Camille Lopez?" X asked, surprised. "What do you know about her?"

The small man carefully lowered the heavy tray onto the table before speaking. "I don't know much, I like to stay in my own business. But I see that lady a lot of times lately."

X pulled a chair out. "Julio, right?"

"Si," he answered, taking the seat X offered and looking pleased that X had remembered his name.

X scooted his chair closer to Julio. "So this woman, Camille Lopez. Where did you see her? Was she here at Corbinians?" X coaxed.

"Yes, sir, she be here in the restaurant a lot of times. My boss, he happy to see her at first. But then she be a problem to him. I hear them fighting a lot."

"Do you know what they argued about?"

"I not sure, but I hear Miss Camille say that if Mr. Bramm not do'a what she tell him he be in big trouble with the menta."

"Menta? Are you sure that's what she said?" Ryan asked. "Could it have been mentor?"

"Si, I think so. My English, she isn't so good. But after that, my boss, he tell me to do whatever Miss Camille aska me to do."

X's interest was definitely piqued. "What kind of things did Camille Lopez ask you to do?"

"Just one time, and I dunno why, but she aska me to make a special ice-cubes. I fill the trays she give me with just a little bit of the fancy water she bring with her. Then she take'd out a bottle from her bag and a drip drip drip she adda some to each little square until it be full.

"Then she coming back to me the next day and now I gotta get 3 bags of the special ice that was delivered and take away from the top so she can puta in the new ice cubes she make."

"Did she take the bags of ice with her?" asked X.

"Si, she come Friday in the afternoon before the big party. After she leave I tell my boss that she is loco and he say, 'Si, she is a real bitch.

'And she be a very dangerous woman too.'"

33

X's Mercedes was screaming through an intersection, Ryan holding on tight.

"Damn. Damn damn damn," X said, gripping the steering wheel. He picked up the radio and yelled over the siren, "I want an APB out for one Camille Lopez. Approximate age is 30. Blond hair, blue eyes, 5 foot 4 inches tall, around 110 pounds."

X was talking to the dispatch officer while Ryan typed speedily on the laptop, retrieving the search X had started in his office after speaking with Arthur Fullington.

"Here we go, Ryan said. "I have a Camille Lopez staying at The Meadowbrook Motor Lodge in Massapequa from July 29th through August 2nd."

"Good work," X said to Ryan, then back to the dispatcher, "We're just a few blocks from there, we're on our way over."

"So you think that Lopez' motive for killing Bramm was what? Jealousy? That he came up with a more diabolical way to murder Henry?"

"He showed her up. I guess it made her angry."

"It's as good a motive as any. Plus it sounds like she was angry that Bramm didn't want to participate in her plan to poison Henry."

Lights and siren on, it took just a few minutes to get to the hotel. The manager on duty, Bradley Muntz, was eager to help.

"Yes, I remember Camille Lopez. There's no way to forget someone like that. She changed rooms twice before she was satisfied."

"We know that she paid by credit card, that's how we knew she stayed here. Do you by chance know where she went after she left here?" X asked.

Mr. Muntz was standing behind the front desk, his name tag failing miserably at covering what looked like a large ketchup stain on his white shirt.

He leaned forward, his big belly preventing him from getting too close to the counter. "When she left, she was with some old lady who lives here in town. I don't know her name, but Ms. Lopez said she met her at St. Rose of Lima's. You might try over there, maybe they can help you."

By the time Ryan said thank you, X was already back in the car honking for him to hurry.

X leaned over from his seat and opened the passenger side door as he put the car in gear. It was already moving when Ryan leapt in, swinging the door shut just as they hit the main road.

"I can't believe it, she was right under our nose all along," X said as he threw the car into third gear, gaining speed.

"Where are you going?" Ryan asked as the car turned right, skidding down a cross street. "The church is two miles up ahead."

"They're doing construction on Bayview; there's always a bottleneck. I'm taking a short cut."

Ryan put a hand on the dashboard as the car revved its way through one small street after another.

"I know you want to find Lopez," Ryan said, "but there are kids in these neighborhoods. You need to slow it down a little."

X turned to Ryan and through the window saw a group of kids standing at the edge of someone's lawn, tossing around a soccer ball.

"Shit," he said, downshifting to second gear and pushing on the breaks. The engine protested, the smell of burnt rubber coming through the vents.

X loosened his grip on the steering wheel and swallowed hard. "This might not make sense, but I blame Lopez for more than just poisoning four people.

"If it wasn't for her, Langly would still be alive."

Ryan sighed. "Could be."

The words felt like a sucker punch to the gut.

"What did you just say?" X asked, feeling somehow betrayed that Ryan didn't understand.

"Langly *could* be alive if it weren't for Lopez." Ryan shook his head, eyes closed. "I hear what you're saying, and God knows I want to beat the hell out of someone every time I think about Langly. But there were a lot of intervening factors between Camille Lopez poisoning the ice and what Calhoon did to Langly."

X smacked the steering wheel, felt the burning sting on the palm of his hand, and then smacked it again harder. Ryan might be right, but X wasn't willing to let go of his anger just yet.

"So what do you think actually happened?" Ryan broke the silence. "Given the fact that Henry was Camille's intended target, how could she have known that he would end up with one of the poisoned bags?"

"I'm not sure. The maid of honor said that Henry's father left an expensive bottle of whiskey in Henry's hotel room the night before the wedding. My guess is that it really came from Camille. She knew he drank a lot and counted on his having a few drinks before the ceremony, made sure he had his favorite ice right there at his fingertips."

"Makes sense," Ryan said just as they pulled into the St. Rose of Lima's parking lot.

But for X, nothing was making sense. And wouldn't, not until he had Camille Lopez in custody.

• • •

The rectory's receptionist practically ran down the hallway, leading X and Ryan to Father Daly's office.

"He's our pastor," she explained on the way. "He'll be able to help you."

She ushered them directly into the priest's office. "Father, these two policemen are here to see you. They said it's important."

Father Daly removed his reading glasses and stood up from behind his desk. He was wearing his Roman collar, the black short sleeve shirt and pants standard issue for Catholic priests.

"What can I do to help you?" he questioned before saying to the receptionist, "Can you please close the door on your way out? Thank you, Cathy."

The door shut noisily, the woman clearly not pleased that she wouldn't be a party to the conversation.

"We have reason to believe that a woman we need to find might have become friendly with one of your parishioners. Does the name Camille Lopez mean anything to you?"

Father Daly dropped into his chair. "Yes, I'm afraid I've had the pleasure of meeting Ms. Lopez. She has been staying with a lovely woman, Monica Adams, who's been a member of the parish for almost 40 years."

"What exactly do you know about Ms. Lopez?" Ryan asked.

"Just that she's been attending services here for a few weeks now and has caused nothing but trouble. She complains about everything and has many of our members upset. And as far as I'm concerned, she's taken terrible advantage of dear Monica."

"How so?" pressed Ryan.

"Well, Monica has given her free reign of her house, her pantry, and her car. From what I've seen and heard, Ms. Lopez hasn't given anything back for such generosity."

X stood stonily by as he listened to the words. "Can we get an address for Monica Adams?"

The priest pressed a button on his phone and asked Cathy for the information. Over the intercom they heard, "79 Elm Street."

"Elm Street?" X paced across the room. "Becca Grande lives on Elm Street, too. Number 82."

"Why, that's right," said Father Daly. "In fact, I got a phone call from Ms. Lopez early this morning asking if I could arrange transportation for she and Mrs. Adams to go into the city for the Fullington funeral. I didn't know Monica even knew the Grande's until then, much less that they were neighbors.

"I got two of our teens to volunteer to drive the ladies into the city. They're good kids; altar boys, in fact."

It dawned on X that the sweet old lady he'd met at the Grande's home was Ms. Adams. With clenched teeth he asked, "Is there any way to get in touch with them? Ms. Lopez is a suspect in Henry Fullington's murder and should be considered dangerous."

Father Daly rose from his desk, staggered back several steps before asking, "Are you sure?" Then, "Oh good Lord. I knew there was something off about that woman, but murder?"

"I don't mean to alarm you, but we really do need to get in touch with those boys. Right away."

"They're probably already on the road," Father Daly said as he reached for the rolodex on his desk. "But I have a cell phone number right here. Here we go; Chris Hill."

"Wait a minute; he's the kid that works for Can-Do Caterers. With Billy." Ryan looked at X, explaining, "I interviewed them."

Father Daly wrote the number on a piece of paper and handed it to X. "They're together today, too. In Chris' Volvo. It's old, maybe an '89; it's a gray wagon. I can check our records and see if we have a tag number."

X pulled his card from his wallet, passing it to priest. "Call me as soon as you can if you find it. I'm going to send a couple officers over to ask you some questions, and a sketch artist. Do you think you can help with a composite sketch of Ms. Lopez?"

"I'd be more than happy to help; I have that woman's face etched in my memory," Father Daly responded as he moved around his desk and opened the door for the policemen, knocking the eavesdropping receptionist onto the ground.

34

Tuesday morning had finally dawned, the day of Henry Fullington's funeral.

Camille watched out the window as, across the street, a sleek limousine pulled away from the curb taking Becca and her mother to Saint Patrick's Cathedral in New York City. Aggravated, she looked at her watch again.

"Where in the world is our ride?" Camille turned around and resumed pacing as Monica sat calmly in her favorite chair, her hands folded in her lap.

"That's what you get when you have to ask for help," Camille continued. "I don't know why Father Daly was so snappish on the phone; he's a priest. He's supposed to always be nice."

"Well, dear, you did interrupt his morning prayers. And it wasn't actually an emergency; you didn't really need to speak with him that very minute."

Camille ceased her marathon stroll in front of Monica's chair, facing her with hands on hips. "So sue me for wanting to make sure we get to Saint Patrick's in time for the funeral. I would have thought the Grandes would invite us to ride with them in the limousine, but nooooo. They dropped us like day old kitty litter."

"It was very accommodating of Father Daly to arrange for someone from the parish to bring us into the city. We should be grateful," added Monica.

"Whatever," Camille huffed and went back to the bay window to sit on its perch. She looked down the street, observing the cars as they passed by. Her heart did a flip-flop when she saw a dark blue Lincoln

Continental slow down right in front of Monica's, but it resumed its speed and continued on. She tried not to be too disappointed, even though she had always loved Continentals and it would have been the second best thing to being in the stretch limousine with the Grandes.

She continued her examination of each car that passed by, unconsciously damning each driver for not stopping to timely pick them up. Her level of frustration was rising as quickly as the minutes ticking by. She was so distracted that she did not notice the old gray Volvo station wagon until it was almost to the house. It looked like it had been through a war zone; it was a rusty carcass of a vehicle with bumpers held on by layers of masking tape. Worse still it farted black plumes of smoke that billowed behind it like a banner saying "everyone in this car is a loser."

She told herself that it would not stop, that it was simply impossible that this atrocity would deliver her to Henry Fullington's funeral. Yet like flies on shit, it parked directly in front of the house.

OK Camille, she told herself. You can handle this. It doesn't matter how you get to Saint Patrick's, just that you arrive.

"Monica, our ride is here. Are you ready to go?" she called out as she went to the foyer and swung open the front door.

And to her utter horror, there stood the two altar boys she'd taken such pains to avoid.

• • •

While Billy McGhee was helping Monica into the backseat of the car, Chris Hill stood at the driver's door, playing catch with the keys.

Camille opened the other rear door, somehow not surprised to see a spring coming through the fabric right where her derriere would soon be sitting.

She gripped the roof of the car, debating on whether or not to complain and risk being recognized, when Chris poked her on the shoulder.

Camille just about jumped out of her skin, startled. She pushed the sunglasses up closer to her face, glad she hadn't grabbed onto the teenager for support, as Chris offered a plastic throw-away cushion with a Yankee emblem on it.

"Here you go, you can use this. I don't really need it that bad," he said, flashing a neon white smile. Camille reached out and took hold of a corner of the offending object with two fingers, inspecting it like it was a skunk.

She leaned her nose closer to the cushion, took a few brief sniffs, and decided it would be the lesser of two evils. She threw it on the spring and got into the car without a word.

Chris shrugged and took his seat behind the wheel. And once everyone was buckled up the car coughed to life and they started the approximately 90 minute trip to New York City.

• • •

Chris was driving west along the Long Island Expressway heading for the city and couldn't get the woman's blue eyes out of his mind. He'd only seen them for a quick second, when she gave him that dirty look about the hole in the back seat. But Billy was right, that Camille Lopez lady sure looked familiar. He was positive he had seen her somewhere before, and not just from St. Rose of Lima's.

Every now and then Chris would use the rear view mirror to try to get a glimpse of the woman sitting directly behind him. He finally got the timing right, catching her when her head was turned toward the window. Her glasses weren't able to hide her profile, and he was able to get a pretty good look. Her face was pulled into a grimace, lines tightly contouring the corner of the eye, her lips pursed. To Chris she looked plain mean.

He poked Billy in the side to get his attention and gestured for him to look backwards. Billy took a nonchalant glance over his shoulder, did a double take, and mouthed the words, "Now I remember. She's that lunatic from the wedding."

Memories are a funny thing. Sometimes you can have zero recollection of something no matter how many times you return and search your psyche. Then some little thing will trigger total and full recall.

Rapid fire recollection jolted through Chris Hill's brain as Billy's words sunk into his consciousness. It was last Saturday morning at Gulf Cove and they had just arrived with the usual crew. They all went into the church and the old man who ran things showed them where they were supposed to set up.

Larry asked him and Billy to set up one of the large tables in the foyer. As the two walked out of the church, the woman who was now sitting right behind him in the back seat was standing near the open side of the van. Chris remembered thinking that it was strange, because she was dressed entirely in black and that seemed kind of weird for a wedding. He approached her, asked, "Excuse me, can I help you?"

The woman had turned around and given him a dirty look, her blue eyes piercing and angry. Chris didn't want her to think he was there to hurt her or that he was some kind of pervert or something. "I didn't mean to scare you; sorry."

She hissed at him, just like a cat, and wandered away. Chris had just blown her off and gone back to work. But now that he thought about it, he remembered that when he got into the van the cover to the big cooler was off, thrown onto the front seat. At the time it wasn't any big deal; he just put it back, even yelled at Billy for being so forgetful.

Chills went up and down his spine as he remembered the gossip he'd heard that morning. Of course the big news was that their coworker, Kenny Mensti, was in fact a drug dealer and had been murdered. But Larry Lafitte had told him and Billy, under the strictest of confidence of course, that the police had been back to the warehouse and strongly suspected that Henry Fullington's killer had somehow added poison to some of the bags of ice.

Oh my God, how could he have forgotten something so important? What if she was the one responsible? He looked over at Billy again but couldn't get his attention. He needed to get in touch with the police.

Chris pulled out his cell phone and scrolled through until he saw Officer Ryan's phone number. He hit dial but then, seconds later, snapped it back shut. How could he tell Ryan what he'd remembered without Ms. Lopez hearing? She was sitting directly behind him.

He decided to text the policeman instead. He carefully put his cell on his right thigh and started typing in his message when Ms. Lopez' arm shot forward and grabbed his wrist.

"What do you think you're doing?" Lopez asked, her voice threatening.

Chris' heart stopped. He'd been caught and now she'd want to kill him too.

"Don't you know it's illegal to text while you drive?"

Chris almost cried with relief as she jerked the sunglasses off of her face, breaking her silent streak. "I don't care whether or not you appreciate your own life but you sure as heck better be worried about mine. The nerve of you young people today."

Lopez snatched his cell and leaned back into her seat. "This is going to stay with me until you get us all safely to Saint Patrick's."

Not knowing how to respond, Chris said "Yes ma'am," which seemed to placate her. He continued driving, wishing he were any-place else in the world besides sharing this cramped vehicle with a psycho.

35

X was back in his car speeding toward New York City, Officer Ryan riding shotgun with the computer still open on his lap.

DiMitri's voice sounded through X's speakerphone. "I've alerted the NYPD, given them a detailed description of Camille Lopez, and told them to be on the lookout in the general vicinity of Saint Patrick's Cathedral. They already have cops there and are taking extra precautions checking out people entering and exiting the area around the Lady Chapel. That's where Henry's funeral is being held. And FYI, it's located right behind the main altar of the cathedral. So far, there are just a few mourners there."

"Thanks for the heads up, but what are you doing at headquarters?" X was weaving around slow traffic as he spoke. "I thought the doctor told you to take it easy for a few days."

"I can do that from here," DiMitri said. "Plus the chief wanted someone to finish going through Langly's notes."

DiMitri's voice cracked as he said the name. "I want to be here. I need to be here."

The words were said so genuinely that X couldn't argue. "I understand. So tell me, what do you have?"

"I just spoke with the Grande's limousine driver. They're about to cross the Triborough Bridge and should be arriving at the cathedral within the next 10 to 20 minutes, depending on traffic." DiMitri paused. "I didn't know if you wanted me to alert him. I didn't say anything."

"Good call. It's probably better to let one of the cops explain everything once they get to the church." X honked his horn at the car in front of him; it was in the far left lane and going 50 in a 55 mph zone. Then he reached forward and turned on the dashboard lights. "Should've done this in the first place," he said under his breath as the red and white beams came to life.

"There's something else." There was a pause before DiMitri continued. "I didn't know it at the time, but now that I've seen the composite sketch of Camille Lopez I realize I saw her the day we went to the Grande's house. Now that I look back, it's obvious that she was avoiding eye contact and rushing to get out of the house.

"I should have known something was going on."

"How could you have?" X said. "We didn't even know we were looking for her yesterday."

"I just feel so guilty. Like maybe I missed a clue. Calhoon told me I wasn't worthy of the uniform; maybe he's right."

X felt his stomach begin to churn as soon as he heard the name Calhoon. "Listen, you can't let anything that bastard said get to you. He was nothing but a manipulative maniac, and you're too good a cop, too strong a man, to allow him to affect you."

"Hey, this is strange, said Ryan, interrupting X's conversation. "I got a text message from Chris Hill, but there's nothing written."

He hit the redial button. "It went straight to his voicemail," he said, frowning. "I hope everything's OK."

• • •

By the time X and Ryan arrived at Saint Patrick's, limousines were starting to accumulate at the front entrance of the famous cathedral for Henry Fullington's funeral.

Ryan approached one of the city cops. "Why the big crowd exiting all of a sudden?" he asked as a throng of people pushed their way through the massive bronze front doors.

The cop tipped his hat, looking first at Ryan then at his watch. "It's 12:30 p.m.; the noon Mass just let out."

X stood on the sidewalk, looking up Fifth Avenue for Chris' car. "This might be them," he shouted as an old Volvo wagon approached the curb.

He motioned Ryan, who rushed onto the street behind the car in case Camille tried to make a run for it. The NYPD cops were everywhere, across the street and on the uptown and downtown corners in the event Lopez broke in any of those directions.

The car barely stopped before it was completely surrounded. Chris and Ryan both immediately put their hands up in the air as X yanked open the back door and yelled, "Don't move and keep your hands where I can see them."

Seconds passed before X staggered backwards. Confusion swept among the police as they realized that an old woman sat in the rear of the car.

Alone.

36

Chris's cell phone had been sitting on Camille's lap and rang eight times in less than ten minutes.

"Who in the world keeps calling you?" she snarled, leaning forward and giving the back of his head a slap. "That's the problem with kids these days; you spend too much time on the phone and not enough time in quiet contemplation."

Chris peeked into the rearview mirror and said, "It isn't my fault; I can't control whether or not my friends call me." He took a deep breath and plunged ahead. "If it's bothering you so much, why don't you just turn it off."

"Now that's the brightest thing you've said all day," she snapped. "How does this damn thing work anyway?"

As she passed her fingers over the phone's surface a screen lit up and showed the names of the people who had called. An Officer Ryan was listed three different times.

Why would a policeman be so anxious to speak with Chris Hill? This couldn't be good. By her approximate calculations, Mark Bramm was either in the process of dying or already dead. What if he figured out what she had done? Knowing him, he'd probably rat her out on his deathbed. And if that were the case, she knew things would start unraveling fast.

Chris took the 96th Street exit of the FDR Drive and drove down Fifth Avenue. They were about 10 blocks from Saint Patrick's, at the southern-most portion of Central Park, stopped at a light. Camille looked to her right and saw the beautiful edifice of The Plaza Hotel, now being converted into condominiums. She felt the distinct quiver of adrenaline that she had come to expect whenever she faced a formidable adversary and the whisper of a voice calling her to flight.

When the light turned green, the cars in front of them came to life and sprinted forward about 20 yards before being snarled in gridlock. Chris gently pressed on the accelerator and the Volvo started to move in pace with the cars, buses and taxis surrounding them.

Camille took a last look up front before grabbing the handle next to her and pushing. The rusty back door didn't immediately open all the way, screeching its protest as she continued to shove against it with her shoulder. Her left foot made contact with the pavement just as Chris slammed on the breaks.

"Camille, what on earth are you doing?" shouted Monica, her small body ricocheting forward before the seat belt caught her and she fell back against the seat.

Camille scooted the rest of the way out of the car amidst blaring horns honking at the traffic delay she was causing. "I just need some air. I'm going to walk the rest of the way. No worries, I'll see you there." Grabbing her bag to her side, she walked away, fading into the crowd.

37

Chris Hill was now sitting on the sidewalk, his body shaking. "Put your head between your knees," Ryan suggested. "It'll calm your stomach."

"There can't be anything left in there," he managed to say. "I think I've puked up everything." His entire body was trembling, his perfect teeth chattering.

X strode over from the small group of city cops he was talking with and squatted down in front of the Chris. "Listen, I don't mean to be insensitive. But you've got to get a grip. This is a matter of life or death."

"She got out of the car, man, about 10 blocks from here. I think she knew I figured out where I'd seen her. I tried to call but she took my phone. I think she might be the one who killed Henry Fullington."

"We know." X reached out, gave Chris' shoulder a reassuring squeeze. "But now we need to find her and we need your help to do it. Are you with me?"

Ryan's shadow fell over them as he leaned down, nudging X with his elbow. "He's in shock; give him a minute."

X stood up abruptly. "Great. Where's the other kid?" He looked around until he saw Billy leaning against the church talking to a police-woman. X was there in three strides.

"She seemed a little anxious about the traffic driving down Fifth and decided to get out and walk the rest of the way," he was saying to the cop.

X introduced himself to her briefly. "Do you mind?" he asked, pointing at Billy.

The cop shrugged and stepped a few feet away, giving X room directly in front of young man.

Billy spoke first. "Is Chris OK? I've never seen him so upset."

"He'll be fine," X said, not really caring if that was true or not. "Now I need you to think. Which way did Ms. Lopez go once she got out of the car?"

"I don't know. She just, like, disappeared into a big group of people."

"Can you remember what she was wearing?" X asked, pressing him for any details.

He chewed on his lip, thinking. "Not really," he finally answered.

The honking horns of the passing traffic were the backdrop to X's impending headache. Frustrated, he finally went into the cathedral where Monica Adams was resting in one of the back pews. As he closed in on her, he could hear her detailed statement to a policeman.

"She has on a black pant suit. Her hair is shoulder length, blond, and she's wearing it down. She got out of the car on the east side of the street at the light on 59th and started walking south towards St. Patrick's. The only thing she took with her was her big shoulder bag; it's black nylon. She keeps her purse in it. The rest of her luggage is in the back of Chris' car; she's due to return to Italy later this afternoon."

Pausing for a breath she added, "You really think she is a murderer?

"Oh my."

38

Camille was used to crowds. They were a persistent annoyance at Vatican City and all of the other beautiful sites around Rome. For years they seemed to swallow her up, making her feel small and vulnerable. But then she met the Raven. He taught her how to mentally rise above circumstances such as that, to exert her superiority and take what she used to consider overwhelming problems and turn them into opportunities. It was one of the many tools he had revealed which could be used to further her destiny.

She now closed her eyes and prayed that her spirit be directed by the many teachings of the Raven. The packs of people on the sidewalk became her shelter. She walked among them feeling safe and secure, totally anonymous. Hiding amongst the ordinary.

In her mind she visualized how she would make her way into St. Patrick's without detection. She had researched every detail about the cathedral and knew its floor plan by heart. And through her contacts at the Monastery Monte Cassino, where she worked just outside of Rome, she had gained access to information otherwise not available to the public. She knew where the employee lounge area was; where the cleaning crew kept their equipment; where the laundry room was located; and where the three secret panels from the main church and into these non-public locations were found.

She didn't need a lot of time for what she wanted to accomplish. In fact, a few seconds would suffice. But she desperately wanted to watch Becca Grande's entrance into the Lady Chapel.

Looking at her watch she saw that she had less than 20 minutes to get in place before the funeral began. Four blocks before St. Patrick's she turned down a side street and went into the first restaurant she came upon, an Irish pub.

The bartender glowered at her when she asked where the lady's room was. "It's only for paying customers," he called as she passed him by. Inside the small cramped space she removed her black jacket and stepped out of her slacks. She hurriedly rolled them together and stuffed them in the trashcan. Out of her bag came the gray dress she had bought on sale last week and a red wig that she had ironically stolen from Becca's closet when they met.

She was back outside walking south on Madison Avenue within minutes. Surrounded by the essence of the Raven she was no longer affected by the likely possibility that she had been found out by the police. There was no power equal to that of her benefactor.

Expecting miracles, one unfolded as she turned back towards Fifth Avenue on 51st Street. Outside a side entrance to St. Patrick's a man was unloading plants and flower arrangements onto a gurney from the back of a delivery truck. She slowed down and looked carefully at a card attached to one of the bouquets that read, "Deepest Sympathies."

Having done her homework, Camille knew that there were no more funerals scheduled at St. Patrick's after Henry's, but six were scheduled for the next day.

She approached the man and asked with authority, "Name of the deceased?"

The man turned around and slowly looked at her, from the tip of her new wig down to the heels of her shoes, then back up again. He smiled, his little eyes and darting tongue reminding her of a lizard. "I don't recognize you. Are you new?"

"Yeah, I just started. Molly is training me."

It had been so easy for Camille to figure out how to gain unobserved access to the cathedral. Molly Megan was the director of funerals. Camille had spoken with her just yesterday, pretending that she was the owner of a small florist shop in Yonkers and had several arrangements for the Baxter funeral which was scheduled for Wednesday, a fact that was posted for all to see in the *New York Times* obituary.

Molly Megan was delighted to explain how floral deliveries were managed, describing a side entrance to the church on 51st Street that accommodated easy access to what she called the arboretum.

Camille learned that to gain entrance one needed only to press zero on the keypad adjacent to the door. There was someone always on duty to answer such a call. Once the delivery was confirmed as scheduled and visual verification was made, via a small hidden camera, the person was buzzed in.

Camille had prepared to go in that entrance by herself; having Mr. Horn Dog here as a diversion would be much safer.

The man's eyes moved to her bust and rested there. "No name tag yet?"

She looked down at her chest, provocatively rubbing the fabric of her dress where a tag would be pinned if she had one. Eventually her big blue eyes returned to the man, his question left unanswered.

"How rude of me," he said, pulling off his dirty gloves. "I haven't properly introduced myself. I'm Barry, as in Barry's Blossoms, he added as he signaled toward the delivery truck with his head.

"Right, Molly told me to expect you," Camille lied. "Your own business; impressive," she said, deciding to lay it on thick.

"I'd love to hear all about it. Why don't we get these flowers out of the hot sun and then I'll give you my number?" She pronounced the last words slowly, the question a tease.

Barry licked his lips and said, "Ladies first," reaching his arm out for Camille to proceed.

"No no, you go on ahead," Camille said, pointing to a vase at the back of the overloaded gurney that was filled with beautiful tall stems. "This one looks like it might topple over so I'm going to carry it in myself. Don't worry, I'm right behind you."

Barry pressed the keypad and looked up at the camera. Camille could hear the buzzing sound as the door opened automatically and quickly followed Barry past an elderly gentleman who monitored the side entrance. Before she knew it they were moving into the inner recesses of St. Patrick's, the big flowering arrangement she carried blocking her face from view.

Once inside, Camille knew she had to move fast. She approached Barry, leaning in to kiss him on the cheek, and said, "I'll be back in a few minutes. Don't say a word to Molly, though. We aren't supposed to fraternize while working." She graced Barry with one final wink, returned the arrangement she was holding to the gurney and was gone.

Camille made her way to the vestment chamber, considered donning one of the robes as a disguise but deciding against it. She would be leaving in a hurry and didn't want to waste precious seconds removing it once she'd accomplished her goal.

No, she would finish her revenge as is. She crossed into the cathedral areas open to the general public and noticed at once that, although she had expected police to be there, there were a lot more than she'd imagined. She was tempted to take this as a compliment of her recent work product, but then remembered not to be prideful. The Raven so appreciated humility as a virtue.

She looked around the church, her eyes searching, before they rested on Becca. Even from a distance she could make out the ridiculous red dress she had talked her into wearing. Henry would be rolling over in his casket at the disrespect. Camille slowly moved to the seventh Station of the Cross which was adjacent to the Lady Chapel. She put a dollar in the donation box and lit a candle, kneeling before the suffering image of Jesus.

From the corner of her eye she saw Monica Adams being escorted to a seat by one of the policemen she recognized from Gulf Cove.

Gulf Cove. Boy did that not go according to plan. What she'd been expecting was for Henry to keel over sometime during his wedding vows from the poison she'd slipped him. She figured that one or two cop cars would show up, and of course an ambulance. No one would realize foul play was involved until an autopsy was performed, and she'd be gone by then, out of the country and free as a bird.

In her script, there were not legions of police crawling all over the place, way too close for comfort. But Mark Bramm just had to grandstand. As soon as she heard the screams from the rear of the church she knew she'd been outdone. She had to admit to a little admiration, tying Henry to the bell the way he had. It was a signature Bramm move.

He loved all things torture, medieval or otherwise, and the more blood and guts the better.

Camille stared back into the candle's flame and allowed the rhythmic dance to quiet her nerves.

Think, think, think, she mumbled to herself. Remember the goal. All you want to do is witness the finale. You probably don't even have to move from this spot. She could smell the lilies that surrounded the Lady Chapel's altar, their scent like the rarest of perfumes.

The slight murmurs within the chapel grew louder and more pronounced as people realized that the bishop had arrived. The mourners began seating themselves, preparing for the service to start.

Henry's father graciously stepped away from a small group presumably offering their sympathies and went to greet the bishop. Camille felt the hairs on the back of her neck stand on end as the two ended up just a few feet from where she was kneeling. Even though she'd never met Arthur Fullington, he was sure to have seen photos of her and she didn't want to risk being recognized. She burrowed her face in her hands, listening intently.

"Arthur, I am so very sorry for your loss. Henry was a fine young man and didn't deserve this tragic and untimely death. Know I've been praying for you," the bishop said. "He's at peace now."

Then someone clearing their throat loudly interrupted the private conversation. "Your highness, how are you? I met you once. I'm Becca Grande; I was supposed to marry Henry, so I'm kind of like his widow."

Camille couldn't resist the temptation. She splayed the fingers of her left hand and tilted her head slightly so she could watch the show.

The bishop's friendly face paled as he set his eyes on Becca. "You are in my prayers, dear," he said patting her hand as the first chords of "Amazing Grace" sounded from the organ. "Excuse me; it looks like we're ready to begin."

Arthur turned to his would-be daughter-in-law, the color draining from his face. "Good Lord, Becca, what happened to your face?"

Becca readjusted the short black veil that did nothing to hide the disfiguration. Large red welts seeped a yellowish substance that she dabbed at with a tissue. Her eyes were almost swollen shut, the rest of her face equally bloated.

Camille watched as the two moved to the rear of the chapel, their voices no longer within hearing range. Camille took a quick moment to get her sightings on the woman who had consumed her every thought for the last several months. Then she removed something from her pocket that was so small it fit into the palm of her hand.

And then she aimed it at Becca.

Nobody seemed to notice the small flash of light coming from her direction as Becca took Arthur Fullington's arm and they walked down the short aisle toward the altar. It was hard to see past the inappropriateness of the dress she was wearing, which made Camille exceedingly happy. But the piece de resistance was Becca's face, her skin a hideous combination of oozing pustules and inflammation. The balm that Camille had rubbed on Becca's face the night before was not meant as a salve. In fact, it was an acid specifically designed to be absorbed by the skin in such a way that any discomfort, burning or other evidence of its potency wouldn't appear until hours later. And the longer it remained on Camille's face the more permanent the disfigurement would be.

Camille positively beamed as she rose and calmly walked out of St. Patrick's Cathedral unnoticed, passing way too many police to even count. She liked the red wig; maybe she'd keep this look when she got to her next destination.

She pulled out the camera and looked at the viewing screen, a picture of her archrival burned in time for posterity's sake. She could have exacted the ultimate punishment on Becca; killing her would have been easy. But allowing Becca to live with the scars of her sins, visible for all to see, seemed a more poetic justice.

Not only had she taken care of Rebecca Grande, but she also extinguished Mark Bramm. Looking back on it she supposed it was her own fault for asking for his assistance. Give a man an inch and he thinks he's a ruler.

She smiled.

The Raven would be well pleased with her creative vengeance.

Tossing the camera back into her bag, she disappeared into the crowd.

39

"She's not going to show." X paced around the check-in area of United Airlines, looking at his watch for the thousandth time. "Her flight leaves in twenty minutes."

X slammed his fist into his other hand, furious that they had somehow let Camille Lopez get away. He was positive she'd show up at the cathedral for the funeral. For all he knew, she had and they just didn't see her.

She didn't turn up at the cemetery, either. His last hope was that she would be here, at Kennedy airport, for her scheduled flight back to Rome. That hope was evaporating.

Ryan waited for the blare of the intercom announcing a change in gate information to stop before saying, "You didn't really think she'd cut it this close, did you?"

"Shit." X walked out of the terminal, kicked the curb hard. Ryan followed a few feet behind.

"I knew this was going to be useless from the second I opened that Volvo door and she wasn't sitting in the back seat like she was supposed to be," X said.

He looked up at the sky as it started to rain. He held his hand out, drops of water splashing off of his skin to the concrete below. "She slipped right through our fingers."

X took a deep breath, needing some fresh air to clear his mind but instead inhaled second-hand smoke. There was a group of people standing nearby in a tight circle, one man attempting to hold a newspaper over their heads, as they puffed feverishly on their cigarettes.

"I haven't even begun to process that Langly is gone," X said, the tobacco laced air reminding him of his friend.

An unmarked Crown Vic pulled to the curb and honked several times before X realized the driver was trying to get his attention. Seeing the passenger window roll down, he approached and looked in.

"Another bust, huh?" Chief Harman sat behind the wheel, straining to turn his large girth toward X.

X hung his head, shaking it wearily from side to side. "I'll track her down, you know I will. There's no way I'm going to let her walk away from this."

The chief picked up a tattered napkin from his lap, patting the perspiration on his forehead. "Uh, I have news about the bride."

"Becca Grande?" he said, surprised. "What now?"

"She was just brought into North Shore Hospital's emergency room. Apparently Lopez tricked her into using some kind of cream on her face that ended up being acid.

"She's going to need extensive reconstruction surgery, skin grafts, the whole works. Her hands are in bad shape too."

X felt like he'd just been kicked in the gut; Lopez was a walking wrecking ball and he'd let her get away. The rain picked up, water now pouring over his head and down the collar of his shirt. For the first time ever he felt decades older than his forty years.

"You need to sleep."

"I will, after …"

"You're not listening to me. I want you to go home. Now," Hartman yelled. "And I don't want to see your face for at least 24 hours. That's an order. The same goes for Ryan."

Then more gently, he said, "We've got APBs out at all the local airports, trains stations, bus routes; hell, we've got people all over the fucking East Coast looking for Camille Lopez. If she surfaces, we'll be there.

"But if she doesn't, I have no doubt you'll track her down so we can throw her ass in jail for the rest of her miserable life.

"But you will not do it until tomorrow."

40

X stood on the sidewalk in front of Corbinian's the next afternoon, the yellow police tape still stretched across the front door. Traffic was slowing down to take a look at the place where someone had been murdered just the day before.

Seconds later Ryan arrived.

"Hey, how're you doing?" X asked, his eyes scanning over Ryan to see if there were any outward signs of the stress the guy had been through over the past day and a half. "I mean really."

"OK, I guess. Sleeping helped. I didn't even hear the kids leave for school."

X sighed. "I hate to admit it, but the chief was right. I needed some down time too."

Silence reigned for a few seconds and X didn't wonder why. What in the world could one possibly say, anyway? Gee, too bad about Langly? It's a shame Lopez got away?

Ryan spoke first. "So they didn't find anything at Bramm's house?" he asked as X dug through his pocket, finally producing the key and a security alarm code number.

"The chief said they scoured it from top to bottom." X chuckled, correcting, "He actually said it was cleaner than he was after his last colonoscopy."

"Well that's an image I'd rather not think about," Ryan said, nose scrunched as X pushed open the front door and entered the restaurant. Everything was still and quiet.

"Why'd you want to come back here?" Ryan asked.

"There was so much commotion yesterday I couldn't really get a feel for the place." He looked around the room. "Strange art work, don't you think?"

On one wall was a display of various swords, knives and daggers. "At least they're under glass; wouldn't want an angry customer getting their hands on one of those," Ryan said.

X moved to another framed weapon, a heavy club with a round spiked medal head. "Look at this one. A mace."

Ryan stood next to X, admiring the bludgeon. "I've always wondered what those things were called. Looks dangerous."

"It is. It was made to penetrate plates of armor; swords didn't cut it."

That got another chuckle, this time from Ryan. Eventually they ended up back at the same table they were at yesterday. X turned on his laptop and started tapping away on the keys while he spoke.

"Do you remember Julio saying that when Lopez first showed up, Bramm seemed happy to see her?"

"You mean the waiter?"

"Sous-chef," X responded absently as he scrolled through a file. "Anyway, I figure that means that they already knew each other before Lopez arrived.

"Arthur Fullington mentioned that Camille Lopez has been living in Rome for the past five years and here," he said, pointing to the screen, "are Bramm's Passport records."

"Twelve trips to Rome in the past four years," Ryan read.

X hit some keys and another file opened. "Here are Bramm's personal credit card receipts for the dates he was in Italy. He stayed at a place just outside of Rome called Monte Cassino. There's a famous monastery there." X crossed his arms over his chest. "And guess what? I just got confirmation that Camille has worked there as a tour guide ever since she moved to Rome."

"OK, so they're in the same place at the same time. How does that help us?"

X sighed. "I don't know. Maybe she gave him a tour and that's how they met. Or he was there for something related to his fascination with ravens and she was either already involved or he recruited her."

Little did X know how close a painting he had just drawn to reality.

41

"**D**o you see that gentleman standing over there, the one in the black suit? He reserved a private tour. You'll be his guide."

Camille looked across the museum and focused on the man. Tall, dark and handsome. She nodded to her boss and went to introduce herself to the tourist.

"Hello, my name is Camille Lopez. I'll be showing you around Monte Cassino today."

The stranger bowed. "Mark Bramm. Pleased to make your acquaintance."

Camille started with the usual spiel. "The monastery was established in the year 529 by Saint Benedict and has a rich history."

"I have a special fondness of Saint Benedict," Bramm said almost right off the bat. "In fact, I consider myself somewhat of an aficionado."

Mark Bramm wasn't exaggerating. He ended up being very well versed in Benedictine history. His questions were quite informed and Camille stumbled more than once in her answers. And for the first time since Henry, she felt her heart skip a beat when she looked into his eyes. They were so dark and penetrating she felt like she could drown in them.

They spent 5 hours walking through the museum and abbey, sharing their mutual interest in Saint Benedict. And by the time the tour was finally over, the sun was already setting.

They were standing awkwardly in the outside square when Bramm said, "I hope you won't think I'm too forward, but perhaps you would like to join me at a lecture I'm attending this evening. It's a rather select group and I think you would fit in perfectly."

Camille blushed. "What's the topic?"

"Saint Benedict, of course. The keynote speaker has developed a rather unconventional approach to his studies. I find his methodology quite stimulating."

"I'd love to join you," she said, taking his arm and willing to go just about anywhere he wanted. She'd been so burned by men in the past. But maybe, just maybe, this time would be different. After all, they already had so much in common.

• • •

Mark Bramm ushered Camille down a final flight of stairs as he explained. "The location of our assemblies is as fundamental as the message we come to hear."

They entered into a darkened room, the atmosphere solemn. There was no chit chat, no coffee bar, wine, cheese or crackers. Bramm looked at Camille, putting his finger to his lips and whispered, "Shush," before leading her to one of the two vacant seats. He took the empty place next to hers.

Camille found herself sitting on a beautifully carved high back chair. The cushioned seat was in rich burgundy velvet, sumptuous to the eye and to the touch. Relaxing against the polished wood, the top of her head reached only halfway to the chair's high back. As she looked around the room at the others present, she thought they all looked a little silly in such a grandiose seating arrangement. Like small children sitting at the grown-up's table. Quite a difference from the humble folding chairs her bible study group used during their weekly meetings.

They were seated in a large circle, a bit unusual for a lecture setting, but it somehow felt right in this environment. Her vision slowly became acclimated to the dimly lit room, dozens of candles providing the only light.

She looked around the room, trying to absorb the detail of the furnishings. There were a series of triptych mirrors, hand carved with twin opening doors in gothic style. They seemed to have been strategically placed along the walls opposite each chair so that every person in the group could see their own image reflected back to them. Because of the way the triptych folded open, it offered a three dimensional view that seemed to distort the physical features of the person it mirrored. Camille wasn't sure if it was because of the faltering light from the candles or from trick glass in different sections of the mirrors. Whatever the cause, the effect was unsettling.

The centerpiece of the room was a sculpted wall hanging that Camille immediately recognized as the image found on the Medal of Saint Benedict.

She was awestruck by the artistry of what could only be described as a brilliant work of art. It was far more ornate than anything located within the walls of the monastery, yet it was infinitely simple. The familiar image of Saint Benedict adorned the center of the sculpture, with a pedestal on either side of him.

On the pedestal to his right there was the infamous shattered cup. The image depicted the story of how a group of monks who were unhappy with Benedict decided to kill him. One evening they offered him a glass of poisoned wine. Just as Benedict made the sign of the cross over the glass as a blessing, it shattered in his hand, falling apart in pieces before he could drink from it. This miracle saved his life.

Camille trained her eyes on the pedestal to Benedict's left, which appeared to be the focal point of the piece of art. Perched on a thorn bush was a raven, with a piece of bread in its beak.

From her studies, Camille knew that a second attempt on Benedict's life was later made by a jealous priest who gave him a piece of poisoned bread. A nearby raven, somehow knowing that the bread was toxic, took it into its mouth and flew away. Again Benedict's life was saved.

Camille's attention returned to the people seated around her. There were ten in all, and only one other woman who was, frankly, both old and fat. Why this made Camille so exceedingly happy she wasn't sure, but being the most attractive female in the room felt wonderful.

Of the men, they were all clean-shaven and well dressed. There was an air of self-confidence in the room, and she hoped that it was contagious. She'd love a little bit of that.

A chime rang somewhere from within the room and everyone quieted. There was total silence for a good long while before a deep, low voice led a meditation.

They were encouraged to feel their breathing, to take in the darkness on their in-breath and push out the light when they exhaled. After a while, they were coaxed along a wonderful journey, both in their minds and their bodies. They were the ripples in an otherwise still lake; the ferocious waves of dark cold waters; the wind tossing about the outstretched petals of a field of wildflowers. Camille had never felt so ascetically alive. After a second and much longer silence, the chime again sounded.

Camille opened her eyes and saw the owner of the voice that had so moved her. She guessed he was in his early fifties, with dark hair and just the slightest bit of silver at the sides. When he smiled, his moustache revealed a deep scar at the corner of his upper lip.

"Greetings, my dear comrades," he said in general, though he rotated around the room to meet each person's eyes with his own in extending a more intimate personal welcome.

"It appears that Mark has brought a companion this evening. Would you be so kind as to introduce her?"

Mark put his hand on Camille's arm. "My fellow journeymen," Bramm bellowed with the style of a polished orator, "I am pleased to present a new but very special acquaintance, Camille Lopez. So deep was our instantaneous connection that I felt compelled to ask her to join me this evening. Camille works at the Monestery Monte Cassino and has extensive knowledge of the writings and ways of Saint Benedict, our benefactor. I believe she makes a strong candidate to join us on our journey."

Camille felt heat rush to her face and she prayed it hadn't turned beet red like it always seemed to when she was embarrassed. She couldn't remember anyone ever speaking about her in such a complimentary way.

She was shocked to see the welcoming looks from the others in the group; everyone seemed to be genuinely happy that she was there. The feeling that she belonged was intoxicating.

Camille, not used to being the center of attention, positively glowed. She had no idea exactly what this group was all about, but she was positive that she wanted in.

The man with the silver streaked hair thanked Mark for the introduction and approached Camille. Her heartbeat quickened as he reached out his right hand and firmly yet gently grasped her chin. His penetrating eyes seemed to devour her soul as he lightly turned her face first to the right and then to the left. Rather than feeling like she was being inspected, Camille felt a pure acceptance pouring from this man.

"I am the Raven." His words had the resonance of a melody, singing the veracity of this appellation. "If you accede to this truth, you are invited to sojourn with us."

Camille was not sure how to respond. The last time she jumped into something without thinking rationally, she ended up married. To be honest, she didn't even understand what this man was talking about. But she felt instantly drawn to him, sensing a protectiveness in him that she had yearned for as long as she could remember.

She was surprised by the sound of her own voice as the words left her lips, spoken with an ardent certainty as she simply said, "Yes."

• • •

Camille found herself on the edge of her seat, listening with rapt attention as the Raven spoke of the journey he was called to lead.

"While the teachings and miracles of Saint Benedict are well known, there is a pearl of inherent wisdom that is palpably missing from most believers. And this crucial insight had been unveiled to me by my namesake."

The Raven moved to a raised dais and pulled a golden cord. A curtain opened, revealing a throne covered by a canopy of burgundy and black silk, interlaced with fine threads of royal blue. He sat, taking his time to settle into the plush pillows, before continuing.

"I once lived a life without true meaning. By society's standards, I suppose you could say I was successful. I had a good paying job, a wife and family, went to church every Sunday, and belonged to the most prestigious country club in the area." He spread out his arms, as if holding his personal history for all to see. "Despite these outward showings of happiness, my every moment was of mere existence. I felt neither fulfillment nor joy."

Camille felt a sting of pain for the man because she intimately knew the heart ache he was talking about. She had been searching for the meaning of her life since she was six years old, when her father walked out on his family leaving she and her mother behind. To this day, Camille believed it was her fault that he left. And her mother agreed.

Her beloved daddy did the unthinkable. He fell in love with another woman, a widow with five children of her own. He tried to explain it to Camille, said she'd always be his little girl but that he was moving away to be with his new family.

Her mother immediately blamed his leaving on Camille. She told her that if she'd been a better daughter, had been a good girl, her father would never have left. Then she would throw out examples of the bad things Camille had done. Like the time she dropped her daddy's favorite coffee mug and it broke into pieces; or the time she had food poisoning and he had to miss watching the Super Bowl to bring her to the emergency room instead.

Camille's father was a liar. He never came back to visit like he said he would and stopped even sending birthday and Christmas cards by the time she was nine. When she tried to reach him to invite him to her middle school graduation, she found out he'd moved to another state with his new family. There was no forwarding address, just a dead end to a deadbeat. Every time she didn't think her heart could break any more, that she couldn't shed one more tear, she'd cry another puddle just missing him.

Camille felt a strange sympathy for this intriguing gentleman she had just met and listened eagerly as he continued telling his story.

"Late one evening, while sitting in my backyard sipping a cognac, I contemplated what this life of mine was really all about. A citronella candle was burning to keep the mosquitoes away and I was enjoying a rare quiet and peaceful moment. I emptied my mind of thoughts and as my senses synthesized I found that I could feel the power of the candle's scent over its small but persistent adversaries.

"My attention turned to the meaning of power. I knew full well that the little gnats that were now being subdued by the citronella had the ability to ruin any and every event, no matter how carefully prepared for. Yet the introduction of one element – the candle- was able to diffuse the little creatures' control.

"Just as I was reflecting on this phenomenon, a raven flew to my side. It was the most beautiful creature I'd ever seen, onyx in color and regal in bearing. Without trepidation it moved to my arm, where its talon's firmly entrenched themselves. There was some pain at first, but as the animal's claws penetrated my skin I felt the mingling of my blood with the power of the raven. An astute awareness overcame me as the bird nested in my flesh."

The Raven's voice was hypnotic as he continued. "I fell into a dreamlike state as I felt myself merging into the form of the raven. Time ceased to exist as I transcended to biblical times and flew to the great prophet, Elijah, at the time he was living east of the river Jordan. In my beak I carried bread to feed the humble man of God.

"Whirls of water then brought me to another biblical figure, Noah. He was on the ark, which rolled and pitched with the violent waters of the flood. I could smell each species of animal present. Yet of these, it was I, the Raven, who was given the vital role of fulfilling God's prophecy. Noah held me in his humble hands and released me into the air. It was within my powers alone to determine whether or not land was near. The safety of the human race depended on the strength of my wings, the acumen of my eyes, the instinctual need for safe haven and nesting."

The Raven stood with majesty and slowly descended the three stairs of the dais, finally positioning himself before Camille.

"My child, I can be your safe haven; allow me to feed you through my teachings."

Again, Camille spoke the simple word. "Yes."

42

The sun was starting to fade as X walked around the side of the house his father had bought when he was just eight years old. He had such happy memories, moving from the small tenement in Flushing to this sprawling estate. Even though his father was gone, there was no question in X's mind of where he wanted to live after he graduated from college. This was his home, where he belonged.

He stopped at the hedges, the lilac in its second bloom, and looked across the yard. As promised, he found Ann sitting on a blanket with a large picnic basket at her side. The way the sun was hitting her red hair made it positively gleam.

She caught him staring at her and grinned. "Do you come here often?" she said as she leaped up to greet him.

X picked her up easily and twirled her in his arms, giving her a kiss before gently returning her to earth.

She reached up, stroking his cheek. "How'd it go today? Any luck with tracking Camille Lopez?"

X pulled off his jacket and tossed it on the ground. "Nothing yet. But we'll find her."

Ann took his hands in hers and sat, pulling him down next to her. She opened the basket and pulled out a bottle of Chardonnay. "I was hoping we'd be celebrating."

"Every day I'm with you is a celebration." They kissed again, deeper this time, before X pulled away. "What's all that?"

Ann handed him the wine opener while she grabbed the folders she'd brought along.

"I've been thinking about the case," she said. "We know that Mark Bramm and Camille Lopez had some kind of association. And that the word raven was significant to Bramm."

"I'll say. He changed his own last name and named his restaurant with words related to raven."

"Have you considered the possibility of a cult that has some connection to ravens?" Ann asked.

"I have," X said. "But I couldn't come up with a damn thing."

"Yes, darling, but what if we put our two heads together and try again. Especially if one of those heads, and I'm talking about yours truly here, has a pretty extensive background in psychology. I spent the entire day doing research."

"Really?" X removed the cork and poured each of them some wine, touched that Ann wanted to help. They clinked their glasses together in a silent toast before X tasted the wine, closing his eyes for a moment to savor the taste.

"Thank you for this," he said. "It's the most relaxed I've been in days."

"I know. And I think that's what your problem is. You've been so immersed with everything that's been going on that you can't see the forest through the trees."

X lay down and rested his head on Ann's lap. The clouds were glorious, the setting sun shading their edges with a rose tint, the light blue sky the perfect backdrop.

"OK, doctor. Point me in the right direction."

Ann started rubbing his temples as she spoke. "Think about Mark Bramm. Of course he's dead and can't tell us anything. But what did his life show you?"

"Well, he's travelled Europe quite extensively. And he and Lopez were in the same small city outside of Rome on more than one occasion." X picked up his head and took a sip of wine, then continued with his list. "He owns a restaurant and has a strange penchant for medieval weaponry. Oh, and he makes murder look like a grotesque art form."

"Good. Now what about Camille Lopez. What do you know about her?"

X thought for a moment. "She didn't want Henry to remarry."

"And why exactly was that? It wasn't necessarily because she wanted to get back together with him, right?" Ann prodded.

"You're right. If Henry were to get married again without the benefit of an annulment, which Camille refused to agree to, Henry would be committing adultery with Becca."

"And ..." Ann urged.

"And... Henry would be sinning and go to hell?" X guessed.

Ann leaned over and kissed his forehead. "That's right. Wouldn't you say that point of view is a little bit extreme?"

"Not necessarily. All good Catholics believe you need an annulment before getting remarried. Unless of course your spouse dies; then you have a clean slate to marry anyone you want.

"Scratch that," X added. "Anyone of the opposite sex who happens to also be Catholic."

"There are other religions that believe the same thing," Ann said. "But I don't know any that would condone murder as a means of preventing a second marriage."

"You know what?" X said, sitting back up, "I think you're on to something here. From what Arthur Fullington told me, Camille Lopez was obsessed with the Catholic Church. Think of it. She's in Rome on some religious pilgrimage when she meets Henry Fullington and falls head over heels in love. She won't give it up in the bedroom unless she's married, so he marries her."

"Gee, that's nice talk," Ann said, batting at his arm.

"Sorry, but think about it. As I remember Camille would have been about 25 at the time. How many 25 year old virgins do you know?"

"I guess you're right," Ann conceded. "Not many."

"It takes three days for Camille and Henry to realize they made a mistake and mutually decide to divorce."

"So Camille's fine with ending the marriage but not with an annulment?" questioned Ann. "Why?"

"Who knows?" X said, wondering the same thing. "If I remember my Catechism correctly, terminating a marriage by divorce doesn't erase the fact that it happened. But an annulment does, at least in the eyes of the church. That distinction must have been important to her.

"So time passes," X continued, "and Henry moves on with his life while Camille stays put in Rome, taking on odd jobs and giving tours at some of the local cathedrals. Other than that, she spent her time in church. Praying, I guess."

"Well that was an obvious waste of time," Ann laughed. "She ended up killing people, for heaven's sake."

"That's the point. Despite all of the outward show of being this morally upright and spiritual person, on the inside she's really a very dark and depraved individual.

"Enter the concept of a raven. Also dark. Satanic even. A symbol of death."

X pushed himself off the blanket, warming to the idea. "What we need to do is find the religious significance of ravens, especially with regard to the Catholic Church. And then look at it to the extreme."

He pulled Ann up and gave her a smacking kiss on the cheek. "I can't believe it, it seems so obvious now."

"Where do we go from here?" Ann asked.

"I think I know where we can start."

• • •

Father Daly sat behind his desk, his fingers pressed against each other and forming a steeple.

"Biblical references to ravens?"

Ann and X sat in the two chairs facing the priest. "I know it's an odd question," X said, "but it could be helpful in finding Ms. Lopez."

Father Daly took off his glasses, absently tapping them against his chin. He was the kind of priest X remembered from his childhood; very gentle with a warm inviting smile that said you can trust me. When he spoke, his words were succinct, as though he didn't want to confuse you with unnecessary verbiage. An upwelling of respect came unbidden just by seeing his Roman collar; X was surprised to find himself missing the church he so rarely attended these days.

"Well, the Bible refers to a raven on a few occasions. The most familiar is the narrative of Noah's Ark.

"Then there's another story in the Old Testament where a raven was sent by God to feed the prophet Elijah during a long drought."

"I think I remember that from Sunday school," Ann said. "I wonder, are there other prophets that, when you think of them, a raven comes to mind?"

"Not necessarily prophets, but saints, yes of course."

X scooted forward on his seat. "Like who?"

"The most obvious is Saint Benedict of Nursia. Ravens saved his life on two different occasions." He put his glasses back on and went to an overstuffed bookshelf, pulling out a thick volume. "There's a monastery dedicated to him just outside of Rome; it's where he died." He turned some pages and looked up. "Here we go; it's located in Monte Cassino."

X was on his feet in an instant. "This can't be a coincidence. Did you know Camille Lopez was a tour guide there?"

"No, she didn't share that with me." He handed X the open book and returned to his chair. "I'm actually a bit surprised by that. She's not the friendliest person to begin with. Plus she has very rigid beliefs. I'd think she would turn people off with her dogma."

Ann grabbed X's sleeve, pulling him back down into his chair. "Are there any other saints that have some kind of association with a raven?"

"You're really testing my memory; it's been a long time since seminary," Father Daly laughed. "I can't pretend to be a scholar of the saints, though I do try to emulate them."

"Anything you can remember would be appreciated," X said.

"Well, there was Saint Vincent of Saragossa, also known as Vincent the Deacon. He was martyred because he refused to throw his bible into a fire. According to legend, ravens protected his dead body from being devoured by wild animals until his followers could recover it. To this day, his shrine is guarded by a flock of ravens; it's known as the Church of the Raven.

"Then there was St. Meinrad. He was a hermit and lived in isolation for well over 20 years. His only companions were two young ravens he supposedly found and tamed. The poor man ended up being beaten to death. Legend has it that his ravens followed the culprits for days, attacking and pecking at them until they couldn't take it anymore and confessed to the crime."

Ann had slowly moved forward to the edge of her chair as she listened, her eyes riveted on Father Daly. "That's amazing."

The priest smiled. "God's ways are not our ways. Who would imagine two small little birds would go to such lengths?

"If you liked that one, you'll love this story," Father Daly said, warming to his audience. "Saint Paul of Thebes reportedly followed an angel of God into the wilderness and remained there for seventy years. Each day the Lord sent him a raven with half loaf of bread to eat. When Saint Anthony the Great went to visit with Paul, the raven appeared carrying a whole loaf of bread, enough to feed both men."

"I'd say your recall of saints is excellent," X said. "I'm shocked that there are so many that have a connection to ravens."

Father Daly motioned for X to pass back the book he was holding. "There are undoubtedly more that I'm not remembering at the moment. If you'd like, I can contact an old friend I went to seminary with; he's a walking encyclopedia about things like this."

"That would be great," X said. "I hate to sound ungrateful, but time is of the essence."

Father Daly rose, leading them to the doorway. I'll call Father Quinn right now. I still have your card; can I have him e-mail you what he finds?"

X took both of the priest's hands in his. "Yes, and thank you. You have no idea how helpful you've been."

43

"**T**his is it." X dropped the file in front of Chief Hartman, pointing his finger at the picture of a huge cathedral.

"Nice church. Why are you so excited about it?"

"Because I'd bet my last penny it's where Camille Lopez is hiding out."

Ryan leaned over the chief's shoulder and read the caption out loud, "Shrine of Saint Cuthbert, Durham, England."

X expounded, "Durham used to be one of the most famous religious and medieval meccas in all of England. Sick people from all over the world went there hoping to be cured; many miraculously were."

The chief glared at X, pushing the file back across the desk. "I'm not in the mood for a history lesson. What's this got to do with Camille Lopez?"

X explained. "That morning, when I confronted Bramm about the significance of his changing his name, he said that he wasn't the raven. The implication is that someone is out there and using that term to identify himself. I also found out that Bramm and Lopez shared a mentor. What I'm suggesting is that this person is the mysterious raven.

"Add to that the fact that both Bramm and Lopez had a special affinity to Saint Benedict, whose history has a strong association with ravens. When you put all of the pieces together, I think there's a persuasive argument that Lopez fled to somewhere that has a similar connection to ravens."

"I heard your theory on this last night, when you called and woke me up from a sound sleep. No need to bore me with all this saint nonsense again," Hartman said, giving the file a second shove.

"I understand," X responded, "but that's how I was able to track down this lead. The saint buried under that cathedral in Durham is also associated with ravens."

Hartman tilted his head, seeming to consider X's theory for just a moment. "Why wouldn't Lopez just go back to Rome, where she came from? We know for a fact she has ties there. This Durham angle is just a guess."

"I asked the same question," Ryan said. "But DiMitri has done a lot of digging and convinced us both that she's not there. First off, it'd be dumb to return; she knows it's the first place we'd look."

"That's true," the chief conceded. "And Arthur Fullington hired a team of private investigators who are combing through Rome and this Monte Cassino place as we speak, looking for her. So far they've come up with nothing."

"DiMitri's investigation confirms that," X said. "She hasn't been seen in Italy by anyone who knows her since she left for the States 27 days ago."

"But why Durham and not any of the other places these dead saints are buried?" the chief questioned.

"Because only Durham has both of the elements we're looking for: an order based on Saint Benedict's teachings and a shrine in memory of a saint whose life story is somehow marked by his relationship with ravens.

"Plus, it so happens that Durham Cathedral hosts an annual retreat that focuses on Saint Benedict and which is coincidentally scheduled for the first weekend of September."

"Not even two weeks from now," Ryan pointed out.

Hartman sat back in his chair and sighed, which X took as a cue to keep on talking, pick up Ryan's line of reasoning and run with it. He knew that if the chief wanted to shut down the conversation, he wouldn't be shy about doing so.

"Then, there's an entry in Bramm's private journal. There's a detailed notation that he spoke with someone named Michael Donavan back in June, and that this person was looking forward to going, and I'm quoting, 'home for the next assemblage.'"

"That same entry mentioned that the Donavan's kids couldn't get used to American football. Only someone from Europe would say that. Yet there's nothing about the kids having to learn a new language. To me, that eliminates all non-English speaking countries in Europe. My guess is that Donavan is originally from England, ergo that's where this next gathering is scheduled to take place."

Hartman stood up, shaking his head. "I don't know, this sounds like a long leap to make. What exactly are you suggesting?"

X moved so he was standing right in front of the chief, looking him straight in the eye.

"You don't need me here right now. Ryan can handle running the investigation; plus he's got DiMitri, who's already trying to track down this Michael Donavan.

"As for me, I was thinking of taking that vacation I postponed. Ann has never been to England; I think it would be fun."

X said it nonchalantly, trying to read Hartman's face. He got nothing. So he added a wink, a little tease, comrade to comrade sharing in subterfuge, strategizing below the radar.

Hartman finally dropped back down into his worn out chair. "This is what I get for having someone who thinks outside the box working for me."

He swiveled the chair back and forth a few times, probably buying time to think up a counter-argument.

"Come on, Frank. I want your blessing on this."

Hartman's face was unreadable, his lips held together in a tight line. He picked up a pencil and seemed to study it for a few seconds before throwing it back on the desk.

"Fine. It'll be a miracle if you find her there anyway. Saints and ravens.

"Sounds more like a football game than anything else."

44

The Raven stood in the cavernous enclave, just one of a very few locales on this earthly domain worthy of his presence.

Flying overhead were approximately forty northern ravens; they had free range throughout the large complex where the Raven came for spiritual respite, their long wings making them quite agile. They soared, tumbling and rolling through the darkened space much like aerial acrobats, chanting their *crau, crau, crau,* homage to their patriarch.

In addition to these, he also kept a small collection of exceptionally unique ravens, miniature species from around the world. There was the little raven, the forest raven, the chihuahua raven and his favorite, the dwarf raven.

Referring to these four as pets did not do justice to the Raven's dedication and love he had for them. Each had its own gilded cage and spent private time with their master learning his ways.

Although most people are familiar with a raven's distinctive deep harsh croak, few know the fascinating fact that ravens can also be taught to speak. It takes patience and practice, but the results are amazing.

The Raven was working with Little Raven when he felt the presence of one of his footmen. He held up his hand as an indication to wait until he completed what he was doing.

"'*I believe in darkness,*'" he prompted the bird to say.

Little raven responded in a squeaky voice, "*I believe in darkness.*"

"Excellent my sweet friend," the Raven pronounced before giving the bird the last remaining piece of dead rabbit he'd used as an incentive for work well done.

The Raven turned his attention to the man bowed in respect, the hood of his cleric gown covering his face.

"Has she arrived?" the Raven asked.

"Yes, Master. She has chosen to dwell where you foresaw."

"And by what name is she now known?"

"Amelia Crau," answered the novice.

The Raven smiled. Hiding amongst the ordinary was instinctive for his flock. In fact it was a matter of heredity. Ravens are in the same family as more well-known and appreciated birds, such as treepies, nutcrackers, magpies and jays. A raven intuitively knows that it can disappear amongst these mundane relatives, lost to the ignorant and fearful eyes of man and thereby giving it the freedom to follow its destiny.

"Give word to Ms. Crau that her master awaits. She is to go to the shrine for evening prayer; she will be led from there."

Again the footman bowed before leaving to do as commanded.

• • •

The Raven sat in the ornate chair, eyes closed, listening to the chant of his flock. His four beloved surrounded him in their masterfully crafted confines, encircling him with an unspoken promise of love and obedience. Man made similar vows when marrying, a ring without beginning or end symbolizing the covenant.

Yet man's word is not trustworthy. Countless marriages now ended in divorce with even more, though not terminating in fact, extinguished in deed. These are loveless unions with jealous, unkind, and impatient participants who pretend that they are taking the higher moral ground by remaining married despite their hatred of their circumstances.

Oh vanity of vanities! If only they knew that by embracing that hatred they could find true freedom.

The Raven stood, removing his shirt so that his scared flesh was available for feasting. He spread his arms in like manner as the one who was hung on a cross. The forty birds flying freely above immediately dove, landing on his body and feeding on his flesh. And instead of losing his life force, as the other one had, the Raven found a new type of existence. One where he could delve into the black hole of space and draw from its unparalleled might. He had the power to release the vast blackness of this void upon his chosen.

As the flock fed on his body he became aroused. He was looking forward to meeting with Camille. She was coming along exceedingly well. Perhaps it was time to share with her her destiny.

45

Camille looked at herself in the mirror one last time before leaving for her meeting with the Raven. Not that choosing an outfit to wear was difficult. It would be blasphemy to wear anything but black in his presence.

But she still wanted to make an impression. She fluffed out the bangs of the red wig, satisfied that it looked like her own hair. Then she undid the top two buttons of the sheer silk blouse she was wearing so that the top of her black camisole was visible. The string of ebony pearls that she wore provocatively clung to her bust line, each bead a shimmering invitation to touch.

The only man she had ever been with was Henry. Since then no one had captured her interest, except for the brief flirtation she had with Mark Bramm. But even that was short-lived, as it was only a few hours later that she found herself in the presence of the Raven and any interest in Bramm vanished.

Camille felt heat rising to her cheeks just thinking about the Raven. But she needed to keep her thoughts G rated, at least for the moment.

She had a rendezvous with destiny, and she didn't want to be late.

• • •

Camille entered the shrine with plenty of time to spare before the 5:15 p.m. service began; the sound of her heels clicking on the marble floor seemed to echo throughout the entirety of the cathedral.

She sat in a pew, made the sign of the cross, and tried to relax. She pulled a rosary from her purse and began the familiar litany. She found a renewed passion in saying these prayers after learning that her master, along with many Christians, regarded the revered raven as an emblem of the Virgin Mary.

Camille held the large bead at the top of her rosary and lovingly recited the words her mentor taught her:

"I believe in darkness, the blanket that surrounds all evil.

I believe in the power of its shadow, the source of hatred and anguish.

Through it all must pass.

From torment to torment; anguish to anguish; true misery to true misery ... "

Camille continued the prayer, fingering the small beads, and lost all track of time as her mind wandered through the teachings that had so profoundly touched her soul. Her life had been so unfocused, so without purpose, before she met the Raven. In retrospect, she could hardly believe how she had swallowed the whole universal religion concept. What a crock! Clearly God did not love all of his children equally. Why else are some born to a fate of poverty, illness and despair while others to one of health, wealth and prosperity? Yet over the ages neither theologian nor philosopher had offered a satisfying response to this reality.

So involved was she in her musings that she was startled when the young man slid into the pew next to her.

"The learned instructor is ready to receive you," he whispered.

Knowing that words were unnecessary, Camille stood and followed the stranger outside.

46

"What a beautiful cathedral." Ann was sitting next to X in the back seat of a cab going through the bustling town of Durham. "And there's the castle, on the other side of the square."

The cabbie looked into his rear view mirror, catching her eye. "Yes, mum, that church has been there since 1093. It houses the Shrine of Saint Cuthbert, who's buried directly underneath.

"The castle was built later, in the 11th century. It was home to the bishops of Durham until 1837, when it was donated to the University of Durham."

The cabbie seemed intent on chatting while he drove. "It tends to baffle tourists because when we talk about the castle, we're referring to the university college. And vice versa."

Ann laughed. "Thanks for mentioning it. I'm sure I would have been one of those who got confused." She looked over at X, who had finished reading through the "Frommer's Guide of Durham" and was now scouring one of the local handbooks produced by the city.

"And here we are," the cab driver said as he pulled in front of an unassuming terraced building with quaint topiary trees in front and a shiny door. "The Grafton House. I'm sure you'll be pleased with it, I've heard nothing but rave reviews."

They entered the boutique hotel, just a few minutes' walk from Durham's historical town center, hand in hand. X had booked the castle suite which was located at the top of the hotel.

"The view is spectacular," Ann said, looking out a window while X tipped the young man who'd carried up their luggage. She took a quick tour of the suite and from the bathroom called out, "They've got an Infiniti tub. I can't wait to get out of these clothes and take a hot bath."

X stood in the doorway, grinning. "As much as I love the thought of you getting naked, I was hoping you'd want to come exploring with me while it's still light. I'd like to get a good look at the town before sundown."

"Give me five minutes to wash up and I'll be ready to go," Ann said, pushing the door closed.

That was perfect for X. It gave him time to study the picture of Camille Lopez that the sketch artist had drawn. The woman staring back at him had crystal-blue eyes, her most striking feature. Otherwise she was nondescript, blonde hair about shoulder length, a fair complexion with an unremarkable nose and ears, no scars or piercings that would make identifying her easier.

He folded the paper and put it in his breast pocket. Lopez had to be here in Durham. She just had to, right?

God he hoped so.

47

The massive double doors to the cathedral's main entrance were open, an outward sign of invitation and hospitality.

"These doors are magnificent," Ann said as she placed her hand on a carving of an angel. "Look at the detail, isn't it …"

She abruptly stopped talking, covering her mouth with her hand.

"Oops. I didn't know there was a service going on," she whispered to X.

X pointed to a sign that read, "Evening Prayer: 5:15 p.m." and then held up his wrist as a familiar anthem floated to the rear of the church: "In the name of the Father and the Son and the Holy Spirit, Amen."

From an alcove above the altar someone started chanting, the chords echoing throughout the cathedral. Ann blinked back tears, putting her hand over her heart. "It sounds like a love letter to God." Speaking softly, she said, "Thank you for bringing me with you to Durham. The entire trip was worth it just for this moment."

They remained in the back of the church, holding hands, until the exquisite voice finished the hymn.

Ann tugged on X's sleeve and pointed to the door. As they walked back outside she said, "I just don't feel comfortable scoping out the church while such a moving service is going on."

"I know; I feel the same way."

They walked over to a low stone wall that made a perfect seating area and relaxed. The famous cathedral was at their feet, the castle turned college just a stone throw away.

"I can't believe I'm going to say this, but I almost hope you're wrong about this whole raven theory," admitted Ann. "The thought that someone would degrade the memory of either Saint Benedict or Saint Cuthbert, would knowingly do anything that might tarnish the image of this cathedral, is sickening to me."

X sighed. "I know." He reached out, brushed a few loose curls back behind Ann's ear, just as the cathedral bells chimed. A group of pigeons that were scattered across the square took flight at the sound, only to land about 10 yards from where they started.

Ann leaned back against X, and he circled his arm around her small body as they sat lazily looking at their beautiful surroundings.

And when the odd looking couple crossed their path and headed south toward the cloister, X didn't give them a second thought.

48

The man Camille was following was wearing a black robe, not unlike what priests wear, with a hood covering his head. They crossed over to the south side of the cathedral and through the cloister to the cathedral close.

"This way," the man said as he slid a key into a back doorway and held it open for her. "Stay close; it's easy to get lost in here."

The man stopped abruptly about 5 minutes later, turning around and eyeing her shoes. "You might want to take those off and leave them behind."

Hands on hips, Camille snapped, "These are brand new patent leather pumps. No way."

"Don't say I didn't warn you," he replied before leading her down a stairwell that must have been at least a quarter mile long. Somewhere along the way, she tossed off her wig, letting her blond hair fall freely around her shoulders.

When they finally reached the bottom she found herself in a dark cave-like room. The young man turned to her, bowed, and headed back for the stairs.

"Wait a minute; you aren't going to just leave me here, are you?" Camille asked.

"It is our master's instructions that you complete the journey alone."

Camille blinked repeatedly, trying to adjust to the darkness. By the time she was able to take stock of the situation, the man was gone.

"I knew the Raven wouldn't leave me in the dark," she said to herself as she noticed an assortment of candles and matches on a table in a small alcove.

Camille grabbed four, thinking that would be plenty, and opened the stylish handbag she'd bought to go along with the shoes. Sadly fashion is not practical and the candles wouldn't fit into the petite clutch.

Camille looked around, realized there was no alternative, and stuffed three of the candles inside the waistband of her skirt. She jumped a few times, glad that no one was watching since she'd look like an idiot, but she needed to make sure the candles were secure and wouldn't fall to the ground.

Satisfied, Camille lit the fourth candle, held it out in front of her and moved forward into the unknown, advancing carefully. The dark tunnel took many turns, the glow of the candle sending eerie shadows against its walls. The temperature seemed to drop with her every step and the slight wind, which at first was only an annoyance, now became a threat to her source of light.

Great, and now she was hearing things too. Could anything else possibly go wrong? It seemed like she'd been down in this hellhole for hours. She'd managed to keep up her spirits when she burned herself trying to protect the candle's flame. She hadn't gotten too upset when she tripped and landed on the graveled earth, snagging her panty-hose. Even when she'd had to squat like a dog to relieve herself, she'd kept a stiff upper lip.

But this new sound that was teasing her senses was making her crazy. She couldn't tell if there was something really out there or if her mind was playing tricks on her.

Not trusting her instincts, Camille inched forward, her hands now waving straight out in front of her and then to the sides in an effort to protect her from the running into whatever might be out there.

There was that sound again, she was sure of it. She stood completely still, barely taking a breath lest it interfere with determining where the noise came from.

She was following the continuous hum when she finally saw a glint of light ahead. With every step the beam grew stronger, almost like the sun rising at dawn. When she finally recognized the distinct chatter of the ravens she smiled broadly; she had found her way. She opened her long forgotten purse and pulled out a comb; just because she'd been crawling through the belly of the earth for the last several hours didn't mean she couldn't look her best.

When she turned a final corner the confined space of the tunnel she was travelling through completely opened up. She stood on the precipice of a huge cavern that seemed to rise to the celestial stars themselves. There, in the midst of the circling ravens overhead was her mentor. He was sitting on the most magnificent throne she had ever seen. The arms and legs were made of pure gold, with elaborate designs of the different species of ravens delicately sculpted throughout. The tassels hanging from the sumptuous burgundy velvet seat cushion were strings of black sapphires, each small stone a symbol of protection and prophetic wisdom.

The Raven nodded in her direction, a sign of permission for her to approach.

She felt her knees start to shake as she moved forward. Nervousness washed over her, and she suddenly realized that she had forgotten all of the wonderful things she had so carefully rehearsed to say to her master.

Stalling for time was not an option. Bowing, she drew near, her mind a blank slate. Then she remembered a verse from the Old Testament and spoke:

"Then I heard the sound of their wings, like the roaring of mighty waters. When they moved, the sound of the tumult was like the din of an army. And when they stood still, they lowered their wings. Above the firmament over their heads something like a throne could be seen, looking like sapphire."

When she was done speaking, she bowed again, waiting for further instruction.

The Raven smiled before picking up a staff that was at his side. It too was made of gold, and its head was a ball of lustrous black onyx.

"My little beauties, did you hear this salutation?" he said to the four caged ravens. "Let us show our appreciation."

The birds flapped their wings furiously, creating a fluttering ovation. Beaming, the Raven opened a gilded box and threw a worm to each.

Turning to Camille, he said, "I see that you have borrowed words spoken by the prophet Ezekiel. I am heartened by this show of respect. You have achieved a level of discernment few others have realized."

He slowly approached and gently tapped the staff on each of Camille's shoulder.

"Come with me, my child. Your time has arrived."

• • •

He was mysterious; exotic; charismatic.

Camille followed a respectful few feet behind the Raven as he toured the grotto, listening intently as he revealed how he was made worthy of the supernal powers he possessed.

He stopped before what looked like an altar. It was a table with a black lace cloth covering it and candles on either end. In the center was what looked like a small skeletal cup, not much larger than an orange. It was protected by a glass dome.

"The first drink I took as a child of darkness came from the skull of the revered raven. This prepared me to become the vessel of its many powers.

"This pristine essence was then nurtured by my plenteous astral travels."

He took a few steps until he came to a white marble inlay on the dirt ground that reminded Camille of a grave marker. Chiseled in the stone was the form of a figure that was half human, half bird. The Raven used his staff to point to the beautiful image. "The Shinto goddess Amaterasu exposed her true self to me in the form of the revered bird, as did the Hindu god Brahma."

Again he moved, this time to another slab of marble which had a large sun etched in the crystallized rock. "I learned, too, that I am the trusted messenger of the sun gods Helios and Apollo."

The next memorial showed the likeness of two ravens circling the earth. "I met the god Odin who had two revered birds, one named Huginn, or thought, the other Muninn, or memory. These flew about the world delivering messages, gathering knowledge and reporting back to the powerful god. So dedicated was Odin to their form that his daughters often took the shape of ravens."

She felt his dark eyes penetrating to her marrow as he explained more thoroughly. "It is through Odin that I was able to cultivate my powers of necromancy, clairvoyance and telepathy."

One of the ravens flying above swooped down, landing on her master's shoulder. He carefully stroked its wings before giving it a gentle push; as if on cue, it soared to the height of the great cavern.

The Raven's mouth widened into a smile, the small scar peeking out from under his moustache as he watched the bird's flight. He stepped towards Camille and for the first time since their introduction he touched her. Putting his hand on her shoulder he said, "Show me that you too can ascend to higher levels. What is it that you are experiencing as we walk this path?"

Camille looked around carefully, noting that there were fourteen of the commemorative tablets. Her mind tumbled to the fourteen Stations of the Cross that the Roman Catholic and Lutheran churches revere. "Master, as we move from one station to the next, I feel as though I'm on a spiritual pilgrimage. Each step on this journey is in devotion to you."

The Raven gave her shoulder a reassuring squeeze before sharpening his hold, his nails piercing her skin. "Well done, my good and faithful servant."

Camille's heart pounded uncontrollably as she felt his touch, at first gentle and then digging for more, thrusting himself through her virginal skin. Her entire body trembled in anticipation for more, God please, more from this deific man.

But instead he removed his hand and continued on to the remaining markers.

Camille took a deep breath, felt the delicious memory of his fingers on her skin slowly start to fade, and tried to pull herself together. If one touch elicited this reaction from her, imagine what was to come. Her determination to be the truest of his followers, to not disappoint, was stronger than ever.

"Of all of my astral journeys, these last two imparted to me my most potent supremacy."

He stood before a stone that was larger than the ones Camille had seen so far. "This is the goddess of battle, strife and fertility, the Morrigan. She takes my form when flying over warriors in battle, and in so doing shares with me the force of her deism."

Camille regarded the intricate war scene sculpted into the marble marker. There were bodies in various stages of death, anguish written on their faces with the help of an expert chisel. With a tear in her eye, she said, "It's magnificent."

The Raven nodded. "Yes, this has always been one of my favorites. I think you will have great appreciation for the last marker."

She followed to the final monument. "The solar deity, Lugh, and the goddess of winter, Cailleach, both favored the revered raven. A mere touch by a bird sent by Cailleach brings instant death."

Camille felt a shiver down her spine as she looked at the image of the old woman, shrouded by a veil. The surface of this marble was not honed, and it looked as though the dark clouds in the background could rise up at any moment and sweep you into their storm.

The Raven finally led her back to his throne and motioned for Camille to sit at his feet as he continued. He spoke in a slow, deep melodic voice, its cadence inducing a light hypnotic trance.

"I am both the sun, the light at the center of our galaxy, and the moonless night, the black hole in the center of the universe. From this black hole in space I draw in mystic energies where they remain, growing in strength, until by celestial revelation I am guided to release them."

Camille drifted into a beautiful haze, swaying back and forth to the sound made by the flapping wings of the forty ravens flying overhead.

"Appraising the people who come through your life is the foundation of being elevated to a journeyman. It allows you to consider whether they might become a viable recruit. Even if they do not possess the qualities to join on our journey, they still might prove valuable in propelling our cause."

The Raven continued. "Sadly I cannot share with you my capacity to soar the skies and nest wherever I choose. Teaching you how to prey on the weak is as close as I can come to giving you wings. Just because a person is found to be undesirable as an initiate does not mean that he or she cannot be useful in other ways; theirs might be the perfect place to nest during your journeys.

"I sanctioned your travels to the United States so that you could crush the luminous future of the man you once married.

"Your industrious efforts in finding an acquaintance that lived in such close proximity as the betrothed was a testament to the success of my teachings."

"Yes, I was able to find the perfect mark. Monica Adams." Camille paused, licking her lips. Why was she having such a hard time pronouncing the words?

He smiled, seeming to note her weak and shaky voice and continued.

"You must always trust in my words and acknowledge that there is nothing called coincidence. Ms. Adams was revealed to you only because of my teachings and omnipotence."

"Yes, sirrrrrr."

"Then there is the business about Mark Bramm. He was among the first of my followers and had a gift of recruiting viable initiates. Although it grieved me to learn of his demise, I was delighted with your enthusiastic implementation of my decrees."

Camille looked up, the image of the Raven becoming hazy. "Survival of the fittest," she barely managed to say.

"I have chosen few to follow me. You, my pet, have earned a privileged position in my order by proving to me your undying devotion to the revelations and beliefs that I have shared with you."

This statement floated to Camille, tickling her sensations but unable to penetrate her clouded mind.

Her tongue felt swollen, too large for her mouth. The effort to reply was too exhausting to even attempt.

The Raven's hand went to a large porcelain bowl that sat at his side and, grabbing the feed inside, threw it onto Camille's bent form.

Camille blinked, confused as the small pellets landed all over her. She bent her head and carefully looked at the small clusters of bird food.

Then she heard the sound of dozens of wings swishing around her body before she felt the first peck of a raven tasting the food.

As comprehension dawned on her, she lifted her head toward her mentor. "Thank you," she mumbled, before resting on the ground.

She lay on her back, with her arms and legs stretched out, so the ravens would have access to the seed that they craved. It felt delicious, like tiny pin pricks all over her body. She could feel each beak's search for the seed, yet also experienced the group as a whole devouring what they could find. The more insistent birds pecked fiercely enough to pierce her flesh, ripping into her skin and tearing it away as they pulled their beaks from one spot to another. The pain mutated into pleasure as she lie there, praying that it would never end.

But when there was no feed left on Camille's clothes or body for the ravens to eat, they abandoned her, loudly squawking *crau, crau, crau,* as they flew back up into the eaves.

Camille inched her body into a kneeling position. She wanted to thank her teacher for ordering the birds to scavenge her body but she couldn't speak. Swallowing was difficult, and her mouth was parched. Her blurry eyes tried to focus on a chalice that had appeared at the Raven's right hand. She panted, her tongue hanging out of her mouth like rabid dog's.

Ignoring her obvious distress, the Raven stood up and walked to one of the four small gilded cages and opened the door. Out popped the rare white necked raven which sat obediently on his shoulder.

The Raven returned to his seat and said "Would you like to drink from the cup?"

Camille opened her mouth to reply, her dry lips splitting, before she heard the bird say in its squeaky voice, "Yes, Master."

"Tell me first, my beloved, in what do you believe?"

The bird responded somewhat mechanically but in a clear voice.

"I believe in darkness, the blanket that surrounds all evil."

Hearing these words, the three birds in the other ornate cages joined in.

"I believe in the power of its shadow, the source of hatred and anguish. Through it all must pass."

"Enough," commanded the Raven.

Turning to Camille, he asked "Are you in anguish, my pet?"

She felt like she was about to lose consciousness. Her mind was reeling; she was not sure what answer he expected from her. Afraid to say the wrong thing, she allowed her body to fall into the welcome void of darkness.

49

"Come on, Ann, I don't want to be late," X called as he waited outside their hotel room.

It had been 48 hours since their arrival in Durham and X had absolutely no leads on Lopez' whereabouts.

So far none of the hotel personnel or shop owners recognized the picture that X had been showing around town. And the hours they'd spent at both the cathedral and the castle, though interesting, did not yield the kind of information he needed.

"Sorry, babe. Just wanted to grab the umbrella." Ann walked into the hallway and, seeing the frustrated look on X's face said, "What? They said it might rain later on."

X sighed. "Sorry. I'm just anxious about meeting this guy. He's supposed to be one of the most knowledgeable historians in the area. I can't believe he's working as a tour guide."

"A private tour guide," Ann corrected. "And he's got to pay for that PhD of his somehow."

"Yeah, well if Mr. Private Tour Guide doesn't help us come up with a solid lead, I'm going to have to call the chief and tell him he was right, that the Durham, England angle is a bust."

Ann looped her arm around his as they walked. "Well, if Camille isn't here, at least you can cross this location off the list of possibilities."

X leaned down, kissed the top of her head. "Thank you for always seeing the glass as half full."

Minutes later they entered the busy Hide Cafe. The room was large with hard wood floors and sleek, modern furniture.

"That must be him, over there in the back," Ann said.

X observed the young man as they crossed the room. He was sitting at a window table with a picturesque view of the River Wear and Old Elvet Bridge, and was wearing a tweed jacket with patches at the elbow and an oxford shirt underneath. His brown hair was pulled into a short ponytail, his eyeglasses slightly retro.

"He looks like a professor," Ann whispered as they arrived at the table.

"Are you Frederick Barnestable?"

The man stood up. "Xavier King, I presume?"

"Yes, but please call me X. And this is my girlfriend, Ann McGuinn," he said as he put his arm around her shoulders.

"Please, have a seat," Frederick offered. "I hope you don't mind, I ordered some scones to nibble on while I waited. Help yourself."

X reached over and grabbed one of the pastries. "Thanks, I haven't had anything to eat yet today."

Frederick signaled for the waitress, who poured them coffee, took their breakfast orders and disappeared into the kitchen.

"So Frederick, tell us a little about yourself," X asked.

"Well, I was born and raised right here in Durham, which is where I did all of my schooling except for my doctorate work. As I mentioned on the phone, I have a PhD in history and philosophy from Cambridge University."

He absently rotated the napkin in front of him as he spoke. "Unfortunately, finding a job hasn't been easy. In the interim, I've been working on having my thesis published. It's quite fascinating, really, on transubstantiation."

"It sounds very interesting," Ann offered.

Frederick laughed. "Ah, I've heard those very same words countless times with much less enthusiasm than you've generously offered. Don't feel badly if you don't find the topic as exciting as I do. Most people don't even know what it means.

"Ah, but that's neither here nor there," he said, waving his hand and setting that subject aside. "You're here on holiday and are looking for a private tour guide. All modesty aside, nobody knows Durham as well as I."

Frederick placed a map of Durham on the table, turned it so everyone could see. "Is there anything in particular that you want to see?"

X put his hand on top of Ann's, saying, "We actually took the general tour of both the cathedral and the castle yesterday. They did a great job, but with so many people in the group it was hard for them to answer everybody's questions.

"What I was specifically hoping to learn more about is the original construction of the cathedral and the castle. I've read up on the literature, of course, and know that there have been a few renovations over the years. But I was thinking that someone with your specific background might have better insight."

"Well you've certainly piqued my curiosity," Frederick responded. "What exactly do you want to know?"

"What I am wondering is whether, over the centuries, anyone has ever speculated that there might be hidden rooms or entrances in either landmark?"

"Well sure, there have been rumors," answered Frederick. "But from a historical standpoint nothing has ever been verified."

X leaned toward the map and tapped his finger, first on the cathedral and then the castle. "If there were to be a hidden room, is it possible that it could be concealed in the eaves? Or even that a dropped ceiling could be hiding it?"

"I dare say it's not very likely. There are volumes written about the aesthetical and structural design of each of the buildings. If there were anything suggestive of such an area it certainly would have been identified by now.

"As for false ceilings, again I would say it's doubtful. I've studied the original construction drawings as well as each improvement or renovation since and there is nothing inconsistent with what you and I see when we walk through the spaces today. I feel fairly confident that every inch of space is accounted for."

Frederick pulled the map aside as the waitress returned with their breakfasts.

X continued the conversation. "So if there is nothing hidden above ground, there would be only one option left. Do you think that it might be possible for a secret area to exist underground?"

"I guess anything's possible, especially given the fact that Durham is located on a peninsula," Frederick said before taking a bite of his porridge.

"How is that relevant?" asked X.

Frederick wiped his mouth with his napkin before answering. "A peninsula's only connection to the mainland is by way of an isthmus. That particular type of terrain appears to be very easily excavated."

Frederick picked up the pepper shaker and placed it on one side of a napkin and then placed the salt shaker a few inches away. "Take Panama, for example," he said, pointing to the napkin. "On one side is the Atlantic Ocean and on the other the Pacific." Taking a knife, he placed it across the napkin linking the two shakers. "The man-made canal which now connects these two waterways bisects the Isthmus of Panama. Any other type of terrain and it would likely have been impossible to excavate a canal at all."

X watched as Frederick rested his chin on his hand. "I've never given it much thought, but I guess what I'm suggesting is that the topography here at Durham would be well suited for excavation. If that's the case, digging underground rooms wouldn't have been terribly difficult to accomplish. Especially on the hush-hush. And who knows, if they dug deep enough there could even be waterways."

X pushed on. "Wouldn't it be easy to hide an entrance that led down to a subterranean level?"

"Sure it would. But locating it would be like finding a needle in a haystack." Frederick took a sip of his coffee. "Why the interest in hidden rooms?"

X put a fork loaded with egg and ham into his mouth and shrugged, letting Ann come up with an answer. "Oh, we just love to solve a mystery even when there isn't one there."

Ann continued to chatter away while X considered what Frederick had just said. When breakfast was done, he asked, "I was wondering if it would be possible for me to see those architectural drawings you mentioned."

Frederick leaned back against his seat, brow furrowed, and crossed his arms across his chest. His hazel eyes didn't blink as he looked at X and Ann intently, the moment of silence becoming embarrassingly long. Finally he spoke.

"Quite frankly, I don't know what to make of you. I was hired to take you and Ms. Ann around town and show you the sites but clearly you are not looking for the typical historical tour.

"I'm not daft," he went on as he scooted forward, leaning his elbows on the table. "You obviously have something very specific that you're looking for. Why not let me in on the secret; perhaps if I know the particulars I could be more helpful."

X looked at Ann, a question in his eyes, and she nodded yes.

"OK," he said. "This is going to sound strange, but I'm looking for some kind of secret group whose focus is on a raven."

Ann quickly added, "Actually, it's the raven's significance in the life of a saint and/or the Catholic Church."

"That's the big mystery? Mate, you should have just come forward and asked," Frederick said as he relaxed back into the chair. "You undoubtedly know the connection between Saint Cuthbert and his ravens; but of course you do, why else would you be here?

"We have a society right here in Durham, Saint Cuth's, as it's known. It was set up back in 1888 by college students who didn't like the living accommodations at the university so they set up a society off campus and lived there. These days it's mostly known for its boat club."

"Yeah, we've checked them out. But that's not really the kind of society we're looking for," answered X. "This group, or club ... whatever you want to call it, would be more like a cult and have far more nefarious objectives. Their view of religion is totally distorted. We believe that a raven is their talisman."

"I'd go even farther," added Ann, "and say it's their god. Or, if not the raven itself, every dark thing that they think a raven represents."

Frederick removed his glasses, seeming to consider what they were saying. "Why are you so intent on finding this cult, or is the raven your point of interest?" asked Frederick.

"We're actually trying to track down a member of the group. She's wanted for questioning by authorities in New York," X answered, electing not to give more details than absolutely necessary.

"And you think she might have come to Durham because of the stories of Saint Cuthbert and ravens?"

"As crazy as that sounds, that's exactly why we're here," X responded. "This woman lived in Rome for several years and was very active with the Benedictine monastery at Monte Cassino. We think that's where she was originally recruited."

"Ah, I see the connection," Frederick said. "Benedict also had a history where ravens held significance."

"Exactly," X said. "When Camille Lopez disappeared without a trace, I started researching other saints who are somehow associated with ravens and whether there were monuments in their honor. Other than the Monte Cassino dedicated to Benedict, the cathedral here in Durham is by far the most famous location."

"You said the name Lopez? Is that the woman you are looking for? Because I know almost every single person in this town and can find out if she's checked into a hotel or a bed and breakfast, maybe even rented a room somewhere. For pity's sake, she could have enrolled in the college and be staying in one of the dorms right inside the castle."

"I appreciate the offer," answered X sincerely, "but I've already done a pretty thorough search. I doubt she'd be using her real name anyway."

"I see," said Frederick as stood up and slung his backpack over his shoulder. "Are we off then?"

"Do you have any ideas?" X asked as he pulled back Ann's chair for her.

"Nothing concrete. But I know where we can start."

50

Calling William Barnestable head of Campus Security would be a misnomer. Though that was indeed his title, the reach of his office included the safety and well-being of tourists visiting the famous cathedral as well. Since both the cathedral and the castle were historic landmarks and in such close proximity to each other, it was determined early on that the term "campus" be interpreted broadly to include the entire area occupied by these monuments. CS worked as an adjunct to the Durham Constabulary, which had primary jurisdiction of the entire city.

William was short and squat with a thick moustache. He was sitting in front of a display of cameras, monitoring a bus that had just stopped in front of the cathedral to presumably drop off passengers despite the signs prohibiting vehicular traffic in the area. He punched a number on his desk phone and spoke. "Kevin, see what the devil's going on over at the church."

Frederick poked his head through the door of the private office. "Dad? Are you busy?"

William swiveled his chair around, his red hair and ruddy complexion decidedly different than Frederick's dark coloring.

"Son, what's got you visiting your old man?" he said as he stood. "You've brought me company I see."

"Yes, this is Xavier King, a detective from the US, and his friend Ann McGuinn. They're here on rather of a hunch, looking for a woman who's wanted by the police back in the States."

"Pleased to make your acquaintance," William said as he greeted the newcomers. "I assume you've contacted the local authorities regarding this matter?"

"Yes, sir and they have a BOLO out for her. Camille Lopez is the name she was using as of last week, but it's likely she's going by something else now." X took the sketch out of his pocket and offered it to the man. "This is what she looks like, though she might have changed her appearance as well."

William took the picture from X's hand and examined it. "Sorry, I don't remember seeing her. Hold on just a minute, let me run her name through my computer." He typed the name and watched his screen come up blank. "No luck."

Just then, a woman wearing a blue uniform with the initials CS written on the back stuck her head through the door. "Sorry to interrupt, but we've got a problem with camera 42."

"Don't tell me it's another college prank," William said. "Someone's panties thrown over the lens? Or is it shaving cream this time?"

"We'll know in five minutes; I dispatched maintenance to check it out."

"Thanks, Katie, keep me posted," William said as he absently pulled at the end of his moustache. Returning his attention to the threesome, he laughed. "I don't get to wear my superman cape too often on this job, but I do stay busy."

"This is actually quite an impressive set up you have," X commented. He looked back at the large room they had just walked through, where there were dozens of desks set up in rows with monitors at each, and additional video screens hanging from the ceiling and against the walls. "How many locations are you monitoring?"

"It depends on what you mean by monitor," William said as he returned to his chair and pointed to the displays in front of him. "Visuals, we have almost 200 between the cathedral and the college."

"Are there any at the castle?" wondered X.

"Castle, college, they're the same thing. The college took over the castle grounds…" He looked up in the air and asked, "What year was that Son?"

"1837."

X ignored Ann, who poked him in the ribs and whispered, "Didn't you hear the cab driver tell us that the other day?"

"But to answer your question," William continued, "yes, we've got video feed from the castle also."

"How else do you keep track of what's going on?"

"Key cards. The students have to swipe them to get in and out of the dorms, the library, cafeteria; the usual. That puts a time stamp in our database so we know who's been where."

Frederick spoke up. "The entrances to the historic buildings in the square have key card access as well, isn't that right?"

"That's true Son. Certain employees who have passed our background check are given the cards."

Frederick asked, "By chance did anything out of the ordinary happen in the past week or so?"

William's chair swiveled so he was looking directly at his son. Crossing his arms across his rather large belly, he questioned, "Like what? We had a couple of suspicious looking bags left unattended that ended up being nothing, two shoplifters we picked up at the cathedral's gift shop, and …

"Well, now that I think of it, there was one unusual thing. Someone used a lost key card over at the college to open one of the doors that's supposed to be locked down for maintenance."

"What does that mean?" asked X.

"When a maintenance or reconstruction and repair project is going on we disable the doors in the area except to the people working that particular job, basically cordoning it off from the public. It's a safety precaution, keeps the general population away from the workers."

"Yet someone was able to gain access?"

"Two someones, actually. But that's the funny thing. We have a camera shot of a man and woman entering the building, but only the gentleman exiting. We never were able to confirm which doorway the woman used to eventually leave the structure."

X felt the first sparks of hope in this otherwise unproductive trip to Durham. He tried to keep his enthusiasm in check, to maintain some professionalism. "Would you happen to still have a copy of that tape?" he asked, knowing this could be the break he'd been looking for.

"Katie," William bellowed into the other room. "Can you retrieve that tape from the day before yesterday of door #666?"

Ann moved closer to X and whispered, "666. That's the sign of the beast in Revelations."

X caught Ann's eyes, nodded. They stood there making small talk with William until the tape was retrieved and put into the monitor, X feeling his palms getting sweaty with every passing second. Within a few minutes they were looking at a grainy image of two people slipping through an entryway.

X leaned over and examined the screen, looking for any resemblance to Camille. "I can't tell if that's her or not," X said, shaking his head in frustration. "Was anyone able to recognize the man?"

William played with the buttons on his control panel, trying to make the image clearer. "No. It's hard to tell if he's wearing a cassock or maybe a choir gown. The employee who lost the card is convinced it was stolen from his wallet while he was in the shower at the gym, even though nothing else was taken."

"Is there any way we can look around that area?"

"I don't see why not," William said as he went to a drawer and pulled out a plastic card. He punched some keys on his computer and inserted the card into a small machine so it could be coded before handing it to X. "That door goes into a wing of one of the college buildings that hasn't been used in years. It's a mess. Every time it's scheduled for renovation something comes up and the project is bumped to a later date."

X reached out and shook Williams' hand. "You've been a great help. Thank you so much."

"No problem," William answered. "I hope you find what you're looking for."

• • •

"What are you looking for?"

X stopped pushing the shopping cart around the campus book-store, looking at the shelves in front of him. "I'm not exactly sure. Anything I think we might need."

He grabbed two rolls of fluorescent tape and, seeing Ann's questioning eyes said, "It'll work better than bread crumbs."

Frederick waited for them at the checkout, talking to a pretty young cashier until they were ready to go. He said his goodbye to the blushing co-ed and turned his attention back to X.

"Got everything you need?"

X put his arms through his brand new backpack's shoulder straps, adjusting it on his back. "Sure hope so."

They crossed the town square, passing the cathedral on their left and heading toward the castle turned university/college. Even though the weather had cooled, the humidity was high. Ann's curls were glistened with moisture.

"The only way you can get to the college is by passing through this medieval gatehouse," Frederick said as he waived to the guard on duty and walked through, the impressive university structure ahead of them.

"These buildings, however," Frederick continued, leading them to the left, "are not open to the public. The gate is locked every evening at midnight to prevent intruders and the guard on duty has discretion of whether or not to let you pass through.

"The door we'll be using is the back entry to where the clergy used to live," explained Frederick as they went down a narrow alleyway, "and also where the chorister school used to be located."

He stopped in front of an old wooden door, nicks and embedded scratches somehow adding to its beauty. The modern door knob with the thin opening for a key card marred the otherwise authentic relic.

"This is it. Are you sure you don't want me to come with the two of you?"

"You're time is better spent researching what we talked about earlier," X said as he faced Frederick. We'll plan on meeting at the library at 6:00 p.m. and decide how to proceed from there."

"Right then," Frederick said as turned away, hunching his shoulders and pulling his jacket close across his body as a rumble of thunder echoed overhead.

51

The door creaked as it opened, small dust balls whispering across the floor as the wind blew in. X stepped inside first, turned on a light and then motioned Ann to follow.

The scent of mildew assaulted their nostrils, the musty scent overpowering. Putting her hand over her mouth and nose, Ann said, "What died in here?"

X pointed to a rolled up carpet that was leaning against the wall of the small vestibule. It was covered with a greenish cottony velvet mold.

"That's disgusting." Ann hurried through the room toward the staircase in front of them, using her other hand to wave fresh air in front of her face.

X was just a step behind her, and now stood between the ascending stairwell that was on his right and the descending on the left. He craned his neck looking up, noticing that there were more balusters missing than still attached to the banister. "It looks like there are five floors above us. I say we start from the bottom and go up from there."

The closer they got to the basement level the darker it became. "There must be a light switch down here somewhere," Ann said, trying to see into the large room once they reached the bottom. "Where's that flashlight?"

"Wait a second I think I've got it." X pulled a string that was dangling above him and the low watt light bulb that was screwed into the ceiling came on. It provided enough light for them to make out another string hanging on the far side of the room.

"Watch yourself," Ann said as she heard him shuffling through the debris on the floor, making his way to the other light fixture. Seconds later it too came on.

"Have you ever seen so much junk in your life?" X said, pulling up what looked like an old tarp. "There's a piano under here." He hit a key and an out of tune note sounded through the room. Opening a nearby box, he added, "These must be what the choir boys wore." He held out an old discolored ruby red robe and brought it towards his nose before sneezing. "Musty. These must have been down here for ages."

Ann was standing in front of a pile of old books that was literally taller than she was. She raised her arm and picked one off the top. "Hymnals," she said, dust flying as she opened the front cover.

"Why would anyone save these?" X kicked at a pile of box springs, the mattresses rotting a few feet away. "They must be remnants from the boarding school."

"Gross, I can feel the bottom of my sneakers sticking to the floor," Ann said as she kicked an empty soda can. The noise spooked a small rodent, which came scrambling from its hiding spot, running right over her shoes.

"Ahh! Oh my God, did you see that?" Ann screamed, jumping from one foot to the other. "It was a big as Caesar."

X pictured his neighbor's dog and said, "Caesar is an overweight terrier; he would be highly insulted if he knew you compared him to a tiny little mouse."

She scrunched her face, hands balled into fists. "It was a rat."

X tried not to laugh and continued walking around the perimeter of the room, his flashlight moving slowly up and down the walls from the floor to the ceiling. "I don't see any joints or hinges, anything that might indicate an access way."

He knocked his fist against the wall. "Concrete. Like the floor. It'd be difficult to penetrate."

"What are you thinking?"

"That even though the obvious place to put an entrance to a lower level would be down here, this room is built like a steel cage. My gut is telling me that we're in the wrong spot.

"Let's go up a floor, and see if we can find anything there."

"You're not going to get any arguments from me," Ann called over her shoulder, already halfway up the stairwell by the time he'd even finished his sentence.

• • •

They had made their way up to the third floor and so far had come up with nothing. Ann stretched, arching her back, and sat down on the ground.

"It's almost noon; are you hungry?" she asked as she dug through the backpack looking for the energy bars, reciting the items she came across. "Band aids, antiseptic cream, a map of Durham, floor plans of both the cathedral and castle; you really thought of everything."

She watched X's back end as he crawled along the base board of the wall, his hands carefully grazing over the surfaces.

"It feels like there's a seam here," he said as he walked his fingers as high as he could reach before standing up. He continued his quest, putting his cheek against the spot. "There's cold air coming from the other side."

"Really?" Ann jumped up and went to X's side, inspecting the wall. "I don't see anything."

X pressed his thumb on the spot. "I can feel a gap in the wall but it's so small I can't get to it. Can you get me the magnifying glass?"

Ann went back to the bag and dragged it closer to X, then dug around inside. "Here you go."

X angled his body so he could get a better view. "Can you aim the flashlight right here?"

As soon as the beam found the right spot X said, "There it is. It's hard to see, but there's a small lever in the very back. Do you have a nail file or something I can stick in there to try and move it?"

"Not on me," Ann said, standing up on her toes trying to see. "What about your Swiss army knife?"

"My back pocket," he said as he stepped back and rolled his shoulders, trying to relax the muscles.

Ann slipped her hand into the back of his jeans and pulled the familiar red pocket tool out.

Using the long blade, X inserted it into the opening and jiggled it up and down until it caught.

There was an almost imperceptible click before a low moan, like a house settling.

"Did you hear that?" X leaned into the wall, put his ear right against it, waiting for the sound to happen again.

Nothing. But he wasn't deterred; he took a few steps back, looking at the section of wall in front of him, imaging where an opening might be. He splayed his hands and moved them along the wall until he felt the slight shift.

Putting his shoulder against the spot, X pushed with all his strength.

"I can feel it giving, but I need more leverage."

Ann moved to his side and put both hands on the wall. "Let's try it again, on the count of three. One, two..."

X planted his feet firmly, bent his knees, and again leaned into the wall, ignoring the ache in his shoulder. He strained as he pushed off his feet, adding as much of his body weight as he could against the solid surface.

The movement was slow, but an angle of open space soon appeared between the room they were in and whatever lay on the opposite side of the wall.

"We've almost got it," he grunted before the section of wall gave way, pushing inward and ending up perpendicular to the rest of the expanse.

"Take a look at that." His eyes were travelling over where the flat wall used to be and where an opening of about four feet by two now existed. Words couldn't describe how excited he was so he laughed instead.

"Can you believe it?" He turned to Ann, picked her up and twirled her around in a circle, laughing some more. "It looks like this long shot of mine might be paying off."

"You did it," Ann said, grabbing his arms to steady herself once he set her back on the floor. "You're amazing."

X was already crouched down and leaning his large frame through the opening. The beam of the flashlight gave him a limited view, but he'd seen enough and backtracked into the room. "There's a stairwell that must lead down to a sub-basement level; it's so far down I can't even see the bottom."

"Let me see," Ann said as she got onto her knees and started crawling through the now visible entryway.

"Wait a minute, what do you think you're doing?" X said, grabbing her ankle and pulling her back towards him. "This is it for you; I'm going alone from here on out."

She shook her foot away from his grasp. "I don't think so. Do you think I came all this way so you could ditch me just when the excitement starts happening?"

"Excitement?" X couldn't believe his ears. "That's hardly a word I'd use to describe Camille Lopez. The woman is a raving lunatic; I don't want you anywhere near her."

Ann moved so she was kneeling right in front of him. "I know you're worried about my safety and I appreciate that. But we don't even know for sure that this is the way to find Camille. And even if it is, we could be hours from locating her. Wouldn't it be smarter for us to stick together, to keep searching until we have proof positive of her location?

"I promise I'll back off if and when the situation gets dangerous."

She tried another tack. "Please?" And then, "You know I'll follow after you anyway; at least if we go together you'll know where I am."

He knew she was right. And by the look on her face, she knew that he knew it.

Despite the little voice warning him that this might not be the best idea, he said, "I want you to promise to stay behind me unless I say otherwise, you hear? And try to remember the way in case we need to retrace our steps and get out of there in a rush."

Ann pulled one of the rolls of fluorescent tape out of the backpack, waved it in the air. "This should make at least that part easy."

Within minutes they were carefully plodding down the stairwell which was incredibly steep and had little tread. There was no banister to hold, just earthen walls on either side making the space feel incredibly confined. X kept up a constant dialogue with Ann, making sure she was doing alright, until they reached the bottom almost half an hour later.

"Look," said Ann, pointing to an old lop-sided table that was leaning against a wall. "Candles and matches."

"Why don't you grab a few and put them in the backpack," X said, squatting down a little so she could reach it. "Just in case."

He waited until he heard the zipper closing before turning back to Ann. "Ready?"

Giving him the thumbs up sign, they moved forward into the dark.

52

Camille didn't know how long she was unconscious; she had long since lost all track of time.

She found herself lying in a puddle of her own urine, caged like one of the birds that the Raven favored. Overhead she heard the wings of the free ravens whipping about wildly.

There seemed to be something on the floor that they were diving at. She tried to clear her eyes so that she could see, her vision still hazy from the drugs the Raven presumably gave her.

She eventually made out the body of the young man who had escorted her from the cathedral. Undoubtedly dead, she wondered why her master had killed him. Frankly, she hadn't liked the guy anyway; as a footman he should have known to be more deferential to her, a journeyman.

Camille watched as a raven landed on the corpse and pushed its beak through the empty eye socket, pulling out a long strand of brain matter before flying away. Undisturbed, she stood up and took stock of her situation. She still had her pocketbook, which contained a little spending money, her hotel room key, a comb and mirror and a package of gum.

She fixed her hair as best she could and popped a piece of chewing gum into her mouth. The fresh mint taste exploded, her taste buds starving for something other than dry dust to placate them.

She finally sat down dutifully, watching two birds fight over the dead man's left pinkie, and wondered when her trusted teacher would return.

53

"Where exactly are we?" asked Ann.

They had followed the dark tunnel for approximately 300 yards before it came to the first fork.

"I think we're under the square and heading toward the cathedral. Can you get some of that florescent tape out and put it here," X said, pointing to the earthen passageway they had just travelled through.

"Do you think it will stick?" Ann pulled a long piece of the neon green and pressed firmly. "Good thing this wall is so dry," she said, patting the strip with her hand.

"Uh huh," X said absently as he studied one of the maps. "Let's bear left. And be careful where you step, the ground's really uneven here," this said as the toe of his boot connected with a rock, sending it sailing through the air.

They continued on for about 15 minutes before they reached the end of the passageway. "Dead end," X pronounced. "Guess we should have taken a right."

Ann looked at the hollow that was the end of the tunnel, a sunken cave wall that looked like something had once battered against it trying to get through. She had the thought, it only lasted a millisecond, but she had it nonetheless; she'd hate to die down here.

She turned, saw that X had already started to retrace their steps, and ran to catch up to him. She reached out and put her hand on his backpack, felt a relieving calm in being so close to him. They walked the entire way back to the fork that way, X leading and Ann right behind him holding onto one of the backpack's straps, a little lifeline that only she was aware of; no need to make him worry about her.

"I'll just put some more tape here," X said once they got to the main tunnel, taking two long strips and crisscrossing them on the wall, "so we know not to go down that way again. "Ready to press on?"

Ann gave the thumbs up sign, and they started off again. She kept her eyes wide open, careful not to take any missteps, and noticed how the dirt walls surrounding them varied in their appearance. At times they were very gritty and scaly and at others had an almost swept, polished look to them.

Their shadows leapt from tiny to gargantuan and back again as they twisted and curved through the tunnel, travelling deeper into the earth. The smell of mold got worse with every step, and the erratic sound of dripping became more constant as moisture collected and fell to the damp ground.

"The ground is getting muddy," Ann finally announced. "Did you notice that?"

"Yeah. I'm not sure if it's because we're heading down toward the water base or whether it's moisture coming from outside. You were right; the forecast is for heavy rain today."

Ann remembered the umbrella that's she'd left with their things at the top of the stairwell. Little good it would do her down here anyway. She shivered, the first feelings of claustrophobia tickling her senses. Being underground was one thing, but imagining the dirt walls getting soaked with water, possibly collapsing under the added weight, was not helping her psyche.

"Are you OK back there?"

"The best," she lied. "Lead on."

54

Camille was starting to get pissed. It seemed like she'd been waiting hours, and still the Raven was nowhere to be seen.

She'd long since unlocked herself from the cage; one bobby pin was all it took to open the padlock. She was now sitting on her mentor's throne, the large chair almost swallowing her small form. She had the miniature raven named Little Forest perched on her arm, giving it small pieces of what remained of the corpse that still lay on the floor. The birds that flew free overhead had all but completely devoured the rest of the body.

Little Forest was a very smart bird, most likely a female she thought. In no time it was repeating her words: My goddess; You are powerful; You can rule.

These statements became a mantra, Camille chanting them lovingly while rocking back and forth. She felt her mind drifting with the words as energy coursed through her veins, moving and pulsing and vibrant, so vibrant that it called her back to the present. And to the awareness that the other three caged ravens had taken up the song as well, each little voice adding a sense of legitimacy to the words spoken.

She wondered about the Raven. How was it that he was the chosen one? No one ever asked her to vote. Did he have some intrinsic qualities that made him uniquely qualified to lead their group?

She pondered this question. He did, in fact, seem to possess powers that she couldn't pretend to have. He had proven to be clairvoyant, many times predicting how the future would unfold and then providing ways to circumvent the inevitable.

He also seemed to have access to resources that she would otherwise never have even known existed. Take this cavern, for instance; who would have guessed it existed. And the undeniably beautiful underground facility in Monte Cassino, Italy.

Camille loved that Benedictine landmark. It was where the scales fell from her eyes and she saw anew. It was true that Saint Benedict was a holy man, but power over evil came not from the man but through the raven.

Saint Benedict must have felt invincible.

Except that one time.

It happened while Benedict was away visiting his twin sister named Scholastica; she was a nun. When he told her that it was time for him to get back to the monastery she begged him to stay longer. Unfazed by her request, he refused.

Scholastica got right down on her knees and started praying. Within seconds a raging thunderstorm materialized that was so violent Benedict was unable to leave until the next morning.

Camille had to give Scholastica her due; when she didn't get her own way she went over her brother's head to obtain the solution she wanted.

Thinking that there was a lesson for her to learn from that story, Camille gently put Little Forest back in her cage before returning to her own.

It definitely would not do for the Raven to find her anywhere other than where he left her.

• • •

Although she was quite awake, Camille was not aware of exactly when or even how the Raven returned to the cavernous area. He seemed to appear out of thin air.

"My pet, are you refreshed after your journey?" he asked, poking his staff through the slats of her cage.

Camille jumped, startled by his voice, before freezing for a moment. Did he know that she'd escaped the enclosure? But since it made more sense that he was referring to the hallucinogenic state she'd been in earlier, she went with that.

"Yes, learned instructor. During this time alone I have replayed in my mind the places I was sent. From the sands of the desert to the lushness of the rain forest I witnessed the heights and depths of your power and control. I saw the true essence of evil, the black anguish and despair that seep from your quintessential being."

"This is good," the Raven responded. "What else did you learn?"

Camille fought the nagging thought that came to mind, namely that she was getting tired of sucking up to this guy. But she had come so far, was so close to attaining what she wanted most; arriving at the highest stratum of power and might. And the only way there was through the Raven.

"Patriarch of darkness, I learned nothing more. I merely confirmed my belief and faith in you as the source of evil and decay and am now more dedicated than ever to dwell in your fold as not merely a journeyman, but as one privileged to the highest of orders.

"Though I thank you for allowing me a taste of the ecstasy you enjoy," Camille continued, "I know that the birds came to me only because of the feed that you provided. Please, when can I become true food for the raven?"

The Raven chuckled, a rare occurrence. "You answer well, my pet, your words thoughtfully chosen. Today you will in fact meet the destiny you deserve."

He looked at her eager expression and turned away, his face hidden from her. "You believe you are prepared to join me in the bliss of the rapture? To bear your flesh to my flock and join me in being raised to the skies, to experience the bliss and delight in the carnage below?"

"Yes, Master, I am ready to take my place next to you."

"Is that pride I hear?"

Confused, Camille answered, "Shouldn't being raised to the highest echelon of journeymen, a place where so sacred few have attained, be celebrated?"

"Yes, I suppose that is true, but never too hastily. There is still one last issue to dispose of before you will be adequately prepared for the privilege."

Camille bit her already split lips to keep from screaming; how dare he throw yet another hurdle in front of her. She pasted on a smile and said, "What might that be?"

The Raven walked slowly around her cage, finally stopping in front of her.

He tapped his chin with a finger, continued tapping away and looking at her like she was some kind of barn animal he was considering buying. "Why don't you tell me how you allowed yourself to be followed into these consecrated grounds?"

"Followed?" Camille shook her head in denial, shocked by the accusation. "That's impossible. Nobody even knows that I'm in Durham. Except of course for the man you chose and sent to the cathedral to bring me here, and he is lying dead at your feet."

It wasn't until the Raven chuckled this second time that Camille recognized its ominous quality. She backed away further into the cage as he lunged towards her. Grabbing hold of the bars, he shook the small enclosure.

"Your disrespect is unacceptable," he screamed, spittle falling from the sides of his mouth, his body trembling with fury. "Are you suggesting that I am somehow to blame for your mistake?"

He leaned forward, his beady eyes peering through the bars that he was now gripping, pushing them back and forth, the veins in his hands bulging and menacing. "Detective Xavier King is presently down in the caverns winding his way toward us even as we speak. You have made an egregious error in your judgment of his capabilities. I directed you not to come into my presence until he was eliminated. Your failure to obey my orders has now compromised not only me but every single journeyman, initiate, neophyte and footman in our sacrosanct circle."

Camille heard the words, but they made no sense to her. She was stunned at the accusation, shocked as she watched her beloved mentor aiming his fury at her. She continued stepping away from him until she felt the cold bars against her back. And there she stood, mutely listening to the Raven's tongue lashing.

"These are the same hallowed grounds that hold the remains of Saint Cuthbert. It has existed for hundreds of years, survived wars and feasts and famines. But now, because of your complete and utter incompetence, it is no longer a secure place for our assemblies and will have to be destroyed."

He took his staff and swung it at the cage, the sound of metal meeting metal reverberating so loudly that the forty ravens overhead went wild, flying and squawking at their master's rage.

He leaned toward the dented cage and spat at Camille. "You have proven to be my greatest disappointment. You honestly thought you deserved to ascend with me to the heavenlies, from where annihilation of the light is finally possible? No."

He screamed out the word, his lips curling up at the edges as the one long monosyllable howled throughout the cavern. "Instead you are worthy of the chaos that will soon consume you."

Camille watched speechlessly as the Raven spun away from her, walking away as though she didn't exist. It was the ultimate betrayal, turning his back on her just like her father had done years earlier. She felt the first seeds of anger pushing their way through her consciousness as the Raven went to the small cages and opened each. The four little ravens flew to sit on his shoulders as he disappeared down one of the long dark tunnels as mysteriously as he had arrived.

● ● ●

The underground tunnel system that William the Conqueror secretly commissioned back in 1060 when the Castle of Durham was built was not elaborate; in fact, its genius was in its simplicity.

There was one main route which went from the northern tip of the island to the southern end and bisected both the cathedral and the castle. Each end opened to a large pool of water which was separated from the river by a rudimentary lock system.

The key passageway had many branches stemming from it designed as a diversionary tactic should the enemy infiltrate the area. Each was in fact a dead-end and intended to take an adversary off course so that the entity in power at the time could effectuate an escape.

As the Raven left the grotto area behind him, he travelled north along that very tunnel system. Not only was this the faster avenue for his escape, it was in the opposite direction that Detective King and the woman with him were travelling. The last thing he needed was a confrontation with them.

55

Camille once again unlocked the padlock and stepped out of her cage, humiliated. How dare that excuse for a man spit at her! She wiped the saliva off of her cheek with the edge of her hand and shook it violently until the pile of spit fell off onto the ground.

Was that thunder she heard? She stood stock still for a moment, craning her ear. Her eyes fluttered closed and she swayed as the sound seemed to move into her body, embracing her. She approached the Raven's throne and once more sat upon it, but this time not as an interloper. She took possession of the chair, claiming it as her own. She settled into the velvet cushion, closed her eyes, and allowed her fingers to walk along each of the golden carved arms. When she finally rested her head against the exquisite brocade back, she emptied her mind of all excessive thought and drew in her breath.

She rocked back and forth, feeling the power of Scholastica merge with her own essence. She lifted her face upward, her white neck elongated and pulsing with renewed vigor, a single long scratch from one of the bird's claws marring the otherwise pristine face. Her skin was torn from just below her ear to her collar bone, a zigzag line that had turned purple at the seams from the ripping and bruising. She gripped the chair, and her body shuddered as she lifted her voice, offering an entreaty.

"I am a proven journeyman, entitled to ascend to the highest of heights and be treated with deference and dignity.

"Woe to he who has turned his back on me. Woe to the imposter who speaks of death and destruction with words and yet whose actions belie this oath. Woe to he who disregards the commitment and dedication of his flock, whose judgment is scarred by fear of his own downfall from omniscience.

"Just as Scholastica proved her superiority over her infamous brother Benedict, may I find like favor and expose the Raven's failings and misdeeds. When all is seen in the perfect shadow of evil, may the transgressions of my foe be revealed and become the cause of his own destruction."

Camille's blue eyes were opened wide and seemed transfixed on an invisible image in front of her. "Then," she bellowed, her chest heaving from the exertion, "shall he become a footstool to me, so that I might rise above his broken remains to the zenith of authority and take control of the remaining journeymen dedicated to the cause."

And as these words were spoken, the raging thunderstorm outside split through the sky, sending torrents of water upon the town of Durham, not dissimilar as happened in the days of Scholastica and her brother.

• • •

Camille leaped from the throne, charged with energy and determination; she was going hunting and the Raven was her prey.

But first she circled the cavern, wondering how he had appeared in front of her without her seeing his approach. There must be a stairwell with direct access to the cave; she couldn't imagine the Raven schlepping through the same filthy muddy tunnels she had used to arrive at this oasis.

Camille searched the obvious places first. There was nothing hidden behind the elaborate wall hangings that decorated the area, and the wall sconces did not shift and magically reveal a covert opening.

When she looked up at the magnificent ravens circling above for inspiration, she noticed one ridge in particular that was about thirty feet from the ground. She moved to inspect the dirt wall directly underneath it and detected something jutting out at about shoulder height. She placed her hand on the cold object and pulled, but there was no movement. She stepped back and looked up, carefully scrutinizing the wall. Then she smiled, realizing that a makeshift ladder had been fashioned from pitons, carefully concealed amid their natural surroundings.

Hiding in plain view. So typical of the Raven.

She hiked her skirt and carefully climbed to the upper landing, verifying her suspicion. Ahead of her was a steep pathway no doubt leading to the city above.

She wondered why the Raven didn't use this way when he left in such a fury. She knew from experience that every move on his part was calculated and deliberate. If he chose the tunnel as his way of egress, there was a damn good reason for it.

Knowing she had to follow him, she climbed back down to the ground level and set off in pursuit.

56

"There's something up ahead," X said. "Do you see the flickering light?"

"What do you think it is?" Ann asked.

X hadn't notice her labored breathing until just then. He turned and watched as she wiped the sweat off her forehead despite the chilly air. "You're winded. Why didn't you tell me I was going too fast?"

"I didn't want to slow you down. I'm fine."

He gave her the once-over, decided they could both use a rest.

"What do you say we take a break once we reach that light," he said. "It looks like it's around one more corner."

Another thumbs up from Ann and a few minutes later they rounded the bend, X leading the way. What he saw in front of him made him stop dead in his tracks; he'd never seen anything like it in his entire life.

Ann was following so closely behind him that she walked right into his backpack.

"Hey," she said as she moved around him. "Watch where you're ..."

The complaint went unfinished as her eyes grew to the size of quarters, her mouth silenced but still wide open. "Oh my God, will you look at this place?"

They stood on the cusp of the huge grotto for a moment before X took a step forward. Hearing the birds above, he looked up. "This place must be at least twenty stories high. It's amazing."

"Is there a ceiling up there?" Ann asked. "It looks like it goes on forever."

X walked further into the cave and pulled a lighter out of his pocket. Raising it above his head, he lit it. "See how the flame's steady? But when I move it down here," he said, leaving it at arm level, "it dances around from the wind coming through the tunnel. I'd definitely say there's a top up there somewhere, and we're at the bottom."

Candles protected by thick crystal glass pillars were everywhere, sending eerie shadows skipping along the walls.

"Is that supposed to be a throne?" Ann asked, pointing to the raised chair.

"I think so. It seems to be the focal point of the room." X moved forward, his eyes adjusting to the filtering light, when the scent of death assaulted his nostrils and he looked down. Before he had the time to warn Ann to stay back, she was at his side, gagging.

"I'm going to be sick." She rushed away with her hand over her mouth, already starting to heave.

X knew he should probably go after her but was riveted to the spot. He knelt as close to what remained of the corpse as possible without getting the blood and guts that were thrown around its perimeter on his pants. It looked like the person had been wearing a robe, but it was now shredded, bits and pieces of its dark cloth spread all over the cavern. The birds no doubt had dropped them haphazardly during flight.

Except for a few lonely clumps of dark hair, the skull looked like it had been licked clean. In fact, there was barely any skin left on the body and it appeared that the birds overhead were just starting to feast on the organs.

"It's definitely not Camille Lopez, unless she is really a he," X called out. He stood up, looking for something to cover the body with, and grabbed the Oriental rug that was on the raised dais. He quickly threw it over the grotesque lifeless form as he saw Ann returning in his direction.

"Are you OK? You look pale," he said as he brushed her cheek with his fingertips.

"I'm better now, but Xavier, what happened to that body? It looked like it was ripped apart."

"My guess is that the person was killed first. The birds scavenged the body after the fact."

"Not just any birds. Ravens," added Ann as one of the large black crows flew just over their heads. Ann ducked and covered while X shooed the bird away.

"Who do you think it was?" asked Ann as she walked around the mound and climbed the three stairs to the opulent seat.

X was about to tell her he had no idea but he'd already lost his audience of one. Ann's eyes, along with her complete attention, were focused on the chair.

"This thing is made of gold; my God, it must be worth a fortune. And look at the jewels decorating the cushion."

She ran her hand over the velvet fabric, her fingers coming to a stop at a string of sapphires. "This is supposed to be a tassel. Can you believe that?" she said, clearly awestruck.

X was poking his finger into one of four birdcages that stood surrounding the throne. "These look a little small for the ravens flying around here."

"You're right, there's no way one could fit in there. Maybe whoever owns this place likes parakeets too."

X put his arm around Ann's shoulder and rotated her so she could see what he just noticed.

"Another cage? But that one is huge; it looks more like a jail cell."

They walked over together, X scanning the ground in front of them to make sure there were no more dead bodies to trip over.

"There's a pair of shoes in there, and a purse," Ann said as X reached in and grabbed them.

He opened the pocketbook and pulled out a comb, mirror and a hotel key. "If I were a betting man, I'd say we just found where Lopez has been stashed lately. With any luck, we're closing in on her."

"Do you think she was a prisoner?" Ann asked.

"I'm not sure. But someone was locked up in there."

Ann slowly moved to one of the marble markers. "Look; the lettering is in Greek." She kneeled down, ran her hand over the engraved words. "I wonder what it says. I don't suppose your cell has any coverage down here, does it?"

X pulled his smart phone from his pocket and flicked the switch. "Nope. And I studied Latin. But I know that if you and I put our heads together ..."

Ann turned, smiling. "You remembered I said that to you?"

"I remember everything about you," X said, hugging her to his side.

Ann's pliant body curled into his own, her warmth seeping through his shirt, a respite from their dogged search. But the reprieve was fleeting, vanishing as X felt Ann's body suddenly go rigid in his arms, heard her shrill scream as it pierced the air.

"Oh my God, what is that?"

57

Camille rushed into the same tunnel she saw the Raven leave by several minutes earlier and almost immediately was able to make out the sound of his heavy footsteps ahead of her. She slowed her pace, planting each foot gently on the ground as she proceeded forward. Having the Raven hear her coming from behind would not do.

Before long she was able to see the light from his candle shining unsteadily, creating silhouettes that danced on the walls, ghosts and goblins careening carefree and mocking those who might be afraid by their presence.

Any sound of movement from ahead stopped and now the Raven seemed to be talking to somebody. She cautiously advanced around a bend, craning her neck so she could get a look at what was going on.

The Raven was on the bank of a big pond of some kind, speaking with a young man who was wearing the robes of a neophyte. They both seemed quite animated, and if Camille didn't know better she would think they were arguing.

But a neophyte would never quarrel with the master. She certainly hadn't. She had always done his every bidding, no matter what he asked of her. Until now.

The two men walked to the far end of the water where the Raven opened what was the first visible door that Camille had seen since being underground. It led to a small room with no other apparent entry or exit.

She needed a better vantage point. Hoping that the Raven would remain distracted, she crawled along the opposite bank. Her beautiful necklace caught on something and snapped, sending the ebony beads rolling away from her. She cursed under her breath; that was her favorite piece of jewelry. Angered anew, she continued inching along until she could eavesdrop on the men's conversation.

They were standing in front of a huge antiquated knob and the new pledge was pleading. "But sir, if I open the valve everything will be destroyed. Not just the tunnels, but the beautiful grotto as well. It is where you nest."

"You have much to learn. My nest is wherever I find myself to be. Now do as I command immediately; start turning the valve."

Camille heard the Raven drone on about how there was no place he could truly call home while he was in this earthly domain and wondered how she could have bought all that crap.

She was almost close enough to make a wild leap at the Raven. She closed her hand around a sharp stone she found nearby and waited for an opportunity to strike.

Suddenly, out of the blue came the small voice of Little Forest, still sitting on the Raven's shoulder.

"My goddess. You are powerful. You can rule."

Camille felt the hair on the back of her neck stand on end as she heard the croaking words; her new two winged friend just blew it for her. She watched as the Raven's face mottled in rage, as he drew away from the neophyte and faced the empty enclave, glaring into the obscure landscape, a look of confusion on his face.

This was it, time to make her move. She shifted onto her knees and then launched herself in the Raven's direction.

She hit him, unawares, square in the chest. He fell straight backward like a domino with her on top of him, and he fell hard. She heard the thud of his shoulders hitting the ground, felt his ribs protesting when her added weight slammed against them and finally cracked once; no twice. It ended up being three times; she'd succeeded in breaking three of his ribs. How he had been able to hold his head up so it didn't slam into the ground she didn't know.

She scrambled away, grabbing for the rock she had dropped as his diaphragm went into intense spasms.

"Oh, poor thing, did you get the wind knocked out of you?" Camille questioned, like she really gave a damn about this man. He was just another traitor, just like her father and Henry. She took a brief glance at the neophyte and saw that he was still at his assigned post but looking like he might soon join the fray. She returned her gaze to the Raven.

"Here, maybe this will make you feel better." Camille pulled her arm back and swung it at his torso, aiming the makeshift weapon at his heart.

The Raven grunted at the blow, though the rock did not penetrate his skin. His breathing was normalizing, and Camille knew he would soon be recovered from the fall and able to fight back.

Changing plans, Camille threw punches at his head hoping that with the rock the impact would be enough to cause at least a concussion, though she was shooting for a skull fracture or brain aneurism.

She was mid-throw when the Raven's arm reached up and grabbed her wrist. Camille dropped the stone and turned to run, hoping that another plan would come to mind later.

"What's the matter, my pet?" The Raven sat up, laughing, as Camille struggled to pull her arm free from him. "Don't you want to play anymore?" With one violent motion, he yanked her back onto the ground before shaking his hand free of her.

The Raven rubbed the spot on his chest where she had hit, seething. "You ingrate; how dare you lift your hand against me." He pushed himself off the ground and kicked her side, his voice rising to a decibel she had never heard from him before as he yelled, "You are worse than a spineless snake; have you no shame at all?"

She instinctively curled into the fetal position as the Raven swung his right leg back before kicking her again, the toe of his black shoe connecting with the same spot he'd just struck. He stretched his arm out, pointing his finger toward the stagnant dank pond. "Slither into the water before I throw you in myself."

Camille's eyes blazed up at him as she pounded the ground with her fist, hating herself for having to do what she was about to do. But she had no choice; the Raven had the upper hand, at least for now. So she swallowed her pride and started crawling toward the pond's edge, its revolting stench making her want to puke on the spot.

"Not fast enough," the Raven shouted as he leaned over and grabbed her around the waist, hoisting her up and throwing her through the air.

She landed hard, face down in the water, every inch of her skin slapping against the surface, stinging as she descended into the murky depths. By the time she re-emerged, the Raven had returned to the far side of the pond where he was looking at her through the scope of a gun, his finger twitching on the trigger.

"What's the matter, pet? You seem surprised." He nodded his head in the direction of the small room, not more than ten yards away. "I keep a cache of toys there, just in case of a situation like this. Clairvoyance, remember? One of my many charms."

Camille's legs were dog paddling, keeping her afloat as she tried to remain calm. She could see the young trainee nearby, struggling with the huge gearshift which abutted the open door, his muscles straining against the heavy weight.

"Not surprised, just disappointed by your choice of weapon, Master. You usually use a more formidable approach in disposing of those no longer in your favor."

"You think I am going to shoot you? No, this," the Raven laughed, waving the firearm wildly about, "is to assure that you stay put while my faithful neophyte prepares for my departure. Your end will come in a torrent, and you will be swept away like that trash that you are."

It looked like junior was making progress with the ancient gearshift that the Raven had commanded him to turn. Camille watched as it slowly rotated, creaking and groaning against the effort. Then, through the open door, she thought she could see the rear wall of the room lower, revealing open air. She shook her head, trying to get the water out of her eyes so she could focus. Did that room lead outside? She saw a sudden flash of lightening split through the sky, giving her a brief glimpse of the raging waters of the River Wear, and knew she was right.

She retrained her eyes on the Raven, who was slowly walking toward the neophyte. Something was wrong with this picture. Seeing her mentor flee into the storm made sense, but what was he talking about when he said she'd be swept away like trash?

As the wheel continued to turn, the gap in the wall widened and the turbulent River Wear started splashing inside. The Raven reached the neophyte and gave him the gun.

"If she makes a move, kill her." Then he waded into the room, the water already up past his knees, and slipped into a harness that must have been hidden somewhere inside.

A cable line whipped back and forth along with the outside winds and it took the Raven several tries before he was able to grab it. Camille was still treading water when he locked his harness into place and turned to her.

"See you in hell," he yelled as he leaped out the ever-widening opening.

He hung for only a millisecond before he disappeared from Camille's sight, likely moving upward along the cable to safety. And most assuredly to more followers who would help him in whatever endeavor he had planned next.

Camille blinked, trying to assimilate what she'd just witnessed. She needed a new strategy, wondered if there were more harnesses in that chamber. If she could get to it before junior shot her.

Suddenly everything exploded as the river violently broke through the breach, rushing forward like a tsunami. The walls of the small room detonated completely as the volcanic blast of water forged ahead. The sound was deafening, and she quickly lost sight of the young man as first the gun and then his body was carried away by the rapid flow. Camille tried desperately to swim away from the onslaught but the undercurrent made it impossible.

As she started bobbing along with the rushing water she had one conscious thought: I will not die.

58

"What in the hell is that noise?" Ann clutched at X's shirt, pulling herself closer to his chest, ducking and burrowing her head beneath his arm.

A tremendous roar came from the tunnel on the far side of the grotto followed by a loud rumble that sounded like it was getting closer; the entire cavern seemed to tremble.

X could feel Ann's body shaking, heard her terror as she stuttered out more words. "That sounds like what people describe when a tornado hits. Xavier, do you think it's a tornado?"

X shook his head, his voice calm and steady despite the terrible roar that seemed to be approaching. "No baby, not down here."

Water started pouring into the grotto from the tunnel at a pace X had never witnessed before. The closest basis for comparison he had was when he was at Niagara Falls years earlier; the power of that waterfall was jaw dropping.

But he'd been watching that fierce flow as a spectator; what he saw now coming toward them was real life, and it was moving at an alarming pace. Within seconds the water was already ankle deep.

"Hurry, let's go back the way we came." Ann tugged on X's sleeve, trying to pull him along with her.

"Not the tunnel. It's too dangerous." X yanked his arm free and started splashing around the cave. He could feel the water flowing throw his sneakers, sucking his feet against the canvas and slowing his progress.

He quickly slipped the shoes off and continued in his bare feet, felt how the hard dirt greedily absorbed the moisture and fast turned into mud. He moved around the perimeter of the grotto, his hands and eyes searching for a means of escape. By the time he came full circle back to Ann, the water was up to their knees.

She was standing in the exact same spot as when he left, arms wrapped across her chest and shivering.

"We need to get to higher ground. Ann, look at me," X said, placing his hands on either side of her face. "This is no time to freak out."

She put her hands on top of his, rubbing them gently. "OK. I'm going to try."

"See that ledge?" he said, pointing to a ridge about fifteen feet off the ground. "I'm going to climb up there first. Make sure you watch where I put my hands and feet. Once I get up there, I want you to follow. You'll only have to climb until I can reach your hands; I'll pull you up from there."

She nodded yes mutely. He clasped her hands and kissed them, then turned to the earthen wall.

There were a few rocks that made for good toeholds as X started scaling the vertical surface. It didn't take long, unfortunately, for him to realize that finding something above him to grip and hold onto was not going to be as easy. It was a slower process than he'd thought, but his hand finally found the side of the ledge. He clawed his fingers deep into the ground, felt the skin under his nails peel back leaving the sensitive nail bed raw. He ignored the pain, continued to push down into the earth until he was sure that he had a solid hold and then pulled himself up and over the ledge.

X was out of breath but didn't waste a minute. He immediately lay down on his stomach, his arms and chest reaching over the ledge toward Ann. "Come on, it's your turn now."

Overhead, the ravens were flying around madly, like kamikaze divers realizing for the first time, deep down, that they were going to die.

He watched as Ann moved toward the dirt wall like a zombie, how she didn't even flinch when one of the birds got close enough for its wings to actually brush across her back. It looked like her body was present but her mind was lost somewhere in abject terror. She reached her arm up leadenly and grasped a stone just above her head.

"That's good Ann. Now try to find a toe-hold around knee level and push yourself up so you can grab onto one of those rocks just above you on your left."

As soon as she lifted her right leg she lost her balance and slipped into the water.

X felt his heart stop until he saw that her head was above the water line; she must be on her hands and knees. He tried to quell the panic, knew it was a useless emotion as he screamed, "Ann, I'm coming."

But before he was even off his stomach she was back up on her feet, blinking the water from her eyes.

"I'm OK," she yelled up.

The adrenaline that had just shot through his system calmed down when he heard her voice; she sounded amazingly strong and steady.

And he could see a shift in her demeanor as well, in her stance. The way she was appraising the wall in front of her looked almost feral from his vantage point. He was so incredibly proud of her as he watched courage overtake her fear.

"Just take a few deep breaths," X called down, though he was talking to himself as well. "You can do it. Just reach for that rock above your right hand and try to pull yourself up."

She did much better on her second try, moving slowly upwards until she finally leveraged her body high enough for X to grip her forearms and drag her onto the narrow shelf of earth.

X pulled her back from the edge until they were against the earthen wall about four feet behind, hugging her, brushing back her wet hair, wanting to inspect every inch of her body to make sure she hadn't hurt herself when she fell. "You did great, Ann," he said as he cradled her head against his chest. "We should be safe here.

"At least for now."

59

Camille's body torpedoed under the current, slamming against something hard; whether it was a wall or the ground she wasn't sure. She was holding her breath, counting the seconds. Seventy-nine, eighty, eighty-one. She wasn't sure how much longer she could hold on. Her chest was burning and she frantically reached her arms up and out in every direction, hoping to break through the water. She felt an undercurrent beneath her and suddenly her body popped through the water like a bobbin. She gasped for air, sucking in the oxygen.

Was that her making that noise? It sounded like someone with severe emphysema struggling for a breath, but with each hoarse raspy lungful of air she felt better until she was finally able to stop worrying about dying then and there. She had business to take care of and anything other than accomplishing her goal, of finding and extinguishing the Raven, was simply not acceptable.

Camille floated along with the upper portion of her torso above the water's surface, trying to use her arms like oars to move left or right; they ended up being more like bumper guards as she smashed into floating debris and walls. With her legs she tried to maintain a constant dog paddle, but because of the water's turbulence she often ended up kicking her feet into the hard ground.

Memories flashed through Camille's mind of when she was a kid. She'd always been an avid swimmer and now some of the basic rules of water safety came back to her. Rather than fighting the treacherous flow, why not allow her body to move along with it as naturally as possible? She turned onto her back and tried to float on top of the current.

Immediately water went up her nose and she sputtered. Wrong direction, silly; head against the current, not feet. She angled herself around and willed herself to remain calm.

This method was definitely not a miracle cure to her problem. She continued to take some hard hits against the narrow confines of the tunnel and the flow often left her submerged, but she basically stayed afloat.

Focus, focus, focus, she repeated to herself as she sped along with the tide. She needed to conserve as much energy as possible and keep her eyes open so she could track her surroundings. She knew that once she reached the grotto she had to be able to somehow get to the exit she'd found earlier.

Otherwise, she was a goner.

60

On hands and knees, Ann and X peeked over the edge of the ridge and watched the torrent below. Water was billowing from the main tunnel at the head of the cave before sweeping through and spilling into the tunnel they had travelled at the opposite end.

"Where is it all coming from?" Ann had to yell to be heard above the din, and even then her words seemed to whip away in the wind.

"It must be the river. It's like a levee was breached or something." X's eyes scanned for a way to higher ground, scoping the upper recesses of the cavern.

Ann scooted backwards until she was flat against the wall again. Pulling her knees up against her chest, she called out, "You don't think the water will reach us here, do you?"

X moved back so that he was sitting next to her. "I don't know." He looked into her eyes, took a breath, and went on. "But just in case it does, we need to be ready. I see something over there," he said, pointing to one of the few ridges above them; it was about 30 yards away and at least twice as far above the ground as where they were. "You stay here and rest while I check it out. If it looks safe, I'll come back for you, and we'll go together."

When he tried to stand up, Ann grabbed at his arm, clinging to him, screaming, "No, you can't leave me here alone."

It tore at his heart, seeing that whatever hold she'd had on her emotions was now gone as tears streamed down her face.

"I'll be back before you know it. Here," he said as calmly as he could as he took off the backpack and put it at her side. "Why don't you have an energy bar while you wait? You'll feel much better with something in your stomach."

She bit her lip and blinked back her tears as he kissed her on the forehead. He saw her lips moving, read them more than heard her say, "Be careful."

Turning away from her was one the hardest things X had ever done. He felt like a major jerk, leaving her so scared and vulnerable. But staying at her side and making pretend things were going to work out alright despite the chaos going on below was not an option.

So he continued his course, not looking back. He moved carefully along the narrow ridge, leaning his body inward toward the wall, hoping that the weight of his body and the laws of gravity would help keep him safely on the ledge.

When X finally arrived directly below the ridge he realized that it would be a lot harder to get to than he thought. Nature hadn't provided nearly as many notches or footholds to grab on to as the wall of earth they'd just scaled.

He looked across the gap toward Ann, put his hand to his mouth and gently blew her a kiss. Then he turned to the unforgiving perpendicular surface in front on him.

X ran his hands over the dirt wall; it was rock hard dry, though in some places water seeping from above loosened the dirt into a thick muddy substance. His progress upward was slow, and he had to mentally remind himself that speed was not a pressing issue at this point. He and Ann were both safely above the fray, at least for now.

X used his trusty pocketknife to cut notches into the earth and then used them as toeholds. Next he would search for anything within arms' distance to grab hold of, pulling himself up higher before making yet another groove for his foot to dig into for stability.

He knew that this was just a test run, and although each step that he progressed was a small victory, it would mean nothing if the climb proved too difficult for Ann when it came time for her to make it.

X's arms were aching by the time he neared the ledge, the sweat falling into his eyes clouding his vision. Ignoring the impulse to rub them, he reached up with his left arm and finally felt the edge of the platform above.

X's fingers found a thick vine and he grabbed on, yanking it to test its strength. It felt steady and strong and X climbed it like the ropes he had in gym class when he was a kid, one hand over the other, slowly progressing until with one last tremendous effort he broke even with the ledge.

Arms exhausted, X shimmied his torso onto the outcropping of solid earth, resting for a brief moment.

And in that moment the edge broke away and X fell, grasping for the vine. His fingers made contact, slipped away, and then found new purchase, his body swaying in midair.

Even as disoriented as he was, X felt the jerk downward. It was only a few inches, and then a few inches more. And then the one connection he had to solid ground gave way.

The moment was suspended in time as X looked down at his left hand, still clutching a small piece of the vine that was now falling past him, its dry roots scratching against X's cheek as they flew by. Then he was tumbling outward, arms and legs flailing. He knew impact was coming, and he tried to brace himself.

But his collision with the water below was far worse than he imagined. He landed flat on his back, his head snapping forward before dropping below the surface. His entire body felt like it had been stung by a thousand bees, and he struggled to resurface before he passed out.

61

Being the head of CS wasn't the most exciting position in the world, if what you considered exciting was solving crimes. Over the years, William had dealt with robberies, rapes and yes, even several murders. But nothing had caught his attention as much as what he was reading about a woman named Camille Lopez.

William googled Xavier King as soon his son and his new friends left his office. From there, information about the happenings at Gulf Cove, Long Island, and the woman named Camille Lopez was abundant. Saying that the New York authorities wanted to talk to Ms. Lopez was an understatement; she apparently was wanted for four murders.

William picked up his cell phone and dialed Frederick, who answered promptly. "Hey, Dad, you caught me just in time. I'm just on my way into the library and was about to turn my phone off."

"Glad I did. Curiosity has gotten the better of me. What makes your Mr. King think that the woman he's looking for is here in Durham?"

"Oh, well it's a bit peculiar, actually. He thinks that she might have been attracted to this particular city because of the cathedral and Saint Cuthbert's affinity to ravens, that there's some kind of cult she's involved with."

"And what services did he hire you for, then? Surely not to give the standard tour."

"No, I'm actually going to be using my background in history and revisit some of the old handwritten journals from the early years, see if I can flesh out any hint of secret rooms or tunnels. X thinks that's where this cult might be meeting. Plus I've got copies of all of the architectural drawings of both the castle and the cathedral on reserve. Maybe I'll spot something I haven't noticed before."

"Sounds safe enough," William said.

"What do you mean by that?"

"Nothing, Son. I'll talk to you later."

William closed his cell phone and looked back at his computer screen, where the grainy image of the two people entering door #666 taunted him.

'Odd,' he thought. 'All the other doors in that building start with the number four.'

He checked his wallet, making sure his master key card was there, and headed for the door calling, "Katie, I'm off for a bit. Take care of business while I'm gone."

• • •

It took only five minutes from the time William walked through door #666 to find the gaping hole in the wall on the third floor. Of course the hard work had already been done; X had apparently first discovered the hidden entrance and then somehow opened it.

William was now moving down the steep stairwell, chastising himself for forgetting a flashlight; he was enveloped in darkness and knew that a fall could be fatal.

William carefully moved his left foot forward until he could feel the step's outer perimeter, nothing but a sudden drop into the blackness beyond its edge. Then slowly he inched downward to the stair below, holding on to the earthen walls surrounding him as he descended, step by step in this same way, until he heard the noise.

It was a horrendous sound, as though a bomb had detonated. William covered his ears, the noise deafening, as the entire shaft rumbled. Disoriented, he fell, toppling down the remaining stairs until he landed on terra firma, thanking God he'd been so close to the bottom.

William rolled over onto his hands and knees until his racing heart, pounding against his chest, finally started to stabilize and with it his breathing.

From the corner of his eye William thought he saw a faint flickering light. He'd been in the dark so long he worried it might be a mirage but he crawled in its direction anyway. When he saw the small table ensconced in the wall he told his mind not to get too excited; he wouldn't believe it until he could feel it with his own hands.

Within seconds William had confirmation. Not only was it a table, it was sturdy enough for him to use to pull himself up. Once standing, he focused on the nearly burned out candle sitting in the middle of the table.

William's eyes were immediately assaulted with pin flashes of light, a virtual kaleidoscope of color so brilliant it was painful. He snapped his eyes closed until the dancing light show calmed and then tried again, this time giving his eyes time to acclimate to his surroundings before reaching for the candle.

Taper in hand, William turned to get a look at where he was. The choppy air current immediately threatened the flame and, not wanting to lose his only source of light, he carefully returned it to the table, pushing it to the deepest part of the alcove where it was sheltered. He saw the row of new candles and was able to get three to stay lit, deciding to leave all but one in the protected niche.

With his hand sheltering that one candle William moved forward, finally recognizing the booming sound that reverberated around the cavern. It was water, and not a babbling brook.

It wasn't until he turned a corner that he saw the unreal image; it looked like a tidal wave had been unleashed. About a foot below where he was standing there was a river that could not be contained in the limited space carved out for it. It was Mother Nature at her worst, a ferocious torrent with wave crashing over wave, the spray drenching his pants, stinging his skin as it slapped against him.

William stood, awestruck by the fury. He was looking upstream, wondering what the source of the onslaught could possibly be, when he noticed something thrashing on top of the current. It was impossible to tell for sure, but he thought he saw an arm break through the water, and then a head; oh dear God, it was a person.

William dropped to the ground, the candle forgotten and the jolt enough to send his glasses flying into the air and break apart. The barreling wind stung his eyes; he squinted, trying to keep the dark form in view. If the body came within reaching distance, he was going to grab for it.

Within seconds he could make out the form aiming directly at him. He lowered his arms into the water and readied himself for impact.

William's game plan formed quickly; take advantage of the current's energy. If he could reach under the torso early enough upstream he could sweep the body toward the shore. And if he got really lucky and the water's momentum was right, he just might be able to hoist the person up to dry land.

62

X's body whipped along with the current, taking a lot of punishment. He couldn't count how many times he'd crashed against the winding channel's walls. He wasn't sure if he'd actually lost consciousness, but he had no memory between the time he hit the water in the grotto and when he re-entered the tunnels. He tried to keep his head above the water, the scenery passing so quickly he almost missed the neon green piece of tape flapping wildly in the wind. He was barreling down the same chute he and Ann had used when they came into the passageway.

He thanked God that he hadn't been sucked into any of the dead end branches, at least not so far. He didn't think it would be humanly possible to survive if that happened. The water, having nowhere else to flow, would pool up to the ceiling. There would be no air and he would die. He fought for random gulps of air, knowing that he had to survive; Ann needed him.

He didn't see the figure that was fast approaching. Suddenly he felt something grab around his body and hold firm. The next thing he knew his upper body was being hauled onto the water's bank. X clawed at the dry ground, helping to drag himself further onto shore while his rescuer reached back down and pulled first one leg, and then the other, out of the flood.

X coughed out the water that had accumulated in his lungs, exhausted. Pain radiated throughout his body, but he didn't think anything was broken. Just in case, he cautiously did a body check, slowly moving his limbs and bending joints. Everything seemed to be in working order.

He gingerly stood up and walked closer to the guy who'd just saved his life.

"I don't know how to thank …" X stopped mid-sentence when he recognized that the man was William Barnestable.

"How in the world did you know where to find me?"

William held up a finger while he took a few deep breaths, finally able to speak.

"After you left my office this morning I did a little digging on this Camille Lopez character and realized that the situation was a lot more dangerous than you let on. It's a good thing I followed my instincts and came looking for you," he added. "You were in some serious trouble there."

"I'm not the one you should be worried about," X said, the relief of being on dry ground short lived. "Ann is still out there. I've got to find her." He heard the hysteria in his own voice, felt it in every beat of his heart.

William rushed past him back to the water's edge, his eyes scanning for another body. "Was she with you? Between the darkness and the water moving so fast I could barely make you out, and you're a lot bigger than she is."

X grabbed on to William's arm and pulled him back several feet. "She's not out there. When I last saw her she was about a mile upstream, on a ledge fifteen feet above water level. It's in a big cavern so I think she'll be safe at that elevation, but she must be scared out of her mind."

"A cavern? This is all insane. I never even knew anything existed down here." Then, looking up into X's eyes, he said, "There's no way you're going to be able to get to her from here. There's got to be another way. Let's get back up to sea level; we'll have come up with a plan by then."

63

Camille knew that her one shot at safety was soon approaching. She wasn't exactly sure what would happen when the comparatively small channel of water she was travelling in met with the large grotto area. She figured that the flow would disperse, and hopefully the power of the current would too. That would be her chance to swim to the spot she'd found earlier; from there she knew she could climb up the side of the grotto.

Reality was not so kind. Just as she was spit into the cavern she got sucked under, where the water spun in a cyclonic frenzy. It was like being in a blender, her arms and legs becoming weapons against each other as her limbs thrashed with the violence of the current. She struggled desperately, but no matter her efforts she could not get her head above water. She tried to remain calm, counting the seconds as she continued to hold her breath.

Camille wasn't sure how much longer she could go without air and for the first time entertained the thought that she was not going to make it out alive. In a panicked effort for air she opened her mouth and instead ended up sucking in water. She felt a crush of burning pain explode across her chest as it went down her airway; she knew it wouldn't be long before she lost consciousness.

Scholastica, she prayed. Where are you?

Her prayer went unanswered as she felt her entire body getting sucked down to the floor of the cave. She tried to get some traction, tried pushing herself off of the ground with her hands, her feet, an elbow, anything to penetrate the current above her. But it was like trying to break through a brick wall; it wasn't going to happen.

And that was when the miracle occurred.

A fierce undercurrent developed out of the blue, whiplashing her body with its powerful force; within seconds it spun her off to the side and out of the eye of the storm.

When her head finally broke through the water she gasped for air, greedily sucking it in. Her stomach heaved, and she threw up the river water that was in her lungs, coughing and sputtering and still not getting nearly as much air as she craved.

It wasn't until she finally got her breathing regulated that she looked around. Camille found herself at the periphery of the cavern and extended her legs straight down, finally able to touch bottom. Even though the water was chest high and the tide was relatively strong, she was able to walk along the outside edge of the cave until she found the makeshift ladder left by the Raven.

He would choke when he found out that she survived because of him. Oh she loved irony. She started her climb upwards, the crazed cries and flapping wings of the forty ravens sounding to her like applause for her good fortune.

64

Ann sat in frozen terror as in her mind's eye she watched a rerun of X falling into the water and then vanishing. Clinically she recognized that she was in shock, and her medical background fought ferociously to regain control of her mind, to squash the paralyzing fear that was overtaking her.

She had to pull herself together. She went through the backpack and forced herself to eat two of the energy bars. Then she opened a bottle of water and took a long sip before throwing it off the ledge. "I hate this," she raged. "X, where are you?" She stood up, the wind whipping around her so wildly that her shirt flapping against her skin stung.

Ann hated heights. But the only thought that frightened her more than having to climb higher up this godforsaken cavern was the thought of remaining where she was. She knew that the gushing flood would soon reach her elevation and she would be swept away just like X had been.

Self-preservation is a strong motivator. So she followed the trail X had taken so recently. She found that if she kept her eyes focused on the narrow path just in front of her the height didn't bother her as much. She made a bargain that after every ten steps she'd reward herself by leaning against the interior wall and resting for a minute. It was during one of those short breaks that her eye caught movement up ahead of her.

At first Ann thought she was imagining it, but no, there was someone ascending the wall on the far side of the cavern. Hope surged through her body, and she screamed out X's name before realizing that the form was way too small to be him.

Ann continued yelling anyway, but whoever it was couldn't hear her with all of the thunderous noise echoing through the cavern. And as the figure reached a ledge much higher than where she was, it simply disappeared.

But that's impossible. Something so real couldn't just vanish into thin air. Was she hallucinating? Yet she was positive that what she'd just seen with her own eyes wasn't a figment of her imagination.

What to do? Ann knew the answer before the question even came to mind. She continued forward on the path until she got to the spot where X had made his ascent. She put her cheek against the wall, said "I love you," but then kept on going. What she needed to do was make her way to where she'd last seen that person; maybe then she could figure out where they went.

Ann slowly moved forward, at times walking, more often crawling. Every so often she allowed herself to look down at the rising water. Even though it terrified her, it did serve the purpose of making her move at a quicker pace. And finally she reached her destination.

Exhausted, she lay face down on the ground, resting her head on her crossed forearms. Then she turned her head toward the wall.

What in the world? She was back on her feet, staring at the solidly constructed rungs that started from somewhere below the raging waters and reached upward toward the upper recesses of the cavern.

She stamped her feet and pulled her hair, cursing God. If only they'd had more time to explore the cave before the tsunami or whatever the hell it was that hit, X would surely have found this spot. Someone had purposefully designed this as a way to reach the higher elevations of the grotto.

She looked up at the trail of rungs. She could do this. All she had to do was take it one step at a time.

Ann slowly climbed her way up to the ridge where the stranger had disappeared. She found herself on a ledge much wider than the one she'd just left behind, and it seemed somehow groomed. There was no loose gravel or dirt; it almost looked like poured concrete.

Then she saw the gap in the dirt wall, more like a small opening to a cave. She put her hands together, praying that it would end up being her means of escape. Everything had been such a huge ordeal up to this point that she never dreamed the next part would be so easy. She tip toed over to the spot, as though she might spook away the vision by her proximity.

Ann walked through the entrance and there, in plain view, was a dirt pathway that led upwards. She was so happy she started crying; even though she didn't know where the trail would lead, she didn't care. There was only one thing she was certain of, and that was her desire to get the hell out of where she was as soon as humanly possible.

Just as she was about start up the trail something caught her attention to her side, a flash of sudden movement. She raised her arm instinctively to protect herself, but not before the blurry form of a person swung a club at her. The last thing she remembered was the pain as it hit her head; then blackness.

65

It had been a spectacular exit: him leaping into the apparent void, only to be held in the cocoon of his harness and lifted out of harm's way.

The Raven smiled at the thought of Camille Lopez being swept away by the flood that was unleashed just moments after his escape. What a wonderful way to get rid of garbage such as her. He took great satisfaction in thinking of the fear she must have experienced before taking her last breath.

That satisfaction, however, was being tempered by the minute. The storm was taking its toll, and while his young initiates were cranking the cable line to raise him up to ground level, he was sitting in the harness like a baby in a wet diaper, drenched by rain and ricocheted about like a feather.

Unbidden came memories of his father.

Liam Gruman. He was a self-made multimillionaire who took advantage of the desperate circumstances of the Post World War II era and created an empire that he left for his son to carry on.

Of course what he'd done wasn't legal, but that was irrelevant. How could one disapprove of the entrepreneurial spirit that Liam possessed?

It had all started here in Durham, in the castle that the Raven was dangling below right this very minute. His father was working as the foreman of a reconstruction project of the famous Norman Chapel when he found a hidden panel behind the altar. And when he went back to investigate in the dark of night when nobody else was present, he discovered not just a large unoccupied space.

What he discovered was an opportunity.

Food was being rationed at the time, which created a niche market opportunity for someone with broad vision and a small moral compass. Liam jumped into the black market business with abandon, using the space behind the Norman Chapel as a pantry for his stockpiles. He taught his only child all the tricks of the trade during his formative years. Life was incredibly good.

And then one day it wasn't.

His father was diagnosed with a rare type of cancer that was already present in five organs. The most the doctors could do was to try and make their patient comfortable until the end came.

Why did he always remember his dearly departed father as he was at the end of his life? Wearing diapers, unable to control his bladder or bowels, suffering one indignity after another.

The Raven looked down at the harness; not an offending diaper, at least not yet for him. But his time would come. Because he had the same cancer that had so mercilessly killed his father.

The cold hard rain continued to pelt his face as he remembered the moment his doctor told him the bad news. His first thought was of exacting revenge on a God that didn't seem to care.

And then the idea was conceived. He would create his own hierarchy of power where he was the almighty ruler, the only source of hope and trust to his followers. He would lead them to the ultimate victory of darkness over light.

Since that day over 30 years ago the Raven was able to amass a huge fortune by continuing the black market business. Equally important, however, was that in doing so he was able to make contact with the very sort of person he was looking for to join his sect. Someone without scruples, disconcerted with the failed promises of an unreliable God.

He laughed, thinking of the fictitious life history he had created for himself and told his followers. They were so eager to be accepted, to belong, that they would have believed anything he told them. The thought of sharing something as personal as the truth with any of those unenlightened beings was simply preposterous.

A loud crack of thunder drew him out of his reverie just as he was being hoisted onto terra firma. He allowed his followers to wrap him in a dry blanket, quite a privilege for those of such a lowly stature, and then led them to the secret castle door that nobody knew about other than himself.

There was one downside of this entryway; he would have to use the common hallways in order to reach his hidden rectory. He hated having to interact with mere mortals of lesser mystical aptitude.

"Got caught in the storm, did you?" said a passerby as the Raven was about to enter the Norman Chapel.

The Raven gave the ponytailed man his most frigid stare as he walked silently by. And as he hastened into the chapel with his three followers in tow he heard the stranger in the hallway call out, "No need to be rude."

66

X crawled out into the third floor room where he and Ann had started their journey hours before and blinked his eyes, trying to adjust to the light. Not that it was very bright; through the window he could see that it was pouring rain outside. William followed a few seconds later, his cell phone in hand.

"Still no signal; I thought it was because we were so far underground, but I guess the weather is messing it up."

X was worn out, the enormity of what he'd been through just now sinking in. "I can't even count how many times I almost died down there; what if something terrible has happened to Ann?"

William approached X's still form, putting a hand on his shoulder. "You can't be thinking that way. If you made it out, so can she."

X looked into the pair of kind-hearted eyes, eyes that bespoke empathy but not pity, and something even more than that. Hope. Then William turned the knife, adding, "Your girl is counting on you."

Those last words hit like a whip, stinging worse than any other pain X could imagine. Ann might need him, right this very minute, and here he was wasting precious time.

"You're right," X said, resolutely shaking off anything but positive thoughts from here on out. He visualized her, safe and sound and busy thinking up ways to torture him for getting her involved in such a mess in the first place. He'd probably lost back rub privileges for months to come.

It felt good when the wheels of his brain started to work again. "Didn't you say you spoke with Frederick right before you came down the hidden stairs? So he's aware that a concealed underground actually exists?"

"That's right," William confirmed, "and he was bound and determined to find documentation confirming its existence, even if he had to pull every single book, map, and private journal in the library looking for it.

"I say we start with him, see if he's come up with anything. I'll bring my people into the loop as soon as I'm able to contact them."

"Agreed. Let's get going," X said, not caring that he was barefooted and his clothes were soaking wet.

Because he had nothing but positive thoughts.

From here on out.

67

It seemed like forever ago that Camille had started up the dirt pathway that she was counting on bringing her up and out of the cave. Exhausted, she realized that she hadn't eaten in days and was likely severely dehydrated as well. She was having difficulty walking, and her feet were dragging.

She decided to take a rest, sitting as gracefully as possible on the hard earth. Just because she was in some underground hellhole didn't mean she should abandon all etiquette standards. She looked down at her once beautiful outfit. The sheer blouse looked more like a used coffee filter, dirt caked in, on, and under it. Her skirt; well, it had lost its shape as soon as she hit the water in that pond.

Thinking about the ordeal the Raven had put her through made her furious. There was that one bright spot, though; taking care of the woman who'd materialized out of thin air.

The memory of holding the club it in her hands, of batting it forward until wood connected with bone, dropping the woman on the spot … well, it just warmed the cockles of her heart.

Camille had no idea who the person was, had never seen her at any of the Raven's assemblies. Oh well, call it a pre-emptive strike. Whoever it was wouldn't be bothering her any time soon.

Usually reliving an attack like that, going over the gory details, refreshed and restored her. But right now Camille simply felt drained. Apparently her brain was as tired as her body. There was nothing but mush between her ears and that fact was alarming. How could she outwit the Raven if she wasn't at her best?

Despite everything that had occurred, or maybe because of it, she was determined to hunt that man down and kill him. Slowly. And painfully.

So she stood back up and continued walking. And her resolve paid off. Within a few minutes she came upon one of the few hand railings that had appeared at intermittent intervals along the trail. She grabbed it with both hands, steadying herself. Mere feet away, the dirt pathway ended with 10 treads embedded into the earth sloping up so sharply that they were almost vertical. It was a harrowing stairwell with only an old worn out rope hanging from insecure looking posts as a guardrail. She looked up to the top and saw a shadow of light spilling from an open doorway. From her angle she could see that there were a few people standing just outside of the door.

Then she heard a voice. His voice.

"I thank you, brethren, for escorting me to my rectory. Now await me in the chapel; I will call for you when I am ready to depart for Rome."

She laughed, the cackling the sound of the insane. So the Raven had made his way through the storm only to fall back into her sights. Saint Scholastica must be watching over me, she thought, giving me another opportunity to debase my tormentor. She took a deep breath, inhaling the wonderful oxygen that she'd never take for granted again, not since the frankly quite upsetting experience in the ferocious waters below.

Camille took advantage of the noise made by the three men as they complied with the Raven's command and left the room. She climbed each step carefully until she was in the hallway, mere feet from her old mentor.

Why he didn't close the door she wasn't sure. But it gave her the opportunity she was looking for.

There stood that good for nothing excuse of a man, clothed to perfection and kicking a pile of wet, discarded garments into a corner.

Camille watched as he looked into a case filled with gold bars, how he smiled at them like he used to smile at her. Then he took a key from around his neck and opened a lock that was on the large refrigerator pushed against the wall.

It seemed odd to have such a large appliance in an office; one of those mini models, maybe. But that thing was huge.

That's when Camille noticed the cooler on the floor. She watched as the Raven covered its bottom with ice before transferring dozens of small vials of liquid from the refrigerator. There was a side compartment which he filled with syringes.

When the Raven turned and saw Camille framing the doorway he dropped the bottle he was holding, small white pills rolling out of its open top. He staggered back a few steps, staring at her like she was a ghost, pointing at her saying, "You."

The satisfaction of seeing the surprised look on the Raven's face when he realized she was still alive was fleeting, trumped instead by the depths of his betrayal.

"You bastard," she raged. "You don't have supernatural powers at all. You just drug us so we'll listen to you."

She advanced on him rapidly, shoving him with everything she had left in her. Not the best strategy, she reasoned, as they both fell to the floor from the momentum.

Then the back stabbing excuse of a man started crawling away.

"Not so fast," she said. She was still on the ground, but was now clutching the briefcase against her chest. "If you want your gold, you better start talking."

The Raven stood up, brushing dust off the sleeves of his jacket and seeming to pay her no mind whatsoever. Camille had gotten used to the many tones he used when speaking, depending on his mood or the circumstances; he now chose patronizing.

"Oh Camille, again you disappoint me. Do you really think I care about that paltry amount of gold? Go on ahead, take it. But I would spend it quickly if I were you; your lifespan has just been dramatically reduced."

She came to her feet and stood perfectly erect, her head held high. "You've tried to kill me before, yet here I am."

She motioned with her head towards the cooler. "I've got to hand it to you, drugging me into believing all of your lies. You must think you're pretty smart."

She walked over to a nearby desk that was stacked with papers and swept them off onto the floor before placing the briefcase on top. That's when she saw the small black weapon and wrapped her hand around its handle.

"I changed my mind; you're not so smart after all."

She turned toward the Raven, the revolver he'd left on the desk in her hand. Baring her teeth, she slowly approached, aiming the .357 Magnum right between his eyes.

68

When they got to the library they spread apart.

"You go to the left, I'll take the right," said William. "Whoever finds Frederick first grabs him; then we meet back here. It shouldn't take more than two minutes, three tops."

X was drawing quite a bit of attention as he hurried through the stacks, his clothes drenched and dirty. One student called out, "Still raining out there?" as he walked by, the words not even registering.

"He's not in there," William said when they hooked back up. "Knowing my son, the only reason he'd stop researching something so important is that he either found what he was looking for and came looking for me or got hungry and went to the cafeteria."

"Lead the way," X said. They rushed down several hallways, the smell of institutional cooking finally wafting in the air.

One more left turn and they were there. The double doors to the eatery were opened and William spotted Frederick right away. "There he is, over there."

X was racing forward before the sentence was even completed.

Frederick dropped the pastry which was midway to his mouth when he saw them approach.

"Good Lord, what happened to you? You look even worse than those poor sods I just saw drag themselves in from the rain."

"I don't have time to explain it all to you right now," X said, the words tumbling out. "Suffice it to say that Ann and I got separated and I need to get back down there.

"Whoever dug out the tunnels and found the cavern must have built a levee or something to keep the river out. Or maybe the point was to access the river in the event of an emergency. It doesn't really matter; all I know is that the entire area is being flooded by the likes of something you'd see in a horror film.

"There has to be another way to get down there," X continued, almost hysterical. "I was pretty disoriented, but I think the water was flowing from the northern part of the island. If I have to, I'll go in where the breach occurred."

William vetoed that idea. "You can't do that; it would be suicide."

As the two men argued the merits of X's plan, the conversation at a nearby table of students caught Frederick's attention.

"You mean we're in lock down mode?" he asked one of the co-eds.

Someone answered. "As of 4:30, the gate was closed to anyone coming in or going out of this area. They say the weather is so bad that they fear a flash flood."

Frederick looked at his watch and then to his new friend.

"X, I saw a group of people not ten minutes ago walking down the hall who looked like they'd just braved the elements. But apparently the gate house has been locked for the past 45 minutes."

"What are you talking about?" X asked. He knew he shouldn't be angry, none of this was Frederick's fault, but he didn't have time to waste on irrelevant trivia.

"Just listen," said Frederick before interrupting the nearby students.

"I didn't mean to eavesdrop, but I heard you say that the gate is closed down. How did you hear about that?"

One of the guys answered. "There was an announcement on the PA system. I'm surprised you didn't hear it."

"I probably had my headphones on," answered Frederick.

"Plus there are signs on the exit doors," added another student, "which is rather thoughtful. No need to bother heading out if you can't pass through the gate anyway."

Then it clicked in X's mind. "If the gate is closed, why would any-one be walking around outside?"

"They wouldn't," answered Frederick. "Unless they didn't use the gate."

"Where were the people you said you saw?"

"They were heading into the Norman Chapel. Follow me, I'll show you."

69

Camille wondered why the Raven seemed unperturbed by having his own gun aimed at him. Instead he laughed, backing away several steps without any outward signs of fear.

"You think I've been drugging you? Well," the Raven conceded, "I actually have, on occasion. Not that you seemed to mind."

Camille brushed her blonde hair away from her face, streaking dirt across her cheek as she snarled at the Raven. "You've said that the only way to experience true ecstasy, to pass through the shadow of evil, is to become food for the raven. If you tell me how you're able to do this, right now, I'll consider sparing your life."

There was amusement in the Raven's eyes as he answered.

"You think it is within your control whether I live or die? You are more naïve than I thought. Can you not see that I am already dead?"

"Clearly you're not dead," Camille said, annoyed. "There you stand, not only talking to me but giving me another load of your crap."

The Raven pointed to the cooler. "But for the marvels of modern medicine, I would have been lying in the grave decades ago. True, I might appear to be alive. But again you are missing the essence of my message.

"If you search the truth you will realize that the state of being alive and being dead are not mutually exclusive."

"What does any of that have to do with being food for the ravens?" Camille sighted the gun on him then repeated her demand. "Tell me why the damn birds dig into your skin and eat but won't touch mine. Or else," she said, taking a few steps forward and putting the gun to her mentor's temple. She leaned in close so she could whisper her final good bye into his ear.

"Oh my God, what is that?" she said, covering her nose and mouth as the awful stench assaulted her nostrils, a dreadful combination of fecal odor, sweat and decomposition. And then a memory flashed through her mind, of recently smelling the same disgusting odor when she was struggling with the Raven at the pond's edge, down in the cavern.

"It is the core of my being, rotting away organ by organ, cell by cell. Mere humans, with their limited capacity to understand, label it cancer. Yet to me it has been a calling, an invitation to examine the lies perpetuated by society's greatest philosophers and thinkers. Instead of slowing draining life away from me, my cancer has prepared me for the total eclipse of the sun and the moon and the stars."

"Excuse me," Camille cut in, stamping her foot, "I hate to interrupt your little speech. Are you trying to say that the only reason the birds eat your flesh is because you're what amounts to a walking cadaver?"

"Are you so unsure of your own ability to interpret my statement that you require verification from me?" the Raven asked. "I am chagrined by your ineptitude but not surprised.

"I do, however, give you points on your choice of words. A walking cadaver. That describes me perfectly."

Camille's stomach recoiled as she backed away from the Raven, suddenly wanting some distance between them. "That's disgusting."

"Your memory is failing you," answered the Raven, laughing at her discomfort. "You have coveted being in my position for years. Nothing has changed."

"Except that I'm holding you at gunpoint," Camille answered, quite pleased with herself. It had taken a lot of doing, but she finally had the tactical advantage over the Raven.

The Raven shrugged his shoulders casually, as if she was nothing but a pesky fly. "What possible harm can the gun do when I have already conceded that I am dead? The question is whether you can do the same. Because if the answer is no, you will have failed the ultimate test of worthiness. It requires relinquishing attachment to all earthly possessions and desires. Instead of living, you suddenly recognize with relief that you are in reality dying."

The Raven ever so slowly approached as he was speaking, the intonation of his words, their cryptic meaning, starting to entrap her mind. Damn him; she needed to stay on her toes, not let him manipulate her.

She was tired, hungry, mad, and her nerves were frayed. So when she heard the unexpected sound of a door banging open, she did what any girl in her situation would do.

Shoot first and ask questions later.

70

Frederick entered the Norman Chapel first. There were three men who stood huddled together at the front of the church, eyeing the newcomers warily. Their clothes were still wet from the rain, their heads cleanly shaven.

"Those are the guys I saw in the hallway, but the tall one is missing."

X was past Frederick and had his hands gripped on the front of two of the men's shirts before they had a chance to respond. He threw them against the wall and held each with a forearm against the throat.

The third man ran down the center aisle like an offensive lineman but had no chance of getting around Frederick and his father. They each grabbed an arm and pulled him back to where his buddies struggled.

X stared down the third guy. "Your friends here have thirty seconds before I crush their windpipes. Unless you talk. Do you understand?"

He nodded.

"There was someone else with you. Was it the Raven?"

The guy looked like he'd been sucker punched as soon as X said the name.

Good; he was on the right track. X added pressure to his captives' throats and immediately their breathing became labored.

"Fifteen seconds left and these two die. Where did the Raven go?"

"Through there", the man finally said, indicating with his head. "There's a door behind the tapestry; just go through and you'll end up in a small hallway. He's in his office, just to the right."

X let go of the two men and ran toward the wall hanging. He grabbed it from each side and tore it away from the elaborate golden rod that it was hanging from. As promised, a hidden entrance was carved into the wall. He put his arms straight out and rammed them against the door, sending is banging open against the far wall

• • •

The sound of the gunshot echoed off the walls.

X instinctively dropped to the ground, minimizing his chances of being hit by a stray bullet. Seeing no one in his direct line of sight, he ran to the open doorway to his right.

There stood the woman he had been hunting for weeks, looking down at the still form of a man, presumably the Raven, lying on the floor. She was holding a revolver and quickly pivoted in his direction.

Lopez looked like a drowned rat. A crazy drowned rat. Her blond hair hung limply in long knotted strands, and mud and dirt were caked all over her wet disheveled clothes. She held the gun firmly and aimed it straight at his chest, though she herself looked a little unsteady on her feet.

X focused on the one thing that truly mattered to him. Judging by Lopez's appearance, she'd been down in the tunnels recently. The likelihood was that another entrance to the caves was close by. And a way for him to get to Ann.

Camille looked almost pleased to see him. "Ah, the infamous Detective King; finally we meet. I suppose I shouldn't be surprised that you're here. You are quite the persistent pain in the ass."

X looked down at the body on the floor, poking it with his foot. "Is he dead?"

Camille Lopez laughed and said in a singsong voice, "Not only is he dead, he's absolutely, positively, undeniably and reliably most sincerely dead."

"*The Wizard of Oz*. I wouldn't have thought you a fan." X peered over her shoulder, adding, "A single shot through the heart. Nice and clean. Doesn't seem like your style."

"I heard you coming and was in a rush; I had to improvise," she answered, shrugging her shoulders. "But now that I have some time on my hands, I can devise something simply delectable for your demise."

"I wouldn't be too sure of that," answered X, inching closer to the mad woman. "I'm here to take you back to the States, where you're going to be convicted of killing four people. You'll get the death penalty and with any hope die by lethal injection. Personally, I'm looking forward to that day."

"Given the fact that I'm armed and you're not, I find your optimism admirable," Lopez smirked.

X heard the footsteps from the hallway and turned just as Frederick and William appeared in the doorframe. He tried to warn them, yelled, "Get the hell out of here, both of you," when Lopez fired a second shot.

X felt the sting across his left shoulder and knew the bullet had grazed him.

"Silence." Lopez screamed the word, each syllable drawn out in a hyenic pitch.

All three men stood stock still, waiting. X didn't know what to expect next and regretted not rushing Lopez the moment he walked into the room.

"I was aiming three inches to the left of your heart, Detective King," Lopez said conversationally, as though they were talking about the weather. "I was a little high, but you can see that I'm not such a bad shot. Next time I'll hit my mark."

She then seesawed back to a yelling rage. "You two," she screamed, indicating Frederick and William, "I want you into the back of the room. Now."

They put their hands up in the air and walked into the small room like they were walking into the gallows, slow wooden movements carved out of despair. X tried to catch their eye, to somehow let them know that the story wasn't over yet. But their somber march didn't give him the chance; they both obviously had their minds elsewhere.

Once they got to the back wall Camille pointed the gun at X, motioning for him to follow his friends.

"You know I can't do that," X said. "I have a sworn duty to take you into custody."

"Blah, blah, blah. My God you men can talk," Camille said irritably. "Listen, I'm trying to do you a favor. When I leave this room I'm going to lock it up tight as a tick so you won't be able to follow me. By the time you figure a way to break out I'll be so far gone you'll never be able to track me down again."

"Do you expect me to believe that?" X said. "Once I'm against that wall you'll execute the three of us without a second thought."

X kept his face passive as he observed William, who was gently shaking his right arm, flexing his fingers, opening and closing his fist. Then, seconds later, a knife slid out from under the cuff of his shirt and into his hand. William elbowed Frederick and whispered some words and within seconds, Frederick started sobbing. It was loud and plaintive and totally annoying.

Camille kept the gun leveled at X, her scream shrill. "Hey you, cry baby. Shut up."

Her head started jerking to the side, quick tiny movements that she didn't seem to be able to control. Maybe a nervous tic, X thought. Or a sign that she couldn't handle the background noise and was getting near her breaking point.

Then, as abruptly as a change in wind direction, she swung back to a relaxed voice. "You," she said, nodding at Frederick, "go get that briefcase on the desk. I want you to close it up tighty tight tight, and bring it to me. And no tricks or the good detective gets one in the chest."

Frederick cautiously stepped around the Raven's dead body, his bawling almost hysterical as he passed by the corpse and approached the small writing table. X hadn't paid the desk much attention, but as he watched his tour guide doing what Lopez had instructed, he saw the gold bars sitting in the briefcase.

Frederick's loud crying was annoying to his own ears, but it really seemed to be wearing on Camille. Her tic reappeared, as did the monosyllabic enunciation as she shrieked, "Can you please stop that whining?" She put her quivering hands against her ears, leaving the gun's barrel aimed at the ceiling. At least momentarily.

X was several yards away from Lopez; the muscles in his legs were cramping, still damp and cold from being down in the tunnels. He prayed they wouldn't slow him down too much as he pushed himself forward at a sprint.

For someone who looked so out of sorts, Lopez's reaction time was quick. She pivoted away from X, turning in time to see William's advance from the far wall with a knife in hand. She had regained firm control of the gun and only needed to move a few inches before she had it pressed against Frederick's throat.

Both men stopped, dead in their tracks.

Lopez pushed the barrel deeper into Frederick's skin, screamed, "Drop the knife or he's a goner."

"Don't listen to her, Dad," Frederick said. His face was pale, the theatrics of crying now over.

Camille smiled, laughter rising from deep in her belly. "Father and son. What a delicious surprise. What guilty pleasure can I dream up for this situation?

"I know," she said, a knowing smile plastered on her face. "Detective, on the floor. Now," she shrieked. "And hands behind your head."

X paused briefly, calculating his chances of being able to rush Camille before she had time to pull the trigger and kill Frederick. But in his gut he knew the odds weren't good. And William was shaking so badly it looked like he might pass out.

"OK, I'm doing it. Just be careful with the gun," X said as he got down onto his knees, grimacing when as put his hands behind his head. Maybe that shot to the shoulder was a little deeper than a flesh wound; his mobility was definitely compromised.

"You. Daddy." Camille stomped her foot until William was looking at her. "Do you want to take your little boy home in one piece?"

William couldn't seem to find his voice until he finally croaked out, "Yes."

"It's your lucky day. I'm in a position to make that happen. All you have to do is eliminate Detective King with that knife you're holding and you're good to go."

William's neck jutted forward. "You've got to be kidding me."

Lopez stuck the muzzle of the gun deeper against Frederick's throat causing him to cough, his Adam's apple bobbing with every breath. He raised his head so that he was looking at the ceiling, his fear obvious.

"It's the detective or your son. If you don't choose, I give you my personal guarantee that all three of you will die."

"She's telling the truth," X intervened. "She's crazy. This is my fight, not yours. Do what she says."

X followed William's gaze as it moved from his own kneeling form on the floor to Frederick. X knew there was only one choice; William would save his son. It was how it should be.

"I have your word you'll let us go?" asked William.

"Cross my heart," Camille answered, holding her arm up in the air like she was swearing an oath in court.

William hung his head, moving toward X. "Sorry, mate. He's my boy, you see."

X nodded up at this man who had saved him from the torrential waters just hours earlier. "I understand, William."

"No, I don't think you do."

X watched as William's hand clenched and unclenched the knife, rotating its hilt with a practiced hand. From his angle on the floor, X couldn't see Camille, but he heard the impatience in her voice when she called out to William, "What are you waiting for? Do it."

X's hands were still behind his head as William raised his right arm into the air, his hand still spinning the knife's handle before grabbing it loosely. X watched as the silver tip descended toward his chest, slower than he would have anticipated. And he saw the last second flip so that the handle was facing his direction.

X only had milliseconds to act. His right hand shot out, intercepting the dagger's hilt. He briefly felt the weight of the knife, not a lot of time to gauge how it would handle once it was airborne, and threw it at Camille.

Lopez looked stunned, her mouth and eyes opening wide, as the knife penetrated just below her shoulder blade. She staggered back several steps before taking a quick peek down at her chest, like she needed confirmation of what her mind already knew. She'd been injured. But even though she looked disoriented, she didn't drop the gun.

Lopez roared like a wounded lion, loud and ferocious, "Stay where you are." She kept the gun steady in her right hand as she pulled the knife out with her left, a sickening sucking sound coming from the wound as blood started dripping down her shirt.

X waited for the bullets that she didn't fire. It didn't make sense; Camille had every incentive to put them down right there on the spot. X knew it was a temporary reprieve, knew how insane she was. There was no way she was going to let bygones be bygones.

Her focus had definitely shifted, though. It was now on the briefcase filled with gold bars, still on the desk. She threw the knife into the hallway and picked up the case with her now free hand. X noticed how the motion made her grimace, saw a fresh spurt of blood oozing from the wound. He might not have killed her, but it looked like he'd done some serious damage.

"On the floor, with the others," she screamed at Frederick as she started backing toward the open doorway, keeping the gun trained on him.

Frederick rushed to his father's side, hugging him. "I'm sorry," he said.

"For what? You're a brave man, Son; I'm proud of you."

X knew that time was quickly running out. But he was counting on Camille's energy running out first. She was losing a lot of blood from the knife wound and looked pale and drained. So he would either engage her in more conversation until she collapsed or get himself killed.

"You look a little wobbly there," X taunted as he stood up slowly, then said to the others in a low voice, "She'll shoot at me first, but she's getting tired so she'll be slow getting off a second shot. Don't wait; rush her as soon as she fires."

Camille, now standing in the hallway, gave a quick glance in the direction of the hidden doorway leading back to the chapel. "Shaken, but not stirred. I am so going to enjoy killing you, Detective."

Her face twitched as she smiled. Then she planted her legs and raised the gun, the universal stance of a marksman ready to pull the trigger.

"Not on my watch, bitch."

71

X saw the surprise register on Camille's face as she turned toward the voice that had come from out of the blue. It was somewhere off to her right, and his stunned mind prayed that what he heard was real.

X bolted through the doorway just in time to see Lopez heft the briefcase and hit his beautiful Ann, dried blood caked across her face, in the chest. Ann fell backwards from the force, clinging onto some kind of roped handrail as she struggled to regain her footing at the top of on an incredibly steep stairwell. He watched in horror as Ann's knees finally buckled and her body fell over the side.

X's heart was hammering in his chest as he ran right past Camille, his only concern getting to Ann. She was clinging onto the old rope, her legs dangling over the precipice and pedaling in thin air.

He reached down to her, straining forward to get closer, but stopped when he felt the barrel of the gun against his temple and heard the unmistakable sound of its trigger being cocked.

"Don't touch her," Camille ordered.

X backed away slightly and turned his head toward Lopez, prepared to plead for Ann's life. Behind the crazy woman he saw William and Frederick tear into the hallway before stopping abruptly, looking like deer in the headlights as they took in what was about to happen.

Time seemed to stop. The discarded knife was still on the hallway floor but too far away to be of any help. Ann was crying out that she couldn't hold on for much longer, the old rope she was clutching starting to unravel. And X was in a stalemate. Move and he died; don't move and Ann died.

And that's when Frederick put his head down like a battering ram and barreled straight forward, aiming directly at them.

X crouched down low just as Frederick smashed into Camille, a hard body hit that propelled her against his bent form. He heard the gun go off, prayed it was a wild shot as Camille toppled over his stooped body, arms flailing as she tried to regain her posture. The weight of the gold bars added to the force of her descent as she crashed downwards, her head hitting the last of the stairs with a sickening thud.

Even in death she did not let go of the briefcase, her body rolling over the ledge of the dirt trail and into the depths of the cave.

"I can't hold on," Ann screamed again as one of her hands slipped away from the corded handrail, leaving her body swinging wildly over the abyss.

X reached back down and grabbed onto her wrist with his good arm, his muscles straining. "I've got you, baby. Just don't let go."

She was biting her lip, tears running down her cheeks. "I'm scared, Xavier."

And then Frederick was at his side, on his stomach, leaning over the ledge and grabbing Ann under her arms, pulling her slowly upwards and finally dragging her over the side and onto solid ground.

Ann didn't collapse, didn't take a second to catch her breath. Instead she crawled into X's open arms, crying and laughing at the same time, running her hands over his body until she rested them on his heart.

"Is it really you?" she whispered just before she passed out.

72

"The doctor said it was lucky he didn't cut himself worse. He only needed 11 stitches, and the tendons and nerves appear to be working just fine."

Frederick was sitting next to his father, comfortably settled at a table in the bar of X's hotel.

William flexed his fingers, flinching at the pain. "I haven't practiced that move in a long time. Guess I got rusty." He picked up his glass, a whiskey neat, and emptied it in one swallow.

Frederick and X both did the same, their tumblers clunking back onto the table in unison.

X grabbed the bottle of Johnnie Walker blue label that sat in the middle of the table and gave them each a refill. "Are you kidding me? You were brilliant. How'd you learn to do that, anyway?"

"I used to juggle; never tried it with a knife before, though." William burped, apologized, and added, "I didn't count on catching the blade end so tightly."

"For a second there I wasn't sure what you were trying to do. Then I remembered you saying you lost your eyeglasses when you fished me out of the tunnels. You were afraid to throw the knife yourself in case you missed Camille and hit Frederick by accident.

"Not that I did a hell of a lot better," X said, cradling his whiskey. "I can't believe I missed her heart."

"She didn't have a heart." Ann, sitting on the cushioned bench with an afghan thrown around her, sipped her herbal tea.

X scooted closer to her, kissing the top of her head. "So, they haven't found Camille's body yet?"

"No, and I'm not sure they ever will," William answered. "I spoke with the Durham Constabulary on my way over here, and they're going on the assumption that both Camille and the briefcase filled with gold ended up back down in the tunnels and were washed out into the River Wear."

X picked up his glass, turning it in his hands. "When I told Chief Hartman the news, I couldn't tell if he was happy she was gone or mad that he wouldn't get the chance to have her executed."

"That's the big boss back home," Ann explained to the Englishmen. "But X worked with a lot of other great cops in tracking Lopez down. There was Officer Ryan, and DiMitri of course."

"Well I heard good news on both their fronts. DiMitri's fully recovered from his injuries and back on the streets with park police, where he wants to be. And Ryan got promoted to detective." X twirled the amber liquid in his glass and put it back on the table. "He's going to be replacing Langly."

It was getting a little easier, saying his friend's name. He knew he'd miss the hell out of him; he already did.

He felt Ann's arm wrap around his waist, give him a gentle squeeze. Langly did have it wrong on one count, X thought. Dating a shrink was the best.

"So Frederick," he asked, "any thoughts on changing your profession to law enforcement?"

Father and son had a good chuckle before Frederick answered. "That is definitely not going to happen. But I am considering my hand at writing, sharing this incredible tale with others.

It's a story of legends, really." Frederick removed his glasses, wiping them with the edge of the tablecloth, and continued. "A secret sect led by the elusive Raven; meetings held beneath historic landmarks; and a case of gold bars out there somewhere.

"Just waiting to be found."

www.ingramcontent.com/pod-product-compliance
Lightning Source LLC
Chambersburg PA
CBHW071249170626
46809CB00001B/141